TIME TRAVEL 101

INTRO TO ETERNITY

THE TIME TRAVEL SERIES

In reading order:

Time Travel 101 - Intro To Eternity

Time Travel 102 - The Cerebral War

(Coming: 2026)

TIME TRAVEL 101
INTRO TO ETERNITY

DANIEL GOY

WICKED INK

PUBLISHING

Time Travel 101 - Intro To Eternity : Book 1
Copyright © 2025 by Daniel Goy

Published by Wicked Ink Publishing Ltd.
www.wickedinkpublishing.com

Cover and book design © 2025 by Wicked Ink Publishing Ltd.
Editors: Raymond Griffiths & Adam Bamford

First Edition: August 2025
Printed in Canada

Library and Archives Canada Cataloguing in Publication

Title: Time travel 101 : intro to eternity / Daniel Goy.
Other titles: Time travel one oh one | Intro to eternity
Names: Goy, Daniel, author.
Description: Series statement: Time travel series ; 1
Identifiers: Canadiana (print) 20250225263
Canadiana (ebook) 20250225271
ISBN 9781998278190 (softcover)
ISBN 9781998278206 (EPUB)
Subjects: LCGFT: Time-travel fiction. | LCGFT: Science fiction. | LCGFT: Novels.
Classification: LCC PR6107.O95 T56 2025 | DDC 823/.92—dc23

TIME TRAVEL 101

INTRO TO ETERNITY

In the war against time,
some destinies are meant to collide.

'My name is Ozymandias, King of Kings:
Look on my Works, ye Mighty, and despair!'

- PERCY SHELLEY

PROLOGUE

Fear.

Fear begins in the *Amygdala*, the oldest part of your brain. All it takes is one synapse to light the flame and quickly unfurl into abject terror in under a second. This wildfire spreads throughout your body, setting alight the *Sympathetic Nervous System*.

Next comes *adrenaline*, your heart beats faster, your breathing becomes heavier, increasing your alertness and sending every organ into overdrive, especially your brain. You see more, you hear more, and all these signals blast through your neurons, slowing time down to a crawl and giving you everything you need to make the crucial decision: stand and fight or run away.

The Big Bang, in actuality, was more like the big scream, an adolescent singularity so scared of the dark that it ran in every conceivable direction to escape it. Fear was present at the dawn of creation and will persist long after we're all gone.

Someday, someone will sit on the shore of the last day of the universe, watching the tide coming to swallow them up in one last mouthful. Whoever that someone may be, human, squid, artificially intelligent super-computer, or transcended entity of pure thought, you better believe that when that final flicker of light fades, it will be met with a pair of urine-filled pants and a scream.

Fear is humanity's greatest asset. Fear ensures survival. Fear is life.

At exactly 4:37 p.m. on February 12th, 2009, no one on earth was experiencing fear more than Jack Phoenix. A young boy of eight years old, eight years old today, as today was his birthday. This was clear to anyone within a half-mile radius thanks to the large *'8 today!'* badge he proudly wore, pinned to his t-shirt. But, right now, Jack was more scared than he has ever been, hiding in the footrest of the back seat of his dad's car, trying his hardest not to breathe and not to be heard, as the monster was still out there, looking for him.

There came a tap on the window above him.

Was this it? Had it found him? He didn't dare raise his gaze to verify his fate. Instead, he covered his eyes with his fingers, hoping that might stop him from being seen.

Another tap.

Jack's curiosity soon became too much to bear, and he couldn't help but peer up through his fingers, searching until his eyes met those of the tapper. His fear subsided at once. It was no monster, only his dad smiling down at him. His dad pulled open the car door, and Jack immediately burst into tears, wrapping his arms around his father so tightly as to never let him go again.

"Jack, it's ok, everything's ok."

Maybe there had never even been a monster. Adults were always telling him he had an 'overactive imagination' after all.

"Is... he... gone?" was all Jack could sputter through breathless gasps.

"He's gone. Everything's going to be ok," replied his

father, and with that, Jack sank his face deep into his dad's woollen jumper.

"Where's mom?" came Jack's muffled voice through the fabric.

"She's busy at the moment, but she's fine. Now come look, I have something to show you."

Jack hesitantly lifted his head, gripped his dad's hand, and stepped out of the car.

Then he saw it, parked in the driveway, only a few metres away: an ice cream truck.

Jack's tear-stained eyes lit up. "Woah."

"Happy Birthday, Jack."

He ran up to the ice cream truck. The faded depiction of *Mickey Mouse* on the side of the vehicle glistened with the promise of all the ice cream Jack could eat, and even more, until he threw up. It was all his, and he could make the rules. No one could tell him how many flakes were too many.

Jack turned back to his father. "Where did you get it?"

"It belonged to a friend of mine. He doesn't need it anymore, so I thought we could take it out for the day. Would you like that?"

Jack's smile beamed. "Definitely," he called back, already jumping aboard.

Jack walked through the vehicle, passing the freezers filled to the brim with ice lollies, the whippy machine with its levers begging to be pulled, and the tubs of sprinkles Jack desperately wanted to dunk his head into.

He took a seat in the passenger's seat while his dad took the driver's. His dad pressed the key into the ignition, and the ice cream truck clunked to life, reversing out of the driveway.

In all of Jack's excitement, he had failed to spot something curious on the pavement, close to the ice cream truck and towards the front door to his house: a man with a bullet through his chest, lying face down on the doorstep, blood still pooling around him as the last spark of life left his eyes. Eyes that would have been very familiar to Jack, as was the familiar scratchy beard, familiar greying chestnut hair, and familiar woollen jumper. In fact, everything about this man was familiar to Jack, for this man was identical in every way to the one currently driving Jack far, far away.

After what felt like an eternity, the pair arrived at their destination: a cliff edge on the outskirts of the city.

"We've arrived," announced Jack's father.

Jack opened the door and climbed down from the truck. "Why did we come here?" he asked.

"Look at that view. Best place in the world to eat ice cream," said Jack's father, and he was right.

Jack looked out over the side of the cliff at the world below, upon a view that stretched on forever. You could see everything from up here, every building and street Jack had ever known, with the sun gently touching the horizon behind.

It was as though his father captured the entire world and miniaturized it. Jack's eyes turned downwards; the cliff dropped abruptly, and he could barely make out the bottom. He quickly stepped away from the edge, suddenly feeling dizzy.

Jack's father joined him, holding two ice cream cones with several flakes jammed into the top and covered with sprinkles and chocolate sauce.

"Cheers," he announced as he held out his ice cream the way Jack saw people do with champagne glasses at fancy dinners. Jack imitated with a 'cheers' of his own and swooshed his ice cream into his father's.

The pair sat on the bonnet of the ice cream truck and tucked into their ice cream cones while enjoying the view from atop the world.

Jack suddenly withdrew from his cone, his chocolate

sauce-covered face all screwed up with disgust. "Ugh, this tastes all metally."

"Tastes fine to me," said his father. "Tell you what, if you finish it all up. I'll tell you a story."

"I'm too old for stories. I'm eight now, remember?" retorted Jack, pointing to his badge.

"You'll like this one, I promise. It's about a man called Jack, just like you."

"Fine," Jack submitted, crossing his arms.

He was secretly a little excited by the prospect. It had been years since his dad told him a story. Still, he refused to show it as he was a mature eight-year-old now, and eight-year-olds hate being told stories.

Jack's dad hopped down from the truck and took a couple of steps towards the edge of the abyss. "It's about a man who did incredible things, saw the impossible, and how one day, he stood right here..."

His father remembered it all—the man, kneeling at the edge of the cliff, bloodied and bruised, shirt torn and soaked with blood.

"...With the devil behind him..."

He remembered the monster standing behind the man, pointing a gun at him, readying his aim.

"...As together, they watched the world end."

He remembered the view, one not too dissimilar to the one he was looking at now, except this one was in flames. A world in ruins, full of screams, ambulance sirens, and the suffocating smell of smoke.

A world set alight with fear.

PART 1
THE BEGINNING

1

CHEST-THUMPING MUSIC FILLED THE NIGHTCLUB AS the drunken crowd swayed into one another. Bright red and green spotlights illuminated the thick fog of alcoholic spirits, sweat, and poor decisions. A warm stench rode the waves of up-stretched arms and across the cramped dance floor until they settled upon Jack Phoenix, who was standing awkwardly a little off to the side.

Jack's rigidly neat brown hair and suit stood out amongst the ocean of laid-back students. He, too, was a student and, despite his self-appointed maturity, was only twenty years old. In fact, he was turning twenty years old tonight, as in only a few minutes, it would officially be his birthday. This was clear to anyone within a half-mile radius thanks to the large *'20 today!'* badge he resentfully wore pinned to his shirt.

The badge and night out had been decided upon by Sam Higgs, a man who also stood out from the other students, but for very different reasons. His bleached blonde hair, with its single greasy dreadlock, swung back and forth above an ensemble comprising a purple blazer, a pair of ripped jeans, a T-shirt promoting a rock concert he never attended, and a generous coating of hipster beads. All this combined made Sam appear like an alien, poorly trying to replicate the look of a student. Sam, for better or worse, was Jack's best friend.

However, unlike Jack, Sam felt very much at home in a nightclub. Perhaps this was because Sam possessed a more outgoing personality than Jack, or perhaps it was thanks to the line of cocaine Sam had snorted in the bathroom moments earlier.

Sam danced like the world couldn't see him, neither in time to the music nor appreciating personal space. The pint of beer he held in his jittering fingers showered onto the dance floor around him, causing him to slip around like a giraffe, taking its first steps. Sam caught sight of Jack and gave him a playful nudge, spilling more of his pint.

"You need to relax," were the accompanying words of wisdom slurred into Jack's ear.

Jack stepped back, ensuring he was suitably out of range of the splash zone.

"I am relaxed," said Jack through gritted teeth, longing to be back home finishing his essay on gravitational fields.

Jack hated nightclubs. They were too loud, too crowded, and how was everybody else immune to the smell? Why did he allow himself to get caught up in another of Sam's great ideas?

"Oh, come on!" bemoaned Sam as someone bumped into him, knocking his drink and leaving a dark, wet stain draining down his shirt.

He darted his head around in search of the culprit. Sam surveyed the dance floor, eyeing the wall of vacant students until he identified the perpetrator descending into the shadow of the crowd. It had to be them.

Sam was never more certain of anything in his life. Sam gripped his plastic cup tightly, pulled his arm back and thrust what little remained of his pint with all his might, soaking his suspect before they could escape.

The sopping wet woman turned to face Sam, her drenched hair coated a face filled with confusion and anger. Sam turned away, desperately attempting to avoid the woman's scorn, and faced Jack once more. Jack was too busy checking his phone to have seen what just transpired. The woman followed Sam's gaze all the way to Jack.

"Hey!" she shouted to Jack.

Jack looked up and saw the damp woman staring back at him. He offered her a smile before receiving a face full of vodka lemonade.

Jack gave Sam a wet, helpless look. Sam simply shrugged and shook his head at Jack, feigning surprise. Jack turned to see the woman talking to a group of large men in rugby uniforms and pointing at the pair.

"Sam…" began Jack.

But Sam was already gone.

The rugby players started towards Jack, and seeing little alternative, Jack ran, pushing his way through the dancing crowd to follow Sam.

"I didn't even do anything!" yelped Jack, to no avail as the hulking group charged after him.

Sam battled through the crowds until he was spat out beside the bar. He was nearly free; the path was clear, yet something made Sam stop dead in his tracks. He froze to the spot, staring at the bar with his mouth ajar as he saw something impossible behind it.

Sam saw himself.

A second Sam Higgs.

This other Sam was identical to him in every way, except he was battered, bruised, and bleeding. Sam watched as his duplicate grabbed a bottle from the bar, and as he did, their eyes met. The club and everything around him dissolved away as Sam stared deeply into himself.

This man wasn't someone who simply resembled him, nor

was it a drug-induced apparition. In this moment of pure clarity, Sam knew the man looking back at him was himself. He had never been more certain of anything in his life. Sam raised his arm, reaching out to himself.

Jack continued weaving through the crowd, his spindly body contorting through every gap he found. Finally, he spotted Sam a few feet ahead. Why did he stop? He wasn't ordering another drink at a time like this, was he?

Jack grabbed hold of Sam for dear life. "What are you doing? We've got to go!"

Sam came crashing back to reality as Jack's terrified face filled his focus with a sickening clarity. He glanced back at the bar, but the other Sam already disappeared. What didn't disappear; however, was the sound of footsteps beating down on the sticky linoleum like the drums of war, heralding the rugby players marching toward them. So, Jack and Sam continued running once more.

Tonight was far from the first time Jack and Sam were forced to run for their lives. In fact, it seemed to be the one constant in Jack and Sam's friendship. Jack long since lost count the number of times Sam dragged him into a dangerous situation before then making said situation infinitely worse, leaving them with but one option: to run.

TAKE, FOR EXAMPLE, A SIMILAR INCIDENT SEVERAL years prior, wherein Jack and Sam were chased from their school. Sam got on the wrong side of some children in the year above, likely having ripped them off with a scam, blamed them for a prank he pulled, or simply thrown eggs at them.

The point being, this became such a standard part of their routine that the exact details of this race to the death were scarcely worth distinguishing from any other. All that concerned Jack at this moment was forcing his twelve-year-old legs to move faster than he ever did in P.E. lessons. Because if he didn't, he would end today with his head stamped into the pavement until his brains shot out his ears, or at the very least have his tie *peanuted* to within an inch of his life.

"Quick, split up!" shouted the twelve-year-old Sam.

Jack intended to shout something in objection but saw his supposed best friend was already gone, having branched away down a nearby alleyway, leaving Jack to the mercy of his aggressors.

Jack, once more left to fend for himself, continued down the street, trying to outrun their threats. Jack weaved through pedestrians and crawled through fences until the shouts finally abated.

Jack used this moment of respite to reach into the breast pocket of his school blazer and fish out his inhaler. He closed his eyes, took two puffs, and tried to calm his breathless gasps, leaning against the cold brickwork of the narrow alley closing around him.

He shot up as he heard the distant rhythm of school shoes against pavement, growing louder by the second. Jack couldn't keep running. He knew he needed to find another way out of this situation. He poked his head from the alley and saw he was standing beside a derelict building with the windows boarded up.

Jack vaguely remembered this once being a bakery, yet now it seemed abandoned. More importantly, he noticed the front door stood ajar, almost beckoning him inside, offering him sanctuary.

He crept inside the building, shutting the door behind him without making a sound. Pressing his weight against it, he prayed no one would find him as he held his breath tight. He listened as the footsteps and shouts muted, and only when

Jack was sure they were gone did he finally allow himself to breathe.

Still unwilling to venture back out, for fear they were waiting on the other side of the door, Jack glanced around his hiding place. In front of him lay a forest of strange technology: large mirrors wired up to computers, tables covered in sci-fi knick-knacks and doo-hickeys, thick cables lining the floor among a scattering of broken glass, and strangest of all, a baby's crib sitting in the corner. Jack noticed a faint aroma of milk and burnt metal lingering in the air.

The gentle hum of machinery vibrated a faint tinge of worry through Jack—this wasn't a bakery, nor was it abandoned. Whatever this place was, Jack knew he didn't belong here, and perhaps, just maybe, it would be less dangerous to open the door and face the gang, who were likely still waiting for him. But they weren't waiting for him. Instead, they located fresh prey and were now closing in on it.

They found Sam down an alleyway, hiding behind some bins and an old mattress. He had nowhere to run.

"Look at the little baby," said the leader. "Too scared to face us, but you can't hide anymore."

But that's where they were wrong. Sam wasn't scared, and he wasn't hiding. He was waiting with a large metal pole he found discarded beside the bin. Sam drew it out and brandished the pole like Excalibur, planting his feet firmly on the ground. He was done running.

"Come on, then!" yelled Sam, through a smile of bared teeth as he swung the pole in wild arches. "Come, get me!"

Sam let out a warrior's roar and charged toward the group, chasing them all back out of the alleyway.

Back in the present, as the clock struck twelve, marking Jack's birthday, the pair celebrated by clambering through the nightclub's fire exit, and rather than finding a metal pole or hiding in an abandoned building, they simply hopped into a taxi outside the club, which Sam promised he would pay Jack back for later.

Sam hung out the taxi window to poke his tongue out at the rugby players, leaving them in his dust. Once they blurred out of view and he sunk back in his seat, his mind returned to the self-portrait he saw behind the bar.

Jack sat beside Sam, staring into the rear-view mirror, convinced they might still somehow catch up with them. He glimpsed his birthday badge glistening in the mirror and tore it from his shirt, dropping it beneath his feet.

The taxi continued, rocking Sam gently to sleep, leaving him to dream about the identity of his impersonator, blissfully unaware of the terrible fate his other self now ensured.

2

THE FOLLOWING MORNING, JACK AWOKE IN HIS BED in the small student house he and Sam rented together and was pleasantly surprised to find he survived the night. Jack showered, brushed his teeth, fifty brushes on each side, and got dressed in his neatly ironed shirt, trousers and socks before scooping up his wallet and keys from his perfectly organized desk.

Jack's rigid morning routine brought him downstairs, whereupon, reaching the bottom step, Jack checked his wallet and keys and fetched the thick bundle of letters wedged in the post flap. Each envelope was oppressively white and official. The lack of any brightly coloured envelopes came to Jack as a relief. *Today is just another ordinary day,* he told himself as he ventured into the kitchen.

The first thing that hit Jack was the unmistakable stench of alcohol turning to vinegar in the stale air. On the floor, Jack found Sam leaning against the cupboards, draped in a blanket, and hugging a washing-up bowl to his face. Today was indeed just another ordinary day.

"Happy Birthday," murmured Sam into the bowl, forcing a level of enthusiasm which Jack didn't meet.

"Rent overdue, utilities overdue, that polar bear you adopted, overdue," said Jack, waving the letters before Sam's eyes.

Sam didn't reply, busy trying to force down the vomit sneaking its way up his throat. Jack dropped the letters onto the kitchen table and walked to where Sam had balled himself. "Could you move? I need to get to the cereal."

Sam tried to shuffle over, but the small amount of movement posed too much for him, and he resumed dry heaving into the plastic bowl.

Jack sighed and leaned over Sam to retrieve the cereal box from the cupboard.

"I think my dealer gave me some bad cocaine last night," choked Sam between retches.

"All cocaine is bad cocaine, Sam. It's cocaine, not a sandwich or a piece of fruit. It's cocaine. You spent money that could have gone towards rent on cocaine."

"Please stop saying cocaine," muttered Sam. "You don't understand. I saw some weird stuff last night. I saw myself-"

"Oh, we all saw you," interrupted Jack, barely containing his irritation. "I saw you, those guys who wanted to kick our teeth in. They got a good look at you."

"But it was another me. What if he's out there ruining my good name?"

"You appear to be doing a pretty good job of that yourself."

"What if it was a clone?"

"What if you were on drugs?" mused Jack with a generous pinch of sarcasm.

Jack opened the fridge and found the milk wasn't in its usual spot. He scanned the refrigerator's shelves, past the Chinese food coated in mold, the crumpled pizza boxes, and the pile of black goo too far gone for Jack to even identify, but there was no milk. Jack slammed the fridge door shut and turned to Sam, finding the milk carton crumpled by his side.

"You drank all my milk?" complained Jack.

"Ah, yeah, I thought it would flush out the toxins, but I think it's only making it curdle," said Sam, hugging the bowl closer to his face. "I'll make it up to you tonight. I've got you the best birthday present ever."

The lid holding in the last vestiges of Jack's contempt and rage for Sam's infinite list of petty annoyances buckled.

"I don't want anything for my birthday. I don't even want to celebrate my birthday. Why don't you, instead, pay the £20 you owe *Bernard* the polar bear?!" argued Jack through a mouthful of dry cereal.

He couldn't deal with any more of Sam's nonsense today and ate breakfast in his room, checking his wallet and keys once more on his way back upstairs.

Jack choked down the last of his cornflakes as he prepared for the day's classes. Of course, Jack had already gone through the background reading for it twice, as well as some research of his own.

Still, he propped his copy of *The Fundamentals of Quantum Mechanics and Astrophysics - Tenth edition* open on his lap to peruse through one last time.

3

"Why is time travel impossible?" Dr Li pondered aloud to an uninterested class.

Dr Li stood behind a well-worn desk at the front of his science lab, a man who may have been 60 or 160 years old. He had a timeless quality to his old age, like a less jolly Father Christmas. His long white beard hung beneath sunken eyes and their many bags, filled with all the things he witnessed but dared not speak of. There was an heir of importance in the way he moved and a calm wisdom in each word he spoke. Unfortunately, this didn't translate to the attention of his class.

"I said, why is time travel impossible?" repeated Dr Li, surveying the rows of lab benches lined with students blankly staring off in every direction but his.

"You." Dr Li pointed his whiteboard marker at a young man whose eyes fluttered as his head slumped. He shot bolt upright, suddenly very awake.

"Because you can't travel faster than the speed of light?" he guessed.

Dr Li threw his pen at the young man, narrowly missing his head.

"Wrong," he announced. "Trick question, time travel is very possible."

Dr Li pulled out a spare pen from the deep pockets of his stained lab coat and walked over to the whiteboard behind his desk, writing $E=MC^2$ in big, thick letters.

"The most famous equation in all of physics. It states that nothing can travel faster than the speed of light because the energy required would have to be infinite. However, there is one thing to which this rule doesn't apply."

Dr Li pointed his pen at a woman staring down towards her lap at a lazily concealed phone. Her head darted upwards as she tried to recall what was just said.

"Neutrinos?" she guessed.

Dr Li again threw his pen. This one hit a lab bench and bounced onto the floor by the woman's feet.

"Wrong. The correct answer is worms. And they do so using wormholes." Dr Li picked up an apple that was slowly rotting on his desk for the past few days.

"Imagine the skin of this apple is the universe. Now, a wormhole allows you to pass from one part of space to another."

Grabbing another pen from his pocket, he dug the pen through the apple. It lodged a few centimetres deep. The apple seemed to provide more resistance than Dr Li hoped for. He jammed it against the desk, drilling the pen in further until finally, the pen popped out the other side of the apple.

"This allows worms to take shortcuts to wherever their little wormy heart desires, faster than the speed of light," continued Dr Li, apple juice dripping down his arm. "The only problem with this is wormholes are tiny, too small for even the most microscopic worm to wriggle through. So how can we make one bigger?"

He pulled out his apple-soaked pen and pointed it at the one student in his class who had been attentively listening to him ramble on for the past hour and forty minutes.

"Um, well..." stammered Jack.

"Come on, I'm running out of pens."

Dr Li shot Jack the slightest hint of a wink, imperceptible to anyone else. It gave Jack the floor, telling him to show this lot how it's done.

"Gravitational pull?" said Jack.

He still couldn't help but flinch a little, worrying this was a trick question and a pen might still come his way. But none came.

"Ding. You'd need a hell of a lot of gravity. Thankfully, cosmic strings are chock-full of the stuff. So if you harness a few cosmic strings and use them to crowbar open a wormhole around you, then, well, you could go anywhere." Dr Li threw his apple onto the ground, smashing it and sending apple shards flying across the room. "Or destroy the universe."

Dr Li continued his lecture, making tangents about time dilation one moment and the best way to grow an apricot tree the next, as though haphazardly flicking through an encyclopedia. Yet somehow, Dr Li seemed an expert in every aspect of everything.

An impossible amount of knowledge crammed into one man. No matter the subject, Jack sat enthralled, hanging off Dr Li's every word, and as he spoke, Jack's mind returned to the abandoned bakery, his secret sanctuary on the day he hid from the wrath of the older boys out for blood.

HE SHOULD'VE LEFT. HE SHOULD'VE TURNED around and walked out the door. No one would've even known he was ever there. The coast was almost certainly clear by now. Yet Jack remained. Maybe he would stay here just a moment longer, he supposed. What would be the harm in being doubly triply sure they were gone? Where was this place he'd found himself, anyway? He decided it couldn't hurt to take a quick look around.

Jack wandered over to a desk covered in peculiar metal objects and picked one up to inspect it. He noticed a trigger and a handle at one end and a few screws, and a staple stuck to the other end. He picked them off and held the device out in front of him as though it were a gun and he was taking down a supervillain.

"Hello," uttered a voice from behind Jack.

Jack froze as fear grabbed hold. Maybe if he didn't turn around, he could simply pretend he imagined it. But he wasn't so lucky, and the owner of the voice grew closer until Jack sensed their warm breath on the back of his neck.

"Well, well, well, caught you red-handed."

How Jack wished he had left when he had the chance.

With a gulp, Jack turned to meet his fate. "Please don't call the police or...or murder me."

Jack looked up into the eyes of the man who would surely tie him up and experiment on him for the rest of his rapidly expiring life. Two big bushy white eyebrows above eyes haunted by time. A man we know of as Dr Li, but for Jack, back then, this man was a stranger who spelt nothing but death.

"Are you threatening me with that thing?" he asked.

Jack glanced down, noticed he was still holding his pretend gun out in front of him, and quickly hid it behind his back.

"No," answered Jack.

"I bet you don't even know what that is," said Dr Li.

Jack wasn't sure if he should answer, although perhaps if he guessed correctly, this man might let him go, like some macabre game show. Unlikely, but what other choice did he have? He slowly brought the device back from behind him and inspected its smooth exterior.

"It's a magnet, I- I think."

"Hmm, that's right," mused Dr Li, almost impressed. He thought for a moment before continuing. "You know, people are magnetic too, just a little, thanks to the iron in your blood. Do you understand?"

Jack nodded, still confused, still terrified.

"Which means if someone could build a strong enough electromagnet, they could do this."

Dr Li flicked a nearby switch, and a giant metal slab behind Jack burst into life, lighting up and whirring like a miniature helicopter. Dr Li cranked up a dial, and Jack suddenly felt something tugging at him—not at any individual part of him, but pulling at all of him, everywhere, and it was getting stronger. Jack tried to pull away but couldn't escape its magnetic pull, like a torrential wind trying to force him back. He tried to take a step forward but found his legs wouldn't budge, trapped in the magnetic field of the whirring black slab.

Pieces of metal whizzed past him and slammed into it in a percussion of screeching hail. The device he was holding furiously wrestled itself from his fingers and flew away behind him, but Jack forced his feet into the ground, refusing to be dragged any closer to the jaws of this terrifying thing. He desperately tried to press on, straining through gritted teeth, but barely moved his foot a single inch.

Dr Li stepped towards Jack, remaining just out of the magnet's reach. "Now, what to do with a thief?" he pondered aloud.

"Please don't call the police. Miss Parker can't find out about this."

"Miss Parker?" asked Dr Li.

"She runs the foster home, please, mister. I really didn't mean to touch your things or even be in here. There were these bullies, and they were picking on me, so Sam put a squirrel into one of their lockers."

Dr Li wasn't faintly interested in Jack's excuses, for he was already formulating a much grander plan for his intruder. He picked up a long, rusted wand from a nearby shelf and presented it to Jack.

"Now, do you know how to use one of these?"

"That's a soldering iron," said Jack, his eyes struggling to focus as the blood rushed to the back of his head. "At school, we once... watched someone use one."

"Good enough. I need an assistant. You help me out around here, and I don't tell anyone about you trying to steal from me. Deal?"

Jack didn't reply, still far too scared, still trying to run free of the magnetic treadmill. Who was this man? What was he going to have Jack do for him? Could he even trust him? That last question would linger in his mind for years to come.

"Deal?" repeated Dr Li, more sternly this time.

The magnetic storm was growing by the second, leaving Jack dizzy, lightheaded and powerless to resist this stranger's offer.

"D-d-deal," stuttered Jack.

Dr Li held out his hand to Jack. "I'm Dr Li."

Jack tried to pull his arm free but was unable to do so.

"Oh, right." Dr Li quickly ran back over to the switch and flicked it off.

The magnetic field trapping Jack dissipated immediately, and Jack fell to his knees as metal rained down behind him. Dr Li stepped over to Jack, arm extended once more.

Jack grabbed the strange man's wrinkled and callused hand and, with a slight hesitation in his voice, introduced himself.

"I'm Jack Phoenix."

"...AND I EXPECT CHAPTER 18 TO BE READ AND FULLY understood before I next see you." Dr Li sat down behind his desk with a resigned sigh and watched as the students shuffled out, all except one.

"Jack, lock the door. I want to show you something," said Dr Li once they were alone.

Jack looked up from the notes he was still frantically jotting down, beamed a smile, and hurried to the door, twisting his key into the lock.

Dr Li pulled out the drawer of his desk. Inside was a keypad and nothing else. He punched a few numbers into the keypad, which made a small joyful ding. Then, the whiteboard behind Dr Li, covered in a collection of notes and stubborn smudges, slid upwards, revealing a concealed room behind—a room filled with computers, mirrors, miniature hadron colliders, and shelves full of half-completed inventions.

Everything Jack had first set his eyes upon in that bakery years earlier, and much more, was right here, distilled into this small, secluded room.

Dr Li walked over to one of the middle shelves and removed a rectangular device with a screen about the size of a mobile phone.

"Close your eyes and hold out your hands," said Dr Li as he booted up his newest invention.

Jack did so diligently, shutting his eyes tightly as he presented his cupped hands, ready to receive.

"Ow," recoiled Jack, peering down at his stinging palm, a speck of blood growing from its centre.

He turned to Dr Li, who was holding a long pin, the tip now coloured deep red.

"What was that for?"

"For this," replied Dr Li as he jammed the pin into a slot on the side of his device.

It burst into life and on its screen was a map with a small blinking dot marking Jack's current location. Dr Li held the device out to Jack, letting him get a good look.

"What is it? A phone?"

"It's a locator; all you need is a drop of blood, and it can track precisely that person's location. When I've finished building it, it'll be all yours. Call it a birthday present."

"Really?" beamed Jack, whilst he was usually opposed to anything birthday-related.

This was an exception. His mind raced with all the uses a device like this could have, like catching criminals and finding people who've gone missing. But best of all, it could stop Sam from running off.

"Anywhere you go, it'll continue to track your location," said Dr Li, pointing to the centre of the map.

Dr Li began to explain how the locator worked and how blood held what he called a 'locality signature' based on the type of oxygen molecule bound by someone's haemoglobin proteins. But Jack's concentration waned, and his attention turned, as it always did, to the small object in the centre of the room. Nestled in a woven tapestry of wires the device sat made of wood and glass, and glowing with a pulsating blue hue as though it were alive.

Dr Li continued to talk about how he needed to stop blood platelets from clogging, and Jack tried his hardest to pay attention, but he couldn't hold it in any longer.

"Is it ready yet?" blurted Jack.

Dr Li snapped out of his explanatory trance and glanced over at the shelf to where Jack was pointing.

"Nearly."

Jack reached out to hold his favourite piece in Dr Li's

museum, hoping to see what progress was made with it, but as he touched its wooden surface, a static electric flicker jumped from the machine, shocking him. Jack recoiled back. The last few minutes hadn't been the best for his hand.

As he glanced back, Jack noticed the small blight of electricity had done something to the machine, as though he tickled it awake. The ancient wooden machine held a glass dome at one end, and within the glass dome lay a miniature antique clock face.

The hands of the clock face twitched, and blue sparks flitted around the glass dome like an angry snow globe, plotting an escape.

"You said that yesterday and the day before, and the day before that," whined Jack.

"We'll get there. You just need to be patient."

"Can't we just test it? Only a few seconds, barely even noticeable."

"Soon," promised Dr Li with an assuring wink. "Now, go, enjoy your birthday. I need to finish up on the locator, anyway- I wonder if a graphene tube might help the blood distribute more evenly..." Dr Li continued his thought, scarcely noticing as Jack left.

Jack wandered through the university, his mind still fixated on the tiny wooden device and all the impossible possibilities it held within.

"Soon..." Jack repeated.

Soon the time machine would finally be ready.

4

Sam made it to his coding seminar, having barely arrived on time. Well, twenty minutes late is still relatively on time, he figured. They expect you to be a little late.

Still feeling the full retribution of the previous night, Sam slumped into the only remaining seat and hid behind his laptop. The room was bright, thanks to its white walls, abundance of lightbulbs and, worst of all, the enormous glass wall through which the sun beamed directly onto Sam, cooking him like an ant under a magnifying glass.

A middle-aged man stood at the front of the class. His name was Greg...Sam was like 90% sure of that. Of course, he couldn't be 100% sure. The guy mentioned it on the first day of term and expected everyone to remember it. There was probably a last name too, but Sam did than his part in retaining the Greg bit.

The few remaining strands of hair on Greg's head were combed tightly over his shiny scalp, fooling nobody, and his large round glasses slid down his nose as the dull sound of his dull voice dragged on about boring, dull stuff, making it impossible for Sam to overcome the throbbing in his head and keep his eyes open.

"People say HTML5 is a lot like a fine wine..." Greg prattled on.

Sam sensed himself going, his eyes closed as he rested his head on his laptop keyboard.

Greg continued, the white noise of his voice growing louder until a hand slammed down on the desk beside Sam's head.

Sam's eyes popped open. "Alright?" he murmured, trying to focus on the blurry lecturer standing above him.

"Were you sleeping?" accused Greg unjustly.

"Pfft me? I can do this class with my eyes closed, so that's just what I was doing." reasoned Sam.

"He was asleep," corrected the voice beside him, and with that, every muscle in Sam's body tensed into a knot. This was the sound of Amir, a huge nerd with an annoying nasal voice which sounded like fingernails scraping across your brain.

Amir shot Sam a snide glare as he straightened the pompous little bow tie around his neck. Amir stood opposed to Sam in every single way and took every opportunity to get Sam in trouble, and right now, was no exception. "And he's been playing *Minesweeper*."

"Shut up, Amir. No, I wasn't," retorted Sam.

"It's on his screen right now," continued Amir's unrelenting tirade of slander.

"What is this? A witch hunt? Let's just get back to computing and-" Sam uttered an involuntary burp. A gurgle of boozy, milky air crept past his lips amid all the stress of these allegations.

Greg's nose twitched as it hit him, his face contorting in disgust. "Are you drunk?"

"Am I...?"

"Drunk, you smell strongly of alcohol. You reek of it."

"Well, I... I'm not newly drunk, if that's what you mean." Sam didn't need this today. He shouldn't be on trial here.

No one was having a go at Amir for snitching, but they were all ready to jump on Sam at the first opportunity for being the tiniest bit hungover. It's not like he was drunk now. Admittedly, he was a little tipsy as he had a couple shots before heading into the seminar, but that's because it's a proven hangover cure and might've helped soak up the toxins from the rotten milk.

The truth was that everyone was clearly jealous that Sam was cool enough to go out drinking instead of staying in his room all day on his computer 'working' like the rest of them.

It didn't matter. Sam knew a way out of this, a sure-fire solution which had never and would never fail. He raised his hand, momentarily holding it in front of Greg's face before snapping his fingers.

"And sleep," commanded Sam.

The world froze, a hundred eyes on Sam, but not in the way he'd hoped.

Sam rose from his desk, closed his laptop, and walked out the door. Or at least, that was Sam's intention. Unfortunately, he forgot to unplug his laptop charger in his haste, and Sam made it only a few steps before the wire snagged tight, sending him tumbling backwards into a crumpled heap.

Sam shot back up like a game of whack-a-mole, hoping to play it off as though he intended to trip, and it was all part of his rebellion. He yanked out the charger, dusted himself off, and once he was back on his feet, Sam's eyes met Amir's, his pretentious smile growing by the second, soaking up every drop of Sam's humiliation.

Amir may have had the upper hand, but Sam had hands too, hands which he used to shove all of Amir's neatly arranged possessions off his desk, sending pens, notebooks and his laptop clattering to the floor. He had it coming for a while.

Sam stood momentarily, deciding what his next move would be. Everyone in the room stared at him in stunned silence. Sam told himself it was a combination of awe and admiration, but couldn't quite make the idea stick. In the epicentre of it all, peering at Sam through a pair of half-moon glasses, was Greg, who was decidedly not awestruck by Sam's actions and boiling over in an explosive shade of red.

Eager to get away from the blast radius, Sam decided his best option, as always, was to run. He fired off through the door, running out along the enormous glass wall as he continued up the path alongside the seminar room. Pausing, he took a moment to catch his breath, and felt the milky cocktail of regret sloshing around his stomach. Sam choked it down, leaning against the large pane of glass to keep himself upright.

Through the glass, Sam noticed everyone still staring at him, rows and rows of students, but it wasn't awe or admiration. The sting of second-hand embarrassment was etched across their faces, clear as could be. With all his might, Sam willed himself not to throw up, refusing to let the last shreds of his dignity slip through his fingers.

Sam turned around to march down the path away from the classroom, off into the sunset, like some cool action hero who didn't even need their stupid coding seminar. Sam managed a single step before his knee buckled, and he doubled over, clutching his stomach as he dry heaved against the pavement.

"Should we-" began Amir.

"Back to work," corrected Greg.

5

Jack walked along the cobblestone path of the church courtyard as he so often did, his feet tapping out a steady, melancholic rhythm, which echoed through the stillness of the winter afternoon. Stubborn patches of white coalesced on either side of the path, bathed in a mosaic of reds and oranges from the church's windows.

A large iron fence with twisted peaks towered over Jack, casting long striated shadows across him. The fence's original green hue was evident only in the occasional remaining fleck of paint. The rest of the paint fell free long ago, giving way to shades of rust beneath.

Jack held a bunch of daffodils under his coat, doing his best to shield them from the cold. His mother always loved daffodils. He didn't know what flowers his dad liked or if he even cared for flowers at all. Too late to ask now, he supposed.

As Jack continued along the path, he passed the regulars he'd become acquainted with over the years. There was Richard Flint, a loving father taken too soon, and Audrey Short, whose life was cut short, not that the inscription took advantage of that obvious pun, which Jack always thought was a missed opportunity.

Soon, Jack reached the rows of stones too old to be deciphered, their engravings worn away with time, no flowers left for them, just lichens and moss consuming the small monuments with no one left to remember.

Each simple stone was likely the only surviving memento to prove someone once laughed so hard they couldn't breathe, burnt the roof of their mouth on a hot piece of food, spent ages getting ready to impress someone they fancied, or lived at all.

Finally, Jack laid eyes upon the one he came for—a simple gravestone, nothing too fancy, and peppered with a fine layer of frost. Jack removed the still-fresh daffodils he brought here yesterday and replaced them with today's daffodils. He sprayed the flowers, as he always did, with a nutrient broth Dr Li helped him create, one which would keep the flowers fresh for months before patting the top of the gravestone.

On the stone, still legible, as Jack often took a toothbrush to ensure this, read: *'Gary Phoenix and his loving wife, Geraldine Phoenix.'* Beneath this was the death date *'February 12th, 2013'*, the one date shared between the pair. Jack walked to the foot of the grave, brushing some wet leaves away as he sat cross-legged.

"It's my birthday today. I'm twenty now," said Jack. "Which also means it's been twelve years since..."

Jack struggled to find the words. His mouth turned dry, and his eyes wet. He didn't want to remember the specifics. He wasn't sure he even could, so he simply gestured towards the grave.

"This...Which I still haven't forgiven you for. Any day you could've picked to go, and you picked my birthday. Although, I suppose it wasn't your choice. I miss you, is all. I miss those trips to France we used to take. I even miss it when you argued. I just miss you being here. I've got Dr Li and Sam, but they're not you. I hope wherever you both are, you're happy."

Jack remembered when he first visited their grave with his grandmother. She took Jack in after all the unpleasantness. Jack remembered how his grandmother would pick him up from school each day, waiting by the gates with a bag of chocolate stars and a small carton of blackcurrant juice.

Jack never once saw the smile fade from her lips, but would sometimes hear her soft cries late at night when she thought he was sleeping. Losing her daughter and son-in-law soon proved too much for her, and then Jack was alone once more. He spent the following few years moving from foster home to foster family, never chosen properly.

"You're too quiet and shy," the care workers would tell him. "You need to make an impression if you want to find a new mommy and daddy."

Jack didn't want a new mommy and daddy, he only wanted his old ones back, so Jack began running away. Not that it would ever take long for him to be found, as he always ran to the same place, the place where he now sat.

Later on, there became a second place he ran to. The old bakery in which Dr Li set up a tiny refuge from the world.

ONE NIGHT, JACK WAS RUNNING FROM WHICHEVER foster family he was with that week, the tears on his red cheeks drowned out by the rain. He climbed in through the window of the bakery and padded through the lab, leaving small puddles with every step.

It was long past midnight, and Jack was sure Dr Li would be at home asleep by now, but it didn't matter. Jack would easily find something to occupy his time until he returned.

While perusing the lab to see what new trinkets he might

find, something curious caught his eye, nestled amongst an overgrown tapestry of wires on Dr Li's desk. A strange wooden object, with a cracked glass dome at one end housing a clock face, the hands of which had broken free and rattled around like the beads of a maraca.

Along the centre of its wooden shell was a brass panel left open on its hinges, exposing even more wires and several burnt-out circuits. Below this panel were three small LEDs, each one dark and dead. Next to the device, Jack spotted a book, an ancient leather-bound tome which, when Jack lifted the front cover, was quickly slammed shut in his face.

"What are you doing with that?" asked Dr Li.

"Nothing, I- I just found it," stammered Jack.

"Promise me, right now, you will never, ever look in this book," said Dr Li, his voice stern and urgent.

"Ok. I promise," said Jack, before his curiosity once more grabbed the wheel. "Why? What's inside it?"

Dr Li leaned in close so no one else in the empty lab might hear and whispered, "Instructions on how to use this." He handed Jack the strange wooden object with its cracked glass dome.

"What is it?" whispered Jack.

"A time machine."

Now, anyone else would've surely scoffed at the idea. But not Jack, for Jack's eyes were already open to the wonder and possibilities contained within this strange place. He'd become accustomed to the inventions and technology that defied all logic and reason, and now, best of all, it was home to a real time machine...

"Or it was...before I broke it," continued Dr Li. "You could help me fix it if you'd like, but the book stays off-limits, ok?"

"Ok." promised Jack, unable to pull his eyes from the device.

Dr Li taught Jack everything there was to know about time and the fourth dimension. Of the teachers, therapists and social workers of Jack's youth, none spoke with as much conviction as Dr Li. He talked to Jack in a way no other adult did, without a hint of pity or condescension. He spoke to Jack as an equal, which caused Jack to aspire to be so.

Dr Li often talked at incredible length with incredible speed about the impossible. Time travel became just another idea to add to the pile, pitched without ceremony and discussed as though it were more commonplace than brushing your teeth. Not that all of it made sense to Jack, or much of it at all, for that matter. Dr Li may have been a genius, but he was still ill-equipped to explain the nuances of quantum mechanics to a twelve-year-old.

Jack believed every word which came out of Dr Li's mouth. He heard many lies from many adults growing up.

"You'll get through this."

"Everything happens for a reason."

"I'm here for you whenever you need me."

Jack saw through each of those lies with ease, but he never doubted the honesty behind Dr Li's words.

Time travel. The idea resonated with Jack at once. Jack had a bone to pick with the past. He and it didn't depart on the best terms, and now Jack might just have a ticket back. He was familiar with the concept from movies and books, but never viewed it as anything more than fantasy. But there it was, with equipment and theories and formulas.

Intrigue rapidly transformed into an obsession, and Jack devoted his teenage years to immersing himself in the subject, assisting Dr Li in his research whenever possible.

At night, as Jack lay in bed, he imagined what he would do with the time machine. He would use it to right the wrongs of the past and retrieve what the world so cruelly took from him and refused to give back. Even if it was all a lie, just a quaint story to calm a young boy's tears, it was a good lie and one that Jack, more than anything, wished to believe.

Soon, Jack would take up residence in the impossible. The paperwork was finalized, and Dr Li became Jack's legal guardian. No more foster families or overcrowded orphanages.

Dr Li sold the old bakery, got a position teaching at a university and bought a cottage down a quiet country road for him and Jack to live in, secluded, peaceful, and safe from the harsh world beyond.

On weekends, Dr Li would escort Jack to the graveyard and wait while Jack cried and talked and cried some more.

When Jack turned 18, he received a full scholarship to the university Dr Li worked at, not that it mattered too much, as Jack already spent all his free time there. When Jack told Sam he was going to university, Sam immediately put in his application, telling Jack how much fun they would have together as university was just one big party.

Sam picked a degree in computer science as, in his own words, "I can already use a computer. What more do I really need to know?"

Jack sat by the grave for nearly an hour, telling his parents about how his university course was going, how Sam almost got them both killed, how Dr Li made him a locator for his birthday, how the time machine was nearly ready and how he would see them again soon.

Jack eventually got up from his spot as the first few spits of rain fell. He kissed the side of the grave and picked up the old flowers as he left, before placing them in front of one of the ancient graves, cracked, illegible and washed away with time.

He would remember them if no one else could.

6

Dr Li sat at his desk, filling the empty lab with the sounds of scraping metal and the hiss of electricity as he worked on the locator. The fumes of the molten solder were getting to him. He leaned back in his chair, deciding a break was in order.

He ran his hand along the drawers of a cabinet behind him, finding the one at the bottom he seldom visited, containing only a box of cigarettes and a lighter. It was decades since he last smoked, yet he always kept a pack within reach in case of emergencies.

As Dr Li stared up at the clock on the other side of the room, he knew this was indeed an emergency. He popped a cigarette in his mouth, lit it, and inhaled deeply, closing his eyes and enjoying his last moment of peace.

As Dr Li's respite began, a knock at the door interrupted him. Sighing and hiding the cigarette behind his back, he thumbed a button on the keypad in his desk drawer. The whiteboard behind him descended into position, concealing its secrets once more.

"Come in."

The door flew open as his visitors entered the class. There were three of them, a girl and two boys, each dressed in hoodies, t-shirts, and jeans. There was nothing noteworthy about them whatsoever, indistinguishable from anyone else walking the halls, but then, that was the point.

The trio strode to the front of the class, their movements synchronized like soldiers to battle.

"Where is it?" demanded the girl.

"Where's what?" replied Dr Li. "You're going to need to be more specific."

"The time machine."

"Oh, that." Dr Li returned the cigarette to his mouth and drew another breath.

He approached the trio of students. Their eyes followed him in perfect unison, an almost inhuman quality to their uniformity.

"What was it? Told they were ecstasy tablets? Thought you'd have a crazy night? That it? Or hell, maybe he's just putting it in the water now," mused Dr Li, looking them over.

He realized it was recent, still relatively fresh. Perhaps it hadn't fully taken effect yet. Wishful thinking, he supposed. Here they were. They knew who he was. They were already long gone.

Dr Li walked towards the door, flicking a few yellow gas taps on the wooden benches along the way and directing them towards the students. They silently filled the room with the sharp smell of noxious fumes, yet the strong odour went unnoticed by the watchful eyes of the three students, each one focused solely on Dr Li.

"He sent you, did he?" asked Dr Li.

This, too, was met with silence. His questions were pointless. Dr Li knew who they were, what they were and why they were there, as this was far from the first time. He thought he would be numb to it by now, yet he sensed the pulse in his neck quicken and every fibre in his body tense. Dr Li continued to talk, hoping to drown out the sound of his own fear.

"Of course he did," said Dr Li, answering for them. He pulled on the door handle, but it wouldn't budge. "Locked it, very sensible."

He stood before them, staring into the three sets of vacant pupils.

"Well, it's not here. More importantly, it's not anywhere. Time travel's not possible," concluded Dr Li with a dismissive shrug.

The three students stopped looking at Dr Li for the first time since arriving and turned their gaze towards the whiteboard. Among the scribblings and equations written in big capital letters were the words '*TIME TRAVEL IS POSSIBLE.*'

Dr Li glanced over at the whiteboard and offered a small, defeated laugh.

"That's just..." Dr Li couldn't find the words. Luckily for him, he didn't have to, as the three students stepped forward, surrounding him.

"Ok," sighed Dr Li, accepting the inevitable.

He took one last puff of his cigarette and flicked it towards the gas taps. A huge fireball engulfed the female student, who was unfortunate enough to be standing in their direct line of sight. A thick wave of heat rippled through the classroom as the flames devoured her.

The two male students charged toward Dr Li. But Dr Li, already one step ahead, snatched a tray from a workbench. He smacked it into the face of one boy and frisbee'd it at the other.

The tray spun through the air before slicing the side of his face. A steady stream of scarlet ran down his neck. It wouldn't be enough to stop them, and with little concern for Dr Li's onslaught, the two boys continued their approach. The first motioned to punch Dr Li in the face, but Dr Li ducked back, dodging the fist before smacking it down onto the lab bench.

Dr Li reached out, his fingers closing around the smooth neck of a glass flask, and he wasted no time shattering it into the boy's head, right above the temple. Shards of glass fired out across the room, and the boy stumbled backwards, dazed. Dr Li seized the opening and charged into him with all his weight.

The boy tripped back into the other as they tumbled to the ground. Dr Li now had the upper hand, or boot in this case, as he stamped it down onto them. Over and over, digging his heal in, hoping against hope it might be enough to incapacitate their unwavering resolve.

An interesting quirk about Dr Li's would-be assailants was how they didn't scream in pain or shout in anger. They remained silent throughout the ordeal. They felt pain; Dr Li was sure of it, but it was as though they physically could not react to it. Nowhere was this more apparent than in the female student who, lest we forget, was still on fire.

The flames chewed away at her flesh like a swarm of piranhas, but rather than try to put herself out, she remained fixated on Dr Li. Her survival was secondary to him and what he held in his possession. She made no sound. Only the crackles of the fire and the BBQ aroma emanating from her roasted body alerted Dr Li to her attempt to sneak up behind him.

Dr Li tried to dive out of her reach, but even as her nerve endings fizzled away, she was too quick for him. She wrapped her arms around him, and the flames spread to Dr Li, joining them in one giant fiery embrace. He struggled to focus through the pain consuming him, unable to wrestle free from her grip. Kicking his legs up against his desk, he propelled the pair of them backwards, slamming her spine against the fire alarm.

The sound of the alarm rang out, the sprinklers switched on, and water rained down, making quick work of the fire. This finally proved too much for the girl as she released Dr Li, sliding off him and collapsing to the floor in a steaming heap.

Dr Li ran to the other side of the room, where he found rows of chemical flasks on the shelves and hundreds of small vials labelled with the initials of his students, used as part of a practical the day before.

He grabbed a handful, trying to make out what was in each, his eyes struggling to see through the downpour of water. Emptying a few vials into a flask, he shoved a cork into the top and shook it until the solution illuminated brighter and brighter.

Just beyond the bench, Dr Li saw one of the male students returning to his feet. Dr Li lobbed the flask at him, which exploded on impact with a blinding flash of white. Dr Li ducked behind the lab bench to shield his eyes from the impossibly bright light, clawing away at his eyelids as it tried to reach inside.

Once the light faded, he peeked back over and saw the same student staggering through the room before slipping on the growing puddles of water and finally falling. Dr Li glanced over at the other boy, bleeding profusely from the head, and of course, he couldn't forget the girl lying face down on the floor, smoke still wafting from her charred and blackened body.

They started it.

Dr Li dragged himself back over to the other side of the class and pressed his hand onto an unassuming bit of wall. A light began running along the wall and under his hand, scanning it.

He pulled his hand away, and a hidden panel in the wall flipped around. Attached to it were an EpiPen and a small metallic disk. He grabbed both and crouched beside the female student. He turned her over and found she was worse than he feared.

Dr Li allowed himself a momentary pang of regret for what he did to her, but what other choice did he have? He pushed the thought to the back of his mind as they were about to be more than even.

"I've got an antidote. I believe this is the one. Two-hundredth time's the charm, right?"

Dr Li jammed the EpiPen into what remained of her melted arm. Behind him, the boy with the bleeding forehead was stumbling over to the wall panel, his reprogramming still forcing him to search for the time machine above all else.

Without missing a beat, Dr Li tossed the metal disk at him, which immediately burst into a blue electrical sphere, hanging in midair and fully engulfing the boy. But it didn't harm or even stop him, for within the charged globe, the boy was still moving towards the panel, only he was moving much slower now.

So, too, the beads of water falling from the sprinklers slowed to a crawl as they met the sphere, the droplets suspended like glass. Time was literally running slower within it.

The antidote spread along the girl's arm and continued through her body. Dr Li silently begged for it to undo the spell placed upon her. After a few endless seconds of waiting, Dr Li watched as the girl opened her eyes, blinking in confusion. She was coming back, humanity ebbing through her once more. Dr Li wasn't imagining it, not this time. He was sure of it. Everything would be different now. He'd found an actual, proper cure.

"How are you feeling?" asked Dr Li, gently taking her hand in his.

The girl punched Dr Li in the face as hard as she could.

Luckily for Dr Li, the adrenaline numbed most of the pain, although it still hurt like hell, but not nearly as much as the terrible realization that there was no way of reversing what happened to them.

He couldn't save them. The fight was already lost. The only positive was that this meant there was little point in fighting fair anymore. Dr Li checked behind him. The boy was about to escape his delayed journey through the blue orb.

Dr Li shot towards the orb just as the boy escaped it.

"Gravity Off!" commanded Dr Li and dove inside.

The falling water hung in the air momentarily before reversing its trajectory, now turning back towards the ceiling. The three students followed with it, flying sharply upwards, as did everything in the room. They collided with the ceiling as stools, microscopes, and entire tables joined them, pummeling them until their bodies could take no more.

From inside the sphere, Dr Li was safe from the sudden lack of physics, gradually travelling upwards at a snail's pace until his head leisurely popped out the top.

"Gravity On!" commanded Dr Li.

Everything in the room fell to the floor with a deafening crash. Dr Li pressed his hand to the orb's centre and closed his fingers around the disc. With this, it popped like a bubble, and time resumed its regular pace. Dr Li wadded through the room, stepping through the carnage and broken bodies of his assailants, half buried beneath the classroom.

The sprinklers still rained down, and the alarm still shrieked. It wouldn't be long before someone would come to investigate, and he didn't particularly want to stick around for it. So, he grabbed the spare key from his now overturned filing cabinet and left.

DR LI'S LAB WAS SOON SWARMING WITH POLICE officers, and a thick barrier of police tape sealed off the corridor to the small crowds of students trying to see what happened inside. Paramedics pulled the three students from beneath the wreckage and were surprised to find all three still resiliently clinging to life despite their ordeal.

Now, it was the investigator's and the forensic team's turn to examine what remained of the science lab. The one in charge of it all was Detective Chief Inspector Sparks, a stern man in his early fifties whose grizzled, stubbled face hid a series of pale white scars beneath. He stood at attention, surveying the scene. His thick arms, like tree trunks, bulged out through the ends of his sleeves and hung stoically by his sides in tight, disciplined fists.

DCI Sparks was once an army corporal, serving several tours in both Iraq and Afghanistan. His time in the army ended many years ago when, during his final stint in Afghanistan, he received news of the sudden death of his wife, and so got the next flight back to be by his teenage daughter's side.

He never returned to the army after, but the army life refused to leave him. He would still wake up long before the sun each morning and train at the gym for two hours before every work shift. With his experience and dedication, it didn't take long for him to be promoted from police officer all the way to Detective Constable Inspector. Regardless of the title, everyone knew him as *Corporal Sparks - a right 'ard bastard.*

A young police officer stood by his side, swaying excitedly in her new uniform as she watched over the crime scene and all the people dressed in white coveralls, picking apart the smallest details of the science lab.

"Any news on the victims, officer?" asked DCI Sparks.

The young police officer started giggling.

"Officer, never been called officer before. I've still got to get used to that."

This was Lucy Sparks, the daughter of DCI Sparks. Ever since she was a little girl, she always wanted to follow in her dad's footsteps. She delighted in telling everyone how she would someday save people and stop bad guys, just like her dad did.

Her uniform was brand new and at least two sizes too big, but it meant she was a real-life police officer. She was investigating a proper crime, likely with actual criminals, and maybe if she tried her absolute hardest, she would be the one to solve it all and save the day. But she was getting ahead of herself.

"Please try to take this seriously," said her father.

"Sorry," replied Lucy, trying to contain her excitement. She quickly flicked through her notebook. "The three victims were taken to the hospital. But none are responsive, so we can't get any statements right now."

"Right, well, why don't you go to the hospital and call me if any of them wake up?" This was an attempt at keeping Lucy out of the way, as her incessant chirpiness was driving everybody insane.

Lucy could tell this was busy work, but she didn't care one bit. She was an actual police officer, and going to the hospital to interview the victims of a crime was something actual police officers did. Maybe the victims would wake up and tell her who did it. She would probably get a medal for that, perhaps not a medal but at the very least, her own desk, maybe even her name in the paper.

She could picture it now: *Officer Lucy Sparks valiantly arrests bad guys. When interviewed, Officer Lucy Sparks modestly shrugged, saying, "It's all part of the job."* Best of all, Lucy thought about her dad and how proud he would be of her.

He would tell everybody he knew, "*That's my daughter, who solved her first case all on her own.*"

Her mind had wandered again. She had to stop doing that, especially if she was going to solve the crime.

"Aye aye, dad- er captain," said Lucy, saluting.

"DCI Sparks," corrected her father.

"DCI Sparks, gotcha," said Lucy with a wink as she hurried out of the room to her next mission.

7

Sam couldn't wait here any longer. He was sitting in the hospital's A&E for nearly fifteen minutes, and enough was enough. He stood up and marched over to the reception desk.

"Excuse me, I've been waiting here nearly two hours, and this is kind of an emergency," exaggerated Sam. "I've been exposed to some expired milk, and it's ravaging my body as we speak. I've been hallucinating; my stomach feels like it's going to explode, and I honestly think I might be dying."

If Sam played this up enough, they would probably give him a note to excuse him from any more coding lessons. A guy in his class got out of lessons for an entire term for a touch of leukaemia, so Sam could surely haggle at least a year off for this.

At this moment, Officer Lucy Sparks walked into the hospital, almost skipping through the automatic doors. She stopped, remembering she needed to be professional.

"Straight face. You can do this. You're an officer of the law," Lucy told herself. She continued past Sam, scarcely noticing him threatening to sue the hospital for his murder, and up to the receptionist.

"Hiya, do you know where I'd find the three students brought in earlier?"

"Woah, woah, woah," countered Sam, the cheek of it, the audacity. Not one more person was going to get seen before him. "I was here first."

"I'm sorry, but this is important police business. I'm a police officer."

Lucy proudly flashed her police badge at Sam.

"Doesn't mean you're above the law. The law of the line," argued Sam, gesturing to himself and no one else.

"Room 212, up the stairs and take a left," said the receptionist.

"Thank you," said Lucy, hastily continuing down the corridor.

Sam was astonished. He stood for a moment, making sure he hadn't dreamt this new level of injustice, but as he stared into the face of the disinterested receptionist, he knew it to be true. A long rant to the receptionist about police getting special treatment followed, how this was a perfect example of police brutality, how they were all responsible for anything that happened to him, and how they would hear from his team of lawyers.

As Sam's rant reached its grand crescendo, he noticed his lecturer, Greg, carrying some cardboard boxes and coming his way. He passed Sam and approached the reception desk.

This was becoming a joke. Why was no one respecting the queuing system?

"Just dropping off the new shipment," Greg told the receptionist. She nodded, and he continued on his way.

Why would Greg be here? Did he follow Sam here after the seminar? Was he spying on him? Sam's imminent milky death would have to wait.

"Greg," called Sam as he followed his lecturer up the corridor.

Greg didn't answer, didn't pause, didn't even seem to notice. He soon ducked inside a storage room, but Sam wasn't about to let him escape easily. He shoved the door open after him, ready to confront his lecturer-turned-stalker.

Inside, Sam found Greg placing the cardboard boxes on a table. Beside him stood three more people, their backs to Sam as they opened the boxes and began sorting through their contents.

The boxes joined the seemingly endless piles of identical ones, filling the small, cramped room stacked to the ceiling in every direction. Sam watched as they moved packets of pills from one box to another, working in hypnotic unison.

Sam soon realized he was standing in this room watching them go about their business for nearly a full minute now, and not one of them acknowledged him.

Was the milk already taken too strong a hold? Was Sam already dead and left to roam this hospital as a ghost?

No, Greg was just being an arse.

"Greg." said Sam, marching over to him.

Greg finally acknowledged Sam with a quick, "I'm busy." He didn't even bother to look up.

"It's funny bumping into you here. Are you volunteering or something?" asked Sam.

"I'm busy," repeated Greg.

"Look about earlier..." Sam trailed off. He couldn't help but notice something about the three people sorting through the boxes.

He realized they were all around Sam's age, two boys and a girl. One with stitches all across their head, another was covered with grotesque burns, and the last, their eyes fully bandaged. These weren't staff or volunteers. These were patients.

What happened here? It was clear this hospital didn't treat its patients well, but Sam didn't think it was bad enough to make its patients work for their treatment. They appeared to struggle to hold themselves up, let alone the boxes.

"Are you alright?" asked Sam, but found no answer as the trio remained silent and continued their work, diligently sorting through the pills.

Maybe the one with bandaged eyes didn't notice him, but the other two had no excuse. Then it dawned on Sam. If his eyes were bandaged, how the hell could he sort through the pills?

"They're fine," said Greg.

"They don't bloody look it. What is going on here?" demanded Sam.

"Excuse me," said Greg in a voice somehow more lifeless and monotone than usual, pushing past Sam as he left through the same door he entered.

"Psst. What's going on? Is he making you do this?" asked Sam, turning to the trio.

Still no reply.

Perhaps they weren't even here. They hardly be the first strange vision Sam saw lately. Then it all made sense to Sam. They were ghosts, and a second, more stomach-twisting conclusion came to him. He, too, was a ghost. Of course, it explained everything. The rugby players got to him last night and beat the life out of him, leaving him to watch his last few moments helplessly, now destined to wander the earth with unfinished business.

Then Sam noticed Greg's clipboard on the table. He

skimmed through it, and as he read, his mind turned from thoughts of ghosts and the otherworldly and focused on the genuine danger carved into each word. Sam needed to get very far away from here. He turned toward the door, now desperately wishing he were a ghost, but it opened before he could reach it.

There stood Greg, holding another pile of boxes. Sam froze, gripping the clipboard tight.

Greg turned from Sam to the clipboard, and a glimmer of emotion flickered across his face, bubbling up above the layers of dullness, one which made Sam want to recede inside himself like a tortoise.

"Give me that now," hissed Greg.

The stress, the injustice, the ghosts and the milk all became too much, and the contents of Sam's stomach, which he was fighting to keep down all day, finally broke free, rocketing upwards. Sam's mouth shot open as all the alcohol, milk, stomach acid, and a few flecks of cocaine fired into Greg's face in a creamy white stream, exorcising any phantoms from Sam's body and leaving Greg's comb-over hair drenched and clumped over his furious features. The cardboard boxes Greg held darkened as the steaming soupy mixture soaked through.

Sam shoved Greg out of the way and darted out of the room, clutching the clipboard to his chest. Sam ran along the corridor, through reception and out the doors, suddenly feeling much better and indisputably alive.

ON THE FLOOR ABOVE, LUCY STRODE PURPOSEFULLY down the corridor, reading the door numbers.

210...211...212.

She found it. Lucy eased the door open, finding a series of beds waiting for her, each one blocked off by a blue curtain.

"Hello?" asked Lucy, but found only silence.

Lucy approached the first curtain, gripped the thin fabric, and pulled it back like a magician, revealing the climax of their act. But as the curtain parted, Lucy found an empty bed where the first of the three students should be.

She approached the next bed and wasted no time in pulling it open.

Abracadabra.

Another empty bed. Another missing victim.

Lucy turned to face the last bed, the final curtain, but as she lifted her foot, she sensed it squelch. She was standing in something sticky, something *red* and sticky. Something red and sticky and coming from beneath the final curtain.

Tearing the curtain free, she revealed the prestige of her magic show.

A final empty bed and a body lying face down beside it in a pool of deep red blood.

No, no, no! She'd arrived too late. Whoever attacked the three students must have returned to finish the job.

She ran over to the body and turned it over, but it wasn't a student. It was a nurse. A fine slice ran along her throat and congealed blood gurgled freely as Lucy lifted her head. Lucy tried to hold the nurse's neck shut, but it was already far too late. Her body was stiff and cold to the touch. She was, most certainly, dead.

A scalpel lay nearby. Whoever did this must've come for the three students; this poor nurse was an innocent bystander. Perhaps she even tried to fight them off in her last moments.

But where were the three students now? Were they captured on CCTV? Or maybe someone witnessed the attack?

Lucy's mind span out of control, and her blood-filled hands trembled, causing the nurse's head to slip from her palms and hit the floor with a wet thud.

"I'm sorry, I'm so sorry." Lucy's voice quivered. "Help, somebody. Please help!"

She grabbed the walkie-talkie connected to the collar of her uniform, her blood-soaked finger slipping on the button as she tried to switch it on, all the while still trying to keep hold of the nurse's throat with her other hand. Hoping she might still make it.

"Immediate backup required at St Margaret's Hospital," said Lucy into the walkie-talkie, trying desperately to remain calm. "I've found a nurse. Her throat's been cut. I- I think she might be dead. The killer could still be here. Please, someone, I don't know what to do. I don't know what to do..."

She released the button and shouted again, trying to get the attention of anyone in the hospital, not daring to leave the nurse. "Please, someone help!"

She held the walkie-talkie close to her face and pressed the button again.

Closing her eyes, she whispered, "Dad?"

8

Dr Li hurried through the bustling train station, weaving in and out of the crowd as he made his way towards platform 4, his head bowed to not draw any unnecessary attention to his singed beard and soaked lab coat. He hadn't stopped since leaving his lab, keeping a steady pace, not too fast, but not suspiciously slowly, either. As long as he kept moving, he would be safe.

Trains were safe, though; lots of witnesses. They wouldn't try anything here.

He boarded the old graffiti-coated carriage just as the doors closed and found it full, surprisingly full. He walked through the carriage and into the next, but couldn't find a single free seat, each one occupied by an endless supply of passengers, chatting and going about their business. As such, Dr Li resigned to holding onto the metal bar and stood while the train rocked him back and forth. With each passing second, the train took Dr Li further away from the university, and Dr Li's breath finally steadied.

In the haste of his exit, he forgot the Time Machine, which remained back at his lab, or at least, what remained of his lab. Still, it was safe for now, locked away, with only him and Jack in possession of the passcode. He removed the locator from his pocket and switched it on. Thankfully, he worked out the last of its bugs before he was rudely interrupted.

After a few moments, the screen lit up, displaying a map still tuned to Jack's blood signature. Jack was at the church graveyard. He was safe, unlike Dr Li.

Dr Li was far from safe. He couldn't go home without risking being followed; this train was seemingly the only safe place left in the world.

Bing Bong.

The speakers above interrupted Dr Li's train of thought as the synthetic voice made its announcement. *"When leaving the train, please ensure that you take all your belongings with you, be they bags, suitcases, or time machines…Hello Li."*

Dr Li recognized the voice at once. The man who sent the three students to visit him, the man he would never escape from, the man who meant nowhere was safe anymore. It was years since he last heard his voice, with its mechanical, inhuman hiss. Yet it still sent a familiar shiver of ice down his spine.

"You can reply," continued the voice on the tannoy, *"I can hear you."*

Dr Li didn't answer. He scanned the carriage, searching for an escape route.

"Don't feel like talking? Twenty years, and you have nothing to say to me? Well, I have something to say to you, Li. Look what I achieved without you. I have total control. I'm everywhere, and I'm everyone."

Everyone in the train carriage stopped, falling silent as, in unison, every one of them stood up from their seats and turned to face Dr Li. Each passenger stared at him with piercing eyes. Old eyes, young eyes, even a baby, struggling to hold its head up, yet still, it fixed its gaze upon Dr Li. The passengers followed his every minor movement through blank expressions with the pin-point accuracy of snakes waiting to strike.

Fighting three of them on his home turf was one thing, but here, they severely outnumbered him. There were at least thirty of them on this carriage, with eight carriages, that made 240 in total. Those odds were insurmountable. Fighting his way out was impossible.

He couldn't escape. Leaving Dr Li with one option. He would have to give him what he wanted: acknowledgement of how great he was, how clever and brilliant his plan was, and how Dr Li was powerless to stop him.

"Yeah, I've seen your little project," said Dr Li, swallowing his fear.

"It's not little though, five thousand people so far…"

"Five thousand people you've hollowed out. These people are as good as dead," said Dr Li, trying to avoid their unavoidable gaze. "This, Toby, is why you will never have the time machine."

"It's inevitable. You're going to give it to me. Nowhere is safe from me. There's nowhere you can go. You've seen what I can do. I could crash this train and kill you right now."

"You won't, because I'm the only person who can use the time machine. You need me."

A momentary pause followed while the voice on the other end of the speaker considered. *"That's not true,"* the voice decided.

"What do you mean?" asked Dr Li, already knowing the answer.

"Well, there's the boy."

Dr Li closed his eyes. Of course, he knew. It was inevitable. "You leave him out of this. He hasn't used it. He doesn't even know how to use it."

"Bring him to me," said the voice. *"Or he dies. Understood?"*

Dr Li didn't reply. Maybe he should take his chances and try to fight his way out. He could overload the locator and send a shockwave through the metal structure of the train. It would almost certainly kill him, too. However, it would be worth it if it meant Jack would be safe. No, he realized that wasn't the truth. Toby wasn't on this train, and as long as he was still out there, Jack would still be in danger.

"Do you understand?! Bring me the time machine! Bring me the boy!" The sound through the speaker system crackled as the voice screeched before becoming calm once more. *"Oh, and mind the gap."*

The speaker system cut off, and everyone on the train returned to normal, continuing their mundane conversations, texting on their phones, and eating their sandwiches as though nothing happened.

Dr Li knew what he would do, what he must do.

Once again, as he always did.

9

Jack received a text from Sam instructing him to meet at their usual spot at 7 o'clock, so Jack arrived at a small, run-down pub at precisely 6:59. It was a weathered old building dating back to the 19th century, and it bore those years well. Generations of drunken gallantry long left their mark.

Centuries of urine and vomit eroded the bricks lining the walls and left a foul odour clinging to the clothes of anyone unlucky enough to pass by. Its windows fogged with grime and cheap chat-up lines, and every surface of its interior was sticky to the touch.

Jack stared up at the large wooden sign above the door and remembered the day he and Sam first saw it. Sam erupted in such a guffaw of laughter at its name that he immediately deemed all over pubs inferior, deciding that this was the only suitable place for the pair to spend their evenings from then on.

Upon stepping inside *The Bell's End*, Jack walked through the dimly lit path he often took, his feet squelching through the damp carpeting. He passed rows of half-conscious alcoholics mumbling into their glasses, being sure to keep his head down to avoid the inebriated gaze of anyone who might be itching for a fight. Jack slid into their usual booth beside the pool table, careful to avoid the spot where Sam liked to stash his used gum, and there he waited.

WHEN IT TURNED 8 O'CLOCK, JACK'S MIND TURNED to worry. Where was he? Sam was usually late, but not this late. He sent him several messages ranging across the full spectrum of Jack's annoyance all the way to concern, with his most recent message simply being, *'Are you ok?'*.

Jack hit send and placed his phone back on the table. He peered around awkwardly, hoping to spot Sam waiting for him at another table, but as he studied the dimly lit pub and its faded Victorian decor, he spotted a man watching him from across the bar. Their eyes met, and Jack instinctively glanced away.

As Jack took a subtle peek back, he found the man staring at him, a scrawny, skinny, lanky man with a gold chain running around his neck and descending into a deep red hoodie. A black duffle bag rested on the stool beside the man. Jack checked behind himself in the hopes the man was eying somebody else, but there was nothing. He was definitely staring at Jack.

Jack returned to his phone, swiping his finger across the menus, hoping that if he didn't look at the man, he, too, might stop staring at him. After a minute, Jack glanced up again and saw the man walking towards him.

Just keep your head down, he thought to himself. *He probably recognizes you from somewhere or wants to ask for your recommendation of pub snacks. There were those little packets of sweet chilli-flavoured peanuts that...*

"Jack?" the hooded man asked.

"Um...yes, I am him...He is me," stammered Jack.

The man placed his duffel bag down and took a seat opposite Jack. "Sam said he might be late."

Sam, of course. The usual explanation for angry glares in pubs. This man was here looking for money, or revenge, or both.

"Oh right, are you a friend of Sam's or..."

"Something like that."

Perhaps this truly was a new friend Sam had made, a big, scary friend with a soul-piercing stare. Maybe he shouldn't judge him solely on his appearance...or his demeanour...or that Jack was yet to see him blink.

"Well, I'll message Sam again, let him know that..."

"Tim."

"Tim. Tim?" Jack ran the name across his mouth. It didn't suit at all.

"Yeah, Tim, what's wrong with Tim?" Tim's eyebrows curled down, and his stare somehow grew even more intense.

"Nothing, great name, tip top...*Tim* top...Erm, I'll let Sam know that...Tim is here. Did you want me to get you a drink or anything?"

"Pint."

"Coming up. A couple of pints for the lads."

Jack shot up and scurried over to the bar. Two pints. Two pints of what? Beer? Cider? Orange juice? He would ask for what was '*on tap.*' That was a thing normal people said.

Jack stood at the bar, momentarily staring towards the door and considering how easy it would be to run away. He wasn't sure why he even agreed to come here tonight. He despised pubs, the noise, the crowds, the inevitable fight Sam would get them in. It was his birthday, after all. He should be able to choose what they did.

Jack decided that if he turned and left, Sam would have to go searching for him for a change. He quite liked the idea of that. But before he could, Jack found the bartender appear before him.

"Alright guv'nor. What can I get you?" asked the oily bartender with a wink.

Too late to run away now.

"Two pints of on tap, please," said Jack, trying to sound normal.

Twenty minutes passed, and Jack was still nursing the foam from the top of his pint as Tim knocked back the final few drips of his. Jack checked his phone, as he was doing religiously every 10 seconds.

"Still no reply from Sam. He should be here any second. Any second now..." said Jack, almost praying, wishing Sam could be here to save him from this situation. "So, how did you and Sam meet? I bet there's a funny story there."

"He saw my number written on a toilet door, and I sold him some weed," replied Tim, not one for funny stories.

"Oh, that's interesting. So you're a, a...a dealer of...drugs?" uttered Jack.

"Yeah."

Of course. An angry drug dealer here for money.

"Is that why you're here now? Is that..." Jack looked around and leaned in, whispering, "Is that what's in the bag?"

Jack knew the answer already. Of course it was. Tim's duffle bag most certainly overflowed with piles of cocaine, marijuana, heroin, and substances Jack had never even heard of.

"No," said Tim.

"Then what is in the bag?" asked Jack, his voice raising an octave.

"It's a secret."

Jack's mind raced. What was Sam buying from this man? Weapons? Guns? Drugs? No, wait, he said it wasn't drugs. Oh God, it was guns then, wasn't it?

This lunatic was sitting across from Jack with a bag of guns, and he just bought him a drink. Jack needed to know what was in the bag.

"You can tell me. I can keep a secret. I bought you that drink, remember? Because we're friends," said Jack, trying his best to sound nonchalant.

Tim unzipped the bag, and dozens of miniature, multicoloured rockets of all shapes and sizes popped out.

"Fireworks?" spurted Jack.

"Yeah, Sam told me he wanted to buy some fireworks for tonight for some birthday thing."

Jack gave a small sigh of relief.

"And he better get here soon. He owes me five hundred quid for this lot," continued Tim.

Jack nearly choked on his drink. "Five hundred pounds for some fireworks?"

"And cocaine," finished Tim.

Jack was going to wring the idiot's neck.

"Boo!" shouted a voice from behind Jack.

Jack almost jumped out of his seat, a tightly wound spring ready to bounce halfway to the moon. As he turned, none other than Sam, standing behind him, holding a clipboard and wearing a cocky grin on his face.

"How are you lads doing?" continued Sam, and before giving them a chance to answer, said, "You two will not believe what I found."

Sam slammed the clipboard down on the table with glee.

Jack wasn't interested in whatever scheme Sam was cooking up right now. He wanted to get far, far away from this undoubtedly murderous, drug-dealing firework salesman.

"Sam, money," said Jack through gritted teeth.

Sam, in his excitement, blocked out Jack and was already into his spiel.

"So my lecturer Greg, right, he's stealing pills from the hospital. I saw him nicking boxes of pills with some shifty-looking people, and I mean real shifty. There was this girl, right, her skin was like properly melted, and this guy with no eyes."

"What are you talking about?" interrupted Jack, losing all patience.

Sam slid the clipboard with all its damning evidence over to Jack. Picking up the clipboard, Jack skimmed through the bundle of paper clamped to it.

"So where is my money, Sam?" asked Tim, uninterested in Sam's grand conspiracy.

"All in good time," replied Sam.

Jack had read enough. "He's not stealing anything. This says they hired him to replace some medicine. He's probably just swapping out expired pills for fresh ones."

"He teaches IT. Why would he be working for the hospital?" said Sam. He already had a list of theories prepared with almost all the dots connected. "He most likely used his computer skills to hack into the hospital mainframe and swap out the drugs to sell them to some gang leader. Tim, you're a gang leader. You know what I'm talking about, right?"

"Yeah, of course," said Tim, although Jack couldn't help but notice a slight hesitation in his voice. "Happen's all the time, but Greg...Ain't got any Gregs working for me. What's his last name?"

Sam shrugged.

"Page," said Jack, answering for him.

"Never heard of him," said Tim.

"You realize how insane you sound right now? Mr Page has been working at the university for years. He's not some secret drug mule."

"Yeah?" Sam pointed at the clipboard. "Then why does it say right here he's handing the stolen pills over to some guy called Dr Tobias Cud?"

"A gang leader with a doctorate?" sneered Jack.

"Hold up," said Tim. "Mate of mine said he got some experimental shit from a guy called Cud. Lovely stuff, he told me, got a deal on it n' all."

"See," said Sam triumphantly. "I told you."

"Well, I..." started Jack. Sam wasn't right. He couldn't be. But what if he was? Amazingly, the documents appeared to support this theory. "Fine then. If you're so sure about this, let's go to the police."

"Nah," said Tim. "I ain't having the old bill looking into my business."

"What do you think we should do, Tim?" asked Sam.

"I say we grab a hatchet. Then we'll trot on down there and do him in. It'll send a message."

"Please don't get a hatchet," begged Jack, sinking into his chair.

"Good point. We wanna be subtle," agreed Tim, swiping some silverware from a small pot on the table. "We'll use a fork. Do him in the neck."

"Sam, say something," whispered Jack.

"I love it," said Sam as he scooped up the remaining silverware. "Maybe a spoon, too? No one ever expects a spoon."

"Please put the cutlery down," sighed Jack. "You can't kill Sam's lecturer."

"Yeah, we can," countered Tim.

"Of course we can," agreed Sam.

"Well, you're not," said Jack. "He probably isn't even doing anything illegal. This is your imagination running wild, as always."

Sam and Tim ignored Jack, muting him out as Sam began formulating a plan. One which Jack was sure would no doubt get them killed.

10

Sam and Tim strode through the frigid night air of the empty university campus with Jack in tow, begging them to reconsider. But Sam and Tim were too busy laughing and goading each other on to listen, bounding under street lamps which shone down on them like spotlights as they passed the grand architecture of the university. All the while chugging down beer bottles and smashing them on the pavement.

Sam kept punching the air, doing his own sound effects to psyche himself up like he was in an old *Batman* cartoon.

"I'd love him to try something," said Sam. "I'd give him one of these. *Pew, wham, bam!*"

Sam was many things, but by no means would he be mistaken for a professional boxer, or someone who took even a single boxing lesson, or stepped foot inside a gym, ever.

Jack began to re-evaluate many of his recent decisions as they reached the university's car park. Why did he encourage this insane conspiracy? Why was he following Sam and Tim here? Why was he still friends with Sam at all?

"Did you really need to bring the fireworks?" asked Jack, needing to start somewhere.

"What? Would you rather we left them at the pub for some toddlers to find?" replied Tim.

"Do many toddlers hang around in pubs? Can't we do this tomorrow? Confrontations are more of a daytime thing. When there'll be, you know, witnesses."

Sam marched over to an old silver car, the only one in the entire car park.

"See, I told you he would still be here," said Sam.

"Please, just think about this for a moment..." began Jack.

Before he could finish, Sam threw his bottle into the driver's seat window. The window shattered with a terrible crash, sending sheets of glass raining down to the tarmac, where they broke into vicious diamonds.

Jack stood in shock, mouth agape, frozen to the spot in a glue trap of fear as the car's alarm blared around him. However, this didn't seem to affect Sam and Tim one iota as they continued laughing like a pair of schoolboys, not beginning to comprehend the gravity of what they just did, gravity which was crushing Jack and forcing all the air from his lungs.

"Well, there's no going back now. We have to go in," said Sam smugly.

"Jesus Christ, Sam, what have you done?!" cried Jack as all the air rushed back. "You smashed the bloody window!"

Jack peered in through the frame of splintered glass and saw the broken bottle of beer lying on the driver's seat, covered in Sam's fingerprints. Even if no one came now, the evidence would soon lead back to them.

"Oh, boo-hoo, he deserves it," said Sam, skipping towards the large sliding doors of the pristine university building, a cascading tower of glass standing proudly, and the next victim in Sam and Tim's tirade of destruction.

Jack prayed for it to be closed. Perhaps the automatic doors would be locked for the night, forcing them to go home. Of course, the dice again fell in Sam's favour, and the doors effortlessly slid open as he and Tim approached them.

Jack hurried after them.

"Ok, ok, we'll go in, apologize, pay for the damage, call it quits. Everybody's happy."

THE TRIO MADE THEIR WAY THROUGH THE MAZE OF identical white corridors towards Greg Page's seminar room.

Maybe it was Jack's loyalty to Sam. Possibly he partially believed the conspiracy. Or perhaps Jack simply noticed the CCTV camera pointing directly at him, forever linking him to whatever was about to transpire. Whatever the reason, Jack continued to follow Sam and Tim despite his better judgement and even his worse judgement, falling further down this rabbit hole of bad ideas.

THEY FINALLY REACHED THE END OF THE CORRIDOR and the door to the seminar room. This was it. The stage was set. Through the small window on the door, Sam saw Greg inside, typing away at his desk on the far side of the room.

"There he is," said Sam, his breath fogging his view.

"You won't be violent, will you? You promised we were just going to talk to him," whispered Jack.

"Yeah, we'll talk to him, then we'll kick his teeth in," said Tim, bringing the conversation up a few decibels.

"No, Jack's right. We should take the subtle approach," said Sam, pressing his face against the glass to get a good look at his arch-nemesis.

As he did so, his weight pushed the door open. Sam lurched back, trying to stop it, but it was too late. The door swung open, and Sam fell face-first into the room.

Greg gazed up from his computer, perplexed by the sudden intrusion.

"Now Tim! Hit him! Hit him!" shouted Sam, scrambling to his feet.

"I thought we were being subtle?" Said Tim.

"Nothing about this is subtle!" cried Jack.

"Fine, fine." Sam dusted himself off and faced his foe. 'Hello Greg.'

"Samuel," replied Greg, confused but not overly concerned by the three men arguing in his doorway.

Sam strolled past rows of computers, swaggering through the room with unearned confidence until he reached Greg's desk, catching a whiff of milky vomit still lingering on his skin. Tim followed close behind whilst Jack hesitantly dipped a toe through the door.

"We've got your little drug report," said Sam, presenting the clipboard. "We know all about your dirty misdeeds. So, here's the deal. You give us a big ol' slice of the money cake, or we go to the police. I think that's more than fair. So, you're going to give us..."

Sam turned to Tim.

"Twenty grand," said Tim.

"Really, that much?" giggled Sam, unable to contain his excitement over his newfound wealth. He turned back to Greg and slammed his hands down on the desk.

"Twenty grand."

"Each," added Tim.

Sam slammed his hands down on the desk again, really getting into it now. "Each! That makes forty grand."

"Sixty," chimed in a meagre voice from the back of the room. "He means sixty."

"Oh, look who wants to be part of the team suddenly," said Sam, swinging around to see Jack, who was still barely through the door.

"Well, if it isn't Jack Phoenix," said Greg. "Don't be shy. Come join us."

He knew Jack's name. How did he know Jack's name? This was becoming a runaway train, speeding towards *Incrimination Station*.

"No, actually, forget I said anything. I'm not part of this," decided Jack, back-peddling.

"Oh, I insist," said Greg. "Come."

Jack obliged, padding into the room with his head bowed.

Greg turned his attention back to Sam, his eyes like fire. "You say you're going to go to the police?"

"We might, we might," said Sam.

"The police belong to us. We are the police. We are everyone," said Greg.

Sam's confidence was faltering now, so he did as he always did and overcompensated.

"Don't threaten me. I hold the cards here, not you. You sit there all high and mighty, but really, you're a dirty drug-dealing lowlife."

"Um..." started Tim, but Sam wasn't about to let anyone interrupt his flow.

"I am the king here, not you. You are staring into the eyes of God, pal. Bow down before me!" commanded Sam, perhaps going too far now.

"So, we'll take our seventy grand, and we'll take it now," he finished, adding an extra ten for good measure.

Greg stood up and slid open the drawer to his desk.

"Here we go, cough up," said Sam.

Greg reached into the drawer, calmly pulled out a revolver, and pointed it at Sam, the barrel steadily focused on his head.

Complete silence washed over for a miniature eternity until Greg gestured to Sam's clipboard.

"Give."

Sam let out a small whimper as he placed the clipboard on the desk. He slid it over to Greg with both hands still holding onto it, too terrified to tell his hands to let go. Greg reached out to grab it when Sam changed his mind, triggering a domino of bad ideas.

Sam hauled the clipboard up as hard as he could, smacking Greg on the chin, knocking his head back and sending the gun flying across the room behind him. Sam struck Greg in the face again with the clipboard, smashing it into his temple with a satisfying thump. Greg stumbled backwards, and Sam darted towards the door. But Greg soon regained his bearings and, more importantly, regained his gun.

Bang.

The deafening sound of a gunshot pummelled Sam's eardrum as he dove to the floor. Greg stepped forward. He no longer cared to listen to these fools. He was simply going to kill them.

Sam crawled behind a computer desk where Jack and Tim were hiding, and the three huddled together as Greg's footsteps grew closer. Sam noticed the deep black hole in the door where the bullet blew through it. It could've been him, and if they didn't think of a plan, it soon would be. He glanced over at Jack, who was holding his chest, breathing heavily and having either an asthma attack or a heart attack. Either way, it wouldn't matter much longer. Finally, he turned to Tim, sitting with his duffle bag pulled tightly against him, hugging it for comfort. Surely, he had a plan.

"Tim, you've been in gunfights before."

"Er, yeah, loads of them," replied Tim, failing to hide his terror.

"So what do we do?" asked Sam.

"Just give him the clipboard," gasped Jack through breathless pants.

"But we don't know how much this could be worth," reasoned Sam.

"Is it worth dying?" said Jack, straining to get his words out.

Another shot blasted across the room and into the glass wall beside them, growing a cascading spiderweb of splintered cracks through it. Time was running out.

Sam noticed a long cable lying beneath him and extending across the floor, leading to an extension lead in the corner. Remembering his trouble with cables earlier, Sam formulated the perfect plan, gripping the wire and pulling it taught.

"I've made a tripwire," he told Tim, "when he trips over, you grab the gun, alright?"

Sam readied his tripwire and held his breath, waiting for his plan to come to fruition. A moment passed, and a shoe stamped down on the cable. Sam followed the shoe up along the grey trouser leg and to the revolver pointed at his face.

"Please don't kill us," whimpered Sam.

A smile grew from the corner of Greg's mouth as he ran his tongue along his bared teeth, like a snake readying for the kill. He pulled back the gun's hammer.

"You brought this on yourself," said Greg, pressing the tip of the gun to Sam's trembling forehead.

Sam closed his eyes.

"Oi," said a voice beside him.

Sam's eyes sprang open to find Tim standing beside him, holding a firework in one hand and a bright pink plastic lighter in the other. He held the lighter beneath the firework, the fuse dancing just above it, ready to be lit.

"Drop the gun and back the fuck up. You do not bring a gun to a rocket fight."

Greg paused but didn't drop the gun.

"You two, get out of here," warned Tim. "This is about to get nasty."

Sam ran, grabbing Jack and pulling him towards the door.

Does Tim know what he's doing? wondered Sam. *Maybe this is a standard Wednesday for him?*

"Stay where you are!" barked Greg, and Sam and Jack obliged.

"You're not running the show anymore," said Tim. "I light this, and we both go up."

"Except you won't," laughed Greg, almost daring him to do it.

This boy was just that, a boy who found himself in a situation far beyond his capabilities. He wouldn't light the firework. Greg was sure of it.

Tim flicked the lighter, and the firework's fuse sizzled.

"Sam, Jack, go!" shouted Tim, not daring to take his eyes off Greg.

Tim's orders were clear, and the pair weren't about to ignore them. They did as they were told and ran out of the room.

Surprise overcame Greg. The boy did it, perhaps he underestimated him.

"Put it out."

"No." Tim didn't believe he could, even if he wanted to.

Frozen to the spot with fear, his entire body seized up. It didn't matter. He had no intention of putting the firework out. He would wipe the smug look off Greg's face...or blow it up.

Greg was done with games. He aimed at Tim's leg and fired the gun without hesitation. The bullet tore through Tim, ricocheting pain across his insides like a pinball, lighting up every nerve in his leg. Tim collapsed to the floor, dropping the firework and clutching his leg while letting out a few profanity-laden screams.

Greg peered down. Where was the firework? The fizzing of its string was still audible and as he listened, he soon realized it was coming from inside the duffle bag.

Tim's and Greg's eyes met once more as they both realized what was coming. They couldn't stop it. They couldn't run from it. Any moment now, the inevitable would come for them both. Tim did his best to shimmy behind a desk, pressing on the pool of blood seeping down his leg and willing himself not to pass out.

With both hands and all the remaining strength he could muster, Tim shoved the desk over. Monitors and keyboards slid and smashed in a violent heap of detached keys and cracked screens, flicking through a flurry of broken colours before fading to black. With his makeshift shield in place, Tim let the pain take him, and he, too, faded to black, slipping out of consciousness.

Across the room, Greg dropped to his knees, digging through the duffle bag, hoping to find which firework was the lit one.

He eventually found it, ripped it free from the bag, and pressed his fingers into the flame, suffocating it. Yet, the fizzing continued. The flame spread, lighting more fireworks, maybe all of them. It was too late. Greg straightened himself, closed his eyes and accepted there was nothing left to be done.

The room erupted with sound and colour as every firework went off at once. Some flew out of the top of the bag, while others tore through it. Each firework carved a unique path of destruction through the room before exploding against the ceiling, floor, or what remained of the glass wall. The lights and electrical equipment burst into flames with explosions of their own.

Nothing was safe from the tsunami of radiant destruction overtaking the room, not Tim and certainly not Greg, trapped in the eruption's epicentre.

As quick as it started, the room fell silent once more. The only sound to be heard was the crackling fires burning through the darkness.

PART 2

THE FUGITIVES

11

Sam and Jack dove out of the seminar room as another gunshot rang out. They froze, and Sam looked back through the small window on the door to the room, where he saw Tim fall to the floor.

"He shot him. He just bloody shot him!"

Jack didn't answer, busy hyperventilating, with almost enough force to propel him from the ground. Jack plunged a hand into his pocket to retrieve his inhaler, hoping it might anchor him back down.

Sam darted his head between the door and the corridor. Should he go back? Should he run? He couldn't leave Tim in there to die, could he?

Luckily for Sam, the decision would soon become irrelevant as an incredible explosion of fifty fireworks ripped through the building. The intense wave of heat threw him backwards in a technicolour rhapsody of blinding brilliance.

Sam gazed up as the door dented and splintered. Then, a stray firework shot through the door, blowing it wide open as it whizzed past Jack and Sam, squealing up the corridor before exploding in a grand fountain of iridescent greens. The explosions finally quieted, but the ringing in their ears remained.

Sam staggered to his feet and walked towards what remained of the door to the seminar room, easing it open. The door snapped from its hinges, falling with a thud and echoing through the eerie silence of the room. Sam peered inside, and Jack soon joined him, sucking on his inhaler. The room lay in ruins, scorched black ash coated everything, and the enormous glass wall on the side of the room shattered into a million puzzle pieces.

Jack sensed the draft from the destroyed wall brush against him, coating him with the pungent scent of gunpowder. The room was noticeably chilly now, despite the several small fires burning around the room. Soft plumes of smoke snaked upwards from the fires, tangling among the freed cables dangling from the ceiling. A scene of destruction, the room became an obstacle course, barely resembling the room they first stepped into only minutes before.

They made their way through, stepping over glass and broken tables while ducking under sparking wires. Jack noticed a computer monitor with a gaping hole in the centre where a firework shot right through it. Jagged computer chips encircled the hole like icicles, and through it, Jack saw something–no, someone.

For, on the floor, huddled beside an upturned desk and covered in chunks of plaster, was Tim. He was no longer holding his leg or screaming. In fact, Tim was no longer doing much of anything, lying in a growing pool of dark fluid.

As Jack approached, he noticed one side of Tim's face was charred. The skin bubbled and oozed as it cooked, the result of a stray firework kissing him on the cheek.

"I-I've found him. He's here," called Jack.

"Is he ok?" Sam called back as he investigated a discovery of his own: Greg, or what little remained of him.

Most of his face was gone, his skin torn from the bone. His eyebrows still pointed downwards like furious arrows towards his eyes, one of which was now reduced to a bloody mess of gristle. His arm dangled loosely, only a few tendrils of tissue connecting it to the rest of him. Sam saw the man's gritted teeth through his absent lips, still vicious, as though he might leap up and start ripping into Sam with those teeth at any moment.

As Sam glanced over the mess of flesh his former lecturer became, and almost felt sorry for him, wondering if he had a family who would miss him.

Then again, this man spent his last few moments trying to murder Sam.

Screw him, Sam thought as he gave his corpse one last kick in the ribs for good measure.

On the other side of the room, Jack sat beside Tim, trying his best to stay calm, practical and, most importantly, not throw up. He placed two fingers on the side of Tim's throat and felt for his pulse. It was faint, but it was there, a tiny beat, clinging to life.

"There's a pulse," confirmed Jack.

Sam kicked away the rubble like a pile of autumn leaves to join them. He peered down at Tim and noticed the deep black stain spilling down his trousers.

"Bloody hell, he really got shot." Sam knelt and grabbed hold of the leg, checking it over.

"No exit wound," he concluded.

"No, *what*?" bemused Jack.

"Exit would. The bullet never came out."

Sam yanked the torn fabric away from Tim's trousers and tied it into a tight bow above the bullet hole. The flow of blood slowed and stopped. Sam turned to Jack with a smile. Even at a time like this, he couldn't help but be a bit smug.

"Stops the circulation," he said. "How do you not know this stuff?"

"I'm sorry, but this isn't a regular occurrence for me," argued Jack, before remembering, there was much more at stake here than Sam's petty one-upmanship. "How close is the hospital?"

"The other side of town," grimaced Sam. "Alright, I'll grab his arms. You get his legs."

The pair heaved up Tim, doing their best to carry him across the charred wreckage, out of the room and onwards through the winding maze of corridors, leaving a breadcrumb trail of blood in their wake.

They struggled to haul Tim down the corridor. He was much heavier than he looked. So heavy, in fact, that they didn't notice they had taken a wrong turn and ended up in the part of the university Jack was more familiar with: the science department. However, Jack wasn't familiar with the police tape now blocking their path.

Jack placed Tim's legs down, walked over to the thick yellow bands stretching from wall to wall, and ducked beneath it towards the door he knew best.

"This is Dr Li's lab," said Jack, running his hand against the door's wooden frame.

He twisted the handle and opened the door, finding the room's interior to be in a similar state to the one he'd just left.

"The lab's been destroyed. Something's happened to him."

"Well, you said he's an inventor. He probably just blew the room up with science, or maybe Greg did it, just like he did to us."

"Tim blew up the room," corrected Jack. "With your stupid fireworks."

"You think the fireworks did this? They couldn't have gone this far, could they? No, wait, this has got all police stuff around it, so it must've happened a while ago unless the police are already here. I can't go down for this. Jack, we need to go. Now."

Jack wasn't listening to Sam. He was busy with Dr Li's upturned, cracked, and soaked desk. Jack wedged open the drawer containing only a keypad and punched in the combination, water growing around each button as he pressed his fingers against them. The keypad made a gurgled wet chime of success, and behind Jack, the whiteboard panel slid open.

He let out a small sigh of relief that the secret room survived whatever transpired here, looking just as he left it. Jack searched the shelves of impossibilities, but the locator was gone, and with it went Jack's hope of finding out if Dr Li was ok, and if he might give them a lift to the hospital.

Everything had gotten too far out of control for Jack to handle anymore. He was almost shot, Greg and Tim were dead or dying, and the cherry on top, Dr Li was missing, potentially in trouble, likely in danger.

For a moment, Jack considered closing the whiteboard up around him, sealing himself in the room, safe from whatever awaited him out there. As much as he couldn't handle what was happening now, he knew this was only the tip of the iceberg, and there was a long way to fall before he reached the bottom. Jack wished he could go back and stop this all from happening.

Jack's head slowly turned to the time machine, comfortably nestled amongst the wires, glowing a deep blue through the veins of its wooden casing.

"Jack, come on!" shouted Sam from outside the room, left to carry Tim by himself.

Jack placed his hands around the time machine, lifting it from its bed. It was small and delicate and a glistening ticket out of this mess. He tucked the device down the side of his boot, where he would often hide things he didn't want anyone to find, ever since Edward, at the foster home, tried to steal his holographic *Charizard*.

With the Time Machine secure, Jack returned to the desk where he squelched one last button on the keypad, resetting the whiteboard to its previous position, before hurrying out of the room to rejoin Sam.

Jack and Sam continued carrying Tim's unconscious body out into the car park. With each step, Tim's body seemed to grow heavier. If it was already a struggle to bring him this far, taking him several more miles to the hospital would be impossible.

Jack lowered Tim to the ground, his back finally giving out. "We can't do this. We've got to call an ambulance."

"And explain all this?" argued Sam, propping up Tim. "People are going to ask questions, Jack, not nice ones, ones where we get put away. You think you'd survive in prison?"

Jack momentarily thought it over as he peered back at the university and the indelible mark of destruction they stamped into it. Then he remembered the odd weight shifting in his boot and his ticket out of here. If only he knew how to use it. For now, Sam was right. They had to get away from here.

Sam scanned the car park for any ideas. Maybe there was a wheelbarrow or something nearby.

There was nothing.

The car park was empty except for Greg's car.

Wait...

Greg's car!

"I've got an idea," proclaimed Sam as he dropped Tim and bounded towards the vehicle.

"No! We are not stealing his car," shouted Jack as he followed Sam, dragging Tim along with him.

Sam halted a short way from the car and turned to face Jack. Sam came up with the perfect solution to fix literally everything, and Jack just shot it down as he always did.

"Listen to me. If we stay here any longer, Tim's going to die. Do you want him to die, Jack? Is that what you want? Is it? After he saved your life?" Sam jabbed Jack with an accusatory finger before directing that finger towards the sagging body at his feet. "You hear that, Tim? Jack wants you to die."

"And how do you suggest we drive the car without the keys?" snapped Jack.

"I'll just hot wire it."

"You don't know how to Hotwire a car, Sam! You need the keys!"

Jack stepped towards Sam, both in full argument mode now.

Just then, Sam noticed something behind Jack, shifting across his peripherals. As Sam squinted, trying to make it out, a terrifying realization hit him. It wasn't something, but someone, exiting through the automatic doors and staggering towards them, following the trail of crimson breadcrumbs.

"He- he might have the keys," squeaked Sam.

Jack turned to see Greg Page staring back at him through his one working eye, limping towards them, shredded tendons still wrapped around his pistol. With some effort, he raised his gun long enough to fire. The bullet struck the back of the car, burrowing through the metal and narrowly missing Sam's head. The pair frantically ducked behind the car, hauling Tim with them.

"What is he? The fucking Terminator!" cried Sam.

"How can he be alive? He hasn't got a face," agreed Jack as another shot blasted through the car.

Greg's mutilated mess of a hand clutched the side of the car, holding himself up as he stumbled around it to find Jack and Sam frozen in place, a couple of rabbits caught in the headlights, staring up at the skeletal silhouette standing in front of them, the grim reaper himself. Every neuron in Jack's mind was singing out a choir of screams, and deep within his boot, a single green LED glowed, coming back to life after so many years.

Greg pointed the gun down at Sam and opened his mouth, his exposed jaw rocking loosely on its hinges as he tried to speak.

"Yo...You..." Bloody coughs interrupted his words, raining down bright red spittle around him.

Finally, the coughing stopped, his single eye rolled backwards in its socket, and he went with it. Greg's body slammed against the tarmac, and his loose arm snapped free, skating towards Jack and coming to rest at his feet.

"Is he...y'know?" whispered Jack.

"I really hope so," whispered Sam.

"The keys," whispered Jack. "Check his pockets."

"I'm not checking his pockets. You check his pockets," retorted Sam, peeling his gaze from their *hopefully* dead foe and turning to Jack.

As his eyes met Jack's, even he admitted Jack was in no state to check anybody's pocket, huddled infantile beside him and hyperventilating once more.

"Ugh, fine!" Sam submitted, crawling over to Greg's corpse. "He's dead, Jack. He can't hurt you."

Greg's eye shot open, twisting in its socket until it found Sam. Sam let out a squeal of fear and slapped his lecturer back to the grave.

Greg's head flopped to the side, properly dead this time.

Sam grimaced as he slipped his hand into Greg's pocket, and after some repulsed rummaging, he fished out his car keys.

However, Sam became fixated on Greg's hand, the one still attached to his body, the one still holding the revolver. Sam thought of all the power the gun possessed. Perhaps he should take it, for his own protection, at least. Sam pressed the tip of his finger against the warm metal of the barrel and sensed its power flow into him.

It would only be a matter of time before this Dr Cud guy came after him for killing one of his dealers. Sam might soon answer the door to his house to fifty heavies armed to the teeth. He needed some insurance. He needed the gun. With his back turned to Jack, Sam wrestled the revolver away from Greg's unabating grip and held the weight of its power before tucking it safely into his coat.

Sam turned back around, holding up the keys proudly. "Got 'em."

He pressed a button on the key fob, and the car responded with a dull thud as the locks unlatched from their mooring. "Shotgun," called Sam as he opened the passenger door.

"What? Absolutely not. You're driving," corrected Jack.

"I can't drive. You know I can't drive. I failed my test eight times. Remember, I had that instructor with the gammy eye. Also, I've had like six beers and that alone..."

"So I've got to be the one to drive your drug dealer in the stolen car of your dead, murderous lecturer, have I?"

Sam gripped the handle tightly and slammed the car door closed, setting his sights on Jack, once more having to shove a spoonful of sense down his throat.

"I don't see many alternatives. Maybe we should ask Tim to drive." Sam grabbed Tim and shook him, hoping to wake him.

"Tim. Tim!" But Tim only sagged listlessly.

"Or we could ask Greg." Sam kicked Greg, hoping *not* to wake him. "Greg. Greg! Y'know, I think they've both got bigger problems at the moment."

Sam grew closer to Jack until they were face to face, ensuring there was no chance for Jack to miss the point he was making. "I have just groped a melty corpse for you. The least you can do is drive the fucking car!"

Jack didn't react other than a slight twitch of his face from where Sam's spittle hit him. Instead, he walked a short way from the car, Sam, the two bodies, and the vast storm of problems waiting for him.

Once there was a suitable distance between them, Jack stopped and, after a moment, let out an almighty scream, releasing all the anguish inside him until his vocal cords couldn't take anymore.

He snatched the car keys from Sam, marching over to the driver's door and its shattered window. As Jack opened the door, the final remaining shards lining the window relented and tumbled to the ground. Jack brushed the glass and the beer bottle from off the seat, allowing it to join the growing pile, and climbed inside.

Sam, meanwhile, laid Tim across the back seats of the car before joining Jack up front, calling out 'shotgun' again for good measure. As he sat down beside Jack, Sam saw he was talking to himself.

"If I don't think too hard about what's happening, everything will be fine."

Sam thought it best not to interrupt him.

"Everything will be fine," repeated Jack, drilling his fingernails into the steering wheel.

Jack pulled away, and together, they drove off into the night.

12

DCI Sparks sipped from his coffee cup as he stood over Greg Page's mangled corpse. He stared down at the perfect puzzle of scattered limbs and viscera, trying to piece together the strange series of events that had occurred here the night before.

They summoned him there for the second time in just twenty-four hours. At this rate, he needed to get his mail forwarded here. The entire university was closed off, wrapped in ribbons of yellow tape, and officers were still turning away the confused students on their way to their morning lectures.

With two explosions and a death count rising, this was like nothing DCI Sparks ever witnessed on the force, in the army, sure, but not here, and he was feeling unsure about his daughter being at the centre, especially after what she witnessed at the hospital. She wasn't ready, but as he saw her running across the car park towards him, he knew she would never admit it.

"They're saying it was a homemade explosive device, suspected terrorist group or plot or something. No other bodies, just a lot of blood. We still don't know if this connects to yesterday's events!" shouted Lucy.

"Keep it down. We don't want people overhearing and getting the wrong idea," said DCI Sparks through gritted teeth, pointing a stern finger toward the growing mass of students.

"Sorry, sorry," whispered Lucy, reaching her father. "There was a camera in the reception. They're going through it now."

"Stop!" barked DCI Sparks, grabbing Lucy as her foot nearly stepped down into the pale remains of Greg Page's face.

As Lucy gazed down, she almost jumped out of her uniform. "Oh God, what happened to him?"

She wasn't ready for this, DCI Sparks decided. He would get her back to the station as soon as he could, assigned to something simple, something safe, something she couldn't step in.

"The blast injured him, we suspect," said DCI Sparks. "Then he wandered out here in search of aid before succumbing to his injuries."

"What about the glass?" asked Lucy.

"Glass?"

Lucy crouched down and pointed out the small pile of glass dotted around the body.

"There's glass everywhere," dismissed DCI Sparks. "The explosion took out the windows. He was most likely covered in broken glass."

"But what about this piece?" asked Lucy, pointing out a deep brown shard of glass and the papery residue stuck to it. "That's not from a window. That's from a beer bottle."

DCI Sparks knelt and turned the piece of glass over with his pen to inspect it, letting out a small "hmmm" as he did so.

Lucy couldn't help but smile. She found something, something no one else did. She made her dad *'hmmm,'* and that was no easy feat.

She was totally ready for this.

13

Jack silently sat in the hospital reception as the fluorescent lights hummed above him, ethereally illuminating the clinical white walls, ceiling, and floor. The thick scent of antiseptic filled the hospital, hoping to conceal the recently departed. Jack sensed everything about this place was unnatural, and every fibre of his being urged him to leave. Yet, here he sat, trapped in this sterile cell.

The hard plastic chair beneath him wobbled every time he shifted his body weight, which he did a lot as he counted the seconds. It had been hours since they'd brought Tim in, and now the sun was rising over the endless night. Not that Jack could tell from the artificial daytime in heaven's waiting room.

Jack stared down the infinite hospital corridor as the occasional doctor or nurse passed through, some casually, some in a hurry. Anyone of them could be busy trying to put Tim back together again. Perhaps he was already dead. What about Mr Page?

He was certainly dead now, despite his refusal to accept it. Jack should have taken him, too. There was enough room in the car. Sam's teacher always seemed relatively friendly from what little Jack interacted with him, and Jack didn't have the right to decide if he should die, even if he were trying to shoot them and possibly a drug dealer, stealing drugs from the very hospital Jack now sat in. Jack thought he should probably tell someone here about that, but who would believe him?

He scarcely believed it himself.

As Jack's thoughts ran away again, he sensed his head thumping, all the stress and pressure, like an angry bull, stampeding through his mind, desperate to break free. He reached down into his boot, and his mind quieted as his fingers met the smooth glass dome of the time machine.

Shielding the device from view, Jack lifted it and peered into the brass clock face, glistening with blue sparks, hoping it might reveal its secrets. Running his fingers over the grooves in the wood, he noticed the first of the three LEDs at the base of the device flickered a pale green. It was working, ready to unlock the door to the past and fix everything. Dr Li taught Jack every formula and mechanism of its function. However, the one thing he didn't teach Jack was how to work the damn thing.

There were no buttons, no controls. Jack wondered if it might be touch sensitive with some kind of haptic feedback or...Bluetooth, of course. The blue glow within the dome was obviously trying to sync up to a device. Jack pulled out his phone to connect to it, but the only thing it located was Sam's phone from across the room.

Sam stood at the reception desk, explaining his conspiracy theories to the uninterested and tired receptionist.

"Look, I need you to run my DNA through your computer so you can tell me if there are any matches, like any secret twins or clones or anything like that."

The receptionist sighed, unperturbed by this man's drunken rambling; she dealt with far worse working nights there.

"As I keep telling you, we don't have that kind of information in our system."

"Let me have a go," said Sam, trying to snatch the mouse from her desk. "I'm great with computers. It's probably just behind a firewall."

A nurse emerged from the corridor, interrupting Sam's intrusions, much to the relief of the receptionist. "Are you the gentleman who brought in Mr Tim Watkins?"

Jack scampered up from his chair to join them, desperate for something to put him out of his misery. "That's us."

The nurse scrutinized the pair, eyeing the blood splattered across their clothes.

"How did you say the incident happened again?" asked the nurse.

"Hunting accident," retorted Sam, hoping to dispel any suspicions.

"You're aware the bullet we removed was from a handgun, not a hunting rifle?"

"We're very unconventional hunters," said Sam with a wink.

"We weren't hunting him." Jack jumped in. "If that's what you were…It was just normal things, like-"

"Bears." finished Sam.

Clearly, the nurse didn't believe them, so there seemed little point in trying to salvage this tale.

"Bears," sighed Jack in agreement. "Is he ok?"

"The operation was successful. We removed the bullet, and we treated the burns. Although there were some complications with the leg."

"Did you cut off the wrong leg?" asked Sam, eyes widening with both panic and intrigue.

"Err, no," said the nurse.

"Did you give him an extra leg?"

The nurse turned to Jack, choosing what seemed like the better option of the two.

"The bullet damaged his femoral nerve, and as a result, your friend may never regain full operation of the leg. You can see him now if you'd like."

Jack nodded, and the pair followed the nurse down the corridor. The very real consequences of last night were now beginning to hit Sam. Tim might not walk anymore. Greg was dead. He may have a secret twin.

It was all getting too heavy for him. Especially now that the alcoholic haze was lifting, leaving only a migraine in its place. Sam ran his hand over the outline of the gun in his pocket and calmed slightly.

At least he had that.

THEY REACHED THE ROOM WHERE TIM WAS BEING treated, another room of cold uniformed white, with a pair of beds fitted with IV drips, heart monitors and a series of oppressive medical equipment. Sat on the furthest bed and facing the window overlooking the car park was Tim, dressed in a light blue gown.

As he heard the footsteps behind him, he stood up before slipping back down again, still unfamiliar with his new arrangement. He scooped up a pair of silver crutches resting by his side and pushed down on them, forcing himself up, and faced Jack and Sam, pushing through the pain evident on his bandaged face.

"Alright lads," said Tim, trying to sound casual as he forced his gritted teeth into a smile.

Pale strips of cotton covered half his face, attempting to hide the oozing charred flesh underneath.

"I'll leave you to it," said the nurse as she turned and left.

"How are you doing?" asked Sam.

"Been better, mate, if I'm honest. But I didn't die, so that's a plus. The doctor said I was legally dead for like 2 minutes, but still."

"What happened?" asked Jack.

"That Greg bloke shot me. Then all the fireworks went mental. I'll tell you what, when I find that bastard..."

"Don't think that'll happen soon," said Sam, hopping onto Tim's bed. "He's dead."

Sam punctuated this revelation by grabbing a grape from a nearby fruit bowl and tossing it into his mouth.

"Oh, shit." Tim fell silent.

It could've been him; it should've been, and suddenly, he remembered all the pain filling his battered frame. Tim took a seat on the side of the bed and shook it away.

"What are we doing about all these drugs? We need to find this Dr Cud and get our money."

"No, this has gone too far already. We're handing the file to the police and letting them deal with it," said Jack, turning to Sam.

As Jack watched Sam casually scoffing fruit, the cogs in his brain clicked together to form a grim realization. "Sam, where is the file?"

"What?" replied Sam through a mouth full of grapes.

"The clipboard, Sam, you know, the one thing that proves we're innocent in all this."

Sam swallowed. "I gave it to you."

"No, you didn't. At no point did you give it to me," argued Jack, his voice rising in pitch.

"Ah, well, one of us has lost it then," dismissed Sam, peeling a banana.

"You idiot, it was the only thing that was going to stop us from getting arrested for actual bloody murder," gasped Jack, leaning into Sam.

"Um, excuse me," said a small voice from across the room.

The three of them turned to find a patient lying in a bed only a few feet away from Tim's. "Sorry, but could I have my fruit back?"

Sam gently placed the bowl of fruit back down on the bedside table between the two beds.

"We're not murderers," assured Jack.

Right on cue, three police officers charged into the room, each one dressed in an array of heavy duty black and white gear, with the nurse following them a small distance behind.

"That's them," said the nurse, pointing at Jack.

A fourth officer, not dressed in uniform and about twice the size of the others, ducked through the doorframe into the room, DCI Sparks.

"Tim Watkins, Sam Higgs, Jack Phoenix," he said. "The three of you are under arrest for multiple counts of terrorism, murder and grand theft auto."

Jack raised his arms in surrender and glared at Sam, as he often did in moments of hopelessness when the odds were impossibly against them, albeit usually because of Sam's actions. Still, Sam was at least quite good at finding a way out.

"Actually, the grand theft auto was just him," said Sam, pointing back at Jack.

"Restrain these men," ordered DCI Sparks.

"Do you mean the handcuffs?" whispered one police officer, a young woman who Sam recognized immediately. The one who thought she was too important to line up behind him yesterday.

"Yes," replied DCI Sparks through gritted teeth before returning to the criminal trio. "You do not have to say anything. But, it may harm your defence if you do not mention when questioned something which you later rely on in court..."

DCI Sparks went on reading the three their rights as the officers approached, handcuffs at the ready.

"This is all a big misunderstanding," babbled Jack, shrinking into himself, desperate to find the correct series of words which might slow the officer's approach and delay the inevitable. "We didn't murder anyone. It's a funny story, actually. He was trying to murder us. Tell them Sam? Tim?"

Tim remained silent. He knew better than to say anything to the police. Start talking, and you'll forget to stop. Your stories contradict each other, and before you know it, you're doing a ten-stretch. That's how they got *Big Gob Barry*. Big Gob Barry's big gob only got bigger once he went to prison and received a *Chelsea smile* from his cellmate. The moral being, don't talk to the police.

Jack continued to ramble and plead with the officers not to arrest them while Lucy placed the handcuffs on Jack's outstretched wrists. She snapped the first cuff on as Jack glanced over at Sam, backing into a corner.

"Guys, look, I'm innocent," said Sam. "I can prove it. All the evidence is right here."

Jack watched as Sam reached into his coat. Did Sam have the documents detailing Greg Page, Dr Cud, and all the illegal drugs, after all? Or maybe he had something even better to prove it. Perhaps he secretly recorded everything on his phone.

However, Jack's hope soon fluttered away as he watched Sam pull the revolver from his pocket and point it at the officers.

The entire room froze, with all eyes now on Sam.

"Ok, can everyone just chill the fuck out for a second?!" said Sam.

To Sam's credit, he was right. When he held the gun, the hierarchy of the situation immediately leaned in his favor.

"Oh great," whispered Jack. His eyes met the terrified patient in the bed next to them. "We're really not murderers."

The officers all backed away slowly, Lucy too, leaving Jack only half-cuffed. DCI Sparks calmly moved his hand down to the radio on his lapel, but Sam spotted him before he could reach.

"Now, if you're about to call for backup. Don't," warned Sam, turning his gun to DCI Sparks and letting his newfound power go to his head. "Hands behind your head, all of you, or, well, you'll make Mr Gun angry, and you don't want that, I don't want that, because when he gets angry, he gets a bit shooty, yeah? A bit blow your fucking head off, ok?"

Jack's eyes scanned the room, searching for a solution, or someone to help or...a way out. His eyes locked onto the door at the other end of the room, the one he entered through moments earlier and the one he could just as easily walk back through. He tried to weigh up a thousand different variables and factors in his mind at once, but the conclusion he arrived at was simple.

He ran.

Lucy was the only one to see Jack escape. Everybody else was busy watching the maniac waving the gun around and making ludicrous threats.

"Now I hope you're all excellent dancers," continued Sam.

Lucy couldn't let Jack, her first real criminal, get away, and this crazed psychopath with the gun seemed far too consumed with himself to even notice her. She made the only right decision a true police officer could make, one she was sure her dad would approve of.

She, too, ran out the door, following Jack.

Tim gave Sam a nudge a few moments later, interrupting Sam's wild monologue of demands for a helicopter and a million pounds, and gestured to where Lucy once stood. Sam snapped back to reality, darting his head around in a sudden panic.

"Wait, weren't there more of you? Ok, Tim, we've got to

go. Where's Jack? Fuck!" Sam searched the room for an escape route and noticed a second door opposite Tim's bed. "Quickly, Tim!"

Sam ran through the door, but Tim didn't follow.

Sam found himself in a small bathroom with a toilet, a sink, and a shower, but nowhere to go except back out the way he entered.

"Fuck!"

Sam stepped out of the bathroom, pointing his gun at the officers once more. "That was a bathroom."

All Tim could offer was a knowing shrug. He wasn't saying a word in front of these officers.

"Fuck it, we'll just go out the other way," said Sam as he shuffled past the officers, dragging Tim along with him, limping behind. "Don't even think about following us or calling for backup, or I'll shoot this whole place down to the ground."

"They already called for backup while you were in the bathroom," muttered Tim, once they were out of earshot.

"Fuck!"

14

Jack sprinted down the corridor, shuffling past patients and doctors as he tugged at the handcuffs dangling from his wrist. They wouldn't budge. Lucy may not have gotten both wrists, but this new bracelet he was stuck with was bound to draw attention.

Where was he even going?

The main entrance wasn't an option. A small army would surely be waiting there by now. He needed to find another way out. He turned a corner and immediately came face to face with his pursuer, crashing into Lucy and knocking them both to the ground. *Not that way*, he thought to himself.

"Hey, stop," shouted Lucy.

Jack scrambled to his feet and darted back along the corridor and down the stairs, his feet leaping two or three steps at a time.

As he glanced back, he found only an empty corridor, which allowed him a moment of respite. Knowing he couldn't outrun her forever, Jack tentatively puffed his inhaler and searched for a place to hide. Scanning the endless white corridor, he spotted a door with a '*staff only*' sign.

Jack approached the door yet found himself hesitant to open it. All his life, he knew not to open a staff-only door. *You can't come in here, it's only for staff. You're not allowed.* The door gloated.

Although, you're also not allowed to extort money from your lecturer, blow up your university, steal a car or run from the police. So, Jack pushed the door open and snuck inside.

The room was dark and full of water tanks and boilers, with rusted pipes reaching out from them in every direction. Jack stepped through, holding his breath, not daring to give away his hiding spot.

The room grew darker as he wandered, and Jack felt less confident in his footing, but he couldn't slow down, or she would find him. Jack's foot snagged on a pipe, and he tumbled forward. His phone slipped from his pocket, and Jack smacked into more rows of pipes as he tried to catch himself, causing a ricochet of chimes to ring out like the keys of a xylophone.

Jack lay on his back, staring into the darkness until the pipes stopped clattering, and all he heard was the sound of his heart once more, beating out the steady rhythm of his terror. A slow creak soon drowned this out as a crack of light descended over him, burning his eyes.

The door was open. She found him.

Jack couldn't risk turning his head to make sure, but he didn't need to. He sensed her presence, sniffing out her prey. Jack remained frozen, staring up into the abyss as the light reflected off a small green sign at the edge of the room: a stick man running through a door—the exit. Jack started crawling as quietly as he could towards it.

The door closed, and the room descended into darkness once more.

"I know you're in here. Just give up," came Lucy's voice, not too far behind Jack.

Jack desperately climbed through the spiderweb of pipes, each one ringing out a reminder of his location as the handcuffs dragged along them. Not that Jack heard anything anymore over the relentless pulsing in his ears.

Reaching the edge of the room, Jack held up a hand, feeling for the handle of the fire exit. Touching the cold metal of the bar, he pulled himself up to his feet and bolted through the door.

Light flooded in, cooking his retinas once more. He glanced back and found the reflection of Lucy's fierce eyes. Only a few pipes separating them now. Jack turned and continued through the door, running for his life, just as the little green man did.

He bolted across the car park, trying to find the half-wrecked car he drove here in. All the while, the sound of sirens grew louder. In the distance, he saw at least ten police cars careering down the street towards the hospital.

Ducking down behind a row of cars, Jack once more attempted to crawl his way to freedom. Loose stones from the chewed-up tarmac dug into his hands and legs as he wriggled between the cars, dragging himself closer to the vehicle that might grant his escape.

As he reached it, Jack fumbled his hand into his pocket to retrieve the key fob. He jabbed the button on the fob to unlock it, not that there was much point in locking the car. It was riddled with bullet holes; the widows were shattered, and frankly, the chances of it being stolen twice in one day seemed minimal.

The headlights flashed as the locks clunked open, and the world around him stood still, as Jack was certain this would be enough to alert a horde of police officers to his location.

Any second, they would be all over him.

But no one came.

So Jack reached up, opened the door, and clambered

inside. Jack jabbed the key into the car's ignition and twisted it. The engine coughed and revved, but wouldn't start. He turned the key again. Still no luck.

No. If Jack were to keep going, so did this stupid stolen car. He would not be responsible for another death.

He turned it again and again, forcing the engine back to life until the car hummed resentfully. Jack gently pressed the gas pedal and drove through the car park. Not too fast, but not suspiciously slowly, either.

Police cars continued swarming around him. Blue and red sirens filled Jack's peripherals, with one siren coming directly towards him. It was too late for him to reverse, or run, or even, at the very least, duck.

Jack had no choice but to keep driving as the police car grew closer and closer. Digging his fingers into the steering wheel, he stared forward and held steady on the pedal.

Then, a tiny miracle occurred, and the police car continued past Jack. The officer inside turned his head away from Jack at the crucial moment and saved him from a life behind bars. Exhaling a long sigh, Jack took another puff from his inhaler, gathered himself and continued driving towards the exit.

He was free.

He wasn't free.

The passenger door tore open, and Jack saw Lucy Sparks running alongside the car, reaching inside.

"Stop!"

"No," blurted Jack as he slammed his foot on the gas pedal, sending the car into a frenzied acceleration. Lucy wouldn't let him go that easily.

"You're not getting away from me!" shouted Lucy, leaning further into the car.

Jack wanted to stop her but couldn't. He wasn't about to push someone out of a moving car. That wasn't him.

However, he found his arm hovering there for a moment as he considered. It would be so easy to give her just a tiny shove.

Clunk.

Lucy snapped the free handcuff swinging from Jack's wrist around her own.

She had him, and he was powerless to stop her. Jack's body didn't receive the message, and his foot pushed down on the acceleration as hard as possible. The car sped along the street, and Lucy had little choice but to jump inside.

"Stop this car now!" demanded Lucy.

"Unlock the handcuffs first," said Jack, trying to negotiate.

"You want me to unlock these handcuffs?" asked Lucy, removing a little key from her pocket before throwing it past Jack and out the shattered window. "Not a chance."

His arms flailed as he tried to catch it, but the key was long gone.

Jack lost, and he knew it, but his foot still refused to leave the pedal.

15

SAM BOUNDED THROUGH THE GERIATRIC WARD AS Tim trailed behind. The distance between the pair was growing, and Sam kept having to slow down for Tim to catch up.

It was not exactly the speedy getaway he hoped for. Sam considered making a break for it and ditching Tim to fend for himself, but that bloody conscience of his got in the way. Too kind for his own good, he decided.

Sam shoved past a baffled audience of elderly patients, before skidding to a stop as he noticed one patient in particular, an old man with a thick grey moustache, yet what caught Sam's attention most was the wheelchair he was sitting in. It was exactly what Tim needed. Plus, Sam's legs were getting tired, as he could probably do with one too.

But where did this hospital keep the wheelchairs?

Well. He knew where they kept one...

Sam grabbed the patient's wheelchair and tipped it up, shuffling the moustached man out as he yelped in surprise and tried to wrestle hold of his chair.

"Sorry about this, but desperate times," said Sam, shaking

the wheelchair as though trying to get the last drops of ketchup out of the bottle.

The patient eventually yielded and slid off the chair, collapsing in an undignified heap.

Tim limped through the ward, catching up to Sam, only to find him standing over the poor, confused man writhing beneath him.

"Sam..." began Tim.

"We don't have time! Get in!" ordered Sam, thrusting the wheelchair at him.

Tim reluctantly took the seat and mouthed "sorry mate" to its previous occupant. Sam grabbed the handles of the wheelchair, kicked his legs back, and shot off, sending Tim careening out of the geriatric ward and into the maternity ward.

Pregnant women screamed with fear as Sam lifted his feet off the ground and hung off the back of the chair. The wheelchair rocketed through an obstacle course of newborn babies and terrified mothers until it shot out into the main corridor once more.

At the corridor's end, Sam saw the hospital's entrance and the police cars beyond it, but that wasn't their destination; Sam had somewhere else in mind first. Sam put his foot down, skidding to a halt, as Tim gripped the armrests to stop himself from flying out.

"It's here," said Sam, pointing to a blank door, seemingly no different from any other.

Sam took a deep breath, pushed the door open, and wheeled Tim inside.

As the room revealed itself, Tim couldn't understand why Sam seemed so enamoured by this place. It was only a supply closet filled with old boxes. They should try to escape, yet Sam was busy digging through these old boxes like it was Christmas morning.

"This is where they had the pills, but they're gone," said Sam. "Whatever Greg was planning with these pills has already happened."

Sam became frantic, tipping over boxes and throwing them across the room in a tornado of desperation. Then Sam saw it, silver foil glistening in the corner of his eye, a forgotten gift hidden behind the Christmas tree. A single packet of bright orange pills. He snatched them and waved them in Tim's face.

"This is it. This proves we're innocent. The police will have no choice but to let us go when we show them these."

"You tried to shoot them," Tim reminded him.

"That's just nitpicking. This is all that matters," said Sam, staring through the clear plastic casing at rows of tiny orange evidence.

Sam lowered the pills and saw something moving behind it, the door handle twisting open. The pair froze as a doctor filled the door frame: a woman in her late sixties, dressed in a long white coat with a stethoscope swinging from her neck and wiry brown hair perched on her head. She seemed unfazed by Sam and Tim. In fact, she called them by name.

"Sam, Tim, you have something which doesn't belong to you."

"How do you know..." began Sam.

"We know everything," she interrupted.

Her glassy eyes were cold and vacant, and the words she spoke weren't her own. She was one of them.

"What are the pills for?" demanded Tim.

The doctor scoffed, "Look at you, crippled, barely able to move, and now you want answers. Even if I were to tell you the intricacies of our plan, your simple minds wouldn't even comprehend it. You're just a toy to us, and a broken one at that. Allow me to finish the job."

She reached out and wrapped her hands around Tim's

neck. He tried to bat her away but wasn't strong enough to stop her hands from tightening around his throat like a python, squeezing the life from him. She possessed an unnatural strength that was far too much for Tim. But not too much for Sam and Tim together as Sam grabbed the handles of the wheelchair and charged forward, knocking her off her feet and slamming her into the wall. She made no sound, no cries of pain. Sam pulled the wheelchair back and slammed it into her again, and again, and again. Still, she didn't make a sound, even when Sam heard something inside her snap.

The doctor dragged herself back up to her knees. Sam should have slammed her again, but at that moment, he was distracted by the wig slipping down her face, revealing patches of uneven hair beneath. She lurched towards Tim, like some feral creature, seizing him in her talons once more. Sam conceded that the people working for Dr Cud showed devotion, but he had something far more powerful: a gun. One that he quickly pointed at the doctor's head.

"I'll do it," said Sam. "Let him go, or I'll do it. Don't tempt me."

The doctor's hands loosened as she laughed.

"Shoot me. I wonder how that'll look. A poor innocent doctor gunned down by a pair of wanted criminals."

Sam didn't relent, continuing to point the gun at the doctor. When Greg held it, it looked so easy.

Was the gun's promise of power a lie? What was the point of having a gun if he couldn't use it without getting into trouble? Did he have the courage to shoot her?

"I don't have all day. If you're going to shoot me, do it already."

He should just pull the trigger. He needed to do it.

This woman was trying to kill Tim, so she deserved it,

right? But what if it didn't work? Were there even bullets left in the gun?

He didn't know how to check or even where to get replacement bullets from. Maybe he should pull the trigger and find out if there were bullets the old-fashioned way. However, then, she was right. The police would hear the shot, and then there would be no way to escape or explain any of this. Telling them about the pills would be pretty much moot at that point. Sam's palms were sweating, and he feared the gun might slip from his hands if he waited any longer.

He needed to stop overthinking it and do it already.

"Time's up," announced the doctor as she pushed the door open. "Help! They're in here. They're trying to kill me."

Sam slammed the wheelchair into her again as hard as he could. Her head smacked the door closed, and she slumped to the floor, her vicious smile lingering on her lips.

They needed to leave, but they couldn't just walk out the front door; they needed to find another way-

What was Sam thinking? Of course, they could go out the front door. Sam tore the coat and stethoscope from the doctor and quickly dressed himself in them.

"They're coming," boasted the doctor, blood seeping through her smile.

Sam did his best to ignore her as he shoved her wig onto Tim's head. Tim, still trying to catch his breath, made little objection.

Sam poked open the door and peered out. It was clear. He calmly wheeled Tim through the corridor. Just a doctor taking his patient for a walk. The corridor wasn't busy, but he heard a stampede of police marching through the maternity ward not far away.

They reached the waiting area, and the automatic glass doors were nearly within reach. Sam could almost taste freedom. He glanced at the receptionist, but she didn't seem to recognize him, which Sam was both grateful for and a little annoyed by.

This proved his theory that there might be another Sam out there, and no one would even notice, but he would have to let it go for now. Instead, Sam focused on the bright morning light of freedom promised by the automatic doors, which was soon quelled by a flurry of blue and red sirens.

Sam was about to face a frankly unfair number of police officers, and he couldn't well threaten them all with his gun. He had no recourse other than to close his eyes and simply keep walking through the onslaught of officers in riot gear charging in, rubbing past him and shouting as they continued inside.

Sam opened his eyes again once he sensed the sunlight on his skin.

Sam's good luck continued as he noticed a car careening through the car park towards them, Greg's car.

Jack pulled through!

Waving his arms, Sam tried to get Jack's attention, but as the car drew closer, Sam saw Jack driving with a police officer in the passenger seat.

What the hell was going on? Did Jack sell them out?

He probably ratted out Sam and Tim for a reduced sentence. It was such a Jack thing to do, only ever thinking about himself. The car drove right past them and continued off down the road.

The selfish bastard didn't even notice them.

16

Jack drove. He didn't know where he was going other than far, far away, hoping to outrun just about everything from the past 24 hours. One thing he was finding it difficult to outrun, however, was the police officer handcuffed to him.

"So what is this? Are you taking me hostage now?" asked Lucy.

Jack didn't answer, continuing to pretend she wasn't there, continuing to pretend the handcuffs weren't there, continuing to pretend what he suspected were the signs of a heart attack weren't there.

He kept staring at the stretch of road ahead; lampposts and traffic blurred past as he let his mind go blank. Yet his mind couldn't help but focus on what she said. *Taking her hostage*—he was hardly taking her hostage. He didn't even want her here. If anything, she was taking herself hostage.

Lucy watched as the man next to her stared silently off into the distance with a murderous focus: calm, malicious, and beyond deadly. A stone-cold killer.

Did he kill the nurse? Was he taking her to the same place he took those three students?

Lucy needed to stop him.

She looked around the car, hoping to find anything that might give her an insight into who this man was. Behind her, Lucy found blood staining the backseats a deep red, and couldn't help but scream at the sight of it.

"Stop the car! Stop this car now!" demanded Lucy, grabbing the steering wheel and wrestling it from Jack.

The car swerved wildly across the road, narrowly missing an oncoming lorry as Jack tried to regain control.

"Are you insane?! You're going to get us both killed," shouted Jack.

Lucy relinquished the wheel. He was right. She had to find another way.

"Look," continued Jack, trying to steady his breaths. "I think we've gotten off on the wrong foot here. Let's start over. My name's Jack."

"Where are you taking me?" asked Lucy, not falling for his games. She knew all about *Stockholm syndrome*.

"I don't know," said Jack.

"Then stop."

"I get you want me to stop the car, I do, but first, let me just explain why I'm innocent in all this because I'm not a bad person...I'm really not." Jack's voice creaked and cracked, trying to hold it together.

As Jack rambled, Lucy remembered the walkie-talkie weighing down her lapel. As part of her standard-issue uniform, she received a pair of handcuffs, a notebook, a pen, a baton and a walkie-talkie. She edged her hand towards the walkie-talkie.

"Please, don't...don't do that," stuttered Jack.

"Why not?" said Lucy, her hand hovering over the walkie-talkie. "What are you going to do to me if I do?"

"I...I don't know," said Jack. He genuinely didn't.

Not wanting to discover precisely what this psychopath had in store for her, Lucy lowered her hand from the walkie-talkie. By the time anyone reached her, this man would have already dismembered and scattered her across several locations, anyway.

Jack stared at her in surprise for a moment. All he did was ask her not to, and she listened. Perhaps he misjudged her, perhaps she was much more reasonable than he'd first suspected. She might even hear him out.

"Thank you," said Jack. "Right, so Sam and Tim, the people you met briefly, they wanted to stop Sam's lecturer from swapping out the hospital's medication for, well, I still don't know what he was swapping them for, but I know it wasn't good."

Jack peered over to check if Lucy was getting all this, but she seemed distracted by the small black stick emerging from her pocket. Jack watched as she extended it roughly a foot and held it to Jack's head.

"Stop the car."

"What is that?" asked Jack meekly.

"A baton," replied Lucy, pressing it into his temple.

Perhaps he misjudged how reasonable she was.

"Ok, let's not go waving that about because you could hurt someone. Please, just listen to my story because if you listen, you might be like, '*Oh, this Jack guy might not be so bad,*' and...you know what, your baton is making me very uncomfortable, so if you could lower it..."

Jack made the mistake of reaching for the baton. Lucy responded by slamming it directly into his mouth.

The brakes screeched, Lucy screeched, and Jack screamed in agony, his free hand gripping his mouth as blood seeped through his fingers.

"Oh, God! Why would you do that?! You baton-ed me!"

Jack let out another groan of pain as his words grew muffled through a mouthful of blood. "Who batons someone in the mouth?!"

Lucy was panting through bared teeth. She did it. She took down a criminal, albeit a criminal, who seemed much less threatening than he did a moment earlier.

"You were trying to kill me," said Lucy.

"No, I wasn't. Ah, this hurts so much!" Jack leant back, eyes watering, blood running down his arm.

"Well, I..." uttered Lucy, trying to find the words. This wasn't exactly the heroic moment she thought it would be.

Jack paused as his tongue located something, something solid. He reached into his mouth and pulled out a tooth with a smattering of gum attached. Jack swayed, nearly fainting at the sight of this.

"My tooth!" he yelped. "You knocked out my tooth."

"You want me to knock out another?" said Lucy, waving her baton again, not liking how close Jack's bloody tooth was getting to her.

"I didn't want you to knock out this one," groaned Jack, leaning back against the headrest.

"Then drive us to the police station. Now!" ordered Lucy.

"Fine, ok. Do I keep the tooth? Can they reattach it?"

"I'm not- I don't know, just drive," ordered Lucy.

Fixated on the tooth and the blood seeping from the hole it left, Jack mindlessly pressed his foot on the pedal.

"Wait!" shouted Lucy, as the car immediately struck a man running across the road.

The man slid sharply along the bonnet and into the windscreen, sending a cascade of deep cracks across it.

Jack hit the brakes, and the man catapulted forward, rolling onto the tarmac beneath.

Could this day possibly get any worse?

"What do we do?" asked Jack.

"We have to get out and help him."

"How?" said Jack, lifting his handcuffed arm.

Lucy quickly realized how short-sighted her plan of handcuffing herself to her enemy had been.

"Just get out of the car!" she shouted as she started trying to climb over him, wanting more than anything to escape this claustrophobic, blood-filled death machine.

The man outside staggered to his feet, dazed and dented. He stumbled over to the car and approached the driver's door, peeking in through the broken window, where he saw Jack staring back at him, more confused than ever, and Lucy gazing up from Jack's lap.

"Dr Li?" said Jack, unable to believe what he was seeing.

"I'm not interrupting anything, am I?" asked Dr Li, peering down at the pair in their strange, compromising entanglement.

Dr Li's face bore scratches and swollen indentations from the car's bonnet, yet he seemed relatively cheerful, all things considered.

Lucy returned to her seat and tried to recompose herself. "You know this man?" she whispered to Jack.

"Sorry about jumping out at you like that. I was afraid I'd lose you," said Dr Li.

"You...you're here, how did you..." began Jack, the thumping pain in his mouth quieting at the sight of his mentor.

Dr Li answered all of Jack's questions by holding up the locator, the blinking dot on the screen still tracking Jack. "I need your help."

Jack glanced uneasily at Lucy, her stern face trying not to falter to the immense confusion.

"I'm kind of in the middle of a thing right now," said Jack, returning to Dr Li. "Not a bad thing, just a thing."

Dr Li seemed almost disinterested in the current situation

Jack found himself in, the lipstick layer of blood growing around his mouth, or the police officer handcuffed to him, and so continued his request.

"We haven't got a lot of time. We need to see a man named Toby Cud..." Dr Li glanced at his watch, its face now smashed. "Now, or it could be too late to fix any of this. Believe me. It wasn't supposed to happen this way. I thought there would be more time. I always think there's more time."

Jack never seen Dr Li in this much of a panic. Was he concussed? Jack briefly considered taking him to the hospital, although maybe not the one he was driving away from.

Wait. What did he say?

"Did you say Toby Cud? Dr Tobias Cud?" repeated Jack.

"You've heard of him?" asked Dr Li.

"He's the reason for all of this," Jack told Lucy. "He's the man you should be arresting." Then, back to Dr Li, "How do you know him?"

"I used to work with him, and if we don't find him soon, he's going to hurt a lot of people."

"Ok." agreed Jack.

Dr Li nodded and walked to the back of the car.

Lucy pointed her baton at Jack once more. "That man is not getting in this car."

Jack remained silent as Dr Li pulled open the back door and climbed inside.

"There's an awful lot of blood back here," said Dr Li as he slid into the middle seat.

Lucy turned her baton to Dr Li. "Get out of this car, or I'll arrest you too."

"Arrest me for what? Getting run over?" said Dr Li dismissively. "Who are you anyway?"

"*Officer* Lucy Sparks," she said, emphasizing the 'officer' part.

"I'm Dr Li. Nice to meet you," he replied, nonchalantly

swatting the baton away. "Now that's all cleared up. Jack, I'm going to need you to take a left up here."

Lucy swung back to Jack. The crazy, concussed pensioner might not appreciate her authority, but at least the man driving did.

"We are going to the police station."

Dr Li snatched the baton from her hand.

"Look, I'm on a tight schedule here, so you'll need to sit quietly while I deal with a very pressing matter. When I'm done, arrest whoever you see fit, but if you try to slow me down..." His face turned grave, and his ancient eyes stared into Lucy. "Well, I wouldn't recommend it. Understood?"

Lucy turned away from Dr Li and faced forward. They were definitely going to murder her.

"So that's a left here," continued Dr Li.

17

Sam wheeled Tim through an estate in search of the house where Tim lived. Tim spoke at great length about his gang of dealers, how he was their leader and how he'd bought them a mansion supposedly not too far from the hospital. Although nearly an hour had passed since Tim told him this, and Sam's footsteps were becoming slower with each stride.

"I say to him, you don't get purer than one hundred percent, mate. Escobar's shit is self-raising compared to this," said Tim, recounting another tale. "But they're not having it, and the deal gets ugly. Next thing you know, I'm taking on thirty of these kung-fu-fuckers with only a plastic spork."

"So what happened?" asked Sam, shifting the focus from his aching legs.

"Well," continued Tim, grandiosely clearing his tender throat. "I do this spinning kick, taking five of them out at once. Then I stab a spork through one geezer's chest. It goes through him like wet toilet paper and comes out through a different guy's spine. Before I know it, I'm walking out with the blow and the fifty-k."

Sam struggled to focus on Tim's tale as their surroundings grew more grim. Tim's directions brought them to what Jack always called *'the rough part'* of the city.

Sam always told Jack it was just him being judgmental. However, the rusted pram lying on the pavement, covered in green sludge, didn't inspire massive confidence.

"It's definitely this way?" asked Sam.

"Yeah, we're close," confirmed Tim.

So, Sam kept going, wheeling Tim through the estate, past a series of overgrown houses boarded up with rotten wood, accompanied by the distant barking of unseen hounds, until they reached a small terraced house at the end of the road.

"This is it," said Tim.

Sam gazed up at the house as he walked up the muddy indentation of grass that made up a driveway. It was derelict and coated in several layers of graffiti depicting various tags and gang insignia. Sam saw a bin bag taped to a shattered window rustling in the wind like a proud flag and a pair of freshly stained underwear resting on the doorstep.

"This is the party mansion?" asked Sam, biting his tongue.

"Of course not," said Tim. "This is just temporary while the mansion gets renovated. I'm having another pool added."

As they reached the door, Tim forced himself out of the chair, straining with all his might to remain upright.

"Stay behind me and don't say a word," said Tim, his voice suddenly severe. "Now give me the gun."

"Why do you need it? I thought you were their leader."

"I am. Now give me the fucking gun!" demanded Tim, fists clenching through the pain.

Sam obliged and handed over the pistol.

Tim straightened his posture, pushed down on his working leg, and knocked on the door. There was a whisper of hushed voices from inside, followed by footsteps approaching the door. Tim realized he was still wearing the ridiculous wig and tore it from his head as the door opened.

A metal chain snapped taut, and a hot stream of stale smoke slithered through the small gap. A shadowy figure appeared through the mist, a man with deep-sunken eyes and lips that were dry and cracked, as dry and cracked as the rest of his skin. The man looked Tim up and down, dressed in his pale blue hospital gown, and tutted.

"Rick..." began Tim.

"The fuck do you want?" said Rick, teeth scraping with each syllable.

Tim's demeanor changed in that moment, his face softened and all the attitude and cold intimidation so ingrained in everything Sam knew about him fell away.

"Look, just let me in, alright? I need to speak to Marcus."

Rick gave a single sarcastic laugh. "Marcus doesn't want to see you. None of us do."

"Come on mate, please let me in," said Tim. "I need to ask him about these." He held up the packet of orange pills.

Rick considered for a moment as he scrutinized the packet.

"Five minutes," said Rick, removing the chain and opening the door.

He paused upon seeing Sam and his doctor's coat flowing open, revealing a T-shirt still damp with blood.

"Who the fuck is this?"

Sam stepped forward with his hand outstretched. "Sam Higgs. M.D."

"Your boyfriend ain't invited," scraped Rick. "Just you."

"Wait here," instructed Tim as he followed Rick inside, and the door slammed shut on Sam.

Sam deflated into the wheelchair as he waited on the doorstep, alone, only the stained underwear for company. Jack had abandoned him, and now Tim, too. Once more, he was an afterthought.

A gun and a medical license didn't change a thing. He felt like a powerless kid. Sam knew he could be a powerful threat, respected and feared by all. If only someone would give him the chance to prove it. It may not come naturally to him the way it did to Tim and his oh-so-scary drug dealer friends.

Admittedly, Sam was unnerved by them, though clearly not as terrified as the owner of the underwear lying at his feet.

Sam had no choice but to wait, left behind like a dog tied up outside a shop, as the distant barking of all the other forgotten dogs rang on.

Tim followed Rick through the veil of smoke of the dimly lit house, forcing his legs to stay upright and not crumple under the immense pressure. He continued past Logan and Robert, both too busy shooting up on the shredded sofa to register Tim's presence.

Not too long ago, Tim spent months barely moving from that sofa, half consciously staring at the TV on the floor, endlessly watching the left side of old films through its burnt-out plasma screen, hoping to escape this place, and now here he was, returning like a bird to his inescapable cage.

Finally, they made it to the kitchen, where they found Marcus sitting at the counter, eating a burrito, guacamole slipping from the end of it and falling down his vest. Upon seeing Tim, Marcus nearly choked.

"What the fuck are you doing back here?"

"Me and my mate, we're in trouble. I thought we could stay here until the heat dies down."

"Well, you thought wrong, didn't you?" said Marcus,

returning to his burrito. "Rick, get this fucking waste-man out of my sight."

Rick tried to grab Tim, but Tim pushed him away, almost losing his balance. He wasn't giving up easily.

"Fine, alright, I'll go. Just tell me, who's supplying you these?" Tim dropped the packet of pills onto the counter.

Marcus put down his burrito, stood up, and walked over to Tim, towering almost a foot above him. He glanced down at the little man, who seemed to shrink more and more in his presence.

"Where did you get those?" hissed Marcus.

"What are they?" asked Tim.

"Get the fuck out of my house," said Marcus, turning his back on Tim.

Tim lowered his trembling hand into his blue gown, wrapped his fingers around the hard metal handle, and pulled out the gun, pointing it at Marcus.

"I don't want trouble. I only need to know what they are and who your supplier is."

Marcus seemed unintimidated by the gun and picked up his burrito once more, taking a bite as he stepped back over to Tim, bending down until he and Tim were face to face.

"You think 'cos you've got a gun it makes you a big man?" laughed Marcus, staring down at the broken man beneath him. "Look at you. You look as bad as when we fucked you up the last time you showed up here. Remind me, how many stitches did you need when we stamped your head to the curb?"

"Sixteen," said Tim, gripping his fingers tighter around the gun until his skin turned pink.

More laughter. Flecks of salsa flicked against Tim's bandaged face, dying it red.

"You're so pathetic."

Tim turned to Rick, who seemed suitably more scared of the presence of a gun. "Tell me what the pills do."

"I don't fucking know, I just sell them," said Rick.

"You sell them for Dr Cud, don't you? Who is he?"

Rick was about to answer when Tim's knee buckled, and he fell to one knee as though about to propose, dropping the gun and gritting his teeth against the burning cries of his leg.

Marcus swiped the gun from the floor and danced the sweaty hunk of mental around in his hands.

"You want to work for Dr Cud? Is that it? You're not worthy of him. The man is a fucking God." Marcus's eyes glazed over. "He is God."

***

Sam had enough. He refused to be left as an afterthought a second longer. In the past day, he battled corrupt doctors, psychopathic lecturers, and even Amir. He could handle a few whacked-out drug dealers.

Stepping up into the wheelchair, he hopped over the rotten fence into the back garden. He then tiptoed around an old fridge, a mannequin, and a variety of other smashed-in objects which didn't belong in a respectable garden until he found the back door. He turned the handle, and the door opened effortlessly, almost inviting him inside.

Sam snuck inside, closing the door behind him just as he found it. He turned to find himself standing in a kitchen beside Tim, Rick, and a new, extra-scary man, menacingly holding his gun. Every one of them turned to face him.

Offering an uneasy smile, Sam reacted.

"And sleep," he commanded, hopefully snapping his fingers.

18

GREG PAGE'S CAR PULLED UP OUTSIDE AN ANCIENT industrial building. The gleaming silver walls which once adorned the building had long since rusted to a murky shade of brown.

Weeds sprouted from every crevice, reclaiming the crumbling, abandoned structure. Yet, the fluorescent lights inside were on. The building was still alive, on life support perhaps, but someone was keeping it running.

"Moonshot Labs," proclaimed Dr Li, introducing the eighth wonder of the world.

He leapt from the car to better admire the building, recalling all the memories entangled within the walls of this place, taking in every little detail as he waited for Jack and Lucy to join him.

"Come on, quickly now."

"Should we go to your side or mine?" asked Jack.

"I am not getting out of this car," huffed Lucy. "There is no way I'm going with two murderers into a creepy building so you can murder me."

Jack turned to her, pleading for her to understand. "We're

not murderers. This Tobias Cud person is the one you need to arrest. He's the real bad guy here."

Lucy paused for a moment, staring into the eyes of this man, his face stained red with his own blood, and his clothes covered in someone else's. Yet right then, for some reason that she couldn't quite explain, Lucy saw only honesty in his eyes.

"If you're telling the truth. Let me call for backup."

Jack glanced over at Dr Li and the building he was about to take them into, the big, dangerous building potentially full of even more dangerous people.

"Fine," he conceded.

Lucy pressed the button on her walkie-talkie and requested as many police as possible to come to Moonshot Labs immediately. She uncurled her fists for the first time since meeting Jack.

"Let's go."

Lucy exited her side of the car and yanked on her arm, pulling Jack with her. If she had to do this, it was damn sure going to be on her terms.

Jack inelegantly climbed through the car after her as hand breaks and gear shifts dragged against his tenderest areas. Eventually, Jack flopped out the passenger door, hardly winning the gold medal for his gymnastic skills.

"See," said Jack, forcing a bloodied smile. "You can trust us. We're all on the same side here."

"Then tell me, why is your friend here visiting this supposedly *bad guy*?"

Jack paused a moment. He hadn't considered this, but he was sure there was a rational explanation and scurried over to Dr Li.

"Um, sorry, minor thing, but why exactly are you trying to find Dr Tobias Cud?"

Lost in thought, Dr Li stared up at the building's ostentatious logo: a giant moon, its bright yellow paint long since chipped away, leaving only a faint outline of its former glory.

Dr Li spent years running from this great lunar insignia, but knew deep down he could never truly escape its orbit. He glanced at his watch, the clock face still shattered. Not that it mattered. He knew the precise time, for he was counting down the seconds since it broke, and those seconds were rapidly reaching their end. It was time to face the man in the moon.

"Dr Tobias Cud." he echoed. "I have to stop him from destroying the world."

This wasn't exactly the rational explanation Jack was hoping for. He turned to Lucy, who only shook her head.

"Pardon?" asked Jack, needing just a smidge more clarification on the whole '*destroying the world*' thing, but Dr Li was once more lost in his thoughts as he wandered over to the entrance and through the automatic doors, the rusted gears doing their best to haul them open.

He stepped into the building, and the familiar scent of the 70s decor hit him immediately. Leather seats, faux wood panelling and vinyl flooring lined the vacant reception, untouched by time and exactly as Dr Li remembered it: a million shades of brown. Despite everything he knew was to come, there was still a comforting familiarity to it.

"Hurry," shouted Dr Li as he hopped over a security barrier beside the welcome desk. "The world won't save itself!"

"I'm sure he's just being melodramatic," Jack told Lucy with a hopeful shrug as he followed his mentor, towing Lucy along with him into the building.

***

DR LI CONTINUED THROUGH THE DECREPIT HALLS OF Moonshot Labs, muscle memory guiding the way as he explained everything to Jack and Lucy at a million miles per hour.

"Toby Cud has been developing a strain of viral analogue which augments human DNA. DNA, which develops new and precise neural pathways..."

Lucy dug her heels further into the ground with every extra bit of nonsense this concussed criminal spouted, hoping to slow her descent into the depths of this building and the insanity of this man's delusion, at least until backup arrived.

"This is too dangerous," whispered Lucy, her voice echoing along the empty corridors. "He's going to get us both killed."

Jack couldn't help but agree.

"Um, Dr Li," he chimed, interrupting the lesson. "I've met a person who works for Dr Cud. His name is Greg Page, and he tried to kill me...a bit. Are you sure this Dr Cud isn't dangerous?"

"Oh, he's extremely dangerous," agreed Dr Li.

Jack leant in close to Lucy. "Did backup say how long they'll be, by any chance?"

Dr Li stopped as he reached the door at the end of the corridor. *Room 14B*, just the sight of it caused every muscle in his body to tense. He pushed open the door and was almost surprised to find himself not immediately riddled with bullets.

No one was home.

"Here we are, Toby Cud's workshop," announced Dr Li as he stepped inside.

The workshop was large, yet claustrophobic, and crammed full of a multitude of half-built contraptions whose exposed wiring reached across the floor and licked at Jack and Lucy's ankles as they hesitantly followed Dr Li inside.

A sharp beam of sunlight shone through a large window and across a curtain of dust, before reflecting off the array of scientific instruments strewn across shelves and dissection tables, instruments which resembled torture devices rather than anything remotely scientific. Jack pulled his arms tightly to his sides, fearing he would need a tetanus shot just from looking at them.

The centerpiece of the room was a large wooden workbench, burnt and stained from years of experimentation, and stretching from wall to wall like a grand dining table, with a feast of Petri dishes laid out along it.

A pair of ornate, velvet-bound mahogany chairs stood at either end of the table, each dyed with an uneven coat of black. A bundle of old newspapers sat in one chair while stacks of test results sat in the other.

As Jack edged along the room's perimeter, he noticed several framed certificates lining the walls, all boasting a myriad of qualifications and scientific achievements, and each in recognition of the same person, Tobias Cud.

"So Dr Cud's not here," said Jack, mostly to confirm it to himself. "That's good. That's not...deadly."

Lucy pulled back on the handcuffs again, beckoning Jack back towards the door. She made the mistake of allowing her curiosity to get the better of her, and followed Jack all the way into the heart of this bizarre torture chamber, but she wouldn't let this go on any longer.

Jack ignored her, busy inspecting a shadow dancing across the wall beside him. As he followed the shadow to its source, he came across a small cage resting in the room's corner, just large enough to house a lab rat.

Surprisingly, despite Jack's almost limitless capacity for fear, rats were an exception. He spent many years in their company working with Dr Li, and in some ways, Jack preferred them to people.

To get a good look, he knelt beside the cage as its inhabitant timidly crawled into the light, sniffing Jack out. As it came into view, he saw this was no mere rat. Repeated experimentation left the poor thing looking as though it were turned inside out, reduced to a tangled web of viscera and wiring, with parts of it entirely replaced with machinery and barely resembling anything living at all.

It locked eyes with Jack and charged at the bars of its cage, gnawing at them with murderous intent. Jack leapt back, adding rats back onto the list of fears, and knocked into Lucy. Their eyes met, and they both agreed without saying a word.

"You know, maybe this is a job for the police," Jack called over to Dr Li as he backed towards the exit.

"Which is why we have Officer Sparks here," Dr Li called back.

"No, you don't. We're leaving," retorted Lucy, yanking on the handcuffs and almost dislocating Jack's arm.

"You can't," said Dr Li. "I'm sorry, Jack, but Toby told me if I didn't bring you here, he would kill you."

The words hung in the air momentarily as Jack tried to make sense of them. His mind stuttered and clunked as it chewed on the unpalatable meaning of what Dr Li just told him, but he simply couldn't swallow it.

"Excuse me?"

"I'm sorry, but he's been watching you and me for a long time. He wants the...you know what."

Jack sensed the block of wood, glass and impossible physics pressing against his ankle. He'd almost forgotten it was there.

"Jack, I need you to trust me," pleaded Dr Li.

"Why didn't you tell me about any of this?" asked Jack in a small, hurt voice.

"Please, Jack, there isn't time. Just do as I say, and I promise we'll get through this."

The distant sound of police sirens growing louder by the second interrupted them, and Lucy's face lit up as she heard their beautiful whirr. Her dad was coming to save her.

"Change of plans," decreed Lucy, almost dancing with excitement. "You two are going to prison, and I'm going home."

Jack lowered a hand towards his boot and the secret within, possibly the only thing capable of fending off the howling storm coming his way. If ever there was a time to use it, it was now.

"I have it," he told Dr Li.

Dr Li's eyes narrowed, his brow wrinkled, and his face seemed older. In that moment, his face bore every year and mistake he ever experienced. However, he didn't say a word. He simply removed Jack's hand from the boot and gripped it in his own.

"I took it," said Jack. "I know I shouldn't have, but I did. Which means we can use it, right? You can make it work. I know you can, and we can go far away from here right now."

Still no reply. Dr Li just stared through Jack.

"I'm talking about the ti…"

Dr Li pressed a finger over Jack's lips and shook his head.

"We can fix this," continued Jack, desperation turning to tears in his eyes. "Please."

The sound of footsteps thundered along the corridor as the seconds ran dry. All the while, Lucy eagerly watched the door.

"I'm in here!"

Dr Li gripped Jack in a tight embrace and whispered a simple instruction into his ear, "Don't let him find it."

He then pulled Jack closer still, hugging him warmly.

"Be better than I was." Dr Li's voice was shaky, and Jack could feel his hands trembling.

The door to the workshop snapped open, and a pair of police officers charged into the room, wearing bulletproof vests, pointing guns, and shouting, "Get down on the ground!"

Lucy dove face down onto the floor, pulling Jack with her. As Jack glanced up, he saw Dr Li was still standing, refusing to back down to the officers who were now screaming in his face and pointing their guns.

"Get down on the ground!" yelled the officers, but Dr Li stood firm.

"Is he here?" asked Dr Li.

"Get down on the ground!" continued the officers.

"Stop," said a voice from the door, bringing with it an icy chill which swept into the room, freezing the officers in place.

All Dr Li could do was close his eyes, hiding behind his eyelids like a child. It was twenty years, and he hoped after all this time, he would feel more prepared, or more accepting at least, but he didn't.

When Dr Li opened his eyes again, he was met with the architect of every nightmare he ever experienced. If evil had a face, he was staring right at it.

Dr Tobias Cud stood before him, with his sickly pale complexion, frown, and wrinkled lip, and sneer of cold command. All of which were punctuated by a path of scars, staples and slabs of silver piercing through his skin and cleaving across his features.

Most of his hair was gone, with only a few scattered clumps clinging onto his scalp, wedged between scar tissue and metal plates. A large titanium contraption ran down the back of his neck and along his spine, tearing through his suit like a stegosaurus. A faded, grey suit, which seemed almost as old as he was and far too large for his scrawny frame, for he'd shrunk over the years, but the suit remained.

Descending through the right sleeve of his suit was an arm encased within a robotic exoskeleton, while his other arm was withered and barely reached past his cufflinks. His trousers were pressed and his shoes polished, for Tobias Cud wished to appear his best for today. The day he would finally get his revenge.

Dr Cud glanced down at Jack, whimpering at his feet.

"You brought him then," said Dr Cud, flashing a wry smile at Dr Li.

"He knows nothing, and the device is too dangerous for anyone to use. It's gone," explained Dr Li.

"Gone?"

"I destroyed it. It's over."

Dr Cud scoffed at this.

"Liar. All you've ever done is lie to me. We were going to do so much. So much. But you lied. And lied. And lied." He raised his robotic arm and grabbed Dr Li by the throat. "You're a liar!" he hissed, lifting Dr Li off the ground.

Dr Li frantically struggled, clawing in vain at Dr Cud's unyielding grip, slicing his fingers to shreds on the jagged metal fist as his desperation grew, fighting for just one more breath.

Jack tried to reach Dr Li to do something, anything to help, but his handcuffed wrist forbid it.

"Never again! No more lies!"

Dr Cud gripped tighter and tighter, and then...

Snap.

Dr Tobias Cud unclamped his hand from around Dr Li's neck, allowing his lifeless body to fall unceremoniously to the ground.

"Noooo!" screamed Jack as the world spun around him in a sickening kaleidoscope of pitch-black hues.

Everything went dizzyingly silent, and the universe blinked out of existence for a moment. When Jack refocused, darkness reformed into shadows, shapes, and finally, to Dr Cud.

This monster, who killed his adoptive father, filled Jack's vision, crouching down beside him to meet his gaze.

"Hello, Jack."

19

The POLICE OFFICERS FOLLOWED THEIR MASTER'S instructions and arranged the pair of grand mahogany chairs beside one another. Lucy struggled and fought as they dragged her toward the chairs.

"Please, you can't just do what he tells you," pleaded Lucy as the officers bound her head, wrists and ankles to the chair, buckling her down with well-worn leather straps. "I know you're good people who've just lost their way, but surely you can see this isn't right."

"Oh, shut her up, will you," bemoaned Dr Tobias Cud, rubbing his brow in frustration.

"You're a disgrace to the uniform!" shouted Lucy, as her mouth was taped shut.

The officers stuck a layer of duct tape over Jack's mouth, too. Although it didn't seem all that necessary, he didn't resist when the officers strapped him to the chair, remaining fixated on the corpse lying on the other side of the room.

Dr Cud stared down into the dead eyes of his very dead nemesis and couldn't help but feel a tad underwhelmed. All those years he spent plotting Dr Li's downfall, he expected more from their last confrontation. Then again, he supposed, the job was only half-done.

He ran his hands across Li's body and found a wallet, a baton, and the locator. The locator rested snuggly in his palm as he inspected the device knowingly, thumbing the screen. The screen lit up, blinking a small dot on its map: Jack's location at Moonshot Labs.

He placed it onto a workbench and turned his attention to his new prisoners and the pair of officers standing diligently beside them, awaiting their next orders.

"Done?" asked Dr Cud.

"Yes, sir," said both police officers in perfect unison, worthy of a *jinx* in any other scenario.

"Good, I'm going to need some privacy now, so I'd like for you both to kill yourselves," said Dr Cud, casually waving them away.

The officers raised their guns to their temples.

Lucy screamed through the tape, trying to beg them to stop, and, for a moment, she swore she saw fear in their eyes.

The officers fell.

Lucy writhed in her seat, fighting against her restraints. The ringing of the gunshots muted her muffled screams and yelps, but not the streams of tears flowing down her face. She couldn't bear to look at them.

This had to be a trick. They couldn't be dead. They just couldn't be.

She noticed something warm and wet collecting around her feet and followed its stream to the bodies, littering the room like discarded toys.

This was no trick.

Beside her, Jack's head flopped forward against the leather strap, for he had fainted.

Dr Cud scrutinized his sleeping prisoner. He knew who Jack was, of course, but now, upon seeing him up close, it became apparent he was merely a boy and perhaps not even worthy of the hatred he harboured for years.

Yet, this simple child took away everything from Tobias Cud, everything he worked his entire life to achieve, as well as his only friend…No, not friend. Dr Li only ever cared for himself, and now he lay dead like all the rest.

Dr Cud flicked Jack's forehead with his fingers until the boy stirred, sluggishly blinking back to life.

Now, with all eyes back on him, he could begin.

Dr Cud walked over to one of the dead officers and reached down to clutch what remained of their head in his robotic, augmented grasp, gripping it tighter and tighter until the skull buckled and cracked open like an egg. He reached inside, and in one swift motion, tore out the brain.

Lucy averted her gaze, twisting her head as far round as it would go, hoping to avoid this grim dissection. Jack had only the slightest awareness of what was happening, slipping in and out of consciousness as his mind fled his body.

Dr Cud held up the brain as he began the monologue he rehearsed many, many times.

"The human brain, the greatest machine in the universe, even with a bullet in it." He jammed his ancient, bony fingers into the brain, piercing his fingernails through memories and cortexes as he searched for the bullet.

He soon found it and, after a few attempts, dug out the dented metal bullet before casually tossing the brain from hand to hand as effluvia dripped onto the floor.

"Malleable. Manipulatable. Rearrange a few neural pathways and receptors, and, oh, you can make someone do anything you like. A walking puppet. Just like *Tweedledee* and *Tweedledum* here, or even Greg Page, you remember him, don't you? He was one of the first. With only a simple pill, I can fix just about anyone."

Dr Cud noticed Jack's attention waning as his head

drooped again, but he knew precisely what would wake him. Squeezing the brain tightly until it bulged through his fingers, Dr Cud dragged the pale lump of grey matter across Jack's face. He was right. This certainly woke Jack up, his eyes now silently wide above the duct tape.

Dr Cud leant in close as he whispered into Jack's ear.

"Are you afraid of me yet?"

He pulled away the tape and awaited Jack's testimony. Jack opened his mouth to speak, and a creamy splutter of vomit convulsed out, running down his chin.

Dr Cud wiped away the small smattering which landed upon his chin and replaced the tape over Jack's mouth, its adhesive properties struggling to cling to his wet lips.

Dr Cud changed tack and turned his attention to Lucy, screaming and writhing behind her restraints.

"Soooo. Whoooo. Areeee. Youuuu?" he asked, studying the young woman.

"We all know the great Jack Phoenix, but you, what are you? Sidekick? Lover? You certainly look familiar." Dr Cud then noticed the handcuffs joining the pair together. "Partners in crime?"

He peeled away the tape from Lucy's mouth, and she immediately spat in his face. Dr Cud wiped away the second load of fluid to hit his face in as many minutes and offered Lucy a coy smile.

Lucy began at once, "I'm a police officer, and you are going to be in so much trouble when..."

Dr Cud hummed a single laugh.

"A police officer. You mean like those two?" he said, pointing at the ex-police officers behind him.

"You're a murderer. You won't get away with this."

"Oh, I think I might."

"You're sick," choked Lucy, unable to hold back the tears.

Dr Cud stopped dead as the words chimed through his

mind, and his grip tightened around his cerebral stress ball until it popped. He leaned in and grabbed Lucy by the lapels of her jacket until the tip of his nose brushed against hers.

"I am not sick!" he hissed. "I am stronger than you ever could imagine."

Lucy recoiled, pressing her head back into the soft velvet lining of the chair. Dr Cud turned away from her, slamming the brain flat onto the workbench. He stood there a moment, hissing through his teeth like a snake.

Noticing the baton beside him, he straightened up and recomposed himself. He returned to Lucy, extended the baton, and dabbed its tip against her throat.

"I'm not sick," repeated Dr Cud, attempting to regain his calculated demeanour.

Dr Cud turned back to Jack, who was still quite docile, and grabbed the tape that had slid down his chin, tossing it to the floor.

"Ready to talk?"

"I don't know who you think I am, but I'm not them." mumbled Jack, slurring his way through his words, like a drunk, or like a man who watched three people die horrifically before having a brain wiped across his face.

Dr Cud slammed the baton into Jack's stomach, and the sharp shock fired along his nervous system, electrifying him awake, more awake than he'd ever been and more scared than he ever thought possible.

"Don't lie to me!" seethed Dr Cud. "I know you've been working with him."

"Who? Dr Li? Yeah, he...he adopted me. I help him out sometimes with his work. But I don't know what you want from me."

Dr Cud took another swing with the baton, knocking a home run into Jack. Powerless to stop the baton, all Jack could do was scream as the full force of Dr Cud's mechanically enhanced strength dented his organs.

"Don't play dumb with me!" retorted Dr Cud. "I know you know about the time machine."

"The what?!" exclaimed Lucy. "Time machine?! Oh my God, you're all insane! Let me out of here! Let me out of here!"

Lucy lurched back and forth in her chair, trying to break free from her restraints. She threw the full weight of her body against its velvet lining, causing the front legs to lift from the floor, hanging in perfect balance for a moment before tipping past the point of no return and taking Lucy down with it.

The intricate carvings of the wood splintered and chipped as it slammed against the floor with a brutal thud. However, Lucy refused to yield as she continued ranting and writhing from the floor; her legs flailing above her.

Dr Cud ran his hand through Jack's hair and gripped tightly, ripping out follicles and eliminating all other distractions.

With all of Jack's attention entirely in his grasp, Dr Cud asked him as clearly as possible, "Where is it?"

Jack felt it pressing into his ankle and tried not to think about it.

"I really don't know what you're talking about. He mentioned time travel a few times, but only as an idea, as a joke. He hasn't built a time machine. No one's built a time machine. It's impossible!"

"It's insane!" concurred Lucy.

Jack tried to press his boot tighter against the chair leg and out of sight, but as he did, Dr Cud noticed a faint blue glow through the cuffs of Jack's trousers. He hadn't seen that perfect shade of blue in so many years, and the sight of it unlocked a flurry of long-forgotten memories.

It was here.

All he needed to do was reach down and take it, but he couldn't, not yet. Dr Cud dug his fingers into Jack's scalp, resisting the overwhelming urge. He needed to be sure it worked first, and for that, there was only one thing to be done. It was a risk, the biggest risk in his entire plan.

Dr Cud relinquished his grip and turned to the brainless police officer at his feet. He leant over and tore the gun away from their stiff hand before returning to Jack and directing it at the boy's forehead.

"Are you afraid?" he asked.

Jack stiffened, gripping the armrests for dear life, unable to do much else.

"Please, I'm begging you, you don't have to do this…"

"Are you afraid?" repeated Dr Cud.

"Yes!" cried Jack, his body positively vibrating. "I'm afraid, very, very afraid. Please, just stop."

"Three," said Dr Cud calmly.

"What? What is it you want?" Jack knew the answer but refused to give it up.

Jack failed Dr Li once today by not trusting him, and now he was being consumed by rigor-mortis. He wouldn't let Dr Li down again, even if it were the last thing he would ever do.

"I don't have a time machine."

"Two."

"What's going on?" shouted Lucy, trying to crane her neck up to see.

She glimpsed the gun, now pressed to Jack's forehead, and fell deathly silent.

Jack reached out and grasped Lucy's hand, clenching it, and she squeezed back.

"One."

Jack closed his eyes.

Dr Cud pulled the trigger. The bullet blasted down the

barrel of the gun and pierced through Jack's brain, killing him instantly.

"What?" exclaimed the much younger Jack, spitting out his third ice cream. "That's how the story ends? He gets shot in the face by the baddie?"

"No, not really. I was just checking to see if you were listening," said his father. "What happened was, Dr Cud pulled the trigger, the bullet blasted down the barrel of the gun and then..."

The small wooden device buried in Jack's boot glowed brighter and brighter until its brilliant blue light shot out in a burst of lightning, climbing up Jack's leg until it swallowed him whole. But it didn't stop there.

It carried on through Jack's hand and over to Lucy's. The blinding fizz of sparks shot up her arm until it engulfed her, too. The cocoon of light snapped shut around them, imploding in on itself until only the two chairs remained.

The bullet continued its trajectory and shot through the chair, burrowing through the velvet cushioning and embedding itself deep within the wood behind.

Dr Cud shielded his eyes from the impossibly bright blue flash until the last sparkle dissipated, leaving nothing in its place.

A crooked smile slowly spread across his face.

PART 3

THE PAST

20

Dr Cud shot Jack, and Lucy was about to be next. She was certain of it.

After what felt like an eternity, Lucy finally opened her eyes and saw that the cold concrete ceiling she was staring at was now replaced by a perfect blue sky. She noticed her body was no longer tied to a chair, and her legs were resting on the ground, on what felt like grass.

She ran her fingers through the thick strands, each of uniform length and slick with morning dew.

It was grass.

Her nose filled with the sweet aroma of fresh flowers, and her ears filled with a dissonant orchestra of serenading birdsongs, percussive car engines, and the distant knell of bells resonating out their long droning toll. Lucy heard bells like these before. They were funeral bells.

She shot up, bursting back to life, and found Jack sitting next to her, still hand-cuffed to her, and she was still holding his hand. She quickly retracted her hand, but Jack seemed too preoccupied to notice. He was darting his head back and forth, studying every atom of his surroundings.

"It works," he said, digging his hand around in his boot.

Beyond her, the full extent of this place came into focus as she saw they were sitting in a graveyard, a path beside them winding into the distance towards a church.

The church bells continued to ring as Lucy's heart raced, each clang of metal resonating through her louder than before and confirming Lucy's fears.

"It works!" said Jack, triumphantly holding up the small wooden block. "We moved, we teleported, we…"

"Died," finished Lucy.

"Hang on. I know this place," continued Jack, not registering what Lucy said, too busy in his excited delirium. "My parents are buried in this graveyard."

"I'm never going to see my dad again," breathed Lucy, the realization of her untimely death now weighing down on her to a crushingly high degree.

"No, wait, hang on," continued Jack, realizing he didn't just recognize the church and the graveyard.

He knew the exact spot where they found themselves, for it was the spot where he spent much of his youth. However, now there was one crucial difference. The grave he knew so well was missing.

"They're alive."

He needed to say it again.

"They're alive!"

He turned to Lucy.

"My mom and dad. They're still alive!"

Jack couldn't help but notice Lucy didn't share his excitement. In fact, she wasn't listening at all. Instead, Lucy was quietly weeping into her hands.

"Hey," said Jack in his best comforting voice, "it's ok."

"How is it ok? How is anything ok? We're dead. I just tried to do my job. I just wanted to make my dad proud." She returned to her hands, unable to stop the tears. "And you got me killed."

Jack held Lucy's wrist, slowly removed it from her eyes, and tried to ignore the snot following the tears down her face. He gripped her wrist and listened.

Fdd...Fdd...Fdd...

"You have a pulse," said Jack, a wide-eyed grin spreading across his face. "We didn't die. I think something far madder happened."

Jack jumped to his feet, pulled Lucy up with him, and guided her along the path through the graveyard, slowing briefly as he passed one grave, which, until now, had always been illegible to Jack.

Now, the once sun-bleached stone regained its lustre, and the engraving, no longer burdened by time, clearly bore the name 'David Summers.' Jack smiled to himself. Maybe he could visit him now that eternity's walls evaporated.

This wasn't what he wanted to show Lucy, so they kept walking until they reached the freshly painted bright green railings, through which Jack and Lucy saw a world that only existed in the faintest recesses of their memories.

Before them lay a bustling street full of people flaunting out-of-date fashion. *Woolworths, Dixons, Virgin Megastores,* each with posters in their windows promoting *Shrek* on VHS, cassette tapes from *Robbie Williams* and *S Club 7* and the brand new *PlayStation 2.*

They saw two children walking hand in hand with their parents. One carried a *Teletubbies* toy as they complained about their aching feet, while the other jabbed away at a *Tamagotchi.*

The family was alive.

The street was alive.

The past was alive.

Jack and Lucy were alive.

"We travelled through time," confirmed Jack, taking it all in. "Early 2000s, by the looks of things."

He could do better than that. It was warm. Mud became grass beneath his feet. The leaves returned to greener shades, once more affixed to their branches, and stretching through the railings, wild bluebells unfurled from their buds, basking in the sunlight.

"April."

Jack glanced down at his shadow casting a short distance northwest, along the grass.

"11 am."

"This isn't possible. None of this is possible," said Lucy, drying her eyes.

"Yet, here we are."

21

ONCE AGAIN, SAM STARED DOWN THE BARREL OF A gun with no plan on how to stop the inevitable bullet coming his way. He thought he should be used to this by now, but with every tiny flicker of Marcus's finger against the trigger, Sam couldn't help but flinch.

Sweat dripped from his neck, down his chest, past his navel, and finally soaked into his trousers. At least, it was mostly sweat. Fear gripped Sam, but confusion overwhelmed him more. He found himself in the kitchen of a drug den that Tim supposedly ruled over, and yet, here Tim was, knelt beside him, next in line for the bullet buffet.

"What's going on here? I thought you were their boss?" whispered Sam.

Marcus burst out laughing.

"This guy? He's an addict. He started dealing for me to pay off his debts. Then we kicked his ass out when we found out what he really was. Isn't that right?"

"Tell me where I can find Dr Cud," said Tim.

"Tobias Cud doesn't want a little cripple like you," said

Marcus, turning the gun towards Tim, baring down on him. "And especially not a dirty, fucking…"

"Stop!" shouted Tim. "Just stop. Look, if you're going to kill us, do it already."

"Do I not get a say in this?" interjected Sam. "Because, personally, I'd rather not get killed."

"Oh look," laughed Marcus, his face inches from Tim's. "The baby's crying."

"I'm not," said Tim, his eyes barely even watering.

"You're such a faggot."

In that moment, something set alight a spark within Tim, and Sam watched as his face twitched and contorted with the same determination which turned the hands of fate in his favour before. Tim pressed down on his leg and forced himself up. The pain tried desperately to fight back, but soon quelled under the unfaltering pressure of Tim's resolve.

"Get down," growled Marcus, shoving Tim back.

Tim resisted. His leg wailed, but he stood firm.

"Fuck you," he said as he turned his back to Marcus and started limping towards the door.

Marcus swung the gun into the back of Tim's head. Tim's mouth filled with the sharp taste of pennies as he collapsed onto the cracked kitchen tiles.

Marcus loomed over him, pistol in hand; he wasn't playing around now. He cocked the gun and…

He didn't fire.

Marcus froze in place, his finger hung still, buffering a single moment from the trigger. A snapshot captured his face, revealing the hate etched on every feature. He didn't blink; he didn't breathe. For somebody far away hit pause on the man's reality.

It took Tim a few seconds to notice something was wrong. Marcus wasn't the type to hesitate. He moved his head from the gun's trajectory and found that it didn't follow, remaining in place, now aiming at nothing. Tim saw Rick behind him, standing in silence with a crooked half-expression on his lips, as he too was engaged in this strange game of *Stuck In The Mud*.

Even the two men on the sofa in the next room froze, although you wouldn't have noticed it. They had stopped, all apart from Sam, who seemed just as perplexed as Tim.

Tim stared into Marcu's vacant eyes and saw them twitching subtly as each frozen man received a signal that consumed their minds. A message informing them that Dr Cud's hypothesis was indeed correct. Fear was the key.

Anything that can yield more fear must be protected, including his friends. At the end of the message, there was a footnote meant specifically for Tim.

"*Timothy,*" began Marcus as he fixed his posture and lowered his gun, now speaking in a voice far more eloquent than his own. "*I believe you were asking about me. You wanted to know who I am.*"

Tim wasn't sure what he was seeing. Just how hard was the knock to the head?

"*I'm a scientist,*" continued Marcus. "*That's how I'm talking to you now. That's what the pills do. They simply allow me to talk to people, to talk to their minds. But I'm not just a scientist. I'm also a survivor, much like yourself. The things you've done today have shown a great strength of character, and I see the toll these people have taken on you. As such, I'd like to offer you a truce. I know what this man did to you. I can feel the pain he caused you. So, allow me to dispose of him for you.*"

Marcus turned the gun around, raised it to his temple and fixed its aim upon himself. Without the slightest hint of hesitation, Marcus pulled the trigger. With a bang and a crack, the light within him went out and red and grey jelly splattered across the wall.

"What the fuck just happened?" screamed Sam, sweat no longer the dominant liquid occupying his trousers.

Tim lurched backwards, away from Marcus's shattered visage, and backed into Rick.

"Shall I dispose of this one as well?" asked Rick.

"No, no more. That's fine," said Tim, choking down the chewy lump rising in his throat and shimmying towards the door.

Sam decided it was time to go with his usual Plan B and pelted through the house, past the two sofa-bound addicts staring vacantly through him.

He kicked open the door and almost shoved Tim through it, catching him in the wheelchair and catapulting him back up the street, far away from whatever the hell happened in there.

Tim glanced back at the house and saw Rick standing at the door.

"I'll be in touch," he mouthed as he faded into the distance.

<h1 style="text-align:center">22</h1>

As the sun set on a day which had refused to end, Sam and Tim passed under rows of waking streetlights and made their way to the house where Sam's family lived. Whenever Sam was in a scrape before, be it with bullies, teachers, or that man whose shed was already on fire long before Sam arrived, he knew he could always run home and hide whilst his mom smoothed everything out for him.

This situation seemed trickier than any he faced before, and he wasn't too sure his mom could fix it this time. He still couldn't process what happened with Marcus. Admittedly, he also couldn't process what happened with Greg, or the doctor, or his clone, or the half a dozen other impossible things which befell him over the past few days. Each one formed a piece of a puzzle that refused to fit together.

Tim stared forward in silence, refusing even to blink, as waiting for him in the darkness was the memory of Marcus, all his words and insults spilling through the mangled crater of his face. He couldn't escape the memory, repeating it over and over like a scratched record. Marcus popping like bubblegum; his head bursting open like a piñata.

Neither Tim nor Sam felt much like talking about what transpired in that house, so the pair conducted the long walk in silence.

Eventually, they arrived at the unassuming house that Sam called home. Sam wheeled Tim along the well-groomed garden path, lined with pansies, until they reached his mother's small allotment of carrots and tomatoes, climbing up along the brick wall towards the window. The curtains were drawn shut, as they always were to keep that nosey postman from spying.

They stopped outside the bright red front door so Sam could ring the doorbell. After a moment, the door swung open, and a young girl answered. She wore a school uniform, and a ribbon knotted around her ponytail.

"You are in so much trouble," she said.

"Shut up, Molly," replied Sam, pushing past her. "You don't know what happened. I haven't even done anything."

Tim awkwardly followed behind, leaving his wheelchair on the porch. The house was clean, yet cluttered with ornaments. China vases and commemorative plates rested on shelves and side tables, each meticulously arranged, dusted and polished.

"You're all over the news. Mom is losing it," said Molly as Sam's mom bustled over from the kitchen.

"Is that my little Sammy I hear?" said Sam's mum, her arms flying outwards as she wrapped them around Sam in a loving embrace.

Sam poked his tongue out at his younger sister. He won.

His mother stepped back and hit Sam on the arm.

"I have been so worried about you. Look, I'm still shaking," she said, holding out her hand. "I've been trying to phone you all day."

"Tim said we needed to get rid of our phones so the police

couldn't track us. That's Tim, by the way," said Sam, pointing at Tim.

Tim forced an awkward smile.

"Your new phone! That was a Christmas present. Oh, what have you gotten yourself into?"

"Nothing, look, it's fine," said Sam, freeing himself from his mother's grip. "We just need somewhere to lie low until everything blows over."

"I've been on the phone to Tracey, and she knows this lawyer who got her off for shoplifting..."

"I don't need a lawyer, and I don't need you telling your friends about every little thing I do," whined Sam, but his mom wasn't listening. She was already feeling his arms and sizing him up. "Look how skinny you've gotten. You haven't been eating properly since living on your own. A mother knows these things. I'll make you boys a nice roast."

"We don't need a roast, mom."

"I, um, I am quite hungry, actually," said Tim timidly from the corner, uncomfortably fiddling with a doily.

"Alright, fine, we'll have a roast," agreed Sam. "But can we not make a big deal out of this?"

"Where's your father? Tell! shouted Sam's mom. "Terry! I swear he's going deaf."

She marched them into the living room to find a middle-aged man dressed in jeans covered in ancient paint stains below a bare chest of matted hair, within which flaky crumbs from a recent sausage roll had embedded themselves. He barely turned his head away from the TV in acknowledgement.

"Are you not even going to say hello? Sammy's here, and he's brought his friend."

"You alright, boy?" replied Sam's dad without getting up. After so many years, the sofa molded to Sam's father like a tortoise's shell.

"We've all been watching you on the news," said Sam's

mom before noticing her husband had changed the channel and was now watching the football. "Oh, turn it back. They want to see themselves on the telly, don't you, Sammy?"

"It's fine, really..." started Sam.

"Put the other side back on. Where'd you put that remote?"

"If he says it's fine," argued Sam's dad, but his wife quickly wrestled the TV remote away from him.

She squinted to make out the buttons on the remote to change the channel and turned the volume up.

"The search is ongoing for the three fugitives seen here." The TV displayed a short piece of grainy CCTV footage taken from the hospital, showing Sam and Tim racing through the hospital with the wheelchair. The footage paused as Sam looked directly at the camera, raising his middle finger.

"Well, that could be anyone," sulked Sam.

"One of the three fugitives is believed to have taken a junior Police Officer by the name of Lucy Sparks hostage. Witnesses reported they saw the officer being dragged into a stolen car, which then fled the scene. Their current whereabouts are unknown."

"Bloody hell," said Sam. "Jack's gone rogue."

"Didn't think he had it in him," said Tim. "Where do you reckon he took her?"

"He couldn't have gone too far," assured Sam.

23

"Should anyone present know of any reason that this couple should not be joined in holy matrimony, speak now or forever hold your peace," said the vicar.

A slight pause as the rows of smartly dressed people sitting in the pews remained silent. The bride smiled through her veil, and her soon-to-be husband smiled back at her. They were ready.

Before the vicar could continue, the ancient wooden doors to the church flew open, and everyone turned their heads to see the doors parting, revealing a man and a woman, drenched in a thick smattering of blood, some of which their own but most was not.

The woman wore a police officer's uniform, while the man wore a coat, shirt and jeans, torn and soaked in sweat and chunks of vomit. Handcuffs united the pair at the wrists, and they possessed a powerful smell that no one in the church quite recognized, for it was the stench of brains.

The woman spoke first.

"Are we dead?" she asked everybody in the church at once.

No one answered. The entire church simply stared at this unholy couple in a sea of stunned silence.

"She means...what year is this?" said the man, stumbling through his words, trying to sound a little more sane.

Still, no one spoke.

He tried again. "Or if someone could point us to the loo?"

He offered a weak smile, revealing a fresh gap between his teeth, bubbling and oozing a steady river of blood down his chin.

An older man in a cravat and braces pointed towards an adjacent door.

"Thank you," said the man, and the pair scuttled off in that direction.

24

Sam's mom brought several plates into the living room, each on its own tray, stacked high with roast potatoes, lamb, Yorkshire puddings, veg and a healthy dose of gravy.

Sam's dad took his tray without looking up from the TV.

Sam took his with a mumbled "thanks," but his mind was elsewhere as he stared at himself on the screen, riding on the back of the wheelchair through the grainy hospital CCTV.

"Mom, I don't have a secret twin I don't know about...do I?" asked Sam.

"No dear, I think one of you is quite enough, don't you?"

Sam sighed thoughtfully as he chewed on a potato. Maybe he imagined it, maybe he imagined everything else too, and it was all going to turn out fine.

Molly grabbed her dinner and went upstairs to eat in her room, away from the endless Sam show.

Tim awkwardly thanked Sam's mom and began jabbing away at the food with his fork. Tim spent the last few years living off kebabs, microwavable chips or, more often than not, simply not eating at all. He nearly forgot how nice food tasted when made with the love of a mother.

For a moment, his mind turned to his own mom, and he wondered what she was doing now, if she was watching him on the news, if she was even still alive. He looked up from his food and saw Sam joking with his father while his mother scolded them for being so rude, and, for just a moment, Tim felt more at home than he did in years.

It wasn't to last, as the familiar sound of police sirens began whirring in the distance until the sound consumed the entire house.

Sam turned to his mother. She rested her dinner tray on the coffee table and walked over to the window, peeping her head through the curtains. She counted at least six police cars and a van parking outside the house and up the street.

Officers began exiting the vehicles, several wearing riot gear, a few holding rifles. She turned back to see Sam ducking behind the sofa and Molly running down the stairs, shouting, "Mom, the police are here!"

Everybody's eyes were on Sam's mom. Even Sam's dad dragged himself away from the television.

She sighed, "Right, leave this to me. I'll sort this."

Sam scuttled out of the room, crawling on his knees from behind the sofa, with Molly and Tim following behind.

Sam's mom opened the front door to greet the host of police officers on her doorstep.

"May I help you?" asked Sam's mom, staring down the officer at the front, gazing past his rifle and riot helmet to the eyes of the young man beneath.

"Are you Rose Higgs?" asked the officer.

"Depends who's asking."

A slight moment of hesitation descended upon them as the officer gestured to the small army of heavily armed police. "The police. The police are asking."

"Then I suppose I am."

"We have a warrant to search the premises. We believe you may be harbouring your son and his associates," said the officer, eyeing the wheelchair beside the front door.

"Excuse me, but I am not letting you lot march through my house. I've just hoovered."

The officer's mouth hung open as he searched for a response, momentarily dumbstruck.

SAM, TIM AND MOLLY HID IN THE GARAGE, LEANING their ears against the door to hear what was being said.

"Tim, what do we do?" asked Sam.

"Um, well…"

"Sam," interrupted Molly. "I don't think Mom can fix this. If you've really done nothing wrong, go out there and tell them the truth."

Sam had a better idea in mind as he stared at the car parked in front of them. The old silver *Ford Fiesta* with the taped-up wing mirror and the 'S' keyed into the side, Sam got grounded for a month after that one.

"I've got it. We'll take the car. I know a shortcut around the estate. We'll lose them easily."

Before anyone could contest, Sam had already thrown open the door and hopped into the driver's seat. Tim limped over to the passenger seat to join him, unsure about this plan, yet devoid of any better ideas.

The car had a strange smell from when Molly filled the cigarette lighter with *Play-Doh*. Sam was well acquainted with that smell over the years, and now that smell would mean freedom.

Sam turned the key, gripped the steering wheel and

checked the mirror, seeing Molly in the back, fastening a seatbelt around herself.

"Molly, get out," ordered Sam.

"I'm coming too."

"No, you're not. You're a child. Mom would kill me if she found out I took you on a car chase."

"Worse than what she'd say if she found out you took her car? You can't even drive."

"You can't what?" interjected Tim.

"I just never...formally passed my driving test is all. Plus, I failed each test differently, so if you add them together, it's basically a pass."

"How many tests have you taken?" asked Tim.

"Eight," answered Molly.

"Molly, get out!" shouted Sam.

"Fine," sulked Molly as she climbed out of the car.

As Molly opened the door to the hallway to rejoin her mom, five police officers pushed past her, filling the garage.

He couldn't put this off any longer. Sam closed his eyes, took a deep breath, and pressed the fob dangling from the keyring under the steering wheel. The garage door rose. The police officers banged their fists against the car, shouting and demanding Sam and Tim get out of the car at once. They pulled on the handles, but the vehicle remained firmly locked.

Sam drove his foot down on the acceleration just as the garage door rose high enough to allow the car through. The wheels spun and the car rocketed forward. Sam had done it. They were through the door to freedom, leaving the police officers behind in the dust.

Their escape was short-lived.

The car immediately crashed into the multiple police cars blocking the driveway.

Tim and Sam jolted forward as the airbags deployed, smacking their heads back into the headrests.

Amidst the confusion and possible concussion, Sam focused his woozy eyes past the deflating airbags and cracked windscreen, and pressed his foot down on the acceleration again. The car revved up and shunted further into the side of a police vehicle, the wheels screeching and smoking, but it was no use.

Arms reached in through what remained of the car and tore the pair from their seats, dragging them across the driveway. Tim glanced up at the hazy figures surrounding him and felt the ground tilting in every direction. Pain quickly replaced Tim's nausea as his face slammed onto the car's bonnet, and an officer handcuffed him. Sam soon followed, shoved down opposite Tim.

Tim could hear Sam's muffled protests through the cold metal of the bonnet, "and sleep, and sleep!"

Sam's mom came running out of the house, shouting for the police officers to let go of Sam as he was 'only a kid' and they 'had no proof.'

Sam's and Tim's eyes met across the car's bonnet as the world spun around them. Neither one had a plan, neither one knew what to do, and despite how much they tried to hide it, both feared what was to come.

25

No matter how much soap and water Jack rubbed into his pores, he could still smell the vomit, the blood, and the brains on his skin. He pressed down on the soap dispenser again, filling his hand with the purple gel and peaked at Lucy beside him, splashing water onto her face.

"Wake up, wake up," said Lucy, willing herself to escape this delusion.

A flush came from one of the toilet stalls behind them, and the door swung open. Jack and Lucy only stared in disbelief at the ghost, who just unceremoniously stepped out from the stall.

"I knew it. I told you. We're dead," confirmed Lucy. "What more proof do you need?"

Before them, Dr Li stood, dressed in a suit and cravat, looking at the pair through eyes much younger than Jack knew. Rakish youth replaced his ancient features, and mere stubble now replaced the pure white beard which once cascaded down his chest like a waterfall. However, all that youth didn't extinguish the weight behind those eyes, and somehow, he seemed to recognize Jack and Lucy. No, it was more than that. He expected them.

"We saw you die," said Lucy, pressing her hand against Dr Li's chest, but her hand didn't pass through his body, which meant he wasn't a ghost...or they both were.

"Well, I'll try not to let it happen again," said Dr Li, reaching past Jack to wash his hands.

He dried his hands and tucked his shirt back into his trousers as Lucy and Jack watched him expectantly. Brushing off any explanation clearly would not cut it.

"Right, fine, ok. So, this is the past. Welcome."

"I get it," said Lucy, everything now becoming quite clear. "You've drugged me."

She turned to the mirror above the sink to inspect her eyes, covering a hand over them to see if they dilated.

Jack reached down into his boot and pulled out the time machine, holding it in his hands and staring at the faint blue light pulsing through its veins. They were truly in the past. This simple wooden object had the power to change the course of history and reshape the entire universe, and it worked, with two of the three green LEDs glowing eagerly.

Dr Li reached into the pocket of his blazer and pulled out an identical device.

"Snap, I'm guessing I'm going to give this to you in the future."

Jack admired the second time machine. Its glass dome was pristine, and the wood glowed with the same blue hue. This must have been the original Time Machine, from long before it broke, Jack realized.

"I hope you're taking good care of it, making sure it doesn't fall into the wrong hands?"

Jack's voice grew low, almost to a whisper. "You mean Tobias Cud?"

"Yes, he would kill me to get his hands on this, and, well... sometimes he succeeds."

"So you really are dead?" asked Jack.

"From your point of view, perhaps."

"But you're still going to die?"

"We're all going to die, Jack. Someday."

Jack hugged Dr Li in a warm embrace, yanking Lucy away from the mirror.

"I'm saying LSD. Definitely hallucinogenic," decided Lucy, having completed her investigation.

Dr Li tore a flyer from the wall advertising a church fate. "Look at the date, 2002."

"Power of suggestion, that paper's blank," countered Lucy. "You're probably not even holding a piece of paper."

Dr Li glanced down at his watch. "Right, ok, fine, you want proof, indisputable proof should arrive, right...about...now."

He pushed open the door to the bathroom to see everyone in the church bustling around, cheering as the sound of an organ chimed through the building. Jack and Lucy walked over to the door to get a better look.

They saw a man and woman through the crowd, the man in a smart suit and the woman dressed in white: the bride and groom with big goofy smiles on their faces. Lucy was still confused, but Jack recognized them at once as a million memories rushed through him.

The faces of the people in the crowd became clearer now, too. He even recognized a few of them, like his grandmother, who raised him all those years. In the centre of them all, with striking clarity, stood his mother and father, alive.

"He's right," breathed Jack. "This is 2002."

"You don't seriously believe...who even are those people?" said Lucy.

"They're my..." Jack struggled to say the word, for if he

spoke it, the illusion might shatter around him, and they would be gone once more.

No, this was exactly how it was in the pictures he saw. The recreation perfectly replicated every detail in the old shoebox of photos, down to the subtle creases in their clothes. A flash of light lit up the church as the photographer preserved this moment in celluloid, capturing those same conversations, same cheers, same excitement that Jack spent years staring at. Somehow, Jack even smelt the celluloid of those old photographs in this place. This was real, no doubt about it.

"The bride and groom. They're my parents," said Jack. "They...they died when I was eight."

"Yet here they are," said Dr Li.

"There's no such thing as time travel," argued Lucy.

She understood how the world worked, and this wasn't it. This was madness. Two criminals weren't about to change her entire perception of reality, especially when there were at least twenty far more plausible explanations for all of this.

However, as she looked at Jack and saw all the hope written across his face, it was clear he truly believed in this. Delusions, drugs, dreams, whatever it was, to him, this was real. She turned to Dr Li.

"I just want to go home."

"Ok. Grab my hand, and I'll take you both home," said Dr Li in a kind voice.

The bride and groom reached the church doors and stepped outside, Jack watching them, longing to be with them, to reclaim the piece of him he was missing. Everything he ever wanted was within reach, literally within touching distance. *So why shouldn't he?*

If he could see them, he could speak to them.

"I'm not going anywhere," said Jack, jerking his handcuffed arm back and pulling Lucy away from Dr Li.

He was going to save them.

26

"It's interesting, your record's clean, other than a case of shoplifting when you were twelve and marijuana possession at nineteen, quite a step up to blowing up buildings."

The detective flicked through Tim's file and placed it back onto the table before taking a seat opposite the most notorious criminal of the past twenty-four hours.

The criminal kingpin didn't answer. The large mirror on the wall, the only notable feature of the claustrophobic room, reflected his blank expression as he stared forward. He would not talk; he would not show weakness, and he certainly would not let her get in his head.

"I don't think you masterminded this," continued the detective. "I think you got yourself mixed up in something and found yourself out of your depth. So now, the question you must ask yourself is, is this really worth going down for?"

Tim remained silent. His mouth was dry, and the handcuffs chaining him to the table itched fiercely, but he refused to move one iota.

"This won't end well for you. Next door, do you think

that-" she glanced at her notes. "*Samuel Higgs* isn't saying anything either?"

This wasn't a bluff.

NEXT DOOR, SAM SAT IN AN ALMOST IDENTICAL room, but unlike Tim, the detective investigating Sam was trying his hardest to get Sam to stop talking.

"He was all like, *I'm going to kill you if you go to the police.* Then he got this gun out and tried shooting us. That's why I kept the gun, as I knew you probably wanted it for evidence. I mean, it's gone now. This psycho drug dealer nicked it and blew his brains out. Anyway, Greg tried shooting us, so Tim gets this firework right..."

Sam continued on and on, beating out each outlandish syllable without pausing for breath.

ON THE OTHER SIDE OF THE TWO-WAY MIRRORS, DCI Sparks watched the pair being questioned, and he was quickly realizing these weren't leaders of a criminal organization at all.

They were idiots, idiots who avoided capture this long simply by luck. One at least had the foresight to keep his mouth shut, while the other lied and lied, digging himself deeper into a hole he could never escape from.

Usually, he would cart them off to the courts, where they would swiftly receive life sentences, and that would be that. But these idiots had his daughter.

She was still out there with one of them, and with every second that passed, she grew further from him. He didn't have time for the standard procedures. He was going to speak to them himself, both of them.

OFFICERS COLLECTED SAM AND BROUGHT HIM TO the same room as Tim. Sam nodded to Tim as he was shoved down onto the seat beside him and chained to the table. Still, Tim didn't reciprocate or even acknowledge Sam's presence, continuing his vow of silence. The officers left, and DCI Sparks stepped inside, locked the door behind him, and took his seat at the table.

"Where is my daughter?" asked DCI Sparks.

He spoke quietly, but with an intensity which made Sam wish he knew the answer.

Sam decided it would be best to match this intensity and, in a gruff voice, said, "I don't know."

Sam's mockery momentarily stunned DCI Sparks. He had Lucy held somewhere and was toying with the leverage he had over him. Maybe he wasn't such a fool after all. DCI Sparks glanced up at the CCTV camera. The usual blinking red light on the side of it stopped, just as he instructed. He reached over, grabbed Sam by the collar, and drew him close.

"Sam, was it?"

Sam could feel the man's warm breath on his face and smelt a hint of whisky in his words. Sam squirmed, nodding in agreement.

"Well, Sam. If you've harmed her, if even a single hair on her is out of place. I will kill you. Do you understand?"

Sam nodded again, this time with terrified enthusiasm.

"Now I'm going to ask you once more where my daughter, Lucy Sparks, is, and if I'm not happy with the answer..." He gripped his fist tight around Sam's collar until the last of the air in his lungs escaped in a small squeak. "We'll keep trying until you give me an answer I am happy with."

DCI Sparks released Sam, allowing him to descend back

into his chair. Sam cleared his throat and chose his words carefully.

"I honestly don't know where she is, or Jack, for that matter. We saw them drive off together, but that's it. Tim will tell you…" Sam glanced at Tim, who was still relatively catatonic. "Or maybe he won't. That's only because there's nothing to tell. We're innocent in all this. You should go after the people with the pills, not us. We haven't even done anything wrong."

"You pointed a gun in my face and threatened to shoot me," said DCI Sparks coldly.

"Yeah, well, Tim murdered Greg," countered Sam, without thinking.

Tim stamped on Sam's foot, the first time he had moved since being here.

"Not murdered…stopped," corrected Sam. "Look, I may or may not have an evil twin, or clone, out there who's probably the one responsible for trying to shoot you, and as for Jack, he won't have done anything to your daughter. He couldn't harm a fly. He's a nervous wreck."

27

Two decades prior, Jack was indeed a nervous wreck, sweating and crying and desperate to get out of the bathroom to save his parents from their fate. There were only two problems in his way: he was handcuffed to Lucy, and Dr Li was blocking the door.

"You can't make me leave. I'm not going back without them," Jack argued.

"You need to understand, Jack, it's not that simple," said Dr Li.

"It is, though. They're right there…" A stark realization hit Jack. "Why are *you* here?"

Dr Li didn't answer, so Jack's mind continued formulating questions.

"Why are you at my parent's wedding? Did you know them? Just how much have you kept from me?"

Dr Li reached out his hand, hoping to calm him. "Please, Jack, I'll explain everything once we're away from here, I promise."

Jack slapped the hand away.

"I'm not going anywhere with you."

In that moment, Dr Li appeared more like a stranger than ever, and Jack realized precisely how little he knew of the man who raised him. So much was hidden from him.

The existence of a maniacal Bond villain out for his blood was merely the tip of the iceberg of secrets Dr Li kept to himself. Every question regarding his past was always waved away, buried beneath scientific distractions and promises of time travel. But no more, not now his parents' lives were at stake.

"Jack," tried Lucy. "I think it would be best if you tried to stay calm right now."

"Why do you care? You don't believe in any of this, anyway. You just want to arrest me," said Jack, turning his venomous glare towards her.

"You know what?" said Lucy. "If you want to stay here, that's fine by me. But I'm going back to the real world."

Lucy reached into her pocket and produced a small key. She plugged the key into the handcuffs, and, with a twist and a click, Jack was free.

"You had a second key this whole time?" said Jack. More secrets. More lies.

"I couldn't let you escape, but I no longer care. I want to get away from all this craziness, so go save your parents, *Marty Mcfly*. I'm going home."

Jack walked towards the door and to Dr Li, the only obstacle between him and his parents.

"Move out of the way!"

"No, Jack. That's not how it works. You can't change the past. You think you're the first person to have lost someone. Well, you're not. Don't you think there are people I'd save if I could? Don't you think Lucy would want to save her mother?"

Lucy's blood suddenly ran cold. She hadn't thought of her

mother in years. She pushed those memories down so deep she almost forgot she still had them.

"How? How do you know about…That?" she asked, her voice quivering.

Dr Li tried and failed to hide his frustration. He was sure this was supposed to be easier.

"I have a time machine. I know everything about everyone," said Dr Li before snapping back to Jack. "I also know time travel because, guess what, I invented it. Everything out there, everything around us, it's like a tape recording of what once was. If you prod the tape, you could damage it and completely change the future you go back to. That's why I'm here, to stop you from doing something stupid. I'm sorry, but you have to leave them."

"You promised," said Jack, his heart almost audibly breaking in two.

"I promised to let you help me build a time machine. That's it. And I won't even do so for another decade, which gives me plenty of time to change my mind."

"But I…I can't let them die," Jack said weakly.

"They already have. They've been dead a very long time."

Lucy stepped over to the sink and stared deeply into the mirror again, forcing herself to wake up from this nightmare.

"Now, it's time we were leaving. I'm taking you both home, and that's final," said Dr Li, holding out his hand.

Lucy returned from the sink and grabbed Dr Li's hand, resigning herself to the chaos. If this would somehow get her home, then so be it.

Jack nodded and reached out his hand. *As if he was going to give up that easily.* Jack shoved past Dr Li and Lucy and tore the bathroom door open, running out into the church after his parents. Dr Li let out an exasperated sigh and chased after him.

Jack ran out of the church and to the courtyard, where his

family and friends crowded around the bride and groom as they were about to enter a white car covered in ribbons. Jack pushed through the crowd, squeezing past relatives to reach the man and woman who would one day become his parents.

"Sorry, excuse me..." stammered Jack.

Their expressions fell at once.

"Oh, you again, what do you want this time?" said the groom impatiently.

Even at his father's scorn, Jack couldn't help but smile. They were real. They could see him. He suddenly felt flustered and almost shy, a child once more.

"First off, I want to apologize for barging in earlier. I didn't know."

"It's fine, really," said the bride, her eyes twinkling, her pristine white gown flowing beneath her like a cloud, her veil encircling her like a halo. She was beautiful and possessed the same kind face that had persisted through Jack's earliest memories.

"Jack!" shouted a voice from the church. Jack turned to see Dr Li shoving through the crowd.

Jack was running out of time, so he leant close, ensuring no single word went amiss.

"On February the twelfth, 2013, it'll be your son's birthday and...and..." Jack stopped, trying to think, but a cloudy haze shrouded his thoughts. He desperately clawed through his mind, searching every corner, but the memory was nowhere to be found.

"I can't remember. Why can't I remember?"

Jack was then rugby-tackled to the ground by Dr Li. The bride and groom shuffled into the car as everyone else watched Jack and Dr Li wrestling on the cobblestones, none wanting to get too close to the bloodied madman or his opponent.

"You can't intervene! You're going to ruin everything!" shouted Dr Li as Jack dug his arm into Dr Li's mouth.

The pair entangled along the pavement, scrambling over one another. Jack tried his best to break free, but it was too late. The car drove out of the courtyard and continued down the road.

Jack eventually stopped struggling and fell limp as he watched his parents disappear once more.

"You're letting them die. It's not fair."

"That's not what I'm doing," said Dr Li as he helped Jack back to his feet.

The fight was over, the crowds dispersed, and Jack and Dr Li walked back to the church.

Inside, they found Lucy sitting in a pew, her hands together, eyes closed, and head bowed. She never really put too much stock into religion before. Her family was Christian, but church was usually only reserved for Christmas, when her dad would accompany her to sing carols. However, the things she experienced today defied any rational explanation, and if time travel...she instinctively rejected the idea as soon as it entered her mind.

Still, if she truly travelled through time, that blew the doors wide open to what may be possible, and religion no longer seemed all that farfetched. Dr Li probably met Jesus Christ and popped around his house for bread and fish. She didn't believe she was dead anymore. Jack was right.

Her heart was indeed still beating, the thumping in her chest impossible to deny, and she was sure heaven wouldn't be this stressful. Lucy was alive, and as much as she wanted to dismiss everything around her as a hallucination, the power of suggestion, or anything she deemed within the realm of possibility, she simply couldn't.

This world was tangible.

She sensed the cold wood of the pew and the ancient smell so deeply woven into the church that her mind couldn't have constructed it. She couldn't deny it any longer. This place was real.

She finished up what she was doing. Was it a prayer? She concluded with an "Amen" regardless.

"Ready?" whispered Dr Li.

Lucy glanced up to find Jack and Dr Li watching her. She unclasped her hands and nodded, shuffling out of the pew to Dr Li's outstretched hand. Jack held the other without saying a word.

Dr Li closed his eyes and concentrated. The time machine flickered and sparked, catapulting the three of them onward through history in a lurid flash of blue light.

28

"TIM WAS THE ONE WHO LET OFF THE FIREWORKS. Am I getting that right?" asked DCI Sparks, leaning back in his chair.

He changed his demeanor, replacing his scowl with feigned intrigue. Scaring Sam and Tim was far from the only trick up his sleeve.

As such, Sam was happy to ramble on about precisely what had transpired that evening as Tim gripped his hand tightly around Sam's thigh, silently begging him to stop. Unfortunately, Sam didn't speak in thigh grips, so continued his incriminating monologue about mind-controlling pills, extortion and the nightmarish firework display that capped the night off, delighted someone finally seemed to take him seriously.

"Do you often buy fireworks from Tim?" asked DCI Sparks.

"Well, Tim is a dealer in many items, but no, usually he sells me..."

"Bahhh!" interrupted Tim, almost involuntarily.

He couldn't take it anymore, and a guttural noise had broken through, piercing his wall of stoicism.

"Everything ok?" asked DCI Sparks. He had him.

"He's fine," dismissed Sam, pulling the spotlight back onto himself. "So, like I was saying, Tim usually sells me..."

"Shut the fuck up!" shouted Tim, throwing his head back in resignation.

"Something to add?" asked DCI Spark, an innocent lilt in his tone.

"Fuck you," spat Tim.

"I'll give you two a moment," said DCI Sparks as he left the room, locking the door behind him.

Tim was furious. A bear in a cage someone had poked and prodded one too many times. He turned to one of the mirrors and pointed at it.

"Fuck you," he said through his reflection before turning to Sam, "and fuck you too."

"Fuck me? Fuck you!" retorted Sam. "I was trying to get us out of this. You never trust me. You didn't trust me at your house, and you're not trusting me now."

"We wouldn't even be here if you hadn't crashed the fucking motor!"

"I didn't see the police cars."

"They were parked in front of you!"

"Well, at least I was trying. We're supposed to be in this together. I thought we were friends."

"You did?" said Tim, his face softening. "You thought we were friends?"

"Well, yeah."

Tim grabbed the table and wiggled it. It wasn't bolted down. That was their second mistake, he thought. Their first being that they believed they could manipulate him. So, with some effort, Tim stood up from the chair.

"If we're in this together, prove it," he said, gripping the table's legs. "Help me lift this."

DCI Sparks watched them through the two-way mirror with interest. What were they doing?

"Get some more officers here, and bring the tasers," he told the officer beside him.

Sam stood up and grabbed the table with a smile. "Where are we taking it?"

Tim pointed at the mirror. "We're leaving."

They dragged the table along the concrete floor; the metal scraping like fingers on a chalkboard. The shackles binding them to the table rattled and howled, unable to hold back their plan.

Once they were in place by the mirror, Tim and Sam gripped the table until their hands lost colour and hauled it up as high as they could. It may not have been bolted down, but it was still heavy, and Tim barely had the strength to hold himself up, let alone a table. The tendons along his arms tightened, and he gritted his teeth down to dust.

"Now," instructed Tim, and they rammed the table into the mirror.

It shattered in a deafening wail, and their reflections scattered into a thousand tiny fragments, each piece cursing them with bad luck. Tim peered through the spider's web of broken glass but found only concrete behind.

DCI Sparks and several other officers watched from the two-way mirror, the one on the opposite side of the room. They shoved open the door to the interrogation room and flooded inside until Sam and Tim were surrounded with tasers aimed at them from every direction.

Sam tried to raise his hands as much as his chains would allow, but it was useless. The tasers popped, electrodes pierced their skin, and a wave of electricity catapulted through them, along their chains and then into one another. Every hair on their bodies shot outwards, and, for a moment, Sam was sure he saw his own skeleton. The pair fell to the floor, writhing in agony, their chains keeping their hands raised against the table in perpetual surrender.

Then, the officers felt a sudden, sharp pull on their tasers as though something were tugging on the electric current. The wires edged away, and the electrodes freed themselves from Sam and Tim, flying towards the centre of the room, hooking on some invisible electric fish and floating in the air.

In a single blink, the air flickered with blue sparks that infinitely grew. The tasers tore from the officer's hands and flung across the room as the charge exploded in a supernova of blinding blue light, and then, as soon as it appeared, it was gone.

In its place stood Lucy, Jack and Dr Li.

They were back in the police station, in one of the interrogation rooms. Lucy felt the floor crunch beneath her feet. She glanced down to find the two men she previously tried to arrest splayed out amongst a sprinkling of broken glass, staring blankly up at her, as was everybody else in the room, none of them able to comprehend what they were seeing, all except one.

"Lucy?" said a voice from behind her.

She turned to find her father standing with four officers surrounding him, awestruck. She ran over and hugged him tight, and he hugged her back. The stern old man's eyes filled. He didn't know how she did it, but somehow, his daughter had answered his prayers.

Beside her, Lucy could hear Jack talking to the two men on the floor.

"We have to get out of here," he told them. "This place isn't safe. The police are working for Dr Cud."

Lucy instinctively pulled back from her father, eyeing the surrounding officers. Jack was right.

"Lucy," said Dr Li. "Come with us, please."

Lucy looked at Dr Li, this bizarre man she still could not figure out. She glanced back at her father, the man she trusted and loved for years, but now doubts were corrupting her mind like a parasite. He wasn't working for Dr Cud. She would know, wouldn't she?

Try as she might, Lucy couldn't shake what she witnessed. Those officers were utterly under his spell. They held their guns to their own heads, and they…

No, she knew her father, and that wasn't him.

Through kidnapping, death and a mountain of impossibilities, her father had been the driving force keeping her going, the hope that she would see him again. Now she had everything she wanted. She wasn't about to let that go.

"I'm sorry," she said. "I can't."

Dr Li's outstretched hand faltered and lowered as the hopeful expression on his face cracked. His lips met and then peeled apart again as he searched for the right words, but couldn't find them.

Dr Li lowered his hand down onto the table, and in a flash of impossibly bright blue light, Dr Li, Jack, Sam, Tim, and the table they were chained to disappeared.

The officers stood silent, paralyzed in utter disbelief at what they just witnessed, all apart from Lucy, who was staring at her father. She peered into his eyes, forcing herself to smile, forcing herself to be relieved, forcing herself to feel safe.

Yet, a quiet unease crept over her like a shadow.

29

Time fractured around them as they propelled through the universe at a speed many times faster than light. Now, the third time experiencing this phenomenon, Jack was sure he would never get used to it. It wasn't unpleasant. He needed to comprehend it for it to be unpleasant, and he certainly couldn't do that.

It was like watching a million snippets from a billion lives across a trillion realities. Like the fastest rollercoaster you could ever imagine, strapped to a rocket. He was falling down a dream, tumbling through déjà vu, and, before he even knew it, it was over, the memory already beginning to fade as he stepped back into reality, a familiar reality.

They appeared inside a small cottage, all wooden beams and exposed bricks, in front of a gigantic fireplace, and Jack knew this place very well. He knew the sofa and the comfiest spot on it, the coffee table with its collage of burnt rings, the soft green carpeting beneath his feet, which clashed with the tall red lamp, the blue curtains and the rest of the room's decor.

Bookcases lined the walls, filled with the musty odour of

stories, which turned to memories as Jack breathed them in. He could breathe again, and the thunder in his chest dulled as this place wrapped around him like a security blanket.

"Do you think they'll find us here?" asked Jack.

"Eventually, but I've kept this place off any records, and they haven't found me yet. You're all quite safe here for the time being," said Dr Li, glancing around at his new house guests and stopping at Sam and Tim and the large grey table connecting them.

"Be right back," he told them and left.

"Right, what the fuck is going on?" said Tim finally. It was about time someone asked.

Jack did his best to explain exactly what the fuck was going on, partly to Sam and Tim, partly to himself. He spoke of meeting Dr Cud, how Dr Li died and came back younger, how he found his parents and how he couldn't save them.

He told them about Lucy, how she turned out not to be so bad after all, and about the time machine and the impossible physics accompanying it. At one point, Tim interjected regarding the smell, and Jack recounted the rotting brain tissue still soaking into his skin.

Jack finished by explaining that all of this had led them to the home where he had lived with Dr Li growing up, in this small, hidden cottage at the end of a quiet, little village.

"So that's why I could never have a sleepover at yours? Because your grandad was some super scientist on the run," realized Sam.

"He's not my grandad, and I think he just didn't like you."

"Oh, thanks."

At that moment, Dr Li re-entered, wearing a thick visor and clutching a buzz-saw. He switched it on and marched towards Sam, the metal teeth of the saw grinding out its ravenous hunger, ready to tear Sam apart.

"He does hate me!" screamed Sam as Dr Li brought the

buzz saw down onto the chain linking him to the table, slicing through it with ease and freeing him.

"There, much better," said Dr Li, lifting his goggles.

"Thanks," choked Sam, struggling to catch his breath.

DR LI PLACED SOME PIZZAS INTO THE OVEN, NOT that he was sure any of them would feel like eating after the ordeal they went through. Things already swerved too far out of control, and it likely wasn't salvageable. But he couldn't simply give up on them. They were beaten, traumatized, and had already made sacrifices. Most importantly, they mattered. So he would still do everything he could to save them.

Sam and Tim sat at the kitchen table beside him, covering themselves in butter. The handcuff chains were broken, but the cuffs were still tightly bound around their wrists. Tim told Sam how you could easily escape handcuffs by dislocating your thumb, but neither were willing to test the theory.

Dr Li watched them buttering themselves like two slices of toast, knowing they would be helpless to save themselves in the end.

UPSTAIRS, JACK CHANGED HIS CLOTHES IN THE ROOM that was once his. His old belongings were all still there, mostly under cables and motherboards and a thousand other abandoned experiments Dr Li conducted there in Jack's absence.

Jack swept them aside and sat on his bed, peering into the mirror on the wall as he tongued at the open gum where his tooth once lived, wincing at the pain. He looked older now; deep bruises formed around the base of his eyes, and exhausted trenches dug along his forehead. He wondered just how much he would age before this was all over.

"Pizza's ready!" Dr Li called up to him.

Jack followed the tangy smell of melted cheese downstairs, where he found a slippery Sam and Tim already tucking into the pizzas and downing a few cans of beer from the fridge. Jack silently sat at the table and dished himself up a slice. He ventured only a few bites, mostly out of polite obligation to keep some normalcy.

Dr Li wheeled a whiteboard over to the kitchen table as they ate and began his lecture. He started by taking out his time machine and placing it on the table. He then beckoned Jack to do the same.

"Same time machine, at different points in its timeline," began Dr Li.

"Already confused," interrupted Sam through a mouthful of pepperoni.

Dr Li picked up both time machines and held one in each hand. "They're the same time machine. This one will get old and become this one."

Sam still had a glazed look in his eye. A toddler being taught quantum physics, *which, come to think of it, isn't much of a metaphor here.*

Dr Li carried on regardless. "The time machine is telepathic. It responds to certain brainwaves, and that's what charges it," he said, directing their attention to the LEDs embedded in the wood; two of the three illuminated green. "I designed it to run on the most powerful brain activity there is: fear."

"It runs on fear?" clarified Jack.

"Like in *Monsters Inc.*?" further clarified Tim. "That's a class film. Got it on pirate."

"Yes, like in Monsters Inc." agreed Dr Li begrudgingly, not appreciating the comparison.

"Except I've tuned this to only run on both mine and Jack's fear," continued Dr Li, turning to Jack. "So once it's got enough charge, someone just needs to touch it and think of a destination, anywhere, anytime and bam! You're there. When you were with Toby, he was going to kill you. You were afraid. You thought you were about to die. What did you think about?"

With some hesitation, Jack said, "I thought of my parents."

A slow realization spread through Jack. It wasn't a coincidence or magical intervention or a sign. He had brought himself back to his parents by his own will.

"Now, it is imperative you do not allow Toby Cud to get his hands on this. He's been trying to steal it from me for longer than I can remember."

"Why not just take him out?" asked Tim.

"Because that would be murder, which is a crime," answered Jack, irritated at how killing became trivial to those around him.

"Easier said than done," answered Dr Li. "He's altered his biology a lot since we first met. This includes reinforced metal implants under his skin, making him more or less bulletproof, and a hydraulic-powered cybernetic arm, providing immeasurable strength. I hid from him for years, but he's begun amassing an army to hunt me down, and armies require people, so he created a drug which allows him to control people's minds."

"The pills!" declared Sam, a little too proud of himself.

"The pills," agreed Dr Li. "They contain a modified viral analogue."

Blank looks. He'd need to simplify this.

"Viruses work by hacking our body's machinery to make more of itself. But what if they told our body not to make more virus, but to make something else, like a receiver or even an entire network extending through your brain?"

"Your body can't just make stuff like that," said Sam.

"Why not? It already makes you, and this would be infinitely less complex. Plus, all the resources are already inside you, copper, zinc..."

"Iron in our blood," added Jack, recounting the first lesson Dr Li ever taught him.

"Exactly, and it all comes together to create a neural link with a transmitter in Toby's head, which he uses to control them."

"Like Greg, and the doctor, and the dealers," said Sam, turning to Tim. "So that's why they were acting like they hated you and called you a..."

"Yeah," said Tim, quickly cutting him off.

"So we need to come up with ideas to stop him. Anyone?" asked Dr Li.

"We kill him," said Tim with no hesitation.

"Ok, no bad ideas," said Dr Li, writing the word '*Murder*' on the whiteboard. "Anything else?"

"We go back in time and kill him," said Tim.

"I'm sensing a theme. I'll just underline '*Murder*' for now."

"We could reverse engineer the drug and find an antidote," said Jack, proposing something a little more sensible.

"Already tried, already failed. Many, many times."

"Come on, it's obvious, isn't it," said Sam. "You have a time machine. Let's go to the future."

"And how would that help?" asked Dr Li.

"Well, in the future, they've got future guns and robots and stuff. So we could use that."

Dr Li tried explaining how they didn't want to interfere with any potential timeline or create a paradox, but Sam was no longer listening.

"Fine, whatever, but you must have some future-y sci-fi weapons around here somewhere," said Sam.

DR LI BROUGHT THE TRIO UPSTAIRS TO THE SPARE room, which he converted into a makeshift lab; a dystopian amount of silver crammed within the small oak frame of the room, wires fizzed along wooden beams, cascading down like vines, past worktops busy with microscopes, half-constructed machinery, Petri dishes brimming with new species of bacteria and a giant bird's nest of crumpled notes and failed plans, piling around everything, like a fresh layer of snow. The centrepiece of the room was a large black monolith, standing proud and patient.

"This is all about twenty years in my future," said Dr Li, surveying the room. "So forgive me if I'm not completely familiar with what everything does."

Sam immediately picked up what he believed to be a handgun from a shelf and aimed it in front of him, closing one eye and sticking out his tongue for accuracy.

"Now this is what I'm talking about, space guns."

Jack snatched the device from Sam.

"Electromagnet," he corrected.

Sam pointed to the ominous slab of black in the centre of the room. "What's that thing?"

"Electromagnet," said Dr Li.

"Is there anything here which isn't a bloody magnet?" complained Sam. "We're supposed to be fighting an army of murderers, not some iron filings."

Dr Li rummaged through the shelves and tables, thinking aloud.

"Broken...unfinished...what was I thinking with that one?"

He picked up what was once a toaster, pulled down on the lever and aimed it at Tim. After a moment, the lever sprung back up, and Tim flinched. However, nothing came out. Dr Li tossed it behind him along with the other broken gadgets.

"What was that supposed to do? What the fuck did you just try to do to me?" argued Tim, but Dr Li was already onto his next invention, one which he knew would work: a small metal disc.

"Oh, I recognize this. Catch," said Dr Li, tossing it to Jack.

Jack caught the disc in his hand, and it burst open, blasting a sphere of blue electricity from its centre.

"Whhhhhhaaaaaa…" Jack tried to say as his voice slowed to a crawl.

"One of my earlier experiments into time travel, it can temporarily slow down time, incredibly unstable, only to be used in emergencies," explained Dr Li as he reached in and tapped the disc floating in the centre.

The sphere imploded, and the disc clattered to the floor.

"You must have some weapons? Guns? Swords? A knife?" tried Sam.

"All useless against Toby Cud," dismissed Dr Li. "If we're going to stop him, we'll need to be creative."

30

Tim and Sam spent the evening drinking beer and tossing the empty cans through the '*frozen football*' as Sam dubbed it.

They played a game where one of them would throw a can into the orb while the other snatches it back using the '*magnetic musket.*' Sam was very proud of the names he invented for Dr Li's inventions. They did this long into the night until the pair passed out on the sofa.

Upstairs, Jack sat in the spare room at a desk, peering down at a microscope. The gentle sound of rain stroked at the window, accompanying Dr Li's old radio, which quietly spoke about the ongoing hunt for the criminals who escaped from police custody and were extremely dangerous.

Jack fed one of the orange pills from Dr Li's collection through a mass spectrometer. The machine buzzed and beeped as it analyzed the pill's wicked contents.

He returned to his microscope, adjusting the dial to focus

it, and watched as each individual cell sprouted tiny metallic protrusions, which grew at a shocking rate towards adjacent cells, connecting them into an obscene network. Jack instinctively lurched back, worried these microscopic abominations might climb up the microscope to attack him with the same malice as their architect.

"I tried to find a cure. It's a dead end," said Dr Li, who stood by the window, watching through the rain for any movement in the darkness.

Jack wasn't giving up so easily. "You said he has robotic implants. Could we maybe hack into them and take control?"

"Maybe," muttered Dr Li, not wanting to reveal that was something else he already tried and failed to do.

"Or an anti-wave? Cancel out the frequency he's transmitting?"

"I wanted to say earlier...about your parents..."

"It's fine," said Jack, quickly shutting him down. "You can't change the past. I get it."

Jack wanted to say how Dr Li coming here, plucking himself from an earlier point in his own timeline, contradicted that, but pushed it to the back of his mind.

"You should get some rest, Jack. You haven't slept in a while. We can think of more ideas in the morning."

"In a minute," said Jack, checking the mass spectrometer results.

JACK WORKED LONG INTO THE NIGHT AS THE RAIN grew stronger. He didn't notice the flash of blue light behind him marking Dr Li's departure, dismissing it as just another burst of lightning.

What Jack did notice was the radio growing louder, rising in volume as something interrupted the broadcast.

"Jack," spoke a muffled voice interwoven with the speaker's static.

The hair on Jack's neck stood on end. He stood up from his chair and crept over to the window, staring into the darkness, but saw nothing. Jack knew the view well, the fields, and the few houses scattered throughout the village.

If you craned your neck, you could even make out the little shop, but not now. Now there was only darkness beneath the weeping sky. There were no streetlights, no headlamps, not even the faint glow of moonlight behind the clouds. The lone and level night stretched far away.

The signal from the radio focused, becoming clearer as the voice spoke again, a voice that was unmistakable.

"I know you can hear me, Jack. We may have gotten off on the wrong foot the last time we spoke."

You mean when you tried to kill me? Jack thought to himself, but didn't bother to answer. Jack knew the voice on the radio couldn't hear him, or at least, he hoped he couldn't.

"I never intended to kill you. I just needed you to show me that the time machine worked, and you did a great job," continued the radio.

Jack's mouth became dry.

"You can't have it," he called out to the darkness.

The radio finished its strange broadcast with a warning. *"I'm coming to collect it."*

Lightning lit up the landscape with the briefest of flashes, and Jack swore he saw someone out there, a shape moving through the rain, but the sky fell dark before he could be sure. Jack pressed his face against the glass, desperate to make it out, and as he did, he felt a distant shuffle of a handle vibrating far below him.

The front door creaked across the silence of the old cottage. Jack looked around the room, finally noticing Dr Li was no longer there; maybe Sam and Tim were gone too, and perhaps he was left here all alone.

Dr Li promised he would be safe here.

Jack suddenly felt the full weight of the past few sleepless nights. He lost the strength to run or to fight and was becoming numb to the adrenaline, which became a permanent fixture in his body. He was trapped.

In the cottage, in the room, in the prison of his own exhaustion. All Jack could do was stand and await fate's approach.

The stairs creaked and groaned, one by one, growing closer, eventually punctuated by the gentle rapping at the door.

Jack didn't answer, hoping he remembered to lock it.

He didn't.

The door opened, and there stood Dr Tobias Cud, with the same gaunt, pale face, same ill-fitting suit, same robotically calculated malice projecting from every single cell of his body.

Rainwater ran down the scarred canals around his dark eyes, past his gnarled lips, and collected along the protrusions of his spine, where it dripped down to the floor like the beats of a clock.

"How did you find me?" asked Jack finally.

Dr Cud held up the small tablet-like locator. "Dr Li left me a parting gift. Now, hand over the time machine."

"No," said Jack, too weak to fight, too weak to run. All he could do was stand his ground.

"Do you know what happens if you say no to me?" said Dr Cud, edging closer to Jack. "I take everything from you. Your friends, the ones sleeping downstairs...will die...in agony...until you give it to me."

However, something Dr Cud missed was that one of Jack's friends wasn't sleeping at all. Sam, awoken by the sound of the door, watched Dr Cud enter the house and make his way up the stairs from the living room sofa. He was yet to be formally introduced to Dr Cud, but connecting the dots wasn't hard.

How many people were half-robot?

Sam slid silently from the sofa, leaving Tim to continue sleeping off his nine beers, and crept upstairs. He tiptoed on the edge of each step, not letting the ancient wood give him away, and pressed his ear against the door, careful not to lean his body weight against it.

"Why do you want it?" asked Jack.

"Your friend, Dr Li, stole my life from me. I want you to take me to the future to find another one."

"You want another life?"

"I want my youth, all the years wasted, following Dr Li. So you're going to take me to a time where they can make me young again."

"Are you talking metaphorically…" Jack stopped.

It was clear Dr Cud wasn't toying with the metaphor. He truly wanted to be young again. The proof was etched into his face, not just by his expression but by the life support system he'd built into his body; every crease, crevice, and fibre grafted by cold metallic alloys were all in aid of extending the limits of this man's mortality.

"What are the pills for?"

Dr Cud was almost within touching distance now, able to smell the sweat growing across Jack's face.

"Are you familiar with the expression '*If you want something done right, do it yourself?*' I thought if I could make the world think like me and give them all a single mind with a single goal, they could create something beautiful. Imagine it, all of mankind, no longer divided, but working together, towards a future where age and illness and death are but a distant memory."

"With everybody under your control, unable to think for themselves. It doesn't sound like a very nice future," said Jack.

"I don't care if you agree with me. I only need you to fear me," said Dr Cud, inches from Jack's face.

He wrapped his ice-cold fingers around Jack's throat, and his metal claws gripped tight as Jack began to splutter and choke, tearing the soul from his body.

Sam kicked the door open. He heard enough. "Let him go!"

Dr Cud released Jack, slamming him down onto the floorboards as he gasped for breath, and turned his attention to Sam.

"Who do you think you're talking to?!" roared Dr Cud, venom coating his words and spittle flying across the room.

Sam didn't actually plan for anything beyond telling him to let go of Jack, which, to his credit, had seemed to work, but now he had to think of something, fast.

Sam eyed the man. He really was as freaky looking as they'd said, his big, scabby head covered in warts and moles and…metal!

Sam slammed his hand down on the controller next to him, and the giant black monolith in the centre of the room hummed to life. Screws and wires flew across the room towards it, followed by a pair of pliers, the locator and the microscope.

A bemused look fell upon Dr Cud's face as he was dragged away from Sam by some invisible force. He reached out his arm in protest and tried to step forward, but it was useless. The machine's pull only became stronger as Sam cranked up the controller's dials.

Dr Cud's feet began to skid along the ground, taken by the magnetic blizzard, whilst Sam offered him a small, cocky smile. Dr Cud slammed into the great metallic slab, pinned to it, unable to resist its pull.

"Yeah! Try your evil shit now. I dare you. Oh wait, you can't!" shouted Sam, triumphantly laughing in Dr Cud's face.

Tim limped hurriedly into the room.

"What's going on?" he said before noticing the man glued to the electromagnet. "I take it this is him, then?"

Jack pulled himself up to his feet, rubbing his throat. Through a stream of coughs, he rasped out the words, "Get back. He's still dangerous."

"Scared of me, even now," mused Dr Cud. "So, what do you intend to do with me?"

Silence fell upon them as they considered.

"Let's piss on him," said Sam finally.

Jack glanced at the man who, mere hours ago, had him tied up, fearing for his own life. But now that the tables were turned, he wished Dr Cud looked as scared as Jack had been... and still was.

However, Dr Cud didn't appear scared at all. In fact, he was smiling.

PART 4

THE INTERROGATION

31

"Are they going to kill him?" asked Jack, his stomach beginning to turn as all the ice cream sloshed around inside him.

"Kill him?" repeated the boy's father. "Is that what you'd do?"

"Yeah, he's the baddie. The baddie always gets killed," said Jack, crossing his arms knowingly.

"Not always. Sometimes good people get killed," said his father, remembering.

32

The scent of fried bacon sizzled through the kitchen and into the living room. It drifted through the morning sunlight, past Tim, who was splayed out on his back, vibrating the sofa with his snores, and settled upon Sam.

The aroma danced around his nose until his eyes flickered open; hypnotized by its alluring scent, he sleepily followed it to the kitchen, poking his head through the doorway.

Inside was Dr Li, frying up bacon, eggs, sausages and a whole host of other breakfast commodities, as fat bubbled and spat from the pans like confetti.

"There's freshly squeezed orange juice on the table," he said without turning around.

"Where did you go last night?" asked Sam, taking a hesitant seat at the kitchen table. "Dr Cud turned up. I stopped him, obviously. No thanks to you."

"Yeah, sorry about that. I couldn't let Toby know I was still around."

"You didn't want to warn us that an evil, murdery, murderer was popping around for tea?"

"I've done nothing but warn you about him," said Dr Li, brushing away the question without actually answering it.

"No, I mean..." Sam noticed Dr Li made tater-tots, his favourite, and forgot what he was asking.

Tim limped in moments later and snatched up the jug of orange juice on the table without saying a word. He glugged it down, spilling a fair amount down himself, hoping this might clear the throbbing in his skull. *Was it six, eight, or fourteen beers in the end?*

Dr Li then presented several plates stacked high with a greasy pallet of mouthwatering colours, glistening yellow yolks, fizzing red tomatoes, and crisped hash browns, almost too picturesque to eat...almost. Tim wasted no time shovelling it down.

"Wait, Jack!" exclaimed Sam, momentarily breaking free of his hunger. "We were supposed to take shifts watching Dr Cud. He's been up there all night."

Sam motioned to rush out and find him, but Dr Li stopped him.

"Jack's fine. I've been monitoring them." Dr Li pointed his spatula at a small television on the counter, which displayed a live feed of Jack, exhausted and scared but still diligently guarding their prisoner.

Sam didn't much like the idea that there were cameras in each room, especially after the state he left the bathroom in last night.

"Have some breakfast, build up your strength and then you can take over," assured Dr Li.

Sam begrudgingly sat back down at the table. The tater-tots were calling to him, as were the bacon, the eggs, the beans, sausages, fried bread and everything else. The choir of food sang a siren's serenade, and Sam could no longer resist.

He dropped a tater-tot into his mouth and could not stop

himself from letting out a hum of joy as its crispy shell gave way to the fluffiest pillow of potato he'd ever tasted.

Dr Li watched as Sam and Tim ate their breakfast, not having the stomach to join them, for it was already crammed full with guilt. He knew he needed to be doing more to help than simply cooking, but what? His mind only drew blanks. So he opened the fridge and scanned its contents. He could get a start on making lunch.

The doorbell rang, and all three of them froze, food hanging from their lips, eyes twitching between one another. Sam drew his magnetic musket and tiptoed from the kitchen, slinking down the narrow hallway. He spotted a fuzzy silhouette through the frosted glass on the front door but could not make out more than a hand reaching for the doorbell again. It rang out, and Sam ducked down, crouching through the carpet.

As he shuffled closer, he became confident that their visitor was only one person...or one robot. Whoever it was, three against one, it wouldn't stand a...*hold on. Where were Tim and Dr Li? The cowards were still in the kitchen.*

Fine, Sam didn't need them, anyway. He could still take down this foe if it came to it. He had stopped Dr Cud without even trying, after all. Sam bit down on the slice of bacon he was holding and reached towards the door, grasping the handle with his greasy fingers. He readied his magnetic musket and pulled open the door.

Standing there before him was Officer Lucy Sparks.

"May I come in?"

33

"I'm fine," were the words Lucy repeated over and over. She didn't need to go to the hospital or see a psychiatrist.

All she wanted was to go home, take a long shower and scrub it all away, not just the remains of the officers whose flesh was embedded in her hair, but the memories too.

Her father drove her from the police station in his car, and there they sat in mutual silence, both meaning to say something, as they both had so much to say, they just couldn't seem to find the right words to unlock their mouths. Neither of them were ever good at the emotional stuff. That was always Lucy's mother's job.

"Lucy..." said her father, finally forcing the word from his mouth, but nothing more came.

"I know," replied Lucy, but she didn't know, not really.

Everything she thought she knew of the man beside her was tainted with doubt. A poison seeping through her thoughts, infecting her mind. Just like the poisoned pill infecting her father. She was being stupid, Lucy told herself, *PTSD* or something. Of course, she could trust her dad; he was the one stable thing in her life. Yet she still struggled to face him all the same.

When they arrived home, Lucy thanked her father, assuring him once more she was fine, and excused herself to the bathroom to take a shower. As the water washed over her, running down her face, she cried. This was the only place she allowed herself to do so as the water could mask the tears, allowing her to hide them, even from herself.

She felt something spongy against her foot and looked down to see a piece of grey matter clogging the drain. A police officer's brain, like her, like her father. Lucy sucked back the tears; she knew she had to help, she needed to be strong, and she needed to do whatever she could to stop Dr. Tobias Cud.

Her father made her dinner. She didn't eat much.

She laid in her bed. She didn't sleep much.

The following morning, DCI Sparks tried to sneak out of the house extra early, but as he got to his car, he found Lucy waiting there, dressed in her uniform.

He tried to find Lucy's eyes, but they evaded him.

"I'm fine," she said, straightening herself up. "I'm a police officer."

Her father knew there would be little point in arguing with her, so he spoke to her the way he would any other police officer, the way he understood. He told her they had a warrant to search the residence of Jack Phoenix and Sam Higgs, and so the pair set off.

WHEN THEY ARRIVED, THE HOUSE WAS SWARMED with officers and investigators conducting their search. However, as Lucy stepped out of the car, every one of them fell silent. Some turned their heads away, pretending not to notice, but some couldn't help but stare.

Lucy kept her head down and pushed past them, avoiding their hushed sympathies. She sensed their eyes drilling into her, following her every movement along the driveway.

"What happened?" asked one of the more confident spectators. Lucy ignored the question and several more as she continued into the house.

The interior of the house was a mess. Every cupboard and drawer hung from their moorings with their contents laid out on the floor, numbered and catalogued. She passed the kitchen, where several cans of cider and an empty milk bottle were being placed into clear, labelled bags.

She made her way up the stairs, shuffling past the forensic team in their white suits, each one turning their attention to what they were doing to gawk at Lucy.

Upon reaching the top of the stairs, Lucy found what she was looking for. She needed to know what kind of man Jack was and if any of what he told her was true. If she was going to find the answers, a good place to start would be his bedroom.

They mostly cleaned out the room. The textbooks and scientific notes which usually adorned the shelves were absent, and the room wore the distinct aroma of bleach and forensic chemicals as every surface was scrubbed for traces of blood and any hope of answers scrubbed away with it. As Lucy approached Jack's desk, she heard a voice behind her that made her jump.

"Gloves."

Lucy turned to see and officer had followed her.

"You forgot to put on gloves," he repeated, holding out a pair. "You don't want to contaminate the evidence and get yourself arrested for association."

Lucy took the gloves, unsure if that was a joke or a genuine suspicion, and began searching the room. All the while, the other officer stood over her, watching her, filling her with unease.

"So, everyone's talking about you," said the officer.

Lucy ignored him, continuing to pull open the drawers in Jack's desk and finding nothing.

"They're saying you appeared with them in a flash of light, and then they escaped. Were they like magicians or something? You must know how they did it."

The drawers were empty. The desk was bare. There needed to be something somewhere.

"You were with them all day. What did they do to you? Did they tell you anything?"

Lucy turned to the closet, and found it as it was, still yet to be picked clean by forensics. Inside lay a trove of ironed shirts, well-folded trousers, and several pairs of shoes arranged in neat rows at the bottom. She seared the pockets of the trousers and ran her hands against the shirts but found no protuberances or secrets.

She motioned to close the wardrobe but found her eyes drawn below, towards the shoes, for that was where he hid it. *The perfect hiding spot*. She buried her hand into the footwear, frantically digging around inside them one by one. There had to be something here.

Lucy touched something tucked down the end of a black dress shoe. Surveying it, she found a small stack of photographs, folded and torn with age and smelling slightly of cheese.

The first photograph was of Jack and Sam as young boys, happily jumping on a bouncy castle. She turned the photo over, and Jack had written '*Sam's 12th birthday*' in biro on the back.

In the second photo, a teenage Jack stood with the older version of Dr Li, looking more similar to the one she saw die. Jack's outstretched hand captured the pair in a selfie, as well as a cottage behind them.

On the back, the inscription read, '*Moving into my forever home at 1 Willow Road.'* Lucy had him. She needed to tell her dad right away.

But then, Lucy noticed the last photo, the oldest and most revisited: a wedding. A bride and groom stood outside a church surrounded by friends and family, and in the background, inside the church and out of focus, she saw something that sent an ice-cold dagger down her spine.

Lucy squinted at the figure, blurred and smudged but unmistakably her. She was in the photo with Jack and Dr Li, exactly as they were yesterday. She turned it over, *'Mom and Dad's wedding, April 8th, 2002.'*

It was true. It was all true.

"Did you find something?" asked the officer.

"No," replied Lucy a little too quickly as she shoved the photos into her pocket.

"What was that?"

"Nothing. Why are you watching me? Did my dad tell you to?" Then, the doubt seized control, and Lucy's voice lowered. "Or did *he* send you?"

"Who?"

"I think you know exactly who."

"I don't know what you're talking about, but if you found something, you need to hand it over."

Lucy ignored his outstretched hand and shoved past him, charging down the stairs. She saw the officers, the detectives, the forensic team, each turning from their business to look in her direction as she passed, but their faces no longer seemed right. In some imperceptible way, she was sure of it.

They were wrong, all of them.

Outside, Lucy found her father talking to a few officers.

"Dad!" she shouted. "Get away from them!"

"What are you talking about?" asked DCI Sparks as Lucy pushed the officers back.

"Dad, we need to get out of here. It isn't safe," said Lucy, tugging at his uniform like a child desperate to go to the toy aisle. "I'll explain everything, but we need to leave right now."

However, her father remained an immovable totem.

"I'm not going anywhere until you tell me what's going on," said her father sternly.

"There are these pills that take over your mind, and he's controlling them all."

Everyone was staring at her now, and more officers and even the forensic team had come out of the house to see. Eyes watching her from every angle, like cameras, each supplying a direct feed to *him*.

"What have those people done to you?" sighed DCI Sparks. "I should never have brought you here today. You weren't ready."

"No, Dad, listen, I promise you, this is all real, really, properly real."

He glanced at her as any father would when his daughter told him a fantastical tale of seeing a unicorn, becoming a fairy, or visiting the moon in a cardboard box. He reached out and held her tightly.

"Whatever they did to you, we can fix it."

Fix, that was the word he had used. Lucy broke free from her father and started backing away.

"Lucy," continued DCI Sparks, "It's ok, you're in shock. You're safe here."

Did his voice sound different? His face looked different. Everything was wrong.

"Stay back!" shouted Lucy. But it wasn't just him. She was surrounded, cameras closing in on her. "Get back, all of you."

Why were they all staring at her? Was *he* controlling every one of them? She needed to get away, somewhere *he* couldn't find her.

Lucy ran down the street, past the rows of police vehicles. She glanced back and saw the officer from the house following her.

"Hey, stop!" he shouted.

Lucy didn't. She only ran faster, turning down the street into a small alcove of wooden fences. It was a dead end, and it didn't take long for the police officer to catch up to her, cornering her.

"I just want to talk," said the officer. "Everyone's worried about you."

Lucy wasn't listening. She was looking for a way out. She kicked at the fence, trying to stomp out a path forward, but the wooden slats were impenetrable.

"It doesn't mean you can steal evidence," continued the officer.

There was no way on; her only way out was back past the officer. Lucy gritted her teeth and charged past the officer, but he wouldn't let her and grabbed her by the arm. Lucy tried to tear herself free, but her footing slipped, and she tumbled down to the wet tarmac.

"Stop," the officer kept saying. He was on top of her now, pinning down her arms.

Lucy struggled and fought like a wild animal in a trap. The officer refused to give her the chance to escape and pulled a pair of handcuffs from his pocket, his car keys and some change coming with it, bursting from his trousers.

Try as she might, Lucy wasn't strong enough to push him off her. He was on her chest, the full weight of him crushing down on her ribs, squeezing out the last whisper of oxygen from her lungs like a tube of toothpaste.

As the final squeak of air fled her body, Lucy choked out, "Are you... Dr Cud...?"

He didn't hear her; he was busy speaking into his walkie-talkie, requesting help. The edges of Lucy's vision darkened as her strength faded, her head fell to the side, and the last thing she saw was the officer's car keys, only a few inches away from her face, before everything went black.

Every thought was consumed by pain until her arms stopped writhing, and her hands fell silent as they couldn't take it anymore, slipping into the darkness and landing on the car keys.

She needed him to get off her!

Lucy plunged the key into his neck. She didn't feel herself doing it; it just happened.

The officer stumbled backwards and slid off her.

Lucy panted, regained her breath, and the light returned to reveal the man beside her. The officer wasn't frightening or intimidating anymore, and Lucy noticed just how young this officer was, even younger than herself.

She stared into the combination of surprise, shock, and fear in the young man's eyes as blood flowed from his neck and across his cheek. His throat gurgled as he tried to speak, but every breath drowned with blood.

From her training, Lucy knew she should apply pressure to stop the bleeding immediately.

She didn't.

Lucy stood up and found her hand was still holding the key. Its tip stained a lurid red. She pressed the button on the fob hanging from it, and a police car not too far from her blinked its headlights in recognition. She calmly walked towards it, the numbing shock guiding her way. The man's gasps for air went unheard by her. Whether someone would find him in time didn't worry her. She didn't think about what she'd just done at all.

Instead, Lucy plugged the wet key into the car's steering wheel and drove away.

She drove in silence, letting the realization of what she'd just done wash over her. The hands gripping the wheel in front of her; the ones soaked in blood were her hands.

She ended someone's life, the worst crime there was, and her addled mind could find only one solution.

So, she followed the address on the photograph.

34

"May I come in?" Lucy asked again.

"No?" replied Sam, the intonation in his voice making it sound like a question.

If it was a question, Lucy swiftly answered it by pushing Sam aside and proceeding toward the kitchen, where she found Tim scooping a forkful of beans into his mouth.

Tim froze in her presence, beans slipping down his fork, but Lucy had no interest in Tim. She had her sights set on the man beside him making sandwiches.

"Where is it?" asked Lucy. "I need it."

"Where's what?" replied Dr Li, scarcely acknowledging her intrusion.

"The..." started Lucy, resenting him for making her say it. "The time machine. I made a mistake, and I need to fix it."

"The time machine is not a pencil eraser. Like I told Jack, the past is delicate, and you can't just go changing things willy-nilly."

"I have to. I did something, and I didn't mean to." reasoned Lucy. "It just happened."

Dr Li turned from the bread to Lucy, seeing the guilt in her eyes, guilt he knew well.

"What happened?"

Lucy wouldn't say it; she refused to allow it to be true and suddenly found it difficult to look Dr Li in the eyes. Averting her gaze from the judgement, her eyes landed on a small television on the counter, displaying a live feed of Jack.

"What is that?" she asked.

Upstairs, Jack stood opposite the man who wanted to kill him, with only a high-frequency magnetic field stopping him from doing so. Jack cleared his throat and gripped the list he'd spent the night constructing.

"I have some questions."

Dr Tobias Cud only stared at him, like a lion eyeing the zookeeper it planned to devour.

Jack didn't need a response. He hadn't finished talking, anyway. He stared down at his list, but not because he was avoiding eye contact with Dr Cud.

Jack wasn't scared of him. There was no reason to be. He was stuck to a magnet. There was no need to fear him at all. *So why was he?*

No amount of reason could expel the dread hiding behind Jack's eyes.

Jack licked his dry lips with his dryer tongue and cleared his throat.

"You're going to answer each question as simply and concisely as humanly possible. If you even are human, that is. Question one, are you human?"

Dr Cud didn't reply. He saw no point in answering the questions of this ignorant child. If Jack wished to see him as some inhuman boogie man, so be it. It would only serve his end goal, anyway.

"You created the pills," continued Jack, skipping ahead. "They seem to contain a modified virus, whose RNA codes for a transmitter which makes people think like you. That's right, isn't it? So, second question, how many people have you infected?"

Dr Cud didn't falter, didn't even blink.

"You're ordering these people to create a cure for ageing. That's what you said."

Still nothing.

"And you want to steal the time machine to give them enough time to do that?"

Dr Cud's face twitched, an almost imperceptible flicker of muscle fibre, but he could feel it. His weak, fallible flesh betrayed him once more. It didn't matter. The boy didn't notice.

But what was he attempting? Was he trying to aggravate him? If so, it was working.

"Third question, how did you even find out about the time machine?"

No, this wasn't an attempt to provoke him; this boy truly believed what he was saying. Dr Li indoctrinated him better than any pill he could produce. Despite his best efforts, Dr Cud couldn't allow these falsehoods to be spoken in his presence any longer.

"I don't want to steal it. I created it. It belongs to me."

"You're lying."

"I am not lying!" erupted Dr Cud as the floodgates burst and his calm composure dissipated. "He stole it from me! We worked on it together for over two decades, and then he took it. Li stole everything from me."

Dr Cud closed his eyes and forced the adrenaline back inside.

"The locator, how do you think I knew how it worked? Because it was my idea."

Jack's eyes flickered to the locator, glued to the metal slab inches from Dr Cud's face.

"Just like the time machine. You know he'll never let you use it. He'll fill your head with promises, but he's a liar. He wants it all to himself." hissed Dr Cud.

Now it was time for Jack's face to twitch, a poker players tell, and Dr Cud had seen it.

"Is that why you murdered him?" asked Jack.

"You think he would let me kill him that easily? That man is not dead; if you believe otherwise, you are truly naïve."

Jack's mind turned to Dr Li, how he had absconded death's grip for now, and how he hadn't been the most open-handed with his gift of time travel. He didn't dare tell Dr Cud about any of it. Just because he was right about those things didn't mean he was right about everything else.

"You tried to shoot me. You tried to kill me. You don't even know me," said Jack.

"I knew you had the time machine. I saw it sticking out of your boot."

Jack sensed the time machine rubbing against his sock even now, itching at him, an itch gnawing along his leg and prickling his back, only growing with each truth Dr Cud spoke.

"Li used to do the same," said Dr Cud. "I've been monitoring you for a while, and I know you're the telepathic link. I needed you to be afraid to ensure it worked."

"And if it didn't?"

Dr Cud didn't answer. He didn't need to. 'Where did it send you?'

"To my mom and dad," said Jack, desperately wanting to scratch away the itch crawling through his skin.

"Running home to mommy and daddy. So that's why he keeps you around. You must be spilling over with fear."

"Shut up," said Jack, the itch now peeling open every cell of his body.

"You have me here, unable to move, and you know what... I bet you're still scared of me."

"Shut up," said Jack again, scratching himself, scraping his nails against his body as the itch spawned offspring, each one crying out for attention as they spread across him.

"Are you afraid of me, Jack?"

"Shut up!" screamed Jack, closing his eyes and holding his hands over his ears.

Suddenly, the door behind him opened, and Jack's scream was met with an even louder one.

"Were you controlling him?!" yelled Lucy with the anger of an army, every molecule in her body bursting into a violent storm.

Jack turned his head to meet her. What was she doing here? Was she talking to him?

Lucy fixed her rage-filled torrent on the man glued to the slab.

"You were controlling him, weren't you? Weren't you? Answer me!"

But Dr Cud didn't. He fell silent once more, with only a small, wrinkled smile on his lips.

"What about my dad? Were you controlling him, too?!"

His smile grew.

"Were you controlling all of them?"

Dr Cud couldn't hold it back anymore, his smile burst open, and he laughed, the cruel laugh of a school bully, feeding on her misery.

"Tell me!" screamed Lucy, now wrapping her hands around his throat.

Her hands were no match for the metal reinforcement of

the old man's neck, which cut Lucy's fingers and only made Dr Cud laugh harder.

"Tell me!"

Sam and Tim appeared in the doorway, having followed Lucy upstairs. After some struggling, they pulled her off Dr Cud. All the while, he went on laughing, and she went on screaming. Lucy refused to take her eyes off him as they dragged her from the room, her face deep red with rage, spit dripping from her bottom lip.

"I'll take over from here," Sam told Jack.

"Ok, yeah, thanks. He's er...yeah...yeah." stuttered Jack as he shuffled past Lucy, Sam and Tim.

His mind was on fire now, his skin blazed, and he doubted everything. Everything Jack had once been sure of was now shrouded in darkness by the shadow of the looming question mark snowballing through his mind, corrupting every memory of his adoptive father. He needed to be alone. He needed to think. He needed...Lightheaded, he stumbled into his childhood bedroom and climbed onto his bed.

As soon as his head met the pillow, the world turned black, and for the first time in a long time, Jack's mind became still.

He needed to sleep.

<h1 style="text-align:center">35</h1>

Sam took over guard duties from Jack, and it was boring, more boring than he thought possible. He wished he still had his phone or anything to distract him from the brain-melting boredom and the orange juice pressing on his bladder; he really should've gone before taking over guard duties.

Sam thought babysitting a serial killer would be exciting, but he was just stuck there on that big magnetic slab, staring forward, not doing a thing. Maybe if Sam poked him, that would get a reaction. Or a *Wet Willy*. He might be an evil robot man, but no one could resist a spitty finger in the ear.

Sam lazily ran his finger along his tongue and brought the finger, dripping with saliva, close to Dr Cud's ear, ready to plug it in, but, to Sam's surprise, the robot man awoke from his stupor.

"Samuel."

"Alright," said Sam excitedly, "are you finally going to do an evil monologue or something?"

"I'm not evil, Samuel. Certainly not compared to the people you've surrounded yourself with."

Sam retracted his finger. "Go on."

"I've gotten to know Jack well, and he's taught me a lot. You know he doesn't see you as an intellectual equal."

"Probably not. The guys like bloody *Einstein*."

"He thinks you're a fool."

"Yeah, he tells me most days."

"He doesn't even view you as a friend."

Sam burst out laughing. "What are you, four years old? Is he not going to invite me to his birthday party?"

Sam licked his finger again and firmly jammed it into Dr Cud's ear canal. He didn't visibly react, but Sam knew.

"You have so much to lose, more than anybody else here," said Dr Cud. "Your parents, your sister, Molly."

"Oh, he knows about my family. He can use *Facebook*," laughed Sam in the most patronizing tone he could muster. "That the best you've got, childish insults and threats?"

Sam sauntered over to the workbench and picked up a pen. He flicked the lid free and shot a wink Dr Cud's way before brushing the pen across the crevices of the old man's forehead.

"Maybe this whole *evil* shtick of yours works with other people, but I'm really not scared of you. You're not at all like I imagined. I mean, you look like my grandad...if he was part washing machine." Sam paused to admire his handiwork. '*Sam Woz Here*' now indelibly scribed onto Dr Cud's forehead.

It admittedly looked a bit off as Sam had to write around the wrinkles and metal bits, but it would do. Sam finished it with a quick sketch of a penis across his temple, completing his masterpiece.

"I've met a lot of dickheads in my time, and you wouldn't even make the top ten," continued Sam. "You've upset Jack, that policewoman too, Louise. I think her name was. They're terrified of you. So yeah, I might not be Jack's intellectual-whatever, I might be a fool, but we are absolutely *best* friends. Do you know why? Because I don't take shit from bullies."

"So now you're threatening *me*?"

"Nah, a threat is something you can't back up. I won't make some big grandiose threat, like *I'm going to kill you and your family and tear your world down around you*," said Sam in his best hammy villain voice. "Or whatever crap it is that you said to them. No. I'm just going to piss on you."

"What?" said Dr Cud; if there was even a spark of humanity left in this man's eyes, Sam could tell its name was Fear.

"No threats," said Sam with a smile. "Just piss."

With that, Sam unzipped his jeans.

No threats.

Just piss.

TIM EVENTUALLY CAME AND TOOK OVER FROM SAM, who returned to join the others.

As he wandered through the house, Sam noticed things were different. The first thing that struck him was the sound, or rather lack of it. It was the excessive silence you would find in an exam or a church. Not that Sam was good at staying quiet in either.

Sam peeked into Jack's room and found him passed out on his bed. Sam gently closed his bedroom door so as not to wake him and continued downstairs. He saw Dr Li flitting around the kitchen, preparing snacks and scribbling down equations on a slew of crumpled paper, and left him to it. Sam continued to the living room, where he found Lucy sitting on the sofa, staring forward, except the television wasn't on.

The television would never be off in Sam's house, serving as background noise, light, and even warmth during winter. It was strange seeing someone sitting on the sofa, staring forward at nothing. Lucy didn't seem to notice he entered the room, so Sam took a seat on the other end of the sofa, trying to see precisely what she was staring at, but found only a damp stain on the wallpaper.

There was a long, unbearable silence, and Sam lasted as long as he could, but it eventually became too much.

"I pissed on him."

Lucy's eyes narrowed as Sam's words woke her from her thoughts. "You did what?"

"Oh yeah, sorry, you're a police officer. I *urinated* on him," corrected Sam. "He seemed like he deserved it."

"He does deserve it," agreed Lucy.

Sam peered at Lucy from the corner of his eye. A slight smile formed on her face, which made Sam smile, too.

Another few minutes of silence passed, and Lucy spoke once more.

"My mom killed herself."

"Oh, um, right..." replied Sam.

What the hell was he supposed to say to that? Luckily for him, he didn't need to say anything.

"My dad was away for months when he was in the army, and my mom was left to take care of me. I don't know if she got lonely or stressed or what, but she started taking pills to help her sleep. Then she started taking pills to stay awake, pills to focus, pills to calm down, pills to be happy. I didn't know about any of this, but I later found a leaflet for *Narcotics Anonymous* in her room, and I put the pieces together. I thought they were medicine or sweets...Then, one day, I was waiting for her to pick me up from school, and she never showed. They found her car at the bottom of the lake not long after. Since then, it's been me and my dad...and he, that man up there. He's taken that from me."

"What did he do?"

"I don't know," said Lucy, her words turning to syrup and struggling to emerge as she remembered every grim detail. "Maybe nothing. But, because of him, I did something I can't take back."

Sam waited through more silence for Lucy to continue, but she never did.

After a little while, Sam grabbed the remote from the coffee table and switched on the television, and with that, the silence was gone, and everything seemed proper once more.

36

TIM LIMPED OVER TO DR CUD, HIS LEG STRANGLING him with each unbalanced step; the bullet had shredded skin, nerves, and muscle tissue and left a hole that would never heal. His cheek was still tender; Tim dared to peel back the bandages for the first time in the bathroom mirror a few moments earlier and witnessed the mess of bubbling blisters and stitches piercing through his skin and trying their best to hold it all together.

He ran his tongue along the inside of his mouth, feeling the wiry ends of the stitches poking in. Tim's ears erupted like an alarm clock, ringing a deafening cry along his punctured drums. He successfully hid his wrecked hearing thus far by keeping quiet, which was probably for the best now there was a police officer around.

Tim was feeling like a prisoner within his own body, chained by the pain, unable to hear, move, or even look at himself. However, he wasn't looking at himself right now. Right now, he was peering at the man to blame for all this.

"You did this to me. What am I going to do to you?" Tim wondered aloud.

Tim searched the desks and shelves for something he could use, his fingers running across pliers, wrenches and wire strippers before stopping briefly at a soldering iron; *that does something to metal, right?*

Maybe Tim could simply plug the bastard directly into an outlet. Tim finally settled on a screwdriver as his weapon of choice. Gripping it tightly, he turned to face Dr Cud, taking in every detail of his chrome features. He noticed Lucy's blood caked around his throat in long, cracked streaks of brown paint. Tim imagined the shade of paint that Dr Cud would produce.

"Now, you might be metal on the inside, but you're still skin on the outside, and skin can cut. See, I used to work with my uncle down at the fish markets. He would have a tank full of cod, and he used to reach in, pluck one out and hold it there, wriggling around in his hands, fighting him. I mean, they don't want to end up down the chippie, do they? So, he gets his knife and starts at the neck, sliding it down and grabbing whatever falls out a bit like a piñata." Tim slowly ran the screwdriver down Dr Cud's neck to his chest as he spoke.

"Little Collin the cod, still alive through all this, keeps fighting. Even when his head comes off, the body just won't stop. Something to do with nerves, I don't know. I'm no fish doctor. I think that even when all that was left was a descaled, deboned fillet, there's still a bit left that believes it might just be able to swim away." Tim's nose turned upwards as the screwdriver reached the top of Dr Cud's trousers.

They were sodden, marked by a large, dark grey patch draining down his leg and the accompanying acidic smell of ammonia.

"Have you pissed yourself?"

"Timothy," said Dr Cud calmly, ignoring the uncomfortable warmth that Sam had gifted him. "You're the person I've wanted to speak to most of all."

"Well, I'd be careful about what you say to me, or I may just rip out that tongue of yours."

"First, I'd like to apologize," said Dr Cud with a disarming sincerity. "How Gregory and some of my newer recruits have treated you was...inappropriate."

"They do what you tell them."

"True," admitted Dr Cud. "However, some small personality traits can persist. Not by design, of course. I'm ironing that out as best I can. May I say, despite everything you've been through, you have faced it with courage and aplomb, and that is to be applauded."

"Well, yeah, you and your shitty little army don't scare me."

"Why should it? You're strong. You've had to be after everything life has dealt you...so unfairly."

"You don't know me, mate. You don't know what I've been through."

"I saw the memories of those men you once considered friends living in that squalor. I saw why you turned to them and how they repaid you when they discovered the truth of who you really are."

Tim fell silent, his eyes freezing into an icy glare, warning of the dangerous road Dr Cud was venturing down.

"Have you told them? Jack. Lucy. Sam. How will they react when they find out the truth?"

Tim turned his gaze down to the screwdriver in his hand.

"We've both been unfairly judged by the world. So I'd like to offer a truce and a proposition."

Tim focused on the screwdriver, gripping its yellow translucent handle harder and harder.

"I can fix you. I'll take you to my lab, fix your leg, repair any damage, and make you stronger than before. No burns, no scars, good as new." proposed Dr Cud, the hiss from his analogue voice box merged with the silky sympathy in his words, a snake offering Tim a bite of forbidden fruit.

Tim's face softened as he looked back up at Dr Cud, his grip on the screwdriver loosening. "You can do that?"

"That's what I do," said Dr Cud earnestly. "I fixed myself, and I've come a long way since then. If you'd like, I could even swap some neurons around in your brain and fix your other... *problem*. How does that sound?"

Tim jammed the screwdriver into Dr Cud's chest. The bubble of rage which lingered since he was first told about therapies or prayer or simply that he should stop trying to get attention finally popped. Tim's body might be broken, but his mind was not, and Tim was sick of being made to think otherwise.

Tim stepped back and dropped the screwdriver from his trembling hand, forcing himself to look, but when he did, he saw Dr Cud was still alive—not a cut, not a scratch, not a single mark, not even a surprised look on his face.

"My epidermal cells are reinforced with nano-alloys in their membranes," said Dr Cud. "But nice try. I'll take that as a no, then?"

Tim's breathing quieted, and the room fell silent, which is how it stayed for the following hour and fifty-two minutes. Tim watched Dr Cud as his mind swarmed with thoughts of everyone who had ever dismissed him, talked down to him, and said he wasn't good enough.

He grew up poor, with no formal education. He lost his dad and then his mom. At his lowest point, he was hooked on every drug he could get his hands on, and yes, despite the best efforts of his family, friends, and everyone he ever met, even himself, Tim was gay.

Now, all the hate and fury and regret that filled Tim's life were concentrated into a single point: the '*W*' Sam drew between Dr Cud's eyes.

Jack knocked gently on the door, slowly pushing it open.

"Hey, um, it's my turn again," he yawned, having awoken from his nap without feeling the slightest bit refreshed.

Tim stood up and limped towards the door, keeping his eyes fixed on Dr Cud until he was out of the room. He staggered downstairs and into the living room, where Sam, Lucy, and Dr Li were all grazing on an endless pile of snacks courtesy of Dr Li and watching television; some show in which a silver-haired woman discovered that the vase she treasured, a family heirloom handed down to her from her grandmother, who had it handed down from her grandmother, was, in fact, worthless.

In any other scenario, Tim would've happily joined them, watched crap tv all day and escaped his thoughts, but this was a pressing matter. So, he grabbed the remote and switched the TV off.

"Hey!" came a harmony of protests, but Tim ignored them.

"I've got something important to say."

Tim suddenly felt the weight of their eyes, looking at him expectantly, just like his mother did on that stupid Christmas Day. However, the people in front of him now wouldn't care. Most barely knew him, and they most definitely had bigger things to focus on.

Come on, Tim. They're all looking at you, he thought to himself. *You've got to say something.*

"I..." began Tim.

Come on, it's not even a big deal nowadays.

"I..." said Tim again.

It was a big deal to mom. 'You brought this on yourself.' That was what she told him. That was what they all told him.

"I think we should kill him," said Tim finally.

"I agree," said Lucy. "It's the only way."

"Er, yeah," said Sam, mimicking Tim and Lucy, although not entirely convinced.

Was this just banter or were they actually being serious?

Sure, Dr Cud was a bad guy and probably deserved it, even if Sam didn't find him particularly threatening, but actually killing him seemed a tad too far.

Dr Li watched them whilst he picked at the cheese platter, consumed by their anger and a newfound thirst for murder on their lips. They were almost smiling with the excitement of some newly graduated reaper.

While this wasn't the solution he envisioned, Dr Li was grateful this whole ordeal might soon end. He could spend the rest of his days trying to find peace with himself and his decisions today. The niggling feeling that he could have done better would likely never leave him.

Even if Toby Cud died here, Dr Li would eventually have to realign with his own timeline, where Toby would still be out there, enacting his plan, causing pain and death, until he would one day kill Dr Li. Perhaps then he would finally find peace.

Tim dragged the whiteboard from the kitchen, wheeling it in front of the television, with its single word still written on it.

Murder.

He grabbed the marker and circled the word several times.

"How are we doing this, then? Because I already tried with a screwdriver, but it turns out his skin is metal, too."

"Right, so, no knives, no guns, nothing that does damage through penetration," said Lucy.

Sam let out a small, stifled laugh at the word.

"So I thought, what if we fill him with bleach?" said Tim, carving the word '*BLEACH*' onto the board.

"Yeah," agreed Lucy, her voice heavy with venom.

"Yeah," agreed Sam, far less confidently. Could they go back to saying *penetration* now?

"Let's fill him up like a balloon!" shouted Lucy.

The aggressive glee was making Sam a little uncomfortable now.

"Or we could drown him..." continued Lucy.

Tim wrote the word '*DROWN*' on the board.

"With bleach!" finished Lucy.

"We could set him on fire," said Tim.

"Let's watch him burn," agreed Lucy.

Sam edged a few inches away from Lucy.

"What if we piss on him again?" propositioned Sam. "We could fill a water gun with piss?"

This wasn't met with the laughter Sam hoped it would. In fact, it was met with daggers. *They really were being serious. They were actually going to kill him.*

"You're the police. Can't you just arrest him?"

"No," said Lucy, pricking Sam with her gaze.

"What if we give him some sleeping pills? Knock him out for a bit," said Sam, squirming a little in his seat.

"No," said Lucy once more. "No pills."

"There are other drugs we could use," tried Sam. "I think there's still some cocaine left."

"We are not getting him all coked up," said Tim.

"What if we go to the future? I bet they'd have good ways to kill someone quickly and painlessly and in a way where they don't even have to be properly dead," said Sam.

"What is with you and going to the future?" argued Tim.

THEY DEBATED OVER THE NEXT HOUR AS THE BOARD

filled with endless ideas for killing, some of which Sam thought drifted into the realms of torture rather than murder.

"I've got it," announced Lucy, her enthusiasm for death still yet to wane. "Electrocution."

"Yes," agreed Tim, revelling in the thought of plugging Dr Cud into the wall and watching him cook. He wrote it in one of the small remaining gaps on the whiteboard.

"I suppose we could," said Sam, this being one of the more rational ideas of late. "It's capital punishment. So we wouldn't be breaking any laws."

"Dr Li?" asked Lucy.

Dr Li wasn't listening, lost in thought and consumed with a cocktail of anxiety, worry and too much cheese.

"Oh, erm...yeah, sounds good." He did not know what he was agreeing to and supposed it didn't matter either way.

"Let's light him up like a Christmas tree!" said Lucy excitedly.

37

"How long do you intend to keep me here?" asked Dr Cud, the light through the window rising across his body as the spotlight behind fell, dying the clouds red and marking almost a full day spent stuck to this magnet, reduced to the playthings of morons.

Dr Cud despised not being in control of his body. He dedicated decades to controlling every facet, but now he couldn't do something as simple as reaching out to strangle the biggest moron of them all.

"As long as it takes," said Jack, trying not to let this man get inside his head again.

He was creating a wall around his mind, an impenetrable barrier where Dr Cud's lies couldn't get to him, for Jack was no longer interested in reasoning with this man. He simply needed to watch him.

"As long as *what* takes?" asked Dr Cud.

Jack didn't respond. He didn't know the answer.

Dr Cud felt the dull ache stretching along his arms. He flushed away most of his pain receptors long ago, but the few who endured whined, desperate to move.

"Do you know the story of King Cnut?" said Dr Cud. "He was a man who, through his arrogance, believed he could stop the tides themselves. You can't stop something that powerful."

"Like getting old?" countered Jack.

Before Dr Cud could respond, Lucy and Tim kicked open the door and barged inside, with Sam trailing a short way behind. Tim was wearing a pair of bright yellow washing-up gloves and holding a DVD player under his arm.

"Jack, it's time," Lucy told him.

"What do you mean, it's time? Time for what?" said Jack.

"Time we put an end to this," said Tim as he limped past Jack, towards the tools.

"What? You don't mean what I think you mean. Sam?"

Sam struggled to make eye contact with Jack. Jack had always been the annoying voice of reason, *Jiminy Cricket-ing* around, telling him he shouldn't be doing this and that.

As much as Sam hated it, Jack was usually right. If he listened to Jack's advice in the pub, they might have avoided all of this. However, he didn't, and so here they were.

"We have to," he muttered.

Jack forced himself between them and Dr Cud, who only watched in silence, enjoying the distraction from the pain and intrigued how this would play out.

"Have you all gone insane? You're going to murder him, is that it? Well, it's not happening. Lucy, this isn't you. You're a police officer. You're not a murderer."

Lucy felt acid rise through her body as Jack spoke. He didn't know what she was, what this monster made her become. "We're doing it."

"Well, I won't let you. I'm not moving," said Jack, putting his foot down and marking a line in the carpet, a line that nobody was going to pass.

Tim tore through the insulated cable of the DVD player

using a set of wire strippers and thrust the exposed copper in Jack's direction.

"Move, or you're getting zapped 'n' all."

"Sure, might as well make it a double murder, a two-for-one special!" shouted Jack. He wasn't moving.

"Sam, grab him," instructed Tim.

"Why me?" complained Sam as he reluctantly grabbed Jack in a bear hug. "I'm sorry, Jack."

"You're not serious!" shouted Jack. "Let me go!"

"I'm really sorry about this," repeated Sam as he pulled Jack away.

"I'm not going," warned Jack. "I'll go limp."

"Come on, Jack, let's be dignified about this."

Jack flopped lifelessly, slopping through Sam's arms like yogurt, as every muscle in his body crumpled, all apart from his mouth, which continued to relent.

Sam struggled and pulled at Jack but couldn't move him, not alone.

"Help me then!" Sam shouted to Tim.

"I ain't lifting him. I can barely fucking walk!" Tim shouted back.

"Lucy, grab his legs," said Sam.

"Do not grab my legs!" Jack continued protesting as Lucy tried to get hold of his legs, screaming and kicking her away in a full-on tantrum.

It took all they could, but together, Lucy and Sam dragged him from the room and down the stairs.

"What would your dad say about this?!" yelled Jack, clawing at the banisters.

"He'll live," said Lucy, unsure if he would or even if he still was.

They got Jack onto the sofa and held him down against the cushions with the full force of their weight, but Jack refused to give in, and his arms and legs flailed wildly in every direction.

"We should tie him up," said Lucy.

"With what?"

"I don't know, rope or something."

"This isn't the sixteen-hundreds," argued Sam. "We don't have rope. Who has rope lying around?"

Lucy looked for something they could use, something rope-like. "Get the cables from the back of the TV. We'll use them."

"Do not tie me up! Don't you dare!" continued Jack's endless protests to deaf ears.

Sam and Lucy bound his wrists with an HDMI cable and his ankles with an extension cord. As the thick cables wrapped around him in knots, Jack finally stopped struggling. Once they finished, Lucy returned upstairs, leaving Sam to guard over his unwanted captive.

"You're actually going to go through with this?" said Jack.

"Well, I think we were going to let Tim do it, but yeah,' said Sam, looking down at his best friend bound in inelegant knots of thick black licorice and stretched out across the sofa. Sam knew it was probably for the best, but as he glanced at Jack's sweaty, red face and at all the disappointment beneath, he couldn't shake the pang of shame digging into him.

"He's the bad guy. Bad guys die," Sam added, partly to himself.

"What then? You're just going to carry on? Go to your lectures? Like none of this ever happened?"

"I imagine there'll be a parade or something, but then, I guess so."

"I always thought deep down you were a good person. An *ass*, sure... but deep down..."

"He's doing bad things, Jack, most of which I don't fully understand, but I know he's killing people and making people kill each other. We've seen it happen. And now, he's started threatening our families. You just don't understand because..." Sam quickly stopped himself.

"Because what?" probed Jack.

Sam didn't respond, but it scarcely mattered. Jack already knew.

"Because I don't have a family, right?"

"I didn't mean it like that."

"You're right," said Jack. "I don't have a family. Not anymore."

Sam couldn't find the right words, but knew he couldn't stay down here. Jack was making him feel all kinds of guilt, betrayal, and, worst of all, that he let his best friend down. Sam muttered a final "I'm sorry" under his breath and returned upstairs.

***

Upstairs, Tim and Lucy were trying to locate a socket to plug the DVD player's wire into. There was the one occupied by the electromagnet, but Tim supposed it probably wasn't the best idea to unplug that.

The pair crawled around the room, pushing things off shelves and shoving desks out of the way. All the while, Tim felt Dr Cud's eyes following him, boring into him, drilling into the back of his skull.

Tim reached his hand around the back of an old bookcase on the opposite end of the room and felt the rectangular outline of a socket. He wasted no time in jamming the plug into it, and, with that, Tim turned to face those hollow, unblinking eyes, silently mocking him.

He took a single step forward and was immediately yanked back by the cord. Pulled taught, the wiring only extended a few feet, not nearly far enough to reach its target.

Those eyes again, laughing at him.

"Get an extension cord!" Tim barked at Lucy.

A small smile formed on Dr Cud's lips, causing the wrinkles around his eyes to dance.

Tim would be the one to wipe that smirk off his face.

He was going to kill him.

He was going to kill Dr Tobias Cud.

38

Jack writhed and lurched with his hands trapped behind him, fighting to free himself from his binds. Unfortunately, all he did was launch himself from the sofa. Jack rolled off the old leather cushions and onto the floor with a thud, leaving himself face down in carpet. He wriggled his body in a wavelike motion, and slowly, feeling more than a little humiliated, Jack peristaltically propelled himself through the forest of un-vacuumed crumbs like a determined worm.

Jack passed the sofa and the coffee table as his flailing legs brought a lamp crashing down behind him, sending his shadow flying.

This didn't slow Jack, for he was resolute in his plan to slither up the stairs and stop any more murders from being committed. He wasn't sure quite how he'd manage it. He could not overpower Sam and Lucy when he had access to all his limbs. It was a problem for later. Right now, he needed to reach for the door handle.

He rolled over to the door and pressed his back against it. Tucking his legs in as best he could and pushed, using every fibre of strength in his brittle frame. With his teeth clamped

234

together and the blood vessels in his forehead close to bursting, Jack forced his muscles to work, pushing until his feet were firmly beneath him. He pressed a single digit against the door handle and found it moved with only the lightest touch, almost as though it were turning on its own...

The door opened onto Jack, sending him crashing to the floor again.

Jack glanced up, and through a face full of scratchy carpet fibres, he saw a familiar pair of ancient boots standing before him.

"Jack!" exclaimed Dr Li, holding a plate of biscuits. "Who did this to you?" He knelt beside Jack and began untying his restraints at once.

"It was the others. They've gone mad. They're trying to kill him."

Dr Li paused, slowly releasing his hands from the thick black cables.

"Why have you stopped?" asked Jack, but the answer was obvious. "Oh..."

"I'm so sorry, Jack," said Dr Li, closing the door behind him and setting the biscuits on the coffee table.

Jack stopped struggling, stopped wriggling, and resigned to his place on the stained green carpet. It was pointless to fight it any longer.

"Did you steal it?" he asked.

"Steal what?" replied Dr Li, as obtuse as ever.

"The time machine, the locator, the slowdown orb thing... Everything."

"Of course not. Whatever he's telling you, it's all a trick."

Somehow, that didn't put Jack's mind at ease. "Why me?"

"Why does Toby Cud want you? Well..."

"Not him..." Jack closed his eyes, buried his face deep into the carpet and asked a question he knew he didn't really want the answer to. "Why did you adopt me?"

"I don't know. From my point of view, I haven't adopted you yet," said Dr Li, another answer which answered little of anything at all. Jack hardly expected anything else. He would have to work it out for himself.

"What you said earlier about having the time machine tuned to my fear, it's not because you trust me, because anyone can operate it. I think you've been using me to charge your machine all this time. Because you think I'm a coward."

"Jack, I..."

Jack still had more to say. The wheels in his mind weren't done turning. "And you were going to give me the locator so you could always know where to find me if you needed a top-up. All the years I lived with you, was the time machine working the whole time? You were at my parents' wedding to stop me from saving them. Why? To keep me frightened? To keep me in your control? You've been manipulating my life since before it even started, just to get close to me..."

Jack realized there was a question he wanted to know the answer to less than any other his mind had thrown at him. A question he would never have imagined having to ask, and yet now, the answer to this question seemed all too clear.

"Did you kill my parents?"

"Jack, I'm not the bad guy here. You have to know that."

"All I know is I've been tied up twice in the last twenty-four hours, and I'm not sure I can tell the difference anymore."

Dr Li, the man who could lecture about the infinite and talk for nearly as long without taking a breath, was now lost for words.

Jack turned his head from the carpet to glance up at his adoptive father and the face he wore, the one Jack knew so well. In it, Jack found the answer to every one of his questions, written in guilt.

"Why are you even still here? You've got them to do your

dirty work for you, and surely I'm miserable enough to fill your stupid time machine. Just go already."

Dr Li considered Jack's request for a moment and nodded.

"If that's what you want," he said, and with a flash of blue light, Jack was alone once more.

Jack heard shouting upstairs, but knew it was futile to intervene. Jack wasn't even sure he wanted to stop them, or Dr Cud, or do anything anymore. So, he did the one thing that seemed like the most reasonable response to a situation like this. He cried, allowing the salt water to wash away every bit of his pain.

A loud crash soon interrupted Jack's tears and a thick orange brick landed beside him with a thud. He turned his head to find the shattered frame of the window, and a hand reached through it, trying to twist open the latch.

Of course, fate couldn't allow him even a single moment of peace.

Jack convulsed and wiggled back towards the door, shouting for help. He leaned against the door and forced himself up again, the adrenaline thankfully doing most of the lifting this time.

"Help!" he yelled.

Jack frantically rubbed his binds against the door handle, trying to hook his fingers around the handle, but his sweaty palms kept slipping free. From this new angle, Jack saw it wasn't just one person on the other side of the window, but five, or six, or ten.

"Release Dr Cud," demanded one of them.

"We've come for our saviour," called another.

Jack yelled louder, the words carving into his throat, "They're getting in!"

He hooked his pinky around the handle and yanked it down as the door shot open, knocking Jack to the floor once more as Lucy and Sam rushed in.

"Oh, fuck!" shouted Sam upon spotting the incoming invaders. He swiped the brick from the floor and lobbed it back through the window.

Bullseye.

The brick met its target and collided with the closest intruder, sending them reeling. Sam peered through the broken window to inspect his handiwork and saw the last thing he expected to see.

These invaders were old, very old. Their average age must've been in the eighties. Elderly men and women dressed in their Sunday best, and each held a matching determination in their vacant stares. Sam supposed that when trying to trick people into taking a strange orange pill without question, after the well of peer-pressured students dried up, OAPs were likely the next best option.

However, these invaders were far more subdued than anyone Sam had faced so far. Greg, the doctor, and the dealers had all been melting pots of pure aggression. As angry as the cast of '*The Golden Girls*' looked, their days of being threatening were long behind them.

Sam looked over the crowd, who seemed better suited to a church fête than a battleground, and felt only bafflement. *One had a Zimmer frame, for God's sake.* Perhaps it was their faulty hearing aids, but they didn't seem to get the message, and the OAPs helped their felled comrade back to their feet, and the invasion resumed, slowly but surely, advancing toward the window.

Sam picked up the broken lamp and tossed it like a javelin through the shattered glass, hitting the one with the Zimmer frame, who swiftly fell like a domino, taking the rest down with them in a procession of shattered hips. It was a sorry sight, and Sam didn't feel great about it. He didn't even shout *strike.*

The doorbell rang, and Sam ran through the hallway,

seeing more shadowy silhouettes of silver-haired soldiers through the front door's frosted glass. It seemed the entire population of this usually quiet village was amassing around the cottage.

A walking stick burst through the frosted glass, revealing this second wave of ancient assailants, who, frankly, seemed even older than the first. Sam dug a hand into his pocket to retrieve the small metal disc he was saving and threw it at the door. The disc erupted as it struck the glass, activating the frozen football. That would slow them down a bit, *well*, slow them down even more.

With that sorted, Sam ran back to the lounge to check on his other spinning plates, who were now back up and ready for round 2.

Behind him, Lucy was busy untying the intricate web of knots entangled around Jack's legs.

"Hurry, they're coming!" complained Jack, squirming around and inadvertently pulling each knot tighter. Lucy untangled the last knot and pulled the extension cord free. Jack sensed the blood rushing back into his feet with a painful fizz.

"Now do my arms," said Jack, but Lucy was already out the door, past the frozen football and back up the stairs, having already achieved her mission.

Lucy reached the top of the stairs and held her trophy aloft.

"I've got an extension lead," shouted Lucy, finding Tim where she left him. "But they're getting in. You need to make this quick!"

Tim plugged in the extension lead and then the exposed cabling. He wrapped his bright yellow gloves around the end of the cable and took one last look at Dr Cud's shit-eating grin; he saw so many people reflected in that grin, and he was about to wipe out every one of them out.

"You're too late," were the last words Dr Cud said as Tim plunged the cord down his throat.

Sparks flew. Dr Cud's body convulsed and glowed as every mechanical element in him lit up in a supernova of overloaded elements. A thick stench of petrol leaked from his bones as they melted, and his cybernetic irises were literally sizzling with agony. Yet his grin remained.

The entire room shone brighter, shrouding them all in a blazing white light, until, one by one, the lightbulbs above them surrendered and exploded, sending sparks and glass raining down around them.

A single defiant spark fluttered through the air and landed atop the discarded plans for an ionic destabilizer; plans drawn on a large, particularly flammable sheet of paper.

Tim continued beating the cord down inside Dr Cud, gagging it further into his throat. Despite the iridescent display, it proved little more than a superficial intervention, as the true core of his igneous frame remained unyielding in its unwavering defiance of any external force.

The fucker wouldn't die.

Then with a *pop*, the electricity surrendered, the entire house went dark, and Dr Cud stopped shaking, stopped glowing, and stopped being attracted to the magnet.

Tim backed away, dropping the wire as he realised the extent of his mistake. He turned to Lucy, whose expression had become grave, and without a word exchanged, the pair retreated slowly towards the door, to not wake the wrath they incurred.

As Tim glanced back, he froze, transfixed upon the furious silhouette of the man he foolishly believed he could kill, the final breath of sunlight reflecting off his smoking pupils, now emblazoned with impatient hate.

Dr Cud stumbled forward and swiped for Tim, his robotic arm lashing out clumsily across the room. Luckily for

Tim, the full force of Dr Cud's faculties was only beginning to return, allowing him to limp out of the way of the mounting tsunami of retribution and follow Lucy downstairs.

Dr Cud stood momentarily, allowing the last of his systems to reboot and the residual static to fade. Every circuit in his body was recharged and rejuvenated by the double helping of electricity now coursing through his veins.

Flexing his fingers, he sensed a strength within him he never knew he could possess. His mind was clearer, his senses more acute. He'd never felt more alive.

He made his way to the door and tried the handle.

Locked.

Even now, these fools underestimated him.

He rammed the door, testing the full limits of his newly overclocked strength. The door rattled in its frame, the hinges groaned, and the wood splintered as it buckled.

Dr Cud paused, his olfactory sensors detecting the warm charcoal scent of something behind him, something burning. He turned to find the mountain of paper strewn around the desk. Erupting into flames and spreading around him, consuming the room. He slammed his fist into the door again, this time more urgently.

***

Tim and Lucy clambered downstairs, past the forest of shrivelled hands slowly groping through the frozen, broken glass of the front door. One particularly wizened hand nearly reached the edge of the frozen football, the tip of their finger brushing against the door handle.

The pair ignored it for now and continued to the living room, finding it much different from how they left it. There was far less furniture for a start, as Sam threw most of it out the window at the shuffling horde of mounting pensioners;

cups, catalogues, cushions and a whole alphabet of other objects catapulted out.

"He's free! He got out! He escaped!" shouted Lucy and Tim in a chorus of mangled panic.

"It's alright though, I locked him in with the fire," finished Tim.

Jack didn't have the words. There were no words. He could only scream. However, the sound of the smoke detector and the banging from upstairs soon drowned him out.

There was only one thing that could save Jack now, his lone life raft in a sea of terror, inside of which his parents were still waiting for him, and it was currently upstairs, about to burn. Blind instinct took over, and Jack shoved his way past Lucy and Tim and, with his hands still restrained behind his back, ran up the pitch-black staircase like a penguin, trying his hardest to ignore the intermittent slam of the door frame and the screeching fire alarm growing louder.

As Jack reached the top step, a burst of flaming orange light cut through the darkness as Dr Cud smashed a hole through the spare bedroom's door. Black smoke poured through the newly made hole in the door, quickly extinguishing the light.

Jack made it to his bedroom, finding the air growing heavier by the second. He reached the small bedside cabinet and swung his body around so his hands could feel through the darkness of the drawer.

Once he got it open, Jack buried his hands through the sea of socks and briefs until he touched the smooth glass dome of the Time Machine at the bottom. He scooped it up in his clammy hands, feeling the grainy indentations of the wood against his fingers.

Who's great idea was it to make a time machine out of wood, anyway?

Jack squinted through stinging pupils, but could no

longer make out the path he took through his room. He took an unsteady step forward, following the trail of playful embers that danced through the smoke like fireflies.

With each invisible footprint, Jack felt himself growing weaker. He took a deep breath of the dark grey fog and felt it burn his lungs before bursting out in a violent stream of coughs.

Hot tar rose in his throat as Jack fought for air, but found only the thick darkness. He pushed on, wading through the pool of fumes, but felt his knee hit the floor, followed by the other, and then, finally, his head. The sound of shattered wood and the incessant screech of the fire alarm pierced through any salient thought he tried to cling to, leaving Jack to drown.

"Jack." he heard someone say, the sound of his own name swaying through the delirium.

"Can you hear me?" The words took on a dream-like quality, ushering Jack into unconsciousness, and he slipped away.

***

Sam burst into the room and found Jack lying face down on the floor, still holding the time machine behind his back. Sam shouted something to Jack, but the sound didn't make it, eclipsed by the smoke alarm, the thumping of the door and Jack's quickly fading consciousness.

"Jack, get up! We need to go!" shouted Sam, clumsily dragging Jack out of the room.

If Jack was going limp again just to spite him, Sam was tempted to leave him there. With a grunt, he hauled Jack onto the landing and paused, watching as the last fragile fibres of wood holding Dr. Cud gave way.

The door flew off its hinges with a blast of heat that sizzled

Sam's eyebrows. Dr Cud emerged through the pitch-black smoke of the fiery inferno, his grey suit quickly becoming ash as bright orange and yellow hues crackled around him. However, they paled compared to the fire within Dr Cud's eyes, a pure white light of distilled wrath.

Fuck that.

Sam wasn't about to face this literal demon, so he snatched the time machine from Jack's hands and clenched it to his chest.

In the blink of an eye, Sam was gone, carting Jack's unconscious body with him through the maelstrom of eternity. Every shade of blue shot past them in an instant until, finally, the whirlpool spat them out under a deep red sky.

Sam took them to the only place he could think of going.

The place where they would surely be saved.

The future.

39

Back in the present, twenty-six years, three months and two days earlier, a burning cottage was becoming overrun with old people. They breached the perimeters and were now shuffling their way inside, toward Lucy and Tim.

Tim wrestled an old woman's walking stick out from beneath her before jabbing it into her face in the most unheroic fencing move imaginable. Lucy punched a pair of reading glasses free from a man's wrinkled nose and slapped out a little old lady's hearing aid.

Together, Lucy and Tim fought through the crowd, kicking and jabbing against walls of wrinkled flesh. There must have been at least twenty of them now, hobbling through the cramped, moonlit hallway. Curious, however, was that they didn't seem to fight back, at least not anymore. In fact, they were barely paying attention to Lucy or Tim at all.

You wouldn't be amiss in assuming this was because of the smokey embers that were now making their way downstairs or the groaning of the weakening rafters in the ceiling, or simply because *the house was on fucking fire*. Yet these people weren't trying to escape the fire. They were following it, climbing the stairs toward the belly of the inferno.

Tim and Lucy pushed against the crowd but found themselves propelled towards the foot of the stairs until they saw precisely what everyone had been so interested in.

Above them, standing atop the staircase, was Dr Tobias Cud. His suit jacket charred away to nothing, and his shirt wasn't too far behind. His face was blackened with soot, and the sporadic wisps of hair on his head looked even patchier than usual.

As he descended the stairs, Lucy noticed he was still very much on fire, barbecuing what little of his skin remained. Each wooden step squealed and snapped as Dr Cud's foot pressed down onto them, and the crowds parted around him, bowing as he passed. Dr Cud soon spotted Lucy and Tim among his worshippers, and his stride quickened, mouthing something inaudible over the chimes of the fire alarm and the roar of the flames.

Lucy and Tim turned from him and attempted once more to fight their way to the front door, furiously battling through an unending tirade of bingo wings. Tim swung the walking stick, and Lucy dug her elbows into several jawbones, sending false teeth flying like confetti.

They soon reached what remained of the door, hanging from its hinges by a kicked-in pile of wood surrounding a punched-in window. Lucy turned back just in time to watch the electromagnetic slab fall through the ceiling, followed by burning beams and smouldering chunks of plaster. It all came down onto the herd of old people, burying half of them in an instant.

Tim grabbed Lucy and pulled her through the door. There was nothing she could do to help them.

They felt the cool evening breeze on their ashen, ash-covered faces and continued up the driveway.

Lucy ran to the police car and dove into the driver's seat. She felt like an imposter inside the vehicle, someone better suited to the back seat, wrapped in chains. Her hands dripped with sweat, and she had to wrestle to get the key into the wheel, dried blood cracking around the keyhole as she forced it in.

Tim hesitated outside the car, just for a second. He still didn't fully trust Lucy not to cart him back to the police station. Even now, literally metres away from a fiery death, his prejudice endured just a little bit, a crumb left on the dirty plate of his mind.

Peering back at the cottage, quickly becoming a pile of burning rubble, Tim decided: *screw the crumb*. He climbed into the passenger seat, staring out the window as Lucy pulled away.

The pair watched as the thatched roof caved in on itself, and a giant fireball of smoke shot into the air, reducing the entire house and everyone in it to kindling.

As the police car drove down the endless country lanes away from the cottage, Lucy saw in the wing mirror the stream of smoke climbing up through the sky, growing like an angry vine to the heavens.

"Do you think Sam and Jack made it out in time?" asked Tim.

"I don't know."

"What about *him*? Do you think he's dead?"

"No."

PART 5

THE FUTURE

40

Jack came to. The first thing he felt was dizziness, followed by pain, lots and lots of pain, shooting upwards from his chest and filling his head like a balloon.

Something was crushing him, steamrolling over his body, and then it stopped. Jack tried to inhale but couldn't as his chest squeezed down once more, harder this time. He felt his ribs fighting to stay in place, as what he could only assume was a blue whale tap-danced across them. Then it stopped again. Then it started again.

Jack tried to gain control of his eyelids and prised them open with a lot of willpower and all his remaining strength. Stinging through the light, his eyes struggled to make out the mess of bright yellow tentacles swaying above him.

No, not tentacles, seaweed maybe?

No.

Oh no.

It was Sam's disgusting, greasy, bleached blonde hair, with its single dreadlock. One Sam claimed he grew for fashion reasons, but Jack was pretty confident it formed on its own accord thanks to his appalling shower schedule, now brushing against Jack's lips. Jack opened his mouth to protest, or at the very least, breathe, but as he did, the dreadlock slipped in. Jack choked and spluttered as it brushed against his tonsils. The hair swooshed upwards, and there was Sam, straddling over his chest and thumping down on him like a jackhammer in a vague approximation of CPR.

"I did it! I saved your life!" Sam shouted into Jack's face, coating him with excited spittle. Sam leapt from Jack's torso to fist-pump the air in triumph.

Jack, un-triumphantly, rasped as he choked down big mouthfuls of air. He was pleasantly surprised to find the air was no longer warm and didn't burn his lungs. With Sam no longer beating down on him like a pair of bongos, Jack could finally get a good look at what was above him.

He saw a bright red sky with twisted branches of black smoke cascading through it. Jack rolled over onto his side and pressed his hands down onto the hard ground. Sam untied his wrists, at least. They weren't in the cottage anymore, that much was clear. Jack found he was lying on a road somewhere, an unkempt road, with chunks of dug-up tarmac piled around him.

Did Sam carry him out of the cottage and up the street?

Jack sat up, dreading what had become of the cottage, but found it gone. Instead, the backdrop to this new nightmare was the crooked remains of a decimated city. Dr Cud couldn't have done all this, certainly not this quickly.

Unless...

Jack noticed Sam was holding the time machine in his triumphant fist.

Of course.

Jack peered out across the colossal wreck, almost resembling Dr Cud himself, with its jagged, warped metal shooting out in every direction.

An old building lay on its side, half-sunk into the earth

before him, encircled by a moat of broken glass. Through the splintered window frames, Jack saw everything inside was reduced to crumbled husks of bricks and timber.

Around the building, the patternless destruction filling Jack's peripherals resembled a million knives pointed directly at him, ready to tear him to shreds. There was an odd familiarity to it all, as though he stood in this wreckage before and could name every scattered stone and twisted lamppost. Jack climbed to his feet to get a better look, gripping a charred wooden plank for support.

His entire body groaned as the strength slowly trickled back into his legs. From his new vantage point, Jack noticed the distant smoke bellowing upwards was coming from several spots along the horizon. This grim machination he found himself in must still be ticking along somehow. There was still something left to burn.

"What is this place?" asked Jack.

"Future," replied Sam.

"No, sure, getting that. What year?" said Jack, his voice echoing through the building's carcass in a chorus of terrified irritation.

"I don't know, future year, I just thought, '*future*.'"

Jack couldn't shake the familiarity clinging to this place, and then he realized why. The weathered plank of wood he was leaning against was a sign, quite a literal one, cracked in half, the paint peeling with age but unmistakable to Jack.

'*The Bell's End.*'

Most of the '*B*' was scratched away, causing the mangled letter to resemble an '*H.*' Which, in its current state, seemed far more fitting.

As Sam glimpsed the sign, the full force of where they were standing hit him. All those nights they spent there, all the drunken stories they shared, all the laughs, the tears, the fights, were now reduced to rubble beneath their feet.

"Oh Sam, what have you done?" whispered Jack.

"What have *I* done? I didn't do this. All I did was save your life," retorted Sam. *"Oh, thank you, Sam. I'm ever so grateful you saved my actual life. No problem, Jack. I know you'd do the same for me…"*

A sudden deep rumbling soon interrupted Sam's performance through the fractured landscape, causing the pair to freeze.

The rumbling continued, louder this time, like someone striking a gong. The sound bounced all around them from ruin to ruin in every direction.

Again, louder still, the sound rang out. The pair didn't know where it was coming from, but one thing was clear: it was getting closer.

Jack stumbled over to Sam and the time machine.

"Ok, Sam, thank you very much for bringing us here, and I mean that sincerely. But I'd like to go somewhere else now."

"Where?" asked Sam, a little too loudly for Jack's liking, causing him to reach out and press his hand over Sam's mouth.

"Just think of anywhere, anything, which isn't this place. Just like you did before." Jack's panicked whispers grew more frantic as the clanging grew louder.

"Home?" muffled Sam from behind Jack's palm.

Jack sensed Sam's warm breath and the wetness of his tongue brushing against his palm. "No, no, not home, somewhere else."

The sound chimed again, deafeningly loud this time. Jack's whole body shook as the vibration reverberated through his skull. Then he saw it, the source of the sounds. Footsteps.

Something was climbing through the wreckage of *The Bell's End*, each step ringing out as a figure, caked in shadow, stepped through bricks, pipes, and cement, crushing each into powder with every heavy footprint.

Jack caught a glimpse as it trudged past the collapsed window frames. He saw the robotic half first, then the fleshy half, stapled inelegantly together. Jack couldn't believe it.

How could *he* be here? Could he have followed them? Or did he simply wait all these years?

"Anywhere else," begged Jack into Sam's ear canal.

Sam tightened his grip on the time machine and tried to think, but couldn't. His mind struggled to focus on anything but the pile of metal and skin staggering toward them. Jack and Sam finally got a good look as it emerged from the pub and stepped into the blood-red daylight.

It wasn't Dr Cud.

"The fuck is that thing?" cried Sam.

Whatever that thing now was, it was once a woman. A long streak of black hair hung down over one side of her face, hair that had matted over the years, now taking on the appearance of an old dishcloth.

She wore a discoloured grey uniform, and poking through her ragged trousers was one fully robotic leg, clanging as she approached. The human side of her face, free from robotic protrusions was almost as grey as her uniform and sagged over her skull. As though what was once flesh died long ago, and only the mechanical elements of her still soldiered on, wearing her remains like an ill-fitting costume. But the soldier on it did, and it was coming for them.

She stopped about twenty feet away, cocking her head to one side curiously. Her vacant eye wobbled precariously in its socket, and a bright red light shone through the tangled dredge of hair beside it, scanning them.

Jack turned to Sam, who was staring wide-eyed with horrified awe, and held his remaining hand over Sam's eyes, now wholly masking his face from the world.

"Don't look at it, don't even think about it. Just concentrate on going somewhere safe."

"Is it still looking at us?" asked Sam.

Jack watched the creature staring back at them, unblinking. Her red light shone over them, glistening as she studied the pair.

"Nope, it's gone," he said, trying to sound reassuring. "Just please hurry."

"Analysis complete," croaked the automated speaker inside the flesh puppet.

The words were disjointed and emotionless, but not unfriendly. To Jack, this was the most terrifying thing he ever heard.

"Go!" screamed Jack.

Blue electricity catapulted out of the device, swallowing Sam and Jack up inside it. The fizzing blue light then collapsed, leaving only a few lingering sparks where they once stood.

The robotic creature cocked its head to the other side, puzzled. At least, she was for a few seconds before the universe reopened in a hail of sapphire hues, and Jack and Sam plopped out right in front of her.

Jack regained his bearings and found himself mere inches away from her cybernetic corpse, staring straight into her loosely hanging eye and its shimmering red counterpart. Her body was bloated and swollen, and at this distance, Jack saw her skin ripple as though something were crawling beneath it.

"We did it," announced Sam, mostly congratulating himself. *He* did it.

Jack lowered his hand from Sam's eyes so he, too, could witness the cold visage of what had once been a person. Sam peered up and down her monstrous form, noting the black cavities along her arms and hands, from where her body tried desperately to rot away, yet it could not.

A strange moment of silence descended upon them. No one moved, no one blinked, no one breathed.

Finally, Sam screamed as loudly as he could, pure terror escaping his body from somewhere deep inside, where all his childhood nightmares lie dormant.

The pair tried to run, but with the reflexes of a caffeinated hummingbird, the woman grabbed hold of them both in a vice-like grip that was all too familiar to Jack. Whatever this woman had become, it was unmistakably the work of Dr Cud.

"Is that really what the future is like?"

The questions were now becoming more frequent. The young boy was on his feet, restless and unable to keep his mind steady for more than a moment.

Six ice creams will do that...or was it seven?

His father thought it might be time to cut him off. Although, as he looked at him, a hyperactive ball of wide-eyed smiles, knowing what this young boy would soon have to face and how brave he would have to be, he thought better of it.

"Well?" said the boy, speaking through full cheeks that might burst at any moment. "Is that really what the future is like?"

"You see, the future differs from the past. It's not fixed. You can change it, or at least I hope you can. But at that moment, yeah, that was the future."

"But that's only if Dr Cud wins," said the boy, beaming a big, creamy smile.

When Dr Cud wins...

41

A young woman named Kirsty stood at the checkout of a supermarket. There were rows of checkouts in front of her and rows of checkouts behind her, stretching out to the furthest reaches of the store, and all unmanned except for hers. Although, it would scarcely make a difference if Kirsty weren't there either.

It was nearing 3AM, and the aisles were deserted. She'd be lucky to see anyone in the shop for at least a few more hours. So, with only the distant whirr of the fridges for company, Kirsty did what she always did and stared forward, watching the clock slowly tick away until it was time to leave.

But tonight would be different. Tonight, a police car screeched through the car park, carrying two people who came running into the supermarket, barely able to wait for the automatic doors to open before tumbling inside.

"Did you see anyone? Did they follow us?" asked the one dressed in a police uniform.

"I don't know. It was just one car. It could have been anyone," replied the one bandaged up and holding a walking stick, spinning back and forth around it as he glanced in every direction.

"Were there people inside?"

"It'd be pretty fucking weird if there wasn't," he said, sarcasm failing to mask his fear.

"You know what I mean. What did they look like?"

"I don't know, people, fucking people. They don't have a big red sign on their heads saying '*we're evil*,' do they?"

The policewoman paused, having spotted Kirsty.

"Hey, you!" she shouted, marching over to her. "Are you one of them? Are you?"

The man limped over, too, a little behind her. "She asked you a fucking question, didn't she?" he yelled.

Kirsty was baffled, not least because there were actually people here.

"Answer the question!" she shouted again.

Kirsty couldn't remember what the question was. Were they robbing her? It seemed unlikely, as one appeared to be a police officer.

"I don't know," said Kirsty, raising her hands in surrender. She hadn't needed to talk to anyone for a while, and the words didn't fall easily from her mouth. "I don't know what you want from me."

Lucy looked at the poor young woman, scared stiff and threatened by her no less. She was supposed to be helping people, not whatever this was. A sharp jolt of guilt caused Lucy to glance away from the cashier. She couldn't just accuse everyone. Perhaps it was just another car.

"Sorry," she muttered as she turned away, walking down an aisle.

Lucy paused as she noticed a familiar box of cereal lining the shelves beside her. It was the same one Lucy used to eat with her father each morning growing up. The cartoon monkey on the box smiled at her, teasing her, knowing she never could eat cereal with her father again, not after the things she did. She tore open the box and shoved her hand inside, chucking a fistful of cereal into her mouth.

Stupid monkey.

"Isn't that, like, a crime?" said Tim, limping after her, either acting as the voice of reason or rubbing it in just how far she'd fallen.

Who the hell was he to talk, anyway? He was still technically under arrest for crimes like...*murder*. Was she wanted by the police now, too? Were they looking for her? Were the people in the car undercover officers?

"I'm going to pay for it," barked Lucy through a mouthful of cereal mush.

"Alright, I was only asking," said Tim.

He was standing too close to her, following Lucy like a lost puppy. Why couldn't he leave her alone for a minute? Why couldn't the entire world be quiet for a single second?

"Where are we going?" asked Tim.

"I don't know," shrugged Lucy, reaching for another handful of cereal. "Whatever aisle has milk."

"And after that? Where the fuck even are we?"

Lucy tried not to think too hard on this. She drove there with no direction in mind other than far away, just as Jack did when they first met. Where could they go?

There wasn't anywhere left in the world that she considered safe. They would always be following. Even if there was somewhere they could go, they no longer had the means of reaching it.

The car's fuel tank was on '*E*' for a while, and Lucy had felt the car start to give up as she pulled into the supermarket car park.

"Look, I'm knackered. We need a plan, or somewhere to go, or just anything. I might even take your dad's help," continued Tim.

"No!" snapped Lucy. "No. Just no." She was tired.

The whirlpool of adrenaline, guilt, and fear she was swept up in could only take you so far. After a while, you had to eat; you had to sleep; you had to stop. But she couldn't stop.

For if she stopped, took even a moment, her mind might return to the thing she dared not think about, the thing she couldn't take back. Her mind flashed to his face, lying there, helpless and confused.

Shut up!

Lucy quickened her pace through the shop. She needed a distraction, and luckily, there was no short supply of those, especially now that she noticed a teenager browsing the pasta and a middle-aged woman checking out the gravy granules. This place had been empty a moment ago.

Lucy found her pace quickening, and upon reaching the end of the aisle and peeking down the next, she counted another three people.

She poked her head down at the one beside that; four more, no baskets, no trolleys, no one holding anything. Each one was simply standing there, pretending to look for something or other.

However, they all already found exactly what they were looking for and were now waiting for her and Tim to make a move, or run, or simply succumb to the weight of it all.

42

THE MECHANIZED CORPSE PULLED SAM AND JACK through the abandoned wasteland towards an ominous stream of black smoke in the distance, her leg ringing out with each uneven step.

They trailed along the ghosts of civilization, passing the broken bones of houses, the stripped remains of cars plundered of machinery, and deep craters in the ground where huge chunks of life were simply eviscerated without a trace. There were no graves, no flowers, nothing to preserve the legacy of those who once occupied this place.

Jack tried not to think too hard about what became of their bodies. He hoped they died painlessly, but as he looked at the thing escorting him, he thought it unlikely. Jack could now smell her fist gripped tightly around his and Sam's arms, a pungent mix of rotting flesh and burning sulphur.

"Anywhere, you could have taken us literally anywhere," whispered Jack.

"Well, sorry, but if there's an evil robot woman in front of me, it's difficult to focus on anything else," argued Sam.

"Correction," said the impassioned voice ahead of them. "I am not a robot. I am a human."

"Is this what all humans are like in the future?" asked Sam.

"Correction, this is the present. The current date is the 16th of May, 2051."

2051, Sam couldn't help but marvel at that. As terrible as this place was, it really was the future. He brought them to the future, albeit not as far as he first thought. After all, this was still in his lifetime. There was probably a cool older version of himself out there, with a beard and biceps. He probably had a scar over his eye from where he'd formed a resistance and taken down Cud's army single-handedly, maybe even a full eyepatch.

Although, on second thought, there didn't seem to be anyone left to form a resistance with. On third thought, wherever this supposed human was taking them would probably end in him dying anyway, so the cool beard, biceps, and scar were becoming less likely by the second.

"Well, you see," started Sam. "2051 is the future for us. We don't belong here, bit of a mix-up, so if you could just loosen your grip a bit, we'll go back to our own time. No hard feelings."

"Correction, you will be taken for testing to identify whether you are worthy of serving our leader, Lord Tobias Cud."

"And if we're not?" asked Sam, but found no response.

"Dr Cud," murmured Jack, looking out over the end of the world. He knew deep down, of course he did. The moment Jack glimpsed Frankenstein's robot, Jack knew *he* was responsible. Dr Cud, living forever at the expense of everyone and everything.

Worst of all, this meant that, in some small part, this was all Jack's fault. Perhaps he should've helped kill Dr Cud while he had the chance. But he hadn't. He tried to protect him and, in doing so, ensured this future.

How many died? How many were left alive?

They resentfully pressed on, arms dragged from their sockets, towards the smouldering beacon. As they drew closer, they found themselves caught in a storm of black soot raining down around them like the call of a volcano. The soot coated the ruins along their path, sucking the light from everything it touched.

Despite the choking darkness, Jack's familiarity with the route only grew, as did the knot in his stomach. With each exhausted stride, he became more sure of their destination and more terrified by it.

Precisely as Jack feared, they soon found themselves beneath the looming shadow of what was perhaps the only building left standing.

"Is that..." began Sam.

"Yeah," confirmed Jack.

They were standing outside the fossilized remains of their university. Its sleek, modern glass aesthetic gave way to an even more contemporary look, shattered chic. Poisonous shards clung to what remained of their metal frames like rows and rows of transparent teeth, ready to swallow them whole.

Their mechanized tour guide marched the pair inside the crystalline jaws of the university and ushered them deep down its pitch-black throat, leading them through the maze of corridors Jack and Sam once knew, only the faint red light of the machine's artificial eye lighting the way.

As they approached the belly of the beast, the ash footprints lining the halls gave way to bloodied ones. Handprints soon followed, smeared along pinboards and posters offering revision tips, indented with deep scratch marks of desperation.

They were far from the first to be brought here.

As they passed Greg's old seminar room, Sam couldn't

help but take a quick peek inside, wondering what became of it and if Greg might still be waiting for him inside.

He pushed on the door, which was repaired since his last time here, and found it wedged on something squishy. Sam tried again, pressing his weight against it and forcing the door open enough to reveal a slither of the room's new contents.

It was more than enough for Sam.

There was indeed something still alive in this new world. *Maggots*. Thousands of them, falling from the piles of decayed flesh, mounting from floor to ceiling of the room. Behind them was a large furnace, burning through the endless supply of offal. This was the source of the smoke, the desecrated remains of those deemed unworthy of *Lord Tobias Cud*.

Sam caught the faintest whiff of the smell consuming the room as it leapt through the gap in the door, wrapped around his throat, and choked at his soul.

The clanking contraption ahead of them pulled him onward, but Sam didn't protest, letting the door swing shut. As it did so, Sam's eyes locked with the piercing red lens of another decaying cyborg inside the room, dressed in a butcher's apron and tending to their collection. The cyborg squinted at Sam, a hint of recognition in its broken face, before it disappeared as the door closed.

Sam turned to Jack with a haunted expression plastered over his face, but Jack only stared back at him quizzically, ignorant of what lay behind the doors lining the corridors. He thought it best to keep it that way and forced an uneasy smile.

Deeper down they went, to where even the fingernails along the walls had given up the fight, the last of hope extinguished, and where light refused to tread. Jack didn't need to see to know where they were headed, and as the robotic corpse stopped, the inevitable was confirmed.

"We have reached our destination," announced their decaying sat nav.

They stood for a moment outside the door to Dr Li's classroom, basking in its cruel irony, except it wasn't irony at all. Where else would Dr Cud place the last level of his hell?

The robotic corpse ran her electronic digits across the wooden door, twitching along the scraps of police tape still clinging to it as she located the handle. She twisted it open and pulled her victims inside.

As they entered, they were met with a flickering stream of unsteady lightbulbs fizzing above them, trying their best to fight against the darkness. The room had power, maybe one of the few places left on earth that did, yet it was cold, like stepping into a fridge. The icy light dripped down onto the cannibalized remains of the lab, now repurposed to suit Dr Cud's dark will, leaving barely a trace of the place Jack knew: the epicentre of scientific endeavour, where anything had once seemed possible.

Yet now, it looked more like a cheap carnival ride than anything genuinely scientific. Half-dissected corpses of failed experiments lay atop every desk. A mass of computers and heavy machinery lined the walls, which blinked and beeped and coalesced into a mess of metallic tendrils at their centre, which weaved across the floor like snakes until they disappeared behind what was once Dr Li's desk. There, Jack saw someone typing away on a keyboard, obscured by the large chair they were sitting in.

"I have located two potential subjects," said the mechanized woman as she dragged Jack and Sam towards the desk.

The chair spun to face them. Jack expected to be greeted by one of the two doctors who had been pulling on his strings his entire life, and wasn't quite sure which of them he wanted to see less. However, found it to be neither, just another mechanically enhanced stranger, plugged into the metal cords.

To Sam, the unblinking fusion of human and machine

staring back at them was more horrifying than anything he could have predicted. Iron enveloped one side of its face like some futuristic phantom of the opera, but the side which remained human was well known to Sam.

"Amir," scoffed Sam, "I see you've achieved your dreams of becoming a computer."

"The guy from your coding lectures?" whispered Jack. "The one you're jealous of?"

"I'm not jealous of him. He's jealous of me."

Amir peered over the cords emanating from his chest and took in his two new subjects. Sam could smell the pomposity oozing from his pores. As he approached, Sam noticed that underneath all the metal, Amir looked the same as the last time Sam saw him, the same smug expression, the same neatly parted hair and the same stupid little bowtie protruding from his grey uniform.

Beneath the rusted coating, Amir was still the same goody-two-shoes Sam knew. He probably volunteered for the upgrade and offered to stay behind after it was done to help stack the chairs.

"Amir. That was my previous designation," said Amir in an impassioned nasally voice as he searched through what little remained of his decomposed mind. "Now, my only designation is to serve Lord Tobias Cud, a privilege that may be bestowed upon you if I deem you worthy."

Sam turned to the cyborg, who was still gripping his arm tightly. "You may as well kill us now, then."

"S-Sam," protested Jack.

He was aching all over and the frozen air was biting at him like a swarm of hungry piranhas.

"What? He is not going to deem us worthy. He hates me. Don't you, Amir? Ever since the time I accidentally knocked that can of Pepsi over your laptop when we first met."

Amir tilted his head, curious. "I don't recall such an event. Who are you?"

Sam's fingers curled. Fair enough, Amir was going to kill him, chop him up into pieces and burn him for fuel, but not so much as remembering him; that was the real insult. "Well, I suppose it has been a while, although you don't appear a day older. why?"

It was true; beneath the augmentation, Amir kept the same youthful sneer, if perhaps a shade bluer.

"I-Immortality," shivered Jack through chattering teeth. "That's what D-D-Dr Cud was trying to do."

"That is correct," said Amir. "These machines keep my body cryogenically frozen. As long as I stay plugged in, my cells are maintained at absolute zero, preserved in perfect stasis."

"I'm pretty sure freezing yourself kills you," chuckled Sam. "Makes sense though. I guess the dead don't age."

"I am not dead," hissed Amir, inheriting a touch of his master's temper. He stood up from the chair and approached Sam, freezing the air around him as he walked.

Sam desperately wanted to leave; he still had the time machine in his pocket, but the robo-woman was still holding onto them. It was all well and good going anywhere in history, but not if you're forced to bring the thing you're trying to outrun with you.

Maybe if he time travelled next to a wood chipper, she might appear inside it and- *no, too risky*. He would need to be smart about this; robots were just fancy computers, and he'd spent the last two years studying computing. He must have learnt somewhere in all those seminars how to beat one.

Amir's computer certainly didn't like it when Sam knocked the can of *Pepsi* over it, nor had Amir, for that matter.

He had no Pepsi.

Then, Sam realized. He didn't need to beat a computer... he just needed to beat Amir.

"Dr Cud asked you to not die, and what bright idea did you have? To make yourself a human popsicle!" laughed Sam. "That's not the over-achieving Amir I used to know. No gold star for you."

"I didn't die," said Amir, frozen spittle flying from his lips, fists raising to his sides.

"What are you going to do? Hit me? Come on, I know you want to. Hit me. Or are you too dead to fight back?" Sam erupted into a flurry of chicken noises, clucking and flapping as much as his restrained arm would allow.

"You always were such a moron."

Sam smiled; he remembered him. "Well, at least I'm not a dead moron."

With that, Amir reached his limit, and his frozen fist flew towards Sam, just as Sam hoped it would. He ducked out of the way, and the fist collided with the face of their captor.

Amir's petrified hand shattered as it sent the mechanized woman reeling backwards, the subzero temperatures momentarily freezing her circuits. Her grip relinquished long enough for Sam and Jack to break free.

"Run!" yelled Sam, and so they did.

They bound out of the classroom and darted as fast as their legs would carry them back along the pitch-black halls.

Amir looked down at his fist, its broken pieces scattered across the floor. With his remaining hand, he tore the cables, anchoring him to his life-support machine, ripping them from his chest. He would show that moron how much life he had in him.

Sam and Jack ran for their lives once more, as they always did. They heard Amir's footsteps closing in on them through the darkness, slamming furiously against the ground. Sam grabbed hold of Jack and held out the time machine, concentrating on being anywhere other than here. He closed his eyes tightly, thinking of his mom, dad, and Molly.

"Sam, no!" screamed Jack, spotting a faint red light piercing through the darkness ahead.

Pain washed over Sam in a dizzying smack to the head. He clattered to the ground as his brain turned about in his skull, screaming out a stinging symphony that ran along his entire body.

Sam opened his bleary eyes, half expecting to see a chorus of birds floating around his head. Instead, he saw a stream of red light slicing through the darkness until it settled on him.

Towering over Sam was another one of Dr Cud's undead minions. Sam crawled backwards towards Jack, who was busy panting out another of his signature asthma attacks. This new aggressor didn't seem interested in following Sam. Instead, it knelt down, picked something off the ground, and held it close to its piercing red pupil.

The time machine!

Neither Sam nor Jack dared to move a muscle. They could only watch this monster through the half-light of its own luminescent eye as it turned the time machine over in its surprisingly human-looking hands.

"Sam!" roared a familiar voice, not from the thing ahead of them, but from behind them.

They were both so transfixed by their current misfortune that they failed to notice the growing clanking of the previous one. Amir soon caught up with them, and his own artificial eye lit up the monster in an unholy crimson spotlight.

Standing before them, in a long, bloodied apron, was the butcher Sam had locked eyes with earlier, and now their eyes locked once more. The small flap of skin composing what Sam thought might've once been a man's face was almost entirely consumed by bolts, cogs and old clock parts.

"Sam," echoed the butcher as it looked up from him and

turned his sights to Amir, his mechanical eye clicking and adjusting to focus on him.

There was a strange momentary standoff where the two cyborgs stared at one another without saying a word.

Then, in one swift movement, the butcher withdrew a pistol from his apron and fired it. A large pellet shot through the air past Jack and Sam, who followed it as though watching a tennis match. The bullet plunged into Amir's chest, embedding itself and sending out a thick current of plasma coursing through his body.

Amir jolted back and forth erratically as his body cooked and exploded, his frozen form fracturing into a million pieces, leaving only a pile of metal, a grey uniform and a singed bowtie on the floor where Amir once stood.

Future gun, Sam thought to himself. He hadn't accounted for just how terrifying the prospect of one might be when you were on the wrong end of it.

The butcher turned his attention to Sam and Jack, looking between them, still pointing his future gun and still holding the one object that could get them home.

"Control, alt, delete," commanded Sam with a click of his fingers. "Enter sleep mode."

It was worth a try.

The robot-man-robot-butcher-thing, whatever the hell it was, raised its surprisingly human, surprisingly small hand to its face and gently tapped it. The metal ingots coating his features folded away, overlapping until they all tucked away inside a small projector on his temple, revealing a human face behind.

"Is this what I think it is?" he said in a profoundly posh accent as he held up the time machine.

Sam and Jack both remained silent.

"Where on earth did you find it?" he continued.

Sam and Jack still didn't reply or even move, fixed to the spot with confusion and terror.

"Are you chaps alright? You look like you've seen a…" He stopped, looking at the time machine once more and then at the two men cowering before him. "Oh, I see. You're not from around here, are you? My apologies."

He tapped more parts of his body, and several latches running down him flicked open. He hopped down and walked over to Sam, leaving a set of mechanical legs behind him. The man in this strange costume birthed was in his early fifties and stood no taller than three and a half feet.

He strode purposefully through the ash, his long apron dragging along the ground behind him. As he reached them, Sam could see there was nothing robotic about him at all. He was human, properly human.

He stopped before Sam and held out a hand, ready to be shaken. "Name's Miles Cross. Sam, wasn't it?"

Sam glanced over at Jack and then back at Miles. He didn't seem evil, and he just killed Amir, both pluses in his book. So Sam shook the man's hand.

"As for you, your name wouldn't happen to be Jack, would it?"

Jack squeaked out a tiny noise of affirmation and nodded.

"Well, isn't that a jolly bit of luck?" said Miles with a smile.

43

TIM AND LUCY WALKED THROUGH THE supermarket as calmly as they could, which wasn't very calm at all. There were now hundreds of them, crowding the aisles, each one patiently watching the pair's every move as they made their way back towards the entrance.

In every direction they looked, more and more eyes stared blankly back. Of course, Tim and Lucy never truly believed they could escape that easily, and as they reached the large sliding doors, their suspicions were confirmed.

A barrier of people stood, blocking the way. Yet, their presence there caused the automatic doors to remain open, making the promise of escape all the more enticing.

Lucy glanced around for an alternative, unguarded escape route. She saw Kirsty still standing at the checkout, panicking and jabbing at buttons on the cash register. The till slid open with a chime and a clunk, and Kirsty fished out a handful of notes.

Kirsty grabbed one divider with her other hand and held it in front of her like a sword to fight these lunatics back. She threw the money at Tim and Lucy, and it clumsily fluttered in the surrounding air.

"Just take the money. Whatever the hell is going on, I don't want any part of it. Take it and leave me alone."

Before Lucy could stop her, Kirsty set off towards the door, reaching the group, and jabbing the divider at them.

"Get out of my way!" shouted Kirsty as they encircled her, closing in until Tim and Lucy could no longer see what was happening.

They heard some confused yells, a couple '*let me go*'s' and finally, a single blood-curdling snap.

The people all shuffled back into their line, leaving Kirsty's broken body crumpled on the floor in front of them.

Lucy stiffened, a horrified gulp of sickening guilt building in her throat. She turned away, unable to look, and walked deeper into the shop.

"Why the fuck did you do that?" shouted Tim at no one in particular.

He wasn't talking to the people ahead of him. Instead, he was addressing the man controlling them.

"She had nothing to do with this. You're here for me and..." he looked round. Lucy was gone. It didn't matter. "You want to go? Let's fucking go. I'll take on all you pricks right here and now."

Tim pressed his walking stick into the ground and stood firm, daring them to try.

A few of them stepped forward, seeming to accept Tim's challenge.

Perhaps he didn't totally think this through; too late to back out now. He looked for something to use as a weapon and found only a fun-sized bar of chocolate. He lobbed it at the approaching opponents to no avail. He needed something heavier than chocolate.

An idea filled Tim's head, and he suddenly knew what he

needed. He was in enough fights in enough bars to know what makes the perfect weapon in a pinch, one that would even the odds a little. So, he turned away and limped down the aisles, pushing through the still, mostly docile crowds of zombified shoppers. Tim doubted they would stay docile for long. They reminded him of one of the drug-induced documentaries he half-watched about beekeeping.

These people were like the bees, all ketamined up with whatever the beekeeper had pumped into them. After a while, the gas wore off, and the bees woke up, and Tim remembered them looking pissed. He need to be ready when these bees did the same.

LUCY TRIED HER HARDEST TO DRIVE AWAY THE thoughts of murder and death and killing and so, so many bodies that she saw in her first couple of days as a police officer. No, not a police officer anymore. She was a criminal, a killer, and if Lucy didn't come here tonight, the woman at the checkout would still be alive.

Lucy caught her bearings and found herself wandering into the kitchenware aisle, one of the few parts of the supermarket that was still relatively quiet. As Lucy scanned the shelves, she found knives, big ones.

So, Lucy grabbed a large, serrated bread knife from the hook and tried to tear through its blister packaging, gnawing at the corners, but the hard plastic wouldn't budge. She needed scissors. Lucy ran her eyes along the aisle until she found the perfect pair...in the same blister packaging.

No exits, no weapons.

Lucy stared down the aisle and found a middle-aged man with a beard and no hair and a twelve-year-old girl with hair and no beard standing at the end, silently watching her.

"Leave me alone!" yelled Lucy as she threw the knife.

The packaging frisbee'd through the air and hit the child between the eyes, knocking her back. Lucy felt another pang of guilt but quickly boarded the door shut. They weren't people anymore. Most likely, they weren't even alive.

There were more of them now, all calmly staring at Lucy like spectators in a zoo. She scooped up more blister packaging and hurled them, sending big armfuls of utensils flying down the aisle.

"Just go away!" screamed Lucy, grabbing the shelving, pulling the whole thing down and burying the gathered crowd.

The fallen shelves wobbled slightly as the people beneath found themselves trapped. With a satisfied smirk, Lucy marched over them and into the next aisle.

This one had toys.

TIM APPROACHED THE SPIRITS, BOTTLES OF ALCOHOL lined shelves piling to the ceiling. He grabbed a bottle of whiskey and unscrewed the cap. Whiskey was Tim's drink of choice if he wanted to appear intimidating to an audience, and he had a pretty healthy audience right now.

"You don't mind?" asked Tim as he took a deep sip, letting it burn his throat. He lowered the bottle and exhaled a small refreshing "aaah."

Tim couldn't hold this off any longer. The bees were swarming, and they were ready to sting. He gripped the whiskey bottle by its neck and shattered it into the side of the shelf with a single flick of his wrist. Whiskey ran down his arm as he presented the remaining half of the bottle: the ultimate pub weapon.

"Back up!" warned Tim, corralling the bees away.

Tim heard a motor buzzing through the supermarket. The crowd turned their attention from Tim to see what was going on, and one by one, each of them went down like bowling pins.

Tim followed their gaze and found Lucy, the queen bee, buzzing loudly and stinging everything in sight. She was charging through, holding a huge motorized gun in each hand and wearing a bandolier of foam darts across her chest. She ran through, screaming away her guilt as she fired her guns wildly, taking down anyone in her path and covering the floor with bodies.

Tim painfully knelt to inspect Lucy's handiwork and saw several foam darts stuck to the face of one of her victims. With some effort, he plucked out a bloodied dart and found a nail jammed through the end of the rubber tip.

Above him, a hail of darts fired over his head, taking down another six who made the mistake of getting too close. She was definitely no police officer Tim had ever seen before, not now she was going full of *Tony Montana-Kevin Mcallister.*

Tim pushed down on his walking and got back to his feet, finding himself caught in a burly man's bear hug. He struggled and shoved, but the man's unrelenting grip grew tighter. Slipping his hand free, he wasted no time plugging the broken bottle into the man.

The man's grip loosened, and he fell off Tim and to the floor, the bottle now firmly embedded into his forehead and filling with blood. Tim didn't have time to decide how he felt about that, as several more bees were already approaching.

He snatched more bottles from the shelf, vodka, brandy, and spiced rum, and lobbed them one after another. Each bottle smashed into a different face, taking them out. However, this didn't deter the amassing army, who simply stepped over the bodies of their fallen comrades to get closer to

Tim and Lucy, overwhelming them and forcing them together.

The pair refused to give in, so with their backs to one another, they spun around, Lucy blasting a storm of bullets and Tim using a gin bottle like a baseball bat.

Click. Click.

Lucy was out of bullets. The gun's motor chewed at the bandolier, but there were no darts left.

Tim reached out for another weapon and found only a single bottle of tequila remained. The rest were reduced to pools of alcohol, blood, and broken glass beneath his feet.

No, it couldn't end like this. Tim refused to accept it, so reached into his pocket and plucked out his last gambit. A bright pink plastic lighter, melted and blackened from the last time, Tim's options were equally thin on the ground, back in the seminar room with Greg. That seemed like years ago now.

But Tim's hand was steady this time.

He remembered the cottage.

He remembered the fireworks.

He flicked the wheel, and it sparked to life, the warm orange glow dancing above his fingers.

"Stop, or we all go up," ordered Tim, and the bees obliged.

Lucy turned to him. This was a bluff, right? He surely wouldn't do it. She saw the fear and the certainty in his eyes. *Please let this be a bluff.*

"I'll do it, I'll fucking do it," confirmed Tim, waving the lighter around.

If the alternative was to become one of them, burning to death would surely be a mercy. Plus, he supposed, with that much alcohol burning up all at once, he might just die drunk. He might not even feel it.

Tim remembered the white-hot sparks of the fireworks raining down on him, melting through his skin, and knew he would feel this too, every horrific second, but he didn't know if he could do that to Lucy.

A day ago, Tim wouldn't have cared what happened to her. She was the police, and she had it out for him like all the rest. But not anymore, they were in this together now.

Shit.

He couldn't do it.

As the flame went out, a small chime echoed overhead, followed by a tinny voice over the PA system. *"Lucy Sparks to checkout four, please. That's Lucy Sparks to checkout number four."*

Tim and Lucy recognized that maliciously arrogant tone at once. *He* had survived.

Tim once again flicked the lighter. All he needed to do was loosen his grip just a little, and this would all be over. He gripped the gold chain around his neck, begging himself to be strong enough to do it.

"I have someone here who wants to talk to you," continued the voice on the PA.

A second voice then spoke, a woman's voice, who uttered a single word. *"Lucy."*

Lucy's brain shivered. She knew the voice. Of course she did.

It was a voice she hadn't heard in a very long time, yet she remembered every inflexion perfectly, as the voice would still sometimes whisper to her in her dreams.

44

Miles escorted Jack and Sam from the university and back through the abandoned ruins of the streets beyond. The projector attached to his face transformed him back into his mechanized visage, and he was once more walking around on his stilt legs, strolling forward with ease, clearly well-versed in this disguise.

The only giveaway was his arms didn't poke through the ends of his shirt sleeves.

"Heads down, keep walking," whispered Miles.

"Where are we going?" asked Sam.

"Somewhere safe from Lord Cud's influence."

"Where is he now?" asked Jack, his eyes twitching nervously along the wreckage, waiting for him to crawl from the shadows.

"Don't have the foggiest idea. There were rumours he died years ago. I think you would be a fool to believe that. I know he's here somewhere, hiding, still labouring away on his cure for death and a working time machine...and here you pair show up with half of that. You two are famous around these parts, and not for good reasons, which means my top priority right now is keeping you safe."

Miles recognized their names from the daily announcement and knew how much Lord Cud hated them. If someone that powerful could dedicate enough of his mind to hate two seemingly inoffensive boys, they must be pretty important. Eyeing the time machine, Miles saw why. They were the key to stopping this.

"What is that?" asked Sam as he trailed off, spying something glistening in the corner of his eye.

He chased after the light like a cat, climbing over rumble and ducking beneath girders, almost entranced by its shine, until he reached its source. Sam found himself before a large marble plinth, on which stood a golden statue of Dr Tobias Cud, standing two stories tall and capturing every fine detail and likeness of the man's splintered body. Except this portrait of him was wearing a crown and ceremonial robes, and he was pulling a suitably pompous expression fitting his attire.

The monument held one fist outstretched to the sky in a grandiose portrayal of his power, because a golden, narcissistic statue clearly wasn't enough to show it already. In its other hand, the statue held something horrifyingly curious: the time machine, immaculately sculpted in gilded majesty.

Sam couldn't help but marvel at the statue, untouched amongst the surrounding craters of destruction, without a single scratch or fingerprint on it.

The others soon caught up to Sam, and Jack read the inscription on the plinth.

"In honour of our bountiful provider, Lord Tobias Cud. Tomorrow is forever in our grasp."

Jack scoffed at it. *Bountiful provider.* What had he provided? Other than the statue, obviously.

"Is this genuine gold?" asked Sam, reaching out his hand.

"Don't touch it!" shouted Miles, but it was too late.

Sam's index finger lightly pressed against the structure's solid gold leg, and Lord Cud's all-seeing eyes glowed red, bearing down on Sam.

Then the entire statue moved, creaking and grinding as it bent down, and the once triumphant fist closed around Sam.

"Sam!" called Jack, banging on the side of the golden fist and trying to force open its giant fingers.

The fist rose, lifting Sam as his legs kicked frantically beneath.

"Do something!" yelled Sam.

"Oh blimey, ok, remain calm," instructed Miles, primarily to himself.

Miles grabbed his future gun from its holster and loaded a pellet into the barrel. He closed one eye, took aim, sticking his tongue out for good measure, and focused on the fist as it rose above them.

Miles pulled his finger back on the trigger and fired. The pellet whizzed through the air and struck the statue's fingernail, getting to work immediately. The fingernail glowed as it filled with the pellet's enormous power.

The statue's grip around Sam weakened, and Sam slipped free, falling ten feet to the ground like a discarded wrapper. He landed on his backside and glanced up to see molten gold dripping down around him, eating through the rubble at his feet.

Sam scurried back, escaping the deadly shower, but Lord Cud wouldn't let Sam go that easily, and the statue opened its mouth to speak.

"*Treason detected! Treason detected!*"

"It's calling for reinforcements! We have to get out of here, chaps! Follow me!" shouted Miles, hoping they could hear him over the statue.

Miles ran, his stilt legs bounding across the desolate wasteland, weaving through fallen streetlamps and ripped-up tarmac, with Jack and Sam haphazardly following, trying their best to keep up.

Behind them, the streets filled with robotic life in a percussive symphony of clunking and scraping as shadows shifted from the darkness, barely a trace of anything human left among their corroded flesh.

Miles reached a manhole cover and heaved it up, forcing it out of the ground with all his strength. He beckoned Sam and Jack over and began climbing down the ladder, deeper and deeper into the darkness. Jack and Sam were initially hesitant to follow. Still, they quickly reconsidered upon seeing the hordes of mutilated cyborgs closing in from every direction.

The pair promptly scampered down the frigid ladder, trying not to slip on its murky coating. Sam pulled the manhole cover back into place just in time as the army of metal feet trampled overhead.

Jack reached the bottom of the ladder and landed in a cold puddle of the foulest-smelling thing he'd ever laid his nostrils upon, gagging as the stretch of sewage hammered its way into him. Miles assured him he would get used to it, but Jack wasn't so sure.

They soon learnt that this wasn't a puddle, but more like a river as they walked for hours through the infinite tunnel of pitch-black filth. With every squelchy footstep, Jack tried his hardest not to throw up.

Sam seemed unperturbed by the smell; he'd encountered far worse. His mind turned to the greying mountains of maggot food in Greg's classroom, and he couldn't help but wonder if anyone he knew might be buried amongst it, maybe even his family.

They eventually saw a tiny speck of light in the distance and followed it to a brick wall, where the light twinkled through the cracks of the mortar. Miles got to work tapping the bricks and as he did so, the bricks lit up, red, blue, yellow, green, yellow again. He operated the wall like a keyboard, tapping on what Jack and Sam soon learnt was a passcode.

Miles completed the sequence, and the brick wall shimmered out of existence, revealing an underground train station on the other side, empty, abandoned and dilapidated, like everything else. This place at least had light pouring down from the overhead fixtures. Something was feeding this place with electricity.

They followed Miles onto the platform, glad to be standing on solid ground again. Jack would have to burn these boots, the socks too, maybe even the feet beneath.

Miles hopped down from the platform and onto the track, where he arranged a large steel barbecue next to an old settee and a couple of deck chairs. Behind it stood a solitary train carriage, stationary and coated in several layers of graffiti and rust. "*Here we are, home sweet home.*"

The carriage door swooshed open as though greeting him back, and Miles climbed in, beckoning Jack and Sam to follow. "This is where the magic happens."

Sam and Jack followed him inside with bated breath, and were met with...the inside of an old train carriage, the only difference was that this one had an old grey blanket laid out across the seats, a few books on the floor and an old 90s computer monitor hooked up in the corner.

Sam could hardly believe it. This wasn't at all the secret base he was promised. The guy didn't even have a pillow.

"Where is everyone? Where's the resistance? Where's your charismatic leader who turns out to be me?"

"There is no one else," said Miles, disconnecting from his disguise, throwing off his apron and climbing onto one of the long rows of seats lining each side of the carriage.

"Just me."

45

THE SOUND THROUGH THE PA SYSTEM CUT THROUGH Lucy's mind like a razor, carving out a very clear path for her, and she knew exactly what she needed to do.

She dropped her guns, snatched the bottle of tequila from the shelf and threw back a long, acrid mouthful. Then, without a word said, she began her long walk through the supermarket as the crowds parted around her like *The Red Sea*. Tim followed as best he could, limping after her.

"Who was that then?" asked Tim. "That voice, you recognized it, didn't you?"

Lucy didn't answer, continuing through the electronics aisle lined with televisions, each one displaying a close-up of a frail woman repeating Lucy's name over and over, beckoning her. Lucy didn't even bother to glance at them. These cheap theatrics would not slow her down.

The crowds continued to part, and as she reached the centre of the supermarket, Lucy found the source of the broadcast. There was the woman who called her name, kneeling on the tiles beside her master like an obedient pet.

Lucy allowed herself only a cursory glance at the woman,

but that was enough to confirm that it was definitely her. No, her sights were on the devil standing over the woman's shoulder, the harbinger of death who took everything there was to take from Lucy. There stood Dr Cud, donning a new suit and biting his lip in anticipation of the grand reunion he organized. Lucy approached him, fear long since replaced with distilled hatred, and met his gaze.

There was a faint hint of disappointment behind the layers of machinery. This wasn't going quite as he expected. No crying, no begging, not even a single word. He went to a lot of trouble arranging this meeting, yet Lucy barely seemed interested in it.

Lucy stared deeply into Dr Cud, face to face with the man she hated more than anything. The supermarket fell silent, perhaps the entire world too, as everyone waited for Lucy to make a move.

After a long moment, she calmly reached into her police jacket, removed a dark plastic cylinder, and flicked it downwards.

Clunk, clunk, clunk.

Three bright blue tiers of hard plastic sprung out the end, and Lucy readied her *lightsaber,* gripping it with both hands and readying herself for battle. There was a *Star Wars* range in the toy section, and Lucy was a dab hand with a lightsaber. Her dad had shown her all the movies soon after her mom…

She gripped tighter, and the toy's cheap speaker hummed.

Tim watched cautiously from a distance. *What the hell was she doing?*

"You're kidding," said Dr Cud, legitimately taken aback.

She wasn't kidding. Lucy swung the lightsaber as hard as she could and smacked it into his face, the boldness of her absurdity knocking him off guard. He wouldn't allow another. Dr Cud held his robotic arm over his face to defend himself, effortlessly blocking the onslaught of strikes whizzing and whirring around his skull. Lucy continued striking the lightsaber, denting it against Dr Cud's robotic features.

Lucy brought it down on him with all her might. Dr Cud shielded himself with his forearm, catching the lightsaber against the side of his wrist and resisting it, forcing the lightsaber back, surprised at how much strength it took. Lucy fought on, pressing the lightsaber into his wrist until the plastic gave. Their eyes locked, their faces inches from one another. Right where she wanted him.

Lucy spat a big mouthful of tequila into Dr Cud's eyes, spraying a stream of spitty orange liquid that she was concealing in her cheeks like a hamster.

Dr Cud stumbled back, blinded behind a layer of liquor, and tripped backwards onto the floor. Lucy dove into him, setting all her rage free, all the pain, and regret, and hate which consumed her was beaten away with every smack of the lightsaber. Her stoic silence was gone. Now she was screaming.

Tim joined her, whacking the more human-looking parts of Dr Cud's anatomy with his walking stick.

Dr Cud took blow after blow, slamming into his body, until the lightsaber bent to a nearly ninety-degree angle, and the walking stick snapped in half. Still, the pair refused to stop.

"Enough!" ordered Dr Cud, the way a headmaster would to an assembly of recalcitrant students. He hauled himself up, shaking off the wrinkles in his suit, and grabbed Lucy's lightsaber, swatting it from her hands.

He tightened his vice-like grip around it until the plastic shell snapped in two and tossed it aside. He shoved Tim backwards into the crowd, and a forest of limbs fired out around him, restraining him.

With no more ridiculous distractions up her sleeve, Dr Cud set his sights on Lucy, snatching her up by her hair and tearing follicles from her scalp as he dragged her over to the woman. His revenge would go as planned even if he had to force it.

"Perhaps you don't recognize her. After all, it's been a while," hissed Dr Cud. "Get a good look."

He held Lucy's head against the woman like a dog presented with its own excrement. Lucy tried to free herself, but the more she struggled, the tighter Dr Cud gripped until the pain forced her to do as she was told.

With little choice, Lucy took in the full extent of the woman: her stick-thin figure made up of skin stretched tightly over bone, her spine hunched over with greying black hair draping over her pale face, her lips which had a sickly blue about them, and her eyes which were sunken into deep, dark rings.

"That's it. Now tell me who she is."

Lucy mumbled something through the sharp breaths of pain.

"I can't hear you!"

"My mom," cried Lucy. "She's my mom."

"You can really see the resemblance, can't you? I completely forgot she was part of my collection. Still, I knew you looked familiar," said Dr Cud, his voice becoming unhinged as it filled with cruel excitement. "She was one of my earliest test subjects. It turns out addicts are the perfect volunteers. When you offer them a pill, they rarely ask what's in it."

Her mother stared at Lucy, and Lucy stared back into her mother's hazel eyes, like a key, unlocking all the memories Lucy tried so hard to forget. Maybe there was a glint of her left inside. Maybe...

"Go on," teased Dr Cud. "Say something to her. I know you want to. Perhaps through the power of love, she'll remember you."

Lucy did indeed want to say something. A small part of

her was screaming out, begging herself to try getting through to her, but she wasn't about to give Dr Cud the satisfaction. Lucy's mother was dead and gone, and seeing her now didn't change that.

"Oh, you're no fun," sulked Dr Cud. He released his grip and tossed Lucy to the ground. "Tie her up. Him too."

His army obliged, scooping up Lucy and Tim with ease, neither one having the fight left in them to struggle.

46

Miles flipped the burgers over. They sizzled as they splashed down on the bubbling fat of the barbecue grill. He pressed the rusted spatula down onto the slabs of meat and a mouth-watering smell spilled out, filling the platform.

After a moment, he slipped the spatula beneath the burgers and peeled them from the grill, charred to perfection. There were no buns, of course. They all passed their use-by dates decades ago. Lots of ketchup, though.

"Here we are, chaps. Delicious," said Miles as he presented Jack and Sam with their paper-plate feasts.

Jack awkwardly smiled, hoping it came across as grateful rather than repulsed. He politely took a bite from the smashed hunk of meat, fighting to get it down.

"What is it?" asked Sam, his skepticism overriding the politeness Jack had fallen prey to.

"Mystery meat," said Miles, ravenously tucking into his own plate of sizzled gristle.

Sam saw meat like this before, in the bowels of the university. He remembered Miles walking through the abattoir in his bloodied apron, selecting the perfect cuts.

"Is this people?" exclaimed Sam, dropping the plate.

At that, Jack gagged and spat out what was in his mouth, using his finger to scrape any remaining remnants from his tongue.

"Heaven's no. What kind of ghastly beast do you take me for? These are rat burgers." assured Miles with a smile.

Jack noticed something out of the corner of his eye: a small, damp bundle of fur with a long, skinny tail scampering down the tracks beside them. He scraped harder at his tongue.

"Miles, no offence," began Sam, absolutely about to offend. "This place, it's great and all...but it's also a massive shit-hole."

Miles sipped from a glass of indiscriminate, murky liquid, trying to hide his disappointment.

"You're living in the sewers," continued Sam. "Eating rat and drinking...what's got to be at least partly piss."

"It's perfectly drinkable," said Miles, trying to claw back a slither of dignity.

"Come back with us. Help us save the world. We can change all this."

Miles looked up at Sam, suddenly beaming. All these years alone, Miles heard nothing so beautiful. The prospect of going back to a world free from nightmares and stopping them from ever happening was almost too much to take.

"You'd take me with you?"

"Of course. It's the least we could do."

Jack fiddled with the time machine in his lap, running his hands along the grooves of its wooden shell. He saw it was fully charged. The three LEDs were bright green, a literal indicator of his fear, cowardice, and lack of control over an unfair world, and now here he was at the very end of it.

As Jack considered the present that awaited them, the present Sam was proposing they revisit, he realized this place really wasn't so bad. After all, they had shelter, light, and all the dead rat they could eat. The LEDs only grew brighter as he thought about returning. Jack felt the dread sewn into his skin growing and knew he could never go back. It would be an unwinnable fight, a death sentence. It wasn't his responsibility. He had no reason to die trying to stop a crazy person. It was someone else's turn.

Jack noticed Miles and Sam watching him expectantly.

"No," whispered Jack under his breath.

"No? What do you mean, no? Of course Miles can come. He took out one of those robot people and the massive statue all on his own. We need him."

"No." Jack repeated, a slight hint of an assertion this time. "We're not going back."

"Has that rat meat gone to your head?"

"If we go back, he'll kill us," snapped Jack. "Look around you. He wins. There's no killing him. There's no stopping him. I think...I think the best thing we can do is hide."

"What, so you'd rather we all just live here for the rest of our lives? Crawling through the sewers like a rat, eating other rats and drinking our own piss? No offence, Miles."

"Of course not, don't be ridiculous!" blurted Jack. 'Erm, no offence, Miles.'

Again, Miles had taken some offence.

"We can go anywhere," continued Jack. "We could even go to a time before any of this ever happened."

"What about Tim, and Lucy, and my family, and everyone we ever knew?"

"It's a time machine. They'll still be there for as long as we like."

"You can't put this off forever," Sam warned him.

"Yes, I can. Of course I can. I have a time machine." Jack let out a sigh. "Why would I expect you to listen to me? You never listen to me."

"Jack," began Sam, his voice growing stern as he got to his feet.

"What are you going to do? Tie me up like the last time I disagreed with you?" scoffed Jack.

"We had to. You were in the wrong. You weren't there for us. If you helped us kill him with all your science knowledge, this would be over by now. You were wrong then, and you're wrong now. You're a coward."

Jack leapt up from his seat at that. It wasn't cowardice. He was being realistic. What Sam possessed wasn't bravery, it was foolishness, always ready to jump gung-ho into everything without once thinking of the consequences.

Jack made his way to leave, but Sam blocked his path.

"Fine. We'll go without you. We don't need a whiny little scaredy cat, do we, Miles?"

Miles kept silent. As much as he wished more than anything to go back, he understood Jack's fear.

"Give me the time machine," said Sam, holding out an expectant hand.

"No." said Jack through gritted teeth as he tried to push past Sam.

Again, Sam stopped him, pushing him back a little harder than he meant to. Jack retaliated by shoving Sam, and the match was lit.

Sam charged at Jack, trying to snatch the time machine from his hands. Jack responded with an elbow to the ribs, and Sam grabbed Jack in a headlock. It was hardly the most formidable battle Miles had ever witnessed.

"Let it go!" yelped Sam as he tried to prise open Jack's fingers.

"No, you can't have it! I'm not going back there! I'm never going back!" yelled Jack, pushing his clammy palm into Sam's face.

Miles eventually stepped in, breaking them up as they rolled back and forth along the tracks.

"Stop this at once! The pair of you are acting like children."

Jack stormed off to the train carriage with a huff.

Sam was about to follow when Miles held out a hand to stop him.

"Leave him," he said. "Give him time."

47

LUCY FELL INTO THE DEEP BLACK SILENCE WITHIN herself. She didn't say a word as they dragged her through the supermarket and shoved her into the back of a van. Nor did she make a peep during the long drive back to Moonshot Labs, where she was once more taken to Dr Cud's lab and tied to the same velvet-lined mahogany chair.

Once more, the soft leather straps tightened around her head, wrists and ankles and buckled her into place at the head of the table.

Lucy felt her face itch. She ignored it.

Lucy saw her mother, the woman she believed to be long dead, standing a few feet away, holding a tray of tools. She ignored that, too.

Try as she might, the one thing Lucy couldn't ignore was the screams coming from across the dining table. For opposite her, Tim was strapped to an identical chair, a mirror image to herself. The only difference between them was Dr Cud started with him.

He tore the bandages from Tim's face and was busy drilling on a new titanium cheek, screwing through the bones of his jaws. The screams and the whirr of the drill soon turned into choked, frantic gasps for breath as Dr Cud forced a clear plastic tube down Tim's throat.

"Nose," said Dr Cud, the way a doctor might speak to a child he had no patience for, and tapped Tim's nose a few times until Tim's breathing became steady.

Tim tried to scream, to shout something threatening with a lot of swearing, but it only caused him to choke once more.

Dr Cud leant back and twisted the dial on a speaker behind him. The calming piano music, gently acting as the soundtrack to this macabre spectacle, played louder, drowning out Tim's spluttered gasps. *Chopin,* his favourite.

This boorish caveman he was working on wouldn't even have the capacity to appreciate it, he thought to himself, but he soon would.

"Now then, I've chosen you to help lead my army, and if you're going to do that, we'll need you fighting fit," said Dr Cud as he plopped down a metallic collumn onto the table, fine electrical tentacles extending from it in every direction.

"So this little fellow here is going to be grafted onto your spinal cord. Then I'll completely scoop out all those silly thoughts in your head using this." He held up a helmet with thick cables dangling from it like a spider's legs. "I'm going to replace them with a perfect copy of my brain. Unlike the rest, you won't just follow my orders. You'll think like me too. I'm gifting you my mind."

Tim gurgled something in protest.

"No need to thank me. I promised to fix you, and I'm a man of my word."

Tim didn't want to be fixed. His uncle once had a dog named Scampi, who used to hump the VCR. His uncle eventually deemed the dog's behaviour too much and took him to the vet to be *'fixed'*. He wasn't the same dog after that.

Tim didn't want to end up like Scampi. Still, Scampi never had a robotic exoskeleton grafted to his spinal cord.

Dr Cud reached for a scalpel from the tray.

"First, I'm going to make an incision, starting from the first cervical vertebrae and going downwards." Dr Cud spoke almost seductively, relishing every moment of this. "You could say it's a bit like...gutting a fish?"

Dr Cud unclasped the strap around Tim's forehead and forced him downwards, jamming Tim's face roughly into the table. He held the scalpel to the back of Tim's neck, but the blade met unexpected resistance, a thin gold necklace draped across Tim's skin like a shield.

As Lucy saw Tim looking helplessly up at her, she couldn't take it anymore.

"It's going to be ok."

Dr Cud closed his eyes in irritation, and the pneumatic tendons in his neck tightened. "How?" he asked, turning to face her. "How is anything going to be ok? Your friend here is about to be turned inside out. Your mother is my puppet. You're going to be next. Everything you ever cared about is mine."

"Someone will save us," said Lucy.

"Who?"

"My dad."

Dr Cud shook his head with gentle condescension. "No."

"...ack...a...Sa..." choked Tim.

"Jack and Sam?" repeated Dr Cud as he retrieved the locator from the tray, dangling it in front of Tim's eyes, the words 'Location Unknown' emblazoned across it.

"They abandoned you. They're not even in this time anymore."

"They're alive," realized Lucy.

Jack and Sam made it out of the house, after all, and with the time machine.

Dr Cud quickly backtracked, stamping out the seed of hope he just planted.

"It doesn't matter. Wherever they are, they're not coming back for you."

"No, they're coming," said Lucy, a hint of strength returning to her. "They're coming, and they're going to save us, and then they're going to kill you."

Dr Cud's eyelid twitched.

"Blind faith," he hissed and returned to Tim, snapping the gold chain from around his neck and holding it up to the light.

Dangling through his robotic fingers was a small, gold-plated capsule, glinting coldly besides a delicate cross. The ultimate symbol of faith in a power who abandons anyone foolish enough to trust it.

"Faith is the denial of the facts in front of you. I don't see Sam and Jack here, do you?" Dr Cud glanced down at the locator, just in case.

"Oh Jack, Sam, come out, come out wherever you are," he called. "Didn't think so!" and let the necklace fall through his fingers.

Dr Cud readied the scalpel and, with no faith left to protect him, dabbed the cold tip against the back of Tim's neck, a tiny bubble of rich red blood sprouting around it.

Lucy closed her eyes tightly, ignoring what was in front of her and chanting to herself.

"They'll save us. They'll save us. They'll save us."

"No, they won't!" roared Dr Cud through gritted teeth, and he plunged the scalpel into Tim.

Blood flowed from the incision, and Dr Cud continued dragging the knife down Tim's back, slicing through skin, fat, and muscle.

Tim screamed the loudest, silent scream and his eyes

watered with impossible pain, but he never closed them, still staring at Lucy, begging her to save him.

48

Sam gripped the handle of Miles' future gun, feeling the weighty combination of steel and sci-fi in his fingers.

"If we're ever going to stand any chance of stopping Lord Cud, you're going to need to become acquainted with this," said Miles. "I take it you have experience with firearms?"

"Of course. Pull the trigger. Things go dead," said Sam smugly.

He closed one eye, poked out his tongue and aimed for the middle of the five cans arranged on a bench as part of a makeshift shooting gallery. Sam stared intently at the can and imagined it was Jack's stupid, idiot face. He locked onto the can, steadied his hand, and squeezed the trigger.

A bang and a shatter.

The bullet missed the cans entirely, instead hitting a tile lining the wall. Sam ran over to the tile to inspect his handiwork.

"You see that?" he shouted back to Miles. "It properly cracked it in half."

He did it; he fired a gun, and he actually shot something.

"Excellent work, Samuel," agreed Miles. "Now, let's see if you can do that to the cans."

"Well, that was just a warning shot to show the cans who's boss." Sam recomposed himself, now much closer to the cans.

He closed an eye, stuck out his tongue, and felt his index finger tingling with power as he pulled back on the trigger. Yet, the cans remained undisturbed, still balanced on the bench.

"I think your gun's broken."

Miles walked over and took the gun from Sam. He fired two shots in quick succession, effortlessly hitting the two end cans and sending them flying.

"Seems fine to me," said Miles as he returned the gun to Sam.

"Sure, make it harder, why don't you?" grumbled Sam to himself, now fixing his aim on the three remaining cans: *three selfish Jacks*.

He took a few more steps forward and fired again. The bullet struck the far side of the platform, shooting out the light above them.

Irritation bubbled through Sam. That one was perfectly on target. He knew it, Miles knew it, even the cans knew it. Sam stamped forward until the tip of the gun almost touched the middle can.

Eye closed, tongue out. He yanked back the trigger.

The can wobbled but remained upright. Sam smacked the barrel of the gun into the can, knocking it to the floor, and returned to Miles, triumphant.

"Sorry about that. Instincts took over. Close combat fighting is probably where my true talent lies."

"Is that so?"

"Yeah, I'm a gold belt in karate, which is actually higher than black." Or at least he might've been if he ever returned after his first karate lesson, wherein Peter Holland unfairly knocked him down when he wasn't ready.

"Hit me," instructed Miles.

Sam stifled a laugh but realized Miles was being serious.

"Oh, no, I'm not punching a dwarf. That seems a bit..."

"Hit me," repeated Miles.

Sam motioned to walk away.

"I can't, that wouldn't be..."

Sam spun around and darted back towards Miles, throwing an unsuspecting punch at him. Miles effortlessly caught Sam's fist, forcing his hand back and twisting his wrist.

"I tap out! I tap out!" shrieked Sam, and so Miles relinquished.

"That wasn't fair. You knew I wasn't ready," complained Sam, rubbing his wrist for any potential sprains.

***

Near to them, inside the train carriage, Jack sat on one of the old, well-worn seats, staring intently at the time machine. The blue glow pulsed through the ancient patterns in the wood. The clock, encased in its glass dome, ticked away the seconds, and the entire device hummed silently in his hands, a soundless choir that tickled with untapped potential.

He thought of all the places he could go, all the lives he could live. He could leave right now, disappear, and never have to think about any of this ever again.

So why didn't he?

His grip loosened. Who was he kidding? He couldn't just run away. Sam, for all his many, many flaws, was right. People needed their help. The entire world did. It was time he faced his fears, returned to where he belonged and said no more!

He stood up from the seat, a newfound motivation ringing through him as he strode towards the train's doors. As he reached them, he heard something that made him pause: the sound of an ancient speaker system crackling into life behind him.

OUTSIDE, SAM HEARD IT TOO, AS THE SOUND flooded the platform from every direction, echoing through the tunnel.

Miles, however, seemed unperturbed, glancing at the clock above the station. *Was it 4pm already?*

The popping static soon gave way to a much worse sound, the familiar venomous cackling of evil in its purest form.

"I know you're out there, hiding from me. I miss you."

"Come here and face us!" shouted Sam, waving the gun.

"Don't waste your breath," said Miles. "He can't hear you. It's a recording."

"It's not just me who misses you," continued the recording. "I have someone with me who really misses you. I keep telling her you're not coming home, but she's sure you would never abandon your friends. Isn't that right?"

A second voice joined, this one a lot more frantic and scared. "Please save us, I'm begging you, he's done something to Tim, I don't...I don't know what, please, just stop him. Jack, Sam..."

"Ok, that's enough. Don't milk it," interrupted the first voice. "Now give me what I want, and we can end this. You know where to find me."

The signal cut out with a sharp hiss, but the words remained, ringing through Sam.

"How does he know we're here?" asked Sam.

"I don't believe he does," said Miles. "That recording plays every day at exactly 4 o'clock on every single speaker, radio, television, you name it. Anything that still works. It's everywhere. I told you, you and Jack are famous, and it would seem Lord Cud's been looking for you for quite a while."

THE YELLOWED COMPUTER MONITOR INSIDE THE train carriage turned itself off. Jack had borne witness to far more than just the sounds of Lucy and Dr Cud. He saw it all.

The fear in Lucy's eyes, the glee in Dr Cud's and the half-dissected remains of the man behind them.

Jack felt a wave crashing over him, filling his lungs and drowning him until he could no longer breathe, suffocating him the way the smoke had, crushing down on his chest the way Sam had and filling him with the impossible terror of which only Dr Cud could instill.

The floor beneath him span, his ears burst with the pulsing sound of his racing heart, and his vision went dark as shadowy lava-like shapes filled his eyes. He tried desperately to breathe, reaching for his inhaler and holding it over his mouth, but could only pull in quick, faint gasps.

As he reached out, his surroundings seemed to recede, causing him to collapse onto the train carriage floor. He tried to stop, tried to calm himself, tried to latch onto anything as his mind filled with fog, turning his thoughts thick and gluey as they, too, slipped from his grasp. He found only a single thought, a memory, and he held onto it as tightly as he could.

"JACK, ENOUGH ARGUING. THERE'S BIGGER SHIT AT stake now. This is serious!" shouted Sam as he ran down the platform towards the carriage. "We have to go back right now!"

Sam stood outside the train, waiting impatiently for the slow-moving carriage doors to open.

He didn't have time for this, so he squeezed his body through the small opening and saw…

49

Jack felt the breath return to his lungs. The air was clean and smelt faintly of sunscreen, but most notably, it was warm. The biting winter of the present and the acidic nuclear winter of the future made way for the still warmth of the past.

Jack got to his feet and found the world around him was rose-coloured, as though he was living in a memory, and as he looked around, he realized he was. He was standing in the restaurant of a French hotel, one he stayed at with his parents as a boy. There were trays and trays of food laid out around him. He remembered this buffet well, the chicken in the sweet, sticky sauce he would never taste again, but here it was, right in front of him, tickling his nose with the promise of peace.

He dunked his hand into the metal tray without thinking, grabbing one fillet and shoving it into his mouth. His tastebuds sang, so much nicer than undercooked rat.

He then noticed the surrounding people and how they weren't moving. The entire restaurant was still as every single person here stared directly at him. He probably should have gotten a plate and waited in line like everyone else.

No, that wasn't it. They were staring at him because he appeared out of thin air through a doorway of blue static. *Yes, that seemed more likely.*

But Jack didn't care.

"Hello," said Jack, addressing the restaurant with a chipper tone. "Or bonjour."

Jack turned to find the chef, mouth agape, on the other side of the buffet tray.

"This chicken is amazing. Is there a way I could get the recipe? Oh, and the burgers, I forgot about these."

Jack fetched a plate.

"You know, my parents brought me here once when I was a kid. In fact, they're probably around here somewhere," continued Jack to his baffled audience as he skipped around them, filling his plate with chicken, burgers, and fries.

He flagged down a waiter. Not that it was necessary. The waiter was watching his every move, along with everyone else. His eyes followed this strange man, covered in ash, blood and sewage, whose clothes were ragged and torn, smiling with unhinged euphoria. Through Jack's smile, he saw his front tooth was missing and the gap it left oozed with infected pus.

"Excuse me, ou est le...ketchup?" Jack asked him.

The waiter didn't answer, but Jack continued unperturbed, trying to recall the little French he'd learnt in school.

"Pour mon french fries? Which I suppose you lot just call fries. I mean, you don't say French burgers or French chicken. French toast, I suppose, but that's a whole different kettle of *poisson*...oh, there's the ketchup."

Jack fetched a bright red bottle from a countertop and coated his fries in ketchup.

Jack bid the waiter, the chef, and the entire restaurant a fond farewell and skipped out through the glass patio doors of the restaurant with his food, almost dancing down the steps backing onto the beach, remembering the way.

As Jack reached the beachfront, he sensed the sun on his skin enveloping him like a warm blanket. His boots sank into the soft sand with each giddy step towards the sun-beds. He spied the perfect one, waiting for him in a quiet spot beneath a large parasol.

Jack kicked off his boots and fell back into the sun-bed. It caught him in an embrace, and all the aches, pains, bruises, cuts, heartache, and fear melted away.

Above him, Jack found not a single cloud in the sky. It was the most beautiful day he ever knew. Children ran along the beach, and Jack saw his younger self in every one of their faces. Seagulls chirped as they flew over the pier, and people gently bobbed through the ocean's waves as they calmly lapped the shores.

Jack gazed out over the sea and the sky as they met in a glorious mirage across the horizon, and all was well. He reached down and grabbed a handful of fries, and for the first time in a very long time, he was at peace.

Then, Jack let out the loudest scream he could, yelling until his lungs gave out and his throat bled. He knocked the plate off his lap as he slid from the sun-bed and onto the sand. Over and over, he screamed, on his knees beating his fists into the sand, kicking up small tufts and cursing the universe.

It wasn't fair. None of this was fair!

Finally, his voice gave out, and he fell silent, collapsing facedown into the sand.

It wasn't enough.

PART 6

THE COWARD

50

"THE CHICKEN WAS SO YUMMY. REMEMBER, YOU tried to make it when we got home, but it tasted like poo."

Jack's father smiled, remembering the flavour, certainly more appealing than the idea of another ice cream.

As he grew older, the memories of his past were falling like autumn leaves, the smiles, the laughter and the joy contained within them, slowly slipping away.

Yet some stubborn memories hid on the tallest branch and remained evergreen, despite how much he wanted to forget them. The pain and the regret of his past remained indelible in his head, only growing as the years went on.

51

JACK WINCED AS THE DRILL BURROWED ITS WAY through his tender face. He wasn't ready for it and wanted to cry out for it to stop. It was already too late to say anything, especially now his mouth was full of machinery.

So, Jack gripped his sweaty palms to the arms of the chair and endured the pain rattling through his skull, screwing his new augmentation into place. He sensed his nerves screaming in agony as they filled with liquid metal. Right as the pain became almost too much to bear, the drilling stopped, and Jack collapsed back into the chair.

"How do you like it?" asked the dentist, holding up a mirror.

Jack inspected his new smile.

"Perfect," he said with a sigh of relief.

The cuts and bruises healed. The lingering smells and the ringing in his ears had washed away, and now his tooth was fixed. Memories alone lingered, yet even those would fade, he reminded himself.

Bang!

Jack shot up, nearly bounding out of the chair and darting

his head in every direction. He found the dentist accidentally knocked the tray holding his equipment, sending toothbrushes and mirrors skating across the floor with a crash. Jack took a deep breath and stilled the thumping in his chest.

"Nothing to worry about," assured the dentist.

As the dentist picked up the tray, he noticed a small collection of drool dripping from Jack's mouth, so he fetched some tissue and dabbed it lightly against Jack's lips.

Jack lurched back, feeling the echoes of brain tissue sliding across his face. Jack tried to compose himself, forcing himself to remain calm, but his body twitched defiantly as adrenaline flowed through him.

"Are you one of them?" whispered Jack.

"I'm sorry?" asked the dentist.

"Nothing," said Jack, climbing out of the chair.

Jack thanked the dentist for his work and quickly made his leave.

***

JACK RETURNED HOME TO HIS CRAMPED ONE-bedroom apartment, although calling it an apartment might be too grandiose a term for it. A *cupboard* might be a more apt description. The place he was living the past few weeks comprised a single room containing a bed which sunk in the middle, an oven which wouldn't turn off, a fridge which wouldn't turn on and a broken sink which doused the entire room anytime Jack tried to use it.

The sporadic patches of wallpaper lining the room were a million shades of brown, stained with years of grease and fat, the carpet was thick and matted like an overgrown garden, and the single window overlooked nothing as it was bricked up years prior.

This was the only place Jack found which didn't require a

deposit or the first month's rent in advance. He started his new life penniless, and the small amount of change he had in his pockets when he arrived donned a monarch scarcely recognizable to anyone in this time period.

People often say that they would invest in this and that if they could travel back in time. Jack never invested in anything in his life, and it wouldn't be any easier now that there was no internet or handy app to do it all for you.

He could explain the forces which held the universe in place, but didn't know where to begin with the stock market. Did he need a stockbroker, or could he break stocks on his own? Even if Jack figured it out, what company would he invest in?

Most of the ones he knew of wouldn't exist for another 50 years, and Jack needed money now. Instead of proudly boasting about how they would go back and invest in *Microsoft* or *Apple*, those shortsighted people would be better off memorizing lottery numbers.

As Jack lay on his bed watching the growing water stain on the ceiling of his new home, he contemplated his choices. Small stalactites of asbestos and plaster, resembling acne, textured the popcorn ceiling around the stain. *They don't make ceilings like this anymore*, Jack thought to himself.

People back in the present were far too busy staring down at their phones to appreciate good ceiling architecture. No one would bother painting the ceiling of that chapel in the present. What was the name of it? The one *Michelangelo* painted.

If only Jack still had his phone, he could've looked it up online in a second. He missed his phone. He missed the internet. He missed everything. Jack quickly dismissed the thought. Phones were overrated, and he would remember the name, eventually.

What Jack really needed was something to do. *Yes, that was it.* He needed to fill his days with something, and by the time the water stain's perimeter reached the ceiling's edge, he decided. He would help people. He might volunteer somewhere, or begin a charity, or become a firefighter...*no, not fire*. If only he still had access to the internet, it would be a lot easier to come up with an idea. Perhaps he could invent the internet a few decades early.

The stain became a leak, and water dripped onto Jack's forehead. In rhythm with the dripping water, the broken clock chimed above the missing window. The clock ticked but never tocked. The cogs still turned, but the hands remained stationary at 4:53. Forever trapped in a foreign time.

Then it came to him, Jack would become a doctor. People would come to him, and he would save their lives. He could help tens, maybe hundreds of people a day doing it.

So, Jack wiped away the rusty water from his brow with a new sense of purpose and set off to the hospital. The same hospital that would one day serve as the backdrop to the moment his life started falling apart, where he escaped both the police and his friends, leaving them to fend for themselves whilst he ran away. That was becoming a habit.

***

JACK SPENT THE NEXT FEW MONTHS WORKING AT the hospital, but not as a doctor; Jack lacked both the qualifications and any proper form of identification for that. Instead, he worked as a janitor, relegated to mopping floors, fixing lightbulbs and cleaning toilets. Yet, Jack did this work dutifully.

Every time he mopped up a spill, Jack told himself he may have also wiped away the name from a headstone. With each lightbulb he changed, Jack prevented an accident and saved a life. Every toilet he scrubbed brought Jack one step closer to redemption.

Jack spent his days wandering through the hospital like a ghost, invisible to both doctors and patients. He worked seven days a week and often through the night. Anything to keep him away from his flat, with its sunken bed filled with bad dreams and its pillow soaked with the orange residue of the unfixable leak.

What he grew to hate most about the flat, however, was how quiet it was, with only the ticks and drips to drown out the silence.

All his life, there was noise, be it the other children in the foster home, Dr Li shouting at some impossible equation, or most recently, Sam.

He would go back for Sam soon. He just needed a few more days. Then he would go back.

52

Two years went by. Birthdays went uncelebrated. Holidays passed unnoticed.

Jack couldn't remember the last time he returned to his flat or even the last time he'd left the hospital, for that matter. Jack set up a rudimentary bed in the hospital's boiler room, comprised of a mattress he was asked to throw out and a pillow and blanket no one seemed to miss.

There, he spent each long night staring up through the thick sheets of cobwebs at the spiders going about their business. The boiler beside him would rattle and complain, and the sound bounced along the network of pipes around Jack's head, keeping his restless mind at bay.

He gave up cashing in his meagre paycheques, living off the discarded, half-eaten meals left by patients, and over time, Jack became even more invisible to the people there, a piece of furniture drifting through the endless corridors of the hospital.

He was never going back. He accepted that now. Time would continue without him, and he would remain. Jack often imagined what it would be like whilst sweeping the long corridors. He imagined realities in which they triumphed, where Dr Li found Sam and Miles, and they saved Lucy and Tim together, stopping Dr Cud and his army with some fancy gadget or simply the brute force of their combined might.

More often, Jack imagined realities where Sam remained in the distant future, forever wondering if Jack would return. No matter how much time Jack spent imagining it and knowing he should go back, he never did.

With each passing day, it became a little easier to stay and a little harder to return. He was looking older now; the shadowy crevices around his eyes sunk deeper, and long, greasy hair and an unkempt beard overtook his face. Jack was sure this was how he would spend the rest of his life.

That was, until the day everything changed, with the simple sound of a baby's cries.

Jack was cleaning the windows of the maternity ward when the crying began, not an uncommon sound in the maternity ward, what with its rows and rows of cribs. However, on this occasion, Jack noticed that the nurse who usually tended to the newborns was gone. He peered over to see which baby was making the noise and found a tiny little thing lying inside a cot, crying and gurgling. *Probably misses its mom*, Jack supposed.

"Hey, it's ok," said Jack, his words came out stringy, being the first time he spoke in weeks. "It's ok, don't cry."

But the baby refused to quiet. Jack reached into the crib, swaddled the baby in its blanket and lifted it to his chest. He held the infant in his arms and began rocking it gently, taking in the fresh scent of talc.

"There, there," repeated Jack as the baby's cries turned to murmurs, which turned to soft breaths.

The baby nestled its head into Jack, and Jack noticed just how cute this little head was, sticking out from the blanket, eyes as big as an owl's, a delicate button nose and only the wispy beginnings of hair adorning its head.

The baby stretched its arm free from the blanket as it got comfortable. From its wrist, Jack noticed a small identity bracelet hanging down. On the bracelet, written in big cursive letters, were the two words Jack wished every day he could scrub from his memory.

Tobias Cud.

Jack felt suddenly light-headed, his past, present and future colliding with vertigo-inducing precision. A million voices crowded Jack's mind, each crying out for his attention.

Kill him!

Why now?!

Raise him to be good!

Why here?!

Swap him with another baby!

Why did it have to be him?!

Grandfather paradox!

Leave!

Run!

All the while, the baby peacefully cooed in his arms, vibrating slightly against Jack's trembling fingers. Jack placed the baby back down into the cot and backed away as though this newborn was still just as much a threat as the last time they met. No, it was a threat, a threat to everyone and everything. This child would grow to be the instrument of humanity's end. The reason Jack was stuck here.

Kill him!

Jack pushed the voices aside, closing his eyes tightly and blocking them out by thinking of the same thing he would always return to in moments of great stress: the thought of his parents, sitting on that beach in France, and the spark of an idea appeared in their kind faces.

Jack sped out of the room as fast as he could, skidding

along the newly polished floor. He sprinted through the corridors of the maternity ward, shoving open every door in his wake until he found what he was looking for, the pair who set the fuse.

It didn't take long to find them, and despite never having laid eyes upon them before, Jack knew them at once. The resemblance may have been faint, but it was still unmistakably there.

A young woman lay in a hospital bed, her wild ginger hair clipped tightly in a bun, revealing a pale, exhausted complexion.

A man with neat black hair and a matching neat black suit sat beside her, holding her hand. They talked and giggled, and the man would periodically ask if she needed him to fluff her pillow or adjust her hot water bottle.

Jack watched them from a distance, waiting for them to suddenly change and sprout fangs and horns. As he continued to watch, they remained as ordinary people. Jack hopped restlessly from foot to foot, looking for a hint of something, anything. His impatience finally got the better of him, and Jack couldn't stop himself from going over to talk to them.

"Excuse me," started Jack, "Mr and Mrs Cud?"

"That's us," said Mr Cud in a distinctly un-evil manner.

"I just wanted to congratulate you on your new baby," said Jack, not exactly sure where he was going with this. "You must be very proud."

"We certainly are," agreed Mrs Cud. "Our little Toby. The doctors always said I wouldn't be able to have any children, but he's our little miracle."

"Mmmm," replied Jack, struggling to agree with her. "So, have you given it much thought for how you're going to raise him? Quite strict, I imagine? Maybe even...oppressively so?" He raised an inquisitive eyebrow at Mr Cud.

"Oh, not at all. I never thought I'd ever get the chance to

be a father," said Mr Cud. "We want to love him and give him the best life we can."

"You read that book on parenting, didn't you?" added Mrs Cud.

"It said to give your child love and patience and…"

"Spoiled. I get it. You're going to spoil him so much he believes there's nothing he can't have, even immortality, at the expense of everyone else," concluded Jack.

Mr and Mrs Cud shot a concerned glance at one another.

"My apologies," said Mr Cud. "But who exactly are you?"

"It's you, isn't it? Just tell me, what is it you do to him?" Jack demanded, his voice becoming more fractured and high-pitched.

Only a confused silence answered his questions. This was pointless. They weren't being helpful at all, lacking even the slightest sprinkling of malice between them. Jack turned, and without saying another word, walked back through the maternity ward.

If it's not them, it's him. It had to be. Some people are just born with the capacity for evilness inside them, lurking in their skulls, begging to come out.

The rush of thoughts bombarded Jack once more, and by the time he returned to his foe, still sleeping peacefully in his crib, Jack knew what needed to be done.

Determination blazed through him, coursing through his veins, as a single thought called to him louder than any other.

KILL HIM!

53

Jack twisted the door lock until it clicked into place, sealing them in. He took a deep breath, steadied himself and grabbed a pillow from the cupboard, ready to confront the one-hour-old infant who would one day take everything from him. Jack imagined his final confrontation with Dr Tobias Cud many times.

A far braver version of himself would look the old mechanical devil in the eyes and tell him *'no more.'* Then, with a sudden burst of strength, he would hit him or strangle him or shoot him and watch those cruel, unfeeling eyes close for good.

Jack struggled to muster up any of the same vengeful strength of his imagined self as he looked down at this helpless infant, its eyes peeping open as it wriggled awake. Those dumb curious eyes stared up at Jack, eyes which showed no fear, no hate and no judgement. Jack readied the pillow, gripping it tightly in each hand. He lowered it over Dr Cud and...

and...

Couldn't do it.

"Stop looking at me like that," whispered Jack, his voice

beginning to falter. "You know what you've done to me, to my friends. Come on, Jack, do this, and it'll all be over. You can go home."

He steadied the pillow again.

"If I close my eyes, I don't have to think about it. I'm just making a bed."

Again, Jack's trembling hands danced over the cot but never lowered.

"Three...Two...One!"

Nothing.

"Three, two, one!"

Still nothing.

"Threetwoone!"

He threw the pillow across the room, heart bashing against his ribs.

There was a long silence as Jack considered his next move, which was soon broken by a soft giggle that twisted around Jack, tightening around him. Dr Cud's first laugh, and it was at him.

"Don't laugh at me!" seethed Jack, shooting the baby a steely glare. "I'm going to kill you. I'm going to do it, OK?"

Jack's anger only seemed to fuel the baby's laughter, and as its innocent joy rang out, the certainty of Jack's words slipped away.

No matter how Jack reshaped the idea, he couldn't make it feel righteous. What he could make it feel like, however, pretty easily, in fact, was baby murder. *Infanticide.* That was the proper name for it. Dr Cud probably did loads of infanticide and didn't think twice about it.

The handle of the door rattled. Time was up. If Jack did it when he was supposed to, it would all be over by now. He still had time, just. He could reach inside the cot, wrap his arms around his tiny neck and...

Jack unlocked the door.

"Sorry," he told the nurse, who was already pushing past him with a tray of bottles. "The handle gets stuck sometimes. I'll see about fixing it."

The nurse scarcely acknowledged him, her attention on the rows of hungry babies. Jack watched her out of the corner of his eye as he returned to the window, wiping the same spot for nearly an hour as, one by one, each baby was fed and changed.

He almost hoped she would call him out, make him leave, absolve him of any responsibility. But she didn't. She simply went on feeding the babies. As she reached Toby, Jack abandoned all pretence of cleaning and was now fully staring at them, watching like a hawk, unblinking as the nurse fed the rubber nipple between his lips. Toby suckled until he drifted off to sleep, unburdened by the nightmares he would cause.

The nurse eventually left, and Jack was once more alone with the audience of babies.

Of course, that was it!

Jack couldn't do it with an audience scrutinizing him, an entire room of witnesses watching his every move. No one could. He needed somewhere more private, away from their judgemental gurgling. Jack scooped up Toby, swaddling him in his pale blue blanket, and slipped out of the room.

As Jack made his way through the hospital, carrying Toby in his arms, he met only the occasional glance in his direction. Right now, Jack was thankful he became invisible to the people working there. He continued, past the reception and out the doors. All the while, Toby Cud slept soundly in his arms, his tiny breaths warm against Jack's chest, safe and secure.

Jack kept walking, unsure exactly where they were going or what he would do when he got there.

54

Jack opened the door to his flat, half expecting someone else to be living there by now. His foot squelched into the shag carpeting, and it became apparent that the leak was the one to take over the residency in Jack's absence.

There was a pungent smell of damp, and spots of mold were growing through the wallpaper. He ran a hand along the bed mattress, heavy and soaked like a sponge, as he searched for the driest area on which to place the sleeping child.

"Right, now you lie there while I find something to murder you with, ok?"

Jack walked over to the kitchenette and found the single knife he owned left on the counter, balanced atop a butter dish. Green and blue spores shrouded the knife like a cocoon. He couldn't stab a baby with a dirty knife. That was simply unhygienic.

Jack took it to the sink and spent nearly ten minutes scrubbing away at the knife until it was beyond spotless. Only now did Jack notice the knife in his hand was a long, serrated bread knife and not the most ideal option for a swift stabbing.

His diet mainly comprised of bread and butter when he first moved there, as it was the only thing he could afford and the only thing he could stomach, and his sole knife reflected this, perfect for cutting bread but little else.

Jack lowered the blade until it lightly rested against Toby's throat, his only option now being to saw into the baby, slowly cutting off his head, and that could take hours. No, Jack decided he would have to go out and buy a new set of knives, extra sharp ones, maybe a knife sharpener too. He would go right this minute.

Although looking at the clock ticking away above him, Jack noticed how late it was getting. It was already 4:53, and the shops would close soon. He would do it first thing in the morning and...

No.

This was getting silly. He needed to just get it over with. But how?

Before he knew it, Jack began speaking his endless trail of thoughts out loud to his soon-to-be victim.

"So, if I kill you before you do any of the bad stuff, then me, or at least this version of me, won't exist because I'd never have come here in the first place, meaning I'll fade away and won't even remember any of this, like in *Back To The Future*. Although, maybe the fact I haven't faded away yet means that killing you won't even work, and the *Parallel Worlds* interpretation of time travel is correct. I know what you're thinking. You think I haven't faded because I'm not going to kill you? Well, that's where you're wrong because I am. I will. I'm just putting it off for a bit, and that's fine. That's normal. It's normal to be hesitant when killing a baby."

Jack began pacing, continuing his soliloquy and waving the knife around as he conducted his thoughts, weighing up the pros and cons of infanticide.

"So, I'm going to kill you and save everyone. Well, not

everyone. There are other people who have done terrible things, other babies I'd need to kill. Baby Hitler, Baby Stalin, Baby Jack The Ripper. Is that what I'm going to become, *Jack The Baby Ripper*? Then again, I read somewhere that Hitler and World War Two actually slowed climate change and overpopulation. Plus, if I were to change the past too much, I might not even be born, creating a grandfather paradox-sized black hole that could swallow up everything. Fine, Baby Hitler can live, for now. Ok, before I do this, are there any positives about your life I haven't considered? Maybe some people you killed were bad people or...No, look, you're a murderer, and you're going to hurt my friends, so if there's even a chance this will save them, I have to try. I mean, not that they even were my friends. Sam betrayed me. Tim is an insane drug dealer. Lucy tried to arrest me and don't even get me started on Dr Li."

Jack lowered his head, turning to face the baby.

"They all would've been able to kill you, though. So why the hell can't I?!"

Jack slammed his fist against the wall, tearing through the sodden wallpaper. That was the truth, wasn't it? As much as he wished it and as much as he tried, Jack simply could never kill Dr Tobias Cud.

Maybe he didn't have to.

Jack scrambled to his knees and dug beneath the bed, sweeping his fingers through waves of soaked carpet until he found a small metal box sealed shut with a padlock. Punching in the combination, his hands slipped excitedly against the dials. With a satisfying clunk, the padlock sprang open.

Inside the box lay the one possession Jack arrived here with. The thing which once represented hope and promise. Now, it served only as a haunting memento of all the mistakes he could never fix. Perhaps, just maybe, Jack could fix one of those mistakes.

He reached inside and pulled out the time machine.

55

THE TIME MACHINE, WHILST BEING A TECHNICAL marvel of physics and engineering, has its limits. For a start, it's powered by telepathic fear energy, which means there are several limiting factors at play.

First, there's only so far you can push the brain's fear centres. In preliminary trials on rats, after being shown enough pictures of hungry cats, their tiny hearts risked giving out, or worse, as with one particularly unlucky rat who evacuated its bowels until it was hollow.

Second, there's only so much fear you can cram into a time machine of this size. The obvious solution here might be to create a bigger time machine, but then it becomes much harder to propel through time and space, making it a delicate balancing act. Plus, a larger time machine wouldn't fit nearly as discreetly down somebody's shoe.

The time machine in Jack's possession couldn't take somebody to the beginning or end of the universe, not that there would be much to see there. In fact, with this time machine, you would be lucky to reach the Middle Ages.

WHICH BRINGS US TO THE YEAR 1474. THE FURTHEST point Jack could reach.

Jack initially thought of the ancient Egyptians but ended up at the British Museum, staring at an exhibit about mummies he once visited as part of a school trip, their toilet paper-covered faces exactly as he remembered them. He even heard his history teacher scalding Sam for his behaviour echoing through the museum.

Jack then tried thinking about the ancient Romans but found himself standing on the set of the film *Gladiator,* in the centre of a grand colosseum, with *Russell Crowe* shouting at him for interrupting his take.

Jack didn't consider just how difficult it was to think of a past he had no recollection of. He only reached the 1950s through good luck and the memory of an old documentary.

Yet, somehow, Sam brought them to the future without ever having experienced it. How did he do it? He simply thought of the future and reached it on his first try. *Everything was always so easy for him.*

Jack planted his feet on the ground, holding Toby under one arm and the time machine in the other.

Eyes closed.

Deep breath.

Jack concentrated with all his might on the past, the distant past, some place far enough back, where nothing that happened would impact something as far away as the present. He imagined people washing in rivers, bails of hay, wicker.

Nothing.

Sam thought of the future.

The future.

Sam literally thought of 'The Future.'

So, Jack thought of *The past*. He imagined those two

words as large as he could, seven cascading monuments towering into the sky, spelling it out.

———

WHEN JACK OPENED HIS EYES, HE WAS THERE, IN THE past: the year 1474.

However, at that moment, Jack only knew it was a time before showers, judging by the smell. As he soaked in his new surroundings, Jack found he was standing in a cathedral, its grand architecture extending all around him, adorned with biblical carvings, crucifixes, and, most notably, people. Lots of people.

Jack appeared before a stunned congregation of thousands, each one staring at him in disbelief. He noticed a preacher beside him, dressed in black, with a golden cross around his neck and an obnoxiously enormous hat on his head.

Jack cleared his throat. "Um...Hi, do any of you speak English?"

There was a long pause until the preacher stepped forward, raising his arms to the sky. "Heaven hath sent an angel to us. What say you, oh blessed one?"

Appearing out of thin air in a burst of light might not have been the best entrance to a less enlightened time. But better an angel than a witch, Jack supposed.

"Right, yeah, so I've got this baby, and I was wondering if someone wanted to do me a big favour and look after him..."

"The angel hath brought us a new messiah!" announced the preacher, raising his arms as the crowd erupted with joyful cheers.

"No, no, not a messiah. Just a normal baby to be treated equally, maybe even slightly less than equal."

Jack's protests were drowned out by cries of, "Our new messiah shall guide us to the light!"

He peered down at Toby, awake and looking out over his newfound followers, gurgling and dribbling triumphantly.

"Ok, this was a mistake. Sorry, I realize that now," sighed Jack.

Jack closed his eyes again and vanished in a flash of divine blue light, taking the new messiah with him.

Confused, the crowd stared at where Jack once stood until one brave peasant called from the back, "The angel has forsaken us."

"It was him!" exclaimed another, pointing at the preacher. "He angered the messiah!"

The preacher tugged at his cross uncomfortably, silently praying for Jack to come back.

"I'm sure the angel will return any moment," he assured his congregation, attempting to calm the growing anger amongst his followers.

56

Jack's mind was blank, void of any iota of a plan. He sat in his damp flat, watching Toby Cud thrash and wail, his chubby limbs flailing, his face red with tears. Jack knew why Toby was crying.

The smell could knock out an elephant, and Jack could feel his shoulders slumping under the weight of Toby's new deposit.

Jack could go. Jack could run away. He was good at that. He could leave Toby here, lock the door, and be rid of him for good. *Someone would only find him and train him to be even more evil*, he supposed, letting out a great, long sigh of acceptance.

Jack held his finger out and Toby reached out for it, gripping it in his little sausage fingers and soon forgot why he was crying. Toby, the miniature dictator who would kill millions, curled into the crease of Jack's arm and drifted back off to sleep.

"Let's get you back to your parents."

THE COOL EVENING AIR HIT JACK AS HE WALKED from his flat. Was it summer or winter now? Jack had long since lost track. He blinked hard, shaking off the drowsy trance he lulled himself into as he swayed Toby back and forth. Its steady rhythm calmed him, filtering out the chaos in his mind as he crossed the road.

Here, destiny would strike Jack once more, this time as a white transit van. The driver applied the brakes, and Jack glanced up just in time to see the van's headlights consume his vision.

Jack flew, and pain fired across his body, but he was yet to feel it. All Jack knew in the moment was surprise. The world blurred around him, wrapping him in an explosive cocoon of shock as he rolled along the bonnet and into the windscreen. Metal shrieked, glass splintered, and all the while, Jack held Toby close to his chest, shielding him from the impact as best he could.

Luckily for Jack, or perhaps unluckily, he had absent-mindedly left the time machine in his favourite hiding place, his boot.

Another important thing to note about the time machine is that for an inter-dimensional teleporter, it was surprisingly fragile, and as Jack's foot crunched through the windscreen, the wooden housing of the time machine split and its glass ball cracked open, allowing time energy to spill out and spurt thick, warm lumps of blue plasma up Jack's leg.

The van driver watched in horror, helpless to stop the man and his baby from slamming into the windscreen, shattering it into a cloudy haze of fractured glass, through which he was sure he saw the man, the baby, and the bonnet of his vehicle disappear entirely in a murky blue cloud of electricity.

He would later recount this story to a pair of sceptical police officers, his wife, his friends down the pub and anybody who would listen for the rest of his life.

Of course, no one ever truly believed him and would either offer more realistic alternatives or simply dismiss him as a liar. Still, he knew what he saw that day.

Jack and Toby rode the van's bonnet, surfing through the deepest depths of the time stream, propelled by the large blue globs spraying from Jack's boot. Each globule grew into a bubble, floating around them like giant baubles from a Christmas tree, and every one of them contained a suspended moment in time. The bonnet skidded along, losing momentum as it screeched an agonizing metallic cry, finally coming to rest...somewhere.

Jack opened his eyes as the tremendous weight of the last few seconds took hold. His ears rang, his brain span, and the entire left side of his body throbbed with red-hot daggers of agony. He peered down at Toby Cud, who seemed completely unperturbed by their ordeal, giggling once more.

Of course, he would find this funny. Jack swallowed hard, his gaze shifting from Toby's amusement to the colourless expanse surrounding them. The road they were standing on was replaced with white, as was everything else, infinitely stretching in every direction. Silent, white, nothingness.

Panic and a shot of adrenaline numbed Jack's pain, and he reached into his boot to retrieve what remained of the time machine. The three LEDs at its base went dark. The blue pulse along the veins and grooves of the wood had flatlined, and the glass ball, once a hive of time energy, had emptied.

"No, no, no, no, no," Jack quietly pleaded.

He closed his eyes, gripped tightly and thought of anywhere, anything, but there was nothing. The time machine was dead, leaving him shipwrecked in this eternal white void.

Toby continued to giggle, but the lack of anything dulled the sound of his small, gurgled laughs.

As hopelessness wove its way through Jack, he noticed something floating in the distance: a shimmering bauble hanging silently in the void. He got to his feet and followed it, half surprised his feet remained on the ground, as beneath him was only more white, yet gravity was still keeping him in place.

As he drew closer, Jack heard a faint voice from inside the spherical ball of plasma, cutting through the silence.

"Just give him the clipboard," said a gasping, wheezing voice.

Jack got closer still and made out a moment reflected in the skin of the pale blue bubble. A memory he knew very well.

"But this thing could be worth..." came another voice.

"Is it worth dying?" interrupted Jack's past from inside the bubble.

Jack's pulse quickened as he watched himself inside the memory, huddled behind a desk, fearing for his life. The terror of that night rekindling within him as he relived every heartbeat.

This was the night everything changed, the night Sam dragged him into the eye of trouble, and the night he first heard the name Dr Cud.

Bang!

A bullet fired from Greg Page's gun, bursting out from the bubble and scarcely missing Jack's head. Jack lurched out of the way, stumbling from the bullet's trajectory and clutching Toby close to him.

He glanced up and found more bubbles materializing in the distance, forming a winding trail through the void, one that might lead Jack back to where he came from. Jack followed the bubbles, each containing a curious visage of days gone.

Lucy chasing him through the hospital.

Moonshot Labs.

Dr Li, dead.

Dr Li, alive again.

Each memory played like a film as Jack continued making his way through the strange theme park attraction of his life.

The arguing.

The fire.

The future.

Jack saw running and panting as he, Sam, and Miles escaped the cyborg creatures. He watched as the three of them retreated into the sewers, just as he recalled, but the bubble didn't follow.

Instead, it continued, showing the army of mechanical corpses growing ever closer to the memory's edge, their pungent smell seeping through. One cyborg paused right against the bubble's skin, almost as though it was staring back at Jack, *but it couldn't actually see him, surely?*

Its blackened, half-decayed arm reached out through the memory, piercing through the skin of the bubble, and the rest of its monstrous form soon joined it, planting its steel feet firmly into the white void.

Others soon followed, a dozen, maybe more, breaking through the boundaries of their domain. They studied their unfamiliar landscape for a moment before locking onto the bundle of petrified terror that was Jack.

From around him, Jack heard a single word ringing out from several bubbles at once, all around him, in every direction, a chorus of Sam's from across his time stream, each echoing the same command: "*Run.*"

So Jack ran, sprinting further along his timeline as the monsters pursued him. A little way ahead, Jack saw a bubble filling with a familiar blinding light, those of a van's headlights speeding towards its surface. He froze as the light intensified, and his grip tightened around Toby.

The vehicle rippled out through the bubble's shell and Jack realized the headlights weren't the same ones which brought him here, despite carrying the same impending dread. This van's garish exterior was decorated with crude depictions of copyrighted characters.

The uncanny portraits of *Mokey Mouse* and *Bags Bunny* stared back at him, frozen in twisted cheer and holding ice creams. With a deafening screech, the ice cream truck veered around Jack, skidding along the non-existent tarmac. Jack glimpsed the man at the helm and was surprised to find it was Sam, steering wildly with one hand and brandishing a gun in the other.

What memory was this? This never happened.

The ice cream truck careened into the amassing army of metallic experiments, mowing them down in a violent flurry before skidding back inside its bubble.

Jack sucked in a sharp breath, trying to process what he witnessed. He certainly didn't remember any of that taking place, but he was thankful for it all the same.

Pressing on, Jack came across a bubble containing only an ancient wooden door, which was yanked open the moment Jack laid eyes upon it. Stepping back, he expected the worst, but saw Tim appear through it, dressed in soaking beige overalls. The remnants from another memory Jack couldn't recall.

"Tim?" asked Jack.

If the mechanical corpses saw him, perhaps Tim could, too.

Tim peered through the bubble, scrutinizing Jack up and down before landing on Toby.

"Bloody hell, Jack," said Tim, "I didn't know you were scared of babies," and he slammed the door shut.

Jack wandered along more bubbles of ever-increasing unfamiliarity, past people he never met and days he never lived, past robots, evil snowmen, and the most beautiful woman he would ever lay eyes falling majestically through the night sky.

However, he was too busy in his own head to notice, frantically piecing the rules of this place together. If the bubbles interacted with him, could he interact with the bubbles? Perhaps they were more than simply prerecorded moments.

Maybe they were doorways one could step through from either side. He only needed to find the right one.

Jack glanced up from his thoughts and wandered into a more familiar section of the gallery of his life: days spent by gravesides, long nights spent crying alone in foster homes, and memories of his grandmother.

Tucked away towards the end of the road, Jack found it. The perfect doorway. The one leading to the moment he always dreamed of returning to.

Jack couldn't help but press his face against it, taking in all the precious snowglobe had to offer. Through it, Jack saw himself as a child, around eight years old...*precisely* eight years old, sitting excitedly in front of a birthday cake.

The sound of his parent's voices filled his ears as they sang to him. With each joyous note, Jack's heart skipped faster. There it was. That was the moment. The impossible moment Jack never quite remembered.

Then, Jack saw someone else join the memory, two shadows creeping into the frame. The monsters who lingered in the back of his mind. Jack pressed a hand against the memory, feeling its nostalgic effervescence as he pushed through to his past.

If he only managed to break through, he might alter the impending events. He could fix everything. His hand slipped inside; the reflective skin stretching and contorting around it, inviting him in. He could do it. He was really going to do it.

Jack paused, his attention suddenly drawn to the sound of

distant explosions vibrating through the void. Fireworks were shooting through the first bubble he met, exploding around him and painting the blank landscape with frantic streaks of colour.

A rocket whizzed past, narrowly missing his face as it skimmed his eighth birthday. The bubble rippled uncomfortably, swelling like a zit until it popped, leaving only the faint scent of birthday cake in its place.

"No!" screamed Jack, his throat tight with desperation.

The fireworks continued launching out in every direction, tracing pathways across the canvas and bursting with more bubbles. Fragments of Jack's past scattered around him as doorways closed. If Jack didn't pick one soon, he would be stuck here forever.

A bubble flickered in the distance, just within reach. Jack sprinted towards it, slowing only as he realized where this exit led. *Not there. Anywhere but there.*

Through its shimmering surface, Jack saw what he was running from all this time: Lucy, moments from the end, waiting for him, pleading for him to rescue her, hope never wavering from her voice.

"They'll save us," Jack heard her saying, over and over, the same thing. "They'll save us."

Jack watched Lucy, trapped at the centre of Dr Cud's cruel web, knowing what he must do but still unable to bring himself to do it.

Beside Lucy, Jack saw Dr Cud, the real one, working on what remained of Tim. His skin was torn open and stitched back together, with his insides rearranged.

Wires stretched from within Tim's skull to a helmet which sat upon Dr Cud's head, and then over to a large monitor. On the monitor, Jack could make out *'95% complete'*. Tim's conversion was well underway.

Dr Cud dropped his tools, and cooly strolled over to Lucy.

His face twisted into an unsavoury grin as he presented a small orange pill to her.

"Do you know what this is?" asked Dr Cud, taunting her with every syllable.

Lucy ignored him, repeating her mantra. "They'll save us."

"This is it, Jack. Last chance before she's gone forever," called Dr Cud, gleefully sure of himself.

Jack glanced down at the infant in his arms, his little face unburdened by hate, and could not comprehend how he ever became that. How could anyone?

Jack turned back to Lucy, watching the nightmare play out as her faith in him continued to ring out. Jack's mind screamed for him to go through, and he wanted desperately to find the strength within himself to do it. However, his feet refused to budge, no matter how much he willed them.

"They'll save..."

Dr Cud grabbed her head and forced the pill into her mouth, digging it down her throat. Lucy broke out in a flurry of coughs and splutters, her eyes wet with pain.

"They'll save us," she choked out.

"No one's coming," Dr Cud assured her one last time. "Right now, that pill is reprogramming every single cell in your body. You have less than a minute before everything you are melts away completely, so I recommend making your final words..."

"They'll save us," she breathed, still refusing to relinquish her trust in Jack as the darkness took her.

"I'm sorry," whispered Jack.

A firework whizzed past him and shot directly into the bubble, popping it and dissolving the doorway into nothing.

Jack's hand fell to his side, heavy with the weight of his cowardice.

Fate gave him one last chance to be brave, and he let it slip away.

57

On the other side of the bubble, the firework continued on, slicing through the past with a dazzling trail of yellow light. It tore through the lab, zipping past Lucy, Dr Cud, and what remained of Tim, and not stopping until it crashed into Dr Cud's equipment.

The firework burst into a shower of sparks, igniting a fire that licked hungrily around the monitor of Dr Cud's grand machine. Dr Cud dropped his scalpel and dove out of the way of the eruption.

"What was that?" growled Dr Cud, his gaze fixed upon Lucy.

Lucy didn't have an answer. She was busy watching the scalpel slowly roll along the table toward her.

Dr Cud yanked the helmet from his head and fetched a fire extinguisher. He wrestled with its hose as he put out the fires, dousing the room in a blanket of white foam until not a single spark survived. Scraping a silver digit across the monitor, and through the foamy smudge, he saw the progress of Tim's conversion was paused at 98%. Jabbing at dials and switches, he dug through the creamy coating of the room to reboot the software.

Lucy used this moment of distraction to crane her neck forward, leaning her head out as far as she could, her arms still tightly strapped to the chair. A bit further, almost there, her shoulders cried out in pain as she nearly pulled herself out from their sockets.

There!

She clamped her teeth down around the scalpel. Lucy then noticed the woman who was once her mother watching her, her passive eyes following Lucy's every move. Their eyes locked on one another, but Lucy's mother didn't utter a word. Was she too far gone even to know what was going on? Or was there one final defiant ember remaining that was still on Lucy's side?

Lucy chose the latter, silently thanked her and started on the wrist straps, carving into them, her head bobbing manically. Lucy carved through the thick leather strap until her wrist slipped free. Now that she was back in control of her arm, she made quick work of the second strap and then the ankle restraints.

She darted over to Tim, his unconscious form splayed out across the table. Fresh machinery bulged through his mutilated flesh, fighting against the stitches. There must be something she could do to help him, anything, *please*.

Lucy leaned in close and whispered into his ear.

"It's ok. I'm going to get you out of here."

She wasn't sure he still heard her or whether there was anything left of him to hear her. Then, Tim made a tiny, weak breath of recognition, containing a single pained word.

"Run."

It wasn't too late. Lucy turned towards the door, hope flaring, until she saw Dr Cud standing in her path, an eyebrow half raised as he blocked her pathetic attempt to escape.

"Sit down," ordered Dr Cud.

Lucy's hand tightened around the scalpel, standing her ground.

"Really?" continued Dr Cud. "What is your plan here? You can't save your friend. Saving yourself is impossible. You took the pill. Every cell in your body is mine. It's too late."

"Tobias Cud," began Lucy as she stepped towards him, brandishing her scalpel. "I'm arresting you for murder, kidnapping..."

"Now you're just being silly," scoffed Dr Cud, offering her a sarcastic, pitied look.

"...Biological terrorism, police corruption..." she stumbled, losing balance, her legs slipping free of her control. Dr Cud was right. She was becoming his puppet.

"...and worst of all, hurting my family."

Lucy glanced over at her mother, then at Tim, and her body gave out. Her hands reached for something to keep her steady but found only the helmet Dr Cud was wearing, her hands closing around it as she fell to the floor, and with the final ounce of control she had left, she placed it on her head.

"That helmet is configured to my brain, you fool. It only works with my brainwaves," said Dr Cud, staring down at her.

"Every cell in my body...is yours," said Lucy, her lips curling into a triumphant smile as her eyes fluttered shut.

A flash of doubt crossed Dr Cud's face. He didn't consider that. How did he not consider it? He accounted for every eventuality, but somehow missed this. His eyes fired to the monitor. Tim's conversion reached 100%. What did she do? She was a fool, an idiot, a stupid child.

Dr Cud turned to the girl's mother, snapping at her with rage.

"Kill yourself!" he commanded. "And make sure it's painful."

Without a word, Lucy's mother exited the lab to perform her task dutifully.

Dr Cud knelt beside Lucy's unconscious body.

"You hear that? I'm in control, not you. I win."

Behind him, Tim stirred, his nose twitching as his reanimated form filled with new thoughts. Dr Cud approached him with some trepidation, staring into Tim, and Tim stared back.

"Timothy?" ventured Dr Cud, a twinge of unease croaking through his artificial voice box.

"Yes, my lord," replied Tim, his words steady and compliant.

"How do you feel?"

"I feel fantastic. My mind is open to so many new ideas."

"Ideas? What ideas?"

"To live forever."

"Good."

"To rule over every one of them," Tim hissed through his teeth, each inflected reflection steadying Dr Cud, allowing him to breathe a sigh of relief.

He glanced over and saw Lucy slowly waking. The pill completed its work, and she was now his slave, ready to receive her orders.

Dr Cud stood tall, soaking it all in, savouring every drop of victory.

Now, nobody could stop him, and soon nobody would even try.

58

Jack sprinted deeper into the endless white void, with Toby pressed tightly to his chest, through the Warzone of fireworks exploding all around him, illuminating his path forward. A single bubble remained, and Jack pressed every ounce of strength remaining into reaching it.

Jack barrelled towards the memory, racing against the fireworks, who all locked their sights upon the glistening treasure. He sensed their warmth on his back as they closed in on him, nearing the finish line. There was no time to check what was on the other side.

It was something, and something was better than eternal nothingness. Jack dove through its iridescent skin, landing on the hard pavement of somewhere distantly familiar.

Behind him, the doorway was gone, leaving nothing but a sizzle of gunpowder. Jack got to his feet and stood on an empty street corner, with houses on one side and a few shops on the other. It was recognizable, but Jack couldn't quite place where.

Then, two boys in school uniform shoved past him, nearly knocking Jack off his feet as they ran for their lives. The puzzle pieces crashed together in Jack's mind as he watched himself and Sam continue running up the street, followed by a group of older teenagers speeding past Jack and after their prey.

Jack knew those teenagers. He knew the street, and he knew this exact day, for it was the one which would change his life forever.

Everything around Jack came into focus, gaining clarity as memories flooded back. Jack passed this street most afternoons when he was young, a backdrop of his youth which long faded from his memory.

Jack began walking, his body stepping along the path as though it were instinct, tracing his younger footprints and leading him straight to Dr Li's lab on the day they first met.

***

JACK SOON FOUND THE OLD BUILDING WITH ITS boarded windows and the distant smell of bread. His younger self was still busy running back and forth along alleyways and bus stops, yet to spy this magical place for a few more minutes.

Standing beneath the shadow of days gone, Jack grasped the door handle and felt a shot of hesitation fire through him. He wasn't sure how Dr Li would react to seeing him again.

Their last interaction didn't end on the best of terms. Jack was angry and threw a long list of accusations at Dr Li, manipulation, lies, even the death of his parents. It was all in the past, years for Jack, decades for Dr Li.

Jack gave a gentle push, and the door opened effortlessly, almost inviting him in, just as it had all those years ago.

Inside, Jack found Dr Li hunched over his electromagnet, adding the final touches.

"There are some diapers over there," said Dr Li without looking up.

Jack walked over to the wall where Dr Li set up a changing

table stocked with diapers and wipes. Next to it stood a crib. Jack spent much of his youth wondering why his mad-scientist adoptive father kept baby stuff in his lab, but now it all made sense. Dr Li always seemed to know exactly what fate would befall Jack long before it happened, and the crib, diapers, and changing station all cemented his omniscience.

Jack laid Toby down on the table and set to work. He'd never changed a diaper, *but how hard could it be?*

Jack undid the straps and was immediately met with a bright yellow fountain of urine streaming into his face with pinpoint precision. Toby giggled, and for a moment, Jack reconsidered killing him.

Dr Li appeared beside Jack and tapped a button on the changing station. Two mechanical arms immediately ejected from either side and swiftly got Toby cleaned, talked, and changed in a matter of moments. Dr Li gently picked up Toby and produced a small glass milk bottle.

"There's a change of clothes for you over there," said Dr Li, pointing at a neatly folded outfit laid out for Jack, the exact clothes he was wearing when Dr Li last saw him.

"What am I supposed to do?" asked Jack, desperation dripping from his voice and urine dripping from his beard.

"I don't know," replied Dr Li as he calmly fed the bottle into Toby's mouth.

"What do you mean you don't know? You had a crib ready. I suppose you know I'm about to walk through that door as a kid. Was that all part of your plan, too? Did you pick this building simply because you knew it was the one I would walk into? You know everything that I've ever done or am ever going to do. I don't know a single thing about you. I don't even know your first name."

"It's just Li," he said, not using more than the minimum number of words he could get away with.

"Stop, just stop," demanded Jack, exasperation turning to

frustration. "What is this really about? Are you torturing me? Is this whole thing a game because I've wronged you in a past life? Are you God? Or the devil? Am I in the matrix? Is this the matrix?"

"It's not the matrix," sighed Dr Li. "I'm only trying to do what's best for you."

"Then help me, tell me, what do I do?"

"I don't know," repeated Dr Li, barely acknowledging Jack as he continued watching Toby gumming away at the bottle.

Jack snatched the bottle from Dr Li and hurled it across the room, shattering it against the wall and prompting a small robotic dustpan to sweep up the glass.

"Tell me!"

Dr Li calmly produced the second bottle he prepared and continued feeding Toby. As he did so, he turned to Jack, glancing at him properly for the first time since he arrived, meeting his pained stare and finally seeing him.

"I don't know," said Dr Li once more. "I know nothing. I don't even know who I am anymore. I only know I need to keep trying to fix everything, and I'm running out of ideas. This isn't the first time I've done this, you know. Every time I go back and try something different, and every time, it ends the same way."

Jack wasn't sure how to respond, seeing the full extent of the pain Dr Li carried, the regrets he tried so hard to bury deep down inside, now bursting from the cracks lining his heart.

"How many times?"

"Fifty," said Dr Li, his tone growing bleak beneath the weight of his failures. "The last time we did this, Tim got hit by a bus, and Lucy got shot. The wheel keeps on turning, and I can't stop it. Each time I account for every possibility and think I have it all planned out, something new gets thrown at me, and everything veers off course again. How was I supposed to know that this time Sam would throw his drink over someone in the club?"

"He did what?" asked Jack, recalling the previous occasion his face had ended up drenched.

"It wasn't supposed to happen. Last time, Sam slipped on his beer and smacked his head, and you had to take him to the ER. That's how you found out about the pills, and you confronted Greg during the day when there were…"

"Witnesses," finished Jack.

It turned out this man was indeed a god, playing an elaborate game of chess. He simply couldn't control his pieces.

"Well, what if we kill him?" said Jack, his attention turning to Toby. "What if we just do it now? Break the cycle."

"Let it go, Jack. You don't kill the baby. You never kill the baby," sighed Dr Li, lowering Toby into the crib.

"Well, what about…"

"Tried it already."

"You didn't even listen to what I was going to say."

"This is the eighth time we've had this exact conversation. Yes, Jack, I've tried leaving him stranded on a deserted island. I've tried locking him in a box at the bottom of the sea. I've tried everything. It doesn't work. No matter what I do, people always end up dead."

So, Jack asked the only question that, at that moment, seemed to matter. "Why do you keep trying?"

"Wouldn't you?" asked Dr Li. "Do you have the broken time machine?"

Jack felt a pang of shame as he reached into his boot and handed over what was left of the device.

"It's even worse than last time," said Dr Li, inspecting the mangled pile of wood, glass, and time.

"Can you fix it?"

"I always do, but it might take a few years, and I'll need some help," said Dr Li, eyeing the door.

It was almost time for a much younger Jack to walk through it, seeking refuge.

"For now, take mine," continued Dr Li as he presented his version of the time machine, pristine and brimming with youthful blue fear.

Jack tried to work out exactly how that made sense, but the timeline tangled in his mind until he thought it best not to question it and simply accepted the gift with a "thank you."

Jack heard faint footsteps coming from outside and turned to face the door. He would arrive at any moment. Jack remembered there was no other man and certainly no baby when he first discovered this place all those years ago. With his time growing short, Jack asked one last question.

"What now?"

"Well," began Dr Li, reaching inside the crib and plucking the sleeping infant for Jack to take. "I recommend putting him back where you found him. Afterwards, get a good night's sleep, maybe a haircut and a shave too, and then put these on."

He lifted the neatly folded shirt and trousers and handed them to Jack.

"You're going to need them where you're going."

"It's not going to change anything, is it?"

"Maybe you'll be the one to break the cycle," said Dr Li with a hopeful shrug.

"In that case, give me something, something you didn't give the other seven."

Dr Li considered and placed a familiar metal disc atop the small pile of clothes.

Jack nodded, his eyes lingering on Dr Li a moment longer. Beneath it all, they were the same. Two tired, broken men filled with regret.

Jack held Toby in his arms, closed his eyes and disappeared in an electric blue whirlwind of renewed hope.

Alone once more, Dr Li walked over to the light switch

and flicked it off. The room was swallowed in darkness, and he took his place in it. His breath was the only thing filling the silence as he waited in the wings, eyes trained on the outline of the door. Any moment now, the curtains would rise, and the play would begin.

After a few seconds, the handle twitched, and a moment later, a young Jack hesitantly entered the room, as he was always destined to do, and the wheel kept turning.

59

Jack placed Toby Cud back where he belonged, swaddled in blankets and gently cooing away among the other newborns in the hospital.

They'd only been gone a few minutes, not long enough for anyone to notice. Toby's timeline would continue with barely a hair out of place. He would still grow old and curdle into the cruel mechanical devil Jack dreaded with every fibre of his soul.

Jack watched as Toby's tiny chest rose and down, blissfully unaware of the days to come.

"I'm terrified of you, you know," said Jack, searching the infant's peaceful features for some sign that he might change for the better, a hint that he might undo the future leading Jack here.

"I know what I have to do," continued Jack. "I have to go back there and try something. I just don't know what. Whatever I do, I'll probably end up dead. Maybe you will. Maybe everyone will."

Jack sensed fate's breath on his neck, sending a shiver down his spine. His seconds were tick-tocking away, and death was calling to him. He tried to ignore it, to find some courage in this quiet nursery.

Jack wondered what his death would be like, whether he might be heroic at the end. As much as he tried, he couldn't quite picture it.

"I kept thinking that one day I'd wake up, and this would all have been some mad dream. I think I would've woken up by now," sighed Jack, his gaze drifting to his hands, weathered with calluses and scars, the nails bitten down the stubs.

A faint tremor ran through them that persisted since the day he arrived in this time. Jack realized just how much they'd aged since coming here.

"Dr Li says he'll reboot everything anyway, go back and try again, so I guess nothing I do even matters. I won't even remember it." Jack clenched his hands into fists, a ripple of anger flexing through them. "So then, why am I still so scared?"

He knew the answer. Every time he closed his eyes, he was reminded of it.

"It's because all the screams and the pain and the dying, it still counts...*they* still count."

Jack reached down and held Toby's tiny hand, his chubby fingers curling gently around Jack's.

"So I need to at least try, don't I?"

Toby didn't answer.

60

"Jack, enough arguing. There's bigger shit at stake now. This is serious!" shouted Sam as he ran down the platform towards the carriage. "We have to go back right now!"

Sam stood outside the train, waiting impatiently for the slow-moving carriage doors to open. He didn't have time for this, so he squeezed his body through the small opening and saw...

Jack, standing before him, *ready*.

"We're going back," said Jack, "and we're going to save Lucy and Tim."

Sam eyed Jack curiously. This wasn't the same man who stormed off in a childish tantrum not too long ago.

"Miles," continued Jack, turning to the man who had just joined them. "Weapons?"

"Just my dart gun and a couple of nine-millimetres."

"What's a nine millimetre? Like a tiny knife?" asked Jack.

"They're guns."

"Even better," said Jack, refusing to miss a beat. "Your dart gun. Will it work on Dr Cud?"

"Only one way to find out."

"Ok," concluded Jack, determination coursing through him. "Grab anything else we might need and let's go."

Sam peered at Jack. It wasn't just a change in his demeanour. He looked different, older, and when he spoke, Sam could swear his missing tooth had returned. Sam was probably imagining it.

Miles returned with his meagre supplies and handed Jack and Sam a gun each, both fully loaded with a fresh supply of ammunition. He turned to the mechanical legs sitting patiently on the seats, the apparatus he created to fit into this unfair world to appear normal amongst those who were anything but. Miles decided to leave that part of himself here. If he was going to save the world, it would be as himself.

Jack held out his steady hand, solid with resolve. Sam placed his on top, and Miles reached up to do the same. As time energy buzzed around them, Miles took one last look out through the train's window at the station he called home and watched as it faded from view, replaced by the electric blue promise of a brighter tomorrow.

Perhaps we should take a break here.

"WHAT? NO WAY, WE'RE JUST GETTING TO THE GOOD part."

The good part...He pondered on that for a moment, staring vacantly through the windscreen of the ice cream truck, watching the sun sink through the horizon. It wouldn't be long now.

"Dad," interrupted Jack, his small hands tugging at his father's jumper. "What happened next?"

"Ok," sighed his father. "Well, the three of them returned

to the present and found themselves outside Moonshot Labs. None of them were ready for what they would find inside."

<h1 style="text-align:center">61</h1>

Jack, Sam and Miles hurried through the corridors of Moonshot Labs, hoping they weren't too late.

Another of the time machine's limitations was that it wasn't very precise. Jack tried his hardest to think of *'the present'* but also *'maybe a bit before the present where Lucy and Tim are still unharmed.'*

He wasn't sure how well that had translated. Why couldn't Dr Li have designed it with a proper interface? Or at least some buttons? The small clock housed within the glass dome read 6 o'clock. Would that be enough?

Jack held the time machine in one hand and a handgun in the other, his fingers contorting around its steel frame as it sat uncomfortably against his palm. He didn't like how it felt: cold and sharp, and much heavier than he imagined.

Jack never wanted to hold one. A combination of moral objections and the fear that it might accidentally go off and blow a hole through him. Except he was a changed man now, a man who may not kill a baby but just might kill an insane megalomaniac hell-bent on destroying the world and everyone who lived there.

They reached the door to the lab, and the trio shot each other one last uneasy glance. This was it. There was no going back now. So, with a deep breath and forcing his hand to remain steady, Jack pushed the door open.

The door creaked through the silent darkness, with no sign of Dr Cud or the carnival of terror that Jack thought would be waiting for him. Only the timid glow of moonlight creeping through the window to illuminate their path between the lab's looming shadows.

The air was heavy with the metallic scent of spilled blood and burnt circuits, which set the hairs on Jack's arms standing on end. His fingers danced over the light switch but decided against it, not wanting to see the full extent of what happened here.

Upon venturing further, they soon found Tim. He was bound to a chair by leather straps, his head resting against the table as whatever took place bore its penance on him.

Sam tore open the straps whilst Jack lifted his head, his fingers feeling the smooth plate of metal where Tim's bandages had once been.

Tim was woozy, and his eyes swayed lazily as he struggled to open them.

"Tim. It's me. It's Jack. We're going to get you out of here."

"Jack," murmured Tim, his voice barely more than a breath.

He knew Jack's name. He recognized him. They weren't too late.

Jack overflowed with relief, his chest swelling as the weight he carried for years finally lifted. The beautiful time machine brought him to exactly where he needed to be, exactly *when* he needed to be.

"Where's Lucy?" asked Jack.

"She's gone..."

"Where? Where did she go?"

"She messed it up...the conversion...he was so angry...but she escaped..."

"She escaped?" whispered Jack, ensuring he heard that right.

"Yeah." Tim's voice faded as his eyes closed once more.

Sam caught Tim's head before it smacked back onto the table.

"It's alright, we've got you," assured Sam. His eyes met Jack's, and the pair shared a relieved smile. They did it.

Miles surveyed the room, scanning every shadow. Something wasn't right here.

"Where's Lord Cud?" asked Miles.

At the sound of that name, Tim's eyes shot open, electrified back to life, urgency filling his voice.

"You've got to get me out of here before he comes back."

Jack and Sam nodded to each other. They didn't want to hang around for him to return, either. Together, they hauled Tim out of the chair, draped his arms over their shoulders, and helped the wounded soldier towards the exit.

Tim wobbled and weaved as he drifted through the outskirts of consciousness until finally, not too far from the door, he collapsed to his knees. Jack and Sam scrabbled to get him back up, but Tim pushed them away. He knelt there, head tucked to his chest, shaking. Was he crying?

No.

As Jack leant in close, he realized Tim was laughing.

Tim got back to his feet with ease, the fresh hydraulics in his leg snapping to attention.

"I'm sorry," said Tim, tears streaming down his unhinged smile. "I can't. It's too funny. Look at your faces."

"Tim?" asked Sam, his voice laced with confusion.

Tim's eyes fizzed. "You haven't worked it out yet? You

simple-minded fools." Tim turned to the door and gestured theatrically.

"Care to enlighten them, my lord?"

The door to the lab swung open, and on the other side stood Dr Cud, with Lucy obediently by his side, her vacant eyes reflecting the moonlight.

Jack and Sam reacted at once, guns drawn and aimed directly at Dr Cud as he strolled into the room, chewing the scenery of his grand reveal.

"Blimey," breathed Miles in dreaded awe. "It's really him."

Dr Cud casually approached them, eyeing down the barrels of the guns to the children behind.

"You're going to pay, you going to fucking pay, you bastard," spat Sam, his voice unsteady with rage.

"Don't be rude now. You wouldn't want to upset me." Dr Cud snapped his fingers, and Lucy diligently stepped forward, holding a scalpel.

There was no anger, fear, or regret in her anymore, for all of it was replaced with a sense of singular duty. In one swift motion, Lucy raised the scalpel. Not to meet Jack, Sam or Miles. Instead, she held the blade to her own throat.

"Oh, this is just too good," boasted Tim.

"Lucy," pleaded Jack, hoping to reach past her programming.

They weren't too late. They couldn't be. This wasn't it.

"Lower your guns," commanded Dr Cud.

A moment passed.

Jack weighed up every option and came to only one conclusion.

He let out a mourned breath and lowered his gun.

Sam bit his lip and followed Jack's lead with a small grunt of reluctance.

Miles refused to do the same, his hand trembling, fighting every shred of fear, trying to force it down. This villain standing over him was far more terrifying than anything Miles had fought before. All those created in Lord Cud's image were merely puppets.

This was the real deal, the stuff of legend, a creature who should only exist in stories designed to scare children into behaving. Yet, here he was, standing before him. Miles stilled his arm and stood firm, refusing to back down.

Dr Cud knelt to Miles' level until they were eye to eye.

"Drop. It." ordered Dr Cud, the harsh sounds of each syllable stretching his lips tightly over his barred teeth.

The gun remained, almost touching Dr Cud's forehead.

"I'm afraid you don't control me," said Miles in a weak but defiant voice as he pulled the trigger.

Dr Cud lurched back as the pellet embedded itself in his forehead, sending a shockwave of electricity cascading through his body. Everyone could only watch whilst Dr Cud stumbled, engulfed in furious bolts of energy that crackled and sparked through him.

Dr Cud fought against it, forcing his hand up to his forehead to rip the crumpled pellet from his head. The pellet came free, the current ceased at once, and Dr Cud recomposed himself. He opened his hand, and the glowing ingot fell through his fingers to the floor.

Miles' heart sank as the pellet bounced along the linoleum and rolled to a stop by his feet. Lord Tobias Cud was indeed far more than Miles expected.

Dr Cud turned his attention to Jack and, more importantly, the item tucked inside his boot.

"Give me the time machine," Dr Cud requested, as casually as one might ask someone to pass the salt.

"No," said Jack, the last flicker of fight left in him. "Turn them back first."

Dr Cud erupted with vicious laughter, and Tim soon joined him.

"I thought you were supposed to be the clever one. If my plan is to make everyone do my bidding, infuse my DNA, and implant myself into their minds...Why would I ever create a way to turn them back?" Said Dr Cud as he watched the final embers of Jack's strength peter into darkness. "Now, hand it over."

Sam placed a hand on Jack's chest, stopping him from doing anything stupid. He heard enough.

"Hold up a second. So, what? You get the time machine, and we get lumped with the zombie twins?" Scoffed Sam, reasserting his gun and pointing it again at Dr Cud.

Sam took Jack's gun from him and pointed that, too, for good measure.

"Well, we don't want them. No deal." Sam swung open his arms, directing the barrels of each gun in opposing directions, one at Lucy and one at Tim.

"By all means, do it," shrugged Dr Cud.

"Do it, Sam, kill us," added Tim.

"Sam..." said Jack.

No, Sam had a better idea. Dr Cud might not care about Tim and Lucy, but there was someone he seemed to care about. Sam turned and pointed his guns at a new target.

"I'll shoot Jack. No Jack, no time machine."

"No, you won't," said Dr Cud, able to read the desperate bluff in Sam's eyes.

"Sam..." tried Jack again.

Sam redirected his guns once more.

"I'll shoot Miles."

"I don't know who that is," said Dr Cud, a tad bemused.

Jack turned to Sam, lowering the guns for him.

"It's over," said Jack, finality in his tone.

Jack stepped forward and placed the time machine into Dr Cud's mechanical fingers, the device humming begrudgingly as it met its new owner.

Dr Cud held it delicately, stroking the wood grains and the warm glass dome. He finally had it. It was all his. Everything he ever wanted was now firmly in his grasp.

As his fingers reached its base, he noticed the trio of LEDs, only a single one glowing a dull green.

"Not so fast," said Dr Cud, grabbing Jack by the arm.

Jack's eyes met Sam's and a knowing look passed between them. Sam shook his head, silently pleading with Jack not to leave, to think of a way out, to at least try to run.

"It's ok," mouthed Jack.

"Are you afraid, Jack?" asked Dr Cud, eyes fixated on the time machine.

"No," said Jack. "Not anymore."

"Well, we can fix that," said Dr Cud, and swung around to point a bony finger at Lucy. "Die."

And so the knell of Jack's screams rang out as Lucy did as instructed.

"I would go into detail, but you're probably too young, and if you think about it, I'm sure you don't really want to know what transpired at that moment.

I could tell you how the scalpel ran along Lucy's throat so effortlessly it looked as though her neck was made of butter, but I won't. I could talk about how the force of blood erupted with such pressure that a drop landed on Jack's top lip, but I won't.

I could explain how her life, her hopes and her memories all fled Lucy's body in an instant, leaving only a hollow vessel that fell to the floor with a dull thud. But I won't. I could go on and on about how fucking unfair it was that Lucy, who started with the purest intentions of anybody in that room, only wanting to help people and make her father proud of her, was now the one lying there dead, while Dr Cud lived.

How he felt no sadness or remorse. How he didn't even seem to show any villainous glee, utterly ambivalent to what he did. But I won't."

JACK DOVE TO THE FLOOR TO CATCH LUCY, PRESSING down on her throat to stem the bleeding. Still, blood continued to pour through his fingers, the last beats of Lucy's heart before it surrendered.

Sam opened fire on Dr Cud, snapping his finger back on the trigger again and again until the clip was empty. Most of the bullets flew wildly, all except one, which hit Dr Cud squarely in the face, ricocheting off him like the striking of a bell.

Dr Cud scarcely noticed the bullets flying his way. All his focus was directed towards the time machine. The single, faint LED was now replaced by three full bulbs of bright green fear.

Jack stared into Lucy's eyes, and they stared back, blindly. She was still warm, and the colour was yet to drain from her features. There must be something he could do, some way to bring her back. Jack blinked tears down onto her, each drop vanishing into the deep, black pools of blood.

What right did he have to feel sad? He was the one who ran away for years, knowing she would die and yet doing nothing to stop it.

Lucy's blank expression betrayed the emotions concealed beneath, an endless epitaph of *why*.

Why did it have to end like this?

Why didn't Jack come for her in time?

Why did she have to die?

Jack didn't have the answers.

The backdrop to Jack's grief blurred around him in fantastical chaos. Sam shouted something, throwing the guns at Dr Cud in a last act of defiance, while Miles tried to pull Sam away with little success.

All the while, Tim went on laughing, manic, untuned laughter that pierced through all else like a jagged knife. Tim's laughter abruptly fell silent as Dr Cud cleared his throat and began speaking, but not to Jack, Sam, Miles or Tim. Instead, he was addressing the world.

A NURSE SOMEWHERE FAR AWAY LIFTED HER HEAD AS Dr Cud's voice broadcast through her mind. She listened intently, ready to obey.

"This is a message to all of you," began Dr Cud.

A flight attendant listened intently as he received instructions, instructions he was compelled to follow.

"I command you to increase production and begin screening the entire population for conversion."

Dr Cud appeared to an elderly man in his dreams, calling to him. The man awoke at once and peered over at his wife, still peacefully asleep beside him.

"Kill any you deem unworthy."

Dr Cud finished his announcement and seized Jack by the collar, tearing him away from Lucy.

"Timothy," commanded Dr Cud. "Kill Sam and the midget."

All joviality stripped itself away from Tim in an instant, and his expression turned serious, murderously so. He yanked the bloodied scalpel from Lucy's lifeless fist and charged towards Miles.

Miles tried to wrestle him off, but he was no match for Tim's new body. With a single, swift stab, Tim embedded the blade firmly into Miles' arm. Sam lunged at Tim, trying to snatch the scalpel from him, but Tim effortlessly shoved Sam back.

Sam and Miles backed into a corner as Tim continued to advance, swiping the scalpel in wild, pendular arcs and howling with laughter.

Dr Cud admired Tim for a moment with pride over what he had created. He pulled Jack in close, and in the blink of an eye, the pair were gone, evaporated into the wild blue yonder, leaving only chaos and blood in their wake.

PART 7

THE REAPING

62

"LUCY'S NOT REALLY DEAD, IS SHE?"

"I'm afraid so."

"She comes back, though, right? They can use the time machine to go back and save her."

"Dr Cud controls the time machine now'"

"Ugh, I hate him. Why is he such a poo-head?"

"I can tell you if you'd like."

<h1 style="text-align:center">63</h1>

You should know Dr Tobias Cud relatively well by now. We've met him at both ends of his timeline, both sides of the spectrum, from innocence to evil.

There was, however, a lot of middle for Toby Cud, years and years of middle. So that's where we're starting this part of the story, right at the beginning of Toby Cud's middle.

It was 1985, Toby was in his thirties, and his ruddy, handsome face was free from the scars and metal that would one day define it.

Although, perhaps not entirely free from metal, as at this moment, he was wearing on his head what looked like, and may well have once been, a colander. Right now, Toby was neither composed, slick, nor menacing. He was instead flailing around in his stained lab coat as bright blue hues pulsated through his skin, and it hurt a lot.

He soon collapsed to his knees, finding it difficult to focus on the circle of mirrors that surrounded him. Each Toby Cud in each mirror screamed, mouths hanging open in perfect synchronicity until their voice cracked and gave out.

Eventually, the switch was thrown, and the energy flow stopped, leaving Toby in a smoking heap on the floor. He unstrapped his colander helmet and flopped onto his back as the pain subsided.

"How was that?" asked Toby in a small, hoarse voice.

"We peaked at twenty-one G's," came the reply. "I hate to say it, but we'll need a larger telepathic field."

"Ok," said Toby, his voice steadying. "Increase the voltage."

"Are you sure? If we increase it any further, it could cause permanent damage."

Toby turned to his lab partner, Dr Li, who was no older than himself, and wearing a matching lab coat that was patterned with a similar rainbow of past experiments.

"Increase the voltage," repeated Toby.

Dr Li nodded and lowered his goggles back over his eyes. "Increasing the voltage."

Toby strapped the helmet on, dragged himself to his feet, and braced himself for the 5000 volts about to fire through him.

Dr Li pulled the switch, and the screaming began once more.

"Don't beat yourself up, Li. We made some real progress today," said Toby as he bit into his tuna sandwich. "We make a good team, me and you. Cud and Li. The first people to travel through time."

Toby's hand spelled out the words, imagining their names written across history.

Dr Li swallowed the final bite of his banana with a pained

gulp. He wasn't too sure about '*Cud and Li*'. The pair worked together at Moonshot Labs for over a decade and had spearheaded many projects together, even ate lunch together in the same spot in the cafeteria every single day.

In spite of this, Dr Li still wasn't convinced their names should be held together in the same breath, for a start it sounded far too much like *Cuddly* for his liking.

"We're still a long way off. I doubt the world will see time travel in our lifetime."

"That hardly matters. It's time travel. As long as it becomes a reality one day, it'll find us." said Toby with a hopeful smile. "But I really do think we're onto something here."

Dr Li took a tentative sip of his coffee as he wondered aloud. "Let's say we could get it working. What would we even do with it?"

"Well, think of all the things you could do, all the lives you could save. You'd have access to the greatest minds in history, as well as the future."

"But what would *you* do?"

"Oh, I don't know. I think I'd like to go back and see if Jesus Christ was all he's cracked up to be."

"I didn't know you were religious."

"I go to church on Sundays, but I think that's more out of habit than anything else."

Dr Li lowered his coffee. "The funny thing is, if you went back, with all your knowledge and technology, people would probably think of you as a god. They might even start worshipping you."

Toby laughed a small dismissive sigh. "I don't think I could handle that sort of pressure."

"Right," said Dr Li, taking another sip. "How's your research coming along? The DNA transfer thingy?"

"It's going great," beamed Toby. "I've nearly got the

embryos to accept the foreign nucleotides. A couple more days, I think, then look out world."

"Mmm," agreed Dr Li as he scooped up his banana peel and empty coffee cup. "Well, I best get back to it."

"Oh, before you go. I've been meaning to ask if you fancied getting a drink or something after work?"

Dr Li rolled the idea over in his mind for a moment, or at least pretended to, before replying with a swift, "I can't tonight, sorry," and left.

"No worries. Some other time then, maybe?" Toby called after him.

"Some other time," promised Dr Li.

Toby sat alone in the cafeteria, finished his sandwich, and returned to his lab. He spent the rest of the day alone with his nucleotides, surrounded by centrifuges, test tubes and microscopes meticulous in their organization, immersing himself in his work as the rest of the world slipped into the background.

Toby left work long after everyone else was gone and travelled home on the same train he always took. He sat in the same spot, jotting half-formed ideas down in his notebook, writing in hurried shorthand as his thoughts raced his pen.

He then made his way to his flat on the sixth floor. Upon opening the door, he called out, "Paprika," and soon, a cat, young enough to still be considered a kitten, came bounding over to him. Toby scratched behind her ear and stroked her salt and pepper fur and she purred happily in response.

"Heya Paprika, were you waiting for me to get home? You're a good girl, aren't you?" said Toby as she nuzzled his ankle.

Toby made his way to the kitchen cupboard, careful to avoid stepping on any eager paws, and plucked out a can of tuna. He decanted the tuna into a bowl and placed it on the floor for Paprika to sink her face into.

Toby reached back into the cupboard to fetch a can of soup for himself, which he poured into a saucepan and heated on the hob until it bubbled with a rich creamy scent.

With their bellies full, Toby and Paprika settled onto the sofa to watch some late-night talk show. Toby occasionally reached for his notebook, adding flashes of inspiration as they came to him, and punctuated each note with a gentle stroke of Paprika's fur, peacefully rising and lowering as she snored.

***

Toby arrived at work the next day long before anyone else, and as he reached his lab, he noticed the door was already unlocked. His heart sank, already knowing what was waiting for him.

As he stepped inside, he once more found the place ransacked and his work ruined. Petri dishes lay shattered on the floor, and research was torn to shreds, littering the room.

Toby closed his eyes and let out a weary sigh. "Those kids again."

With a quiet resignation, he fetched a broom from the corner and began sweeping up the mess. Starting once more from scratch.

64

"Please, Tim. Just listen. You don't need to do this," begged Sam as he and Miles dodged the savage swings of Tim's scalpel, dripping with hate and a fair smattering of Miles' blood.

But Tim's mind was no longer his own.

Miles' torn shirt sleeve was turning a bright shade of red, and he was losing feeling in his arm. He wrapped his hand tightly around the gash along his biceps and felt the blood pulsing through his fingers.

Another stab of the blade, this one grazing Sam's cheek as he did his best to limbo out of its path.

"Tim, mate, I know you," panted Sam, refusing to give up on him. "You've gotten out of worse than this. You can fight it."

The knife danced in the air as Tim continued his pursuit, a sick imitation of joy stretching across his armour-plated jaw.

"Why would I want to stop when I'm having so much fun?"

Sam and Miles had nowhere left to run, pressed against the cold concrete walls. Miles swallowed down the pain and fear tightening around his throat and slid a hand down into his pocket, where he retrieved a pellet and loaded it into the chamber of his gun. He appreciated Sam's unwavering belief in his friend, but sentimentality wouldn't help them here.

"That little toy of yours didn't work on Lord Cud, and it won't work on me either, because I am him," hissed Tim.

Well, there was only one way to find out. Miles locked eyes with Tim, raised his weapon and fired a pellet into Tim's neck with expert precision. The pellet pulsed a wave of furious red current through Tim, forcing him back. Tim shook violently until black smoke spilled from every orifice.

Half-cooked, Tim stiffly collapsed to the floor as the pellet finished its work.

"Is...Is he dead?" whispered Sam, edging towards Tim.

Tim suddenly shot awake and sat bolt upright like a meerkat, darting his head in every direction.

"Sam?" murmured Tim, as though waking from a dream.

Sam raised his own gun at this. "Don't try that again. Do you really think I'm that much of an idiot? You might look like Tim, but you're not him."

"I am Tim, and mind where you're pointing that fucking thing, will you?"

"Tim!" Sam's suspicions fell at once, and he threw his arms around him, hugging Tim tightly.

"Alright, alright," complained Tim, not exactly returning the embrace, but not pushing Sam away either. "What the hell is going on here?"

Sam turned to Miles, who was devoid of any answer. He stared back, blank with disbelief. This wasn't possible.

Tim got to his feet. A new man, or more accurately, an old one. He glanced down at his hands, stapled together around an entire load of macabre robotic instruments. However, they were still his, and he was regaining control. It was all coming back to him now.

"She did it," whispered Tim, almost to himself.

A familiar pain etched its way up Tim's leg, no longer numbed by the software, and he revelled in it. The pain meant he was himself once more.

The universe was quick to rebalance the scales of fate, and the sound of distant footsteps cut through the sweet reunion, lots of them echoing down the corridor and charging straight toward the lab.

Sam readied his gun and made his way to the door.

"Let's do this."

"Absolutely not!" exclaimed Miles, blocking Sam's path. "We have three guns, two of which are devoid of bullets. That's hardly enough to make it out of here, and even if we could, believe me, it won't be any safer outside."

"Well, what are we supposed to do?" asked Sam, the growing percussion of footsteps rattling through him.

Without another word, Miles reached up and slammed his fist against a panel embedded in the wall. The door beside them whirred and shuddered as it locked into place.

"These door's seal magnetically. Lord Cud's paranoia might come in handy for once. Should be enough to keep them out for a while."

"Then what?" asked Sam, but he already knew the answer.

65

IT WAS 1993, AND TOBY CUD RECENTLY TURNED forty years old. His hair was growing thinner than he cared to admit, and the shadows around his eyes grew a shade darker. Yet, one aspect of his appearance remained unchanged: the colander he wore on his head.

The colander grew more technically sound over the years, equipped with many relays and surge protectors, meaning experiments were now only *very* painful instead of unbearably so.

After another afternoon spent being Dr Li's guinea pig, Toby couldn't help but notice something curious about one monitor angled just out of his sight line.

"That's strange," said Toby, squinting at the screen. "It only looks like it's recording *your* brainwaves. It doesn't seem to pick up on mine at all. Do we need to reconfigure it?"

"No, it's fine," said Dr Li in a quick, dismissive tone.

"Are you sure, because..."

"It's fine," snapped Dr Li, a little harsher than intended. "I made a few modifications, that's all. I decided it would be best to tune the telepathic field solely to my fear receptors."

"Oh, right," said Toby in a small, hurt voice.

"That way, nobody can use it without my strict supervision," continued Dr Li, scribbling notes on a clipboard, purposefully oblivious to Toby's disappointment.

"Not even me?"

"It's safer this way."

"Of course. I understand," said Toby, forcing a smile. "You can't have just anyone using it willy-nilly."

Toby couldn't help but wonder what exactly the point of today's torture session was if his brainwaves weren't even being recorded. No, he trusted Dr Li and was sure there must have been a good reason.

After a long silence hanging heavy around them, Toby took a deep breath and worked up the courage to ask the question he would ask Li every week.

"Me and a few of the guys are going bowling tonight if you're interested?"

Dr Li didn't turn from his monitor.

"Can't tonight, busy." He stopped making up proper excuses some years ago. Bowling, badminton, drinks down the pub. No matter what Toby asked of him, the RSVP would always read the same.

"Some other time then," agreed Toby, forcing another smile.

TOBY SPENT THAT EVENING BOWLING ALONE. HIS reservation for two was non-refundable, and there was always the possibility Dr Li might still show.

He tossed the ball down the aisle, and to his surprise, knocked down a strike. For a fleeting moment, excitement replaced his loneliness. When Toby glanced around for someone to share in his moment, he found only the indifferent gaze of the staff, boredom palpable on their faces.

Peering up at the screen, it now blinked Dr Li's name. Toby returned to the row of bowling balls and grabbed another as the pins reset. He would take Dr Li's turn for him, just to get him started.

66

Sam sat by the window and watched the sun rise over a new day, one filled with chaos, sirens, screaming, and dying. The street below was a procession of smashed windows and kicked in doors.

Few buildings remained standing, most were now mere skeletons of charred wooden beams and rubble. Sam watched as people fled, fell, and died, their corpses littering the roads unceremoniously, like fallen leaves. Some died quickly and almost mercifully, whilst others fought back and paid a far higher price. Deep purple hues indelibly imprinted on their skin and terror stamped into their final expression.

As the sun rose higher in the sky, the fires went out, and the screams fell silent. The fight was over, and the victor was clear. Sam's mind fixated on his family, his mom, his dad and Molly, and a million scenarios played out in his head. He could almost hear their voices calling out to him, growing more distant with each imagined fate. Sam told himself they were safe, believing anything else would've sent him mad.

He wanted to leave. He wanted to go home and make sure

his family were safe. However, he heard the uniformed breaths of the army on the other side of the door, still patiently waiting for them.

Miles said that as long as the electricity held, that door was impenetrable. The fluorescent lights above them were indeed still working, illuminating a harsh spotlight over the decaying lab and Lucy's senseless body, shrouded in a dark brown cocoon of dried blood.

Sam had laid a lab coat over her face, and they all said a few words, but it wasn't proper. They couldn't bury her, couldn't cremate her. Instead, they were trapped with this constant reminder of their failure splayed out across the floor, and worst of all, she was starting to smell.

She believed in Sam. He couldn't imagine why, but she did. She begged for his help, yet Sam didn't even know the first thing about her. She tried to open up to Sam back at the cottage, to share her past with him, but Sam wasn't the shoulder she needed then, and he certainly wasn't now.

Sam knew she had a dad. He might be out there now, searching the wreckage for any sign of her. More likely, he already shared the same fate as his daughter. Sam peered over at her, facing his mistake.

Lucy's pale features poked out from beneath the lab coat, and only now Sam notice her beauty, the delicate porcelain features that he played a part in breaking. Sam felt a deep knot of shame. He wished he got to know her better and silently thanked her for believing in him.

In another life, perhaps.

Sam checked the locator again. He'd found it on the makeshift surgical table, buried amongst the various tools, computer components, and pieces of Tim. The locator screen lit up and once more displayed the words '*Location Unknown.*'

Jack was lost.

Across the room, Tim's mind began to wake, and so did the pain. Fighting off the plague in his head left him with the worst hangover he'd ever felt, but he wasn't able to stop the dreams. They were vivid and aggressive as Dr Cud's desires, hate, and fear whispered through him.

Dr Cud's consciousness was dripping back into his, drop by corrosive drop, and the leak was getting stronger. The dam he built in his mind was weakening, and it wouldn't be long before the darkness washed Tim away entirely.

Tim wasn't alone in this fight, however, as a bit of Lucy's mind was still in there with him. He sensed her soul inside him fighting on like a bright glimmer through the darkness, forcing Dr Cud back and buying him a little more time.

As Tim opened his eyes, Miles met him, standing over him with his gun ready, just in case.

"He's awake," called Miles.

Sam felt a flash of hope, but didn't allow himself to give in to it.

"Tim?" asked Sam, sure that whatever spell turned him back would already be broken.

"It's still me," groaned Tim, stretching out his aching joints, making sure they were all still his own.

"Incredible," said Miles, studying Tim with fascination. "There is simply no explanation for it."

"It was Lucy," said Tim. "Dr Cud filled me up with computer chips and then tried shoving his mind into me too, but Lucy got in the way of the upload before it finished. So somehow, when you shot me, we could fight it together."

Sam's hope swelled. Not only was Tim back, but maybe a bit of Lucy survived. There was probably some futuristic sci-fi gadget somewhere around here that could put her in her own body and bring Lucy back for good.

A deep frown grew along Miles' brow as he thought.

"It seems I briefly inhibited the part of Tim that was machine, allowing his true consciousness to take over." The tempo of his words grew slower as they reached their inevitable conclusion. "If what you say is true, then it's only a matter of time…"

Miles trailed off, unable to finish. He was used to dealing with monsters, but somewhere over the years, he forgot there was once humanity in there as well. Every experiment he fought, each one of them was once a person like Tim.

How many of their deaths was he personally responsible for? Thousands, at least. Was their consciousness still in there, too, hiding away?

"It's alright, I know," said Tim. "I can feel him. He's trying to take over again."

"No," said Sam.

He had a taste of hope and he wasn't about to lose it now.

"We saved you. I saved you. You can fight it. You have to. Or we could shoot you again? Miles, where's your gun?"

Miles simply shook his head. "It would kill him."

"I'll be fine," said Tim with a smile, though it didn't reach his eyes. "I won't let him win without a fight."

Tim's eyes then drifted to Miles' haphazardly bandaged arm. In a sickening flash of memory, Tim saw the scalpel in his hand, its blade dyed red, and the helplessness in Miles' face, and a wave of shame rushed over him.

The repercussions of last night's misdeeds, the bastard sidekick to any hangover, be it cocaine, ecstasy, an evil wizard's mind control, or that '*one last can of special brew*' which stole his body away from him, it didn't matter, the responsibility for what he had done to Miles lingered.

"Sorry about the arm," said Tim.

Miles looked down at the unappealing mass of torn flesh stretching up his arm.

"Nothing a bit of super glue and a few stitches couldn't fix," said Miles with a chipper smile.

The mood needed desperately to be lifted, and Miles found the perfect solution.

"I believe I saw a drinks cabinet around here somewhere. I think we could all do with one."

67

As the trio made quick work of Dr Cud's surprisingly well-stocked drinks cabinet, Tim sensed the man's influence growing stronger, in subtle, insidious ways. The occasional twitch of a finger, the odd dark thought. He felt it in his bones, literally, thanks to his new metal skeleton, a replica of the one inside Dr Cud and the one which would soon be welded into anyone deemed worthy enough.

You may wonder what compelled Toby Cud to turn himself into a discount Halloween costume. To answer that, we need to take another detour along his timeline.

It was 2002, and, nearing his fiftieth birthday, Toby Cud was still working at Moonshot Labs.

He still wore the same old lab coat, fitting ever looser on his hunched shoulders. He saw Dr Li wandering through the halls, albeit far less often, and he was still alone. Toby tried to ignore how empty the halls became. A lack of funding stripped the life from the place. Once a teeming utopia,

Moonshot Labs was now a mere skeleton crew of faces he no longer recognized. Yet Dr Cud soldiered on, exactly as he always did.

The only difference to his rigorous routine on this day was that today, he left his lunch on the train. He was so engrossed with his notepad that he almost missed his stop.

Upon noticing the doors to the train were about to close, he jumped up and bounded out the carriage only to watch his sandwich, crisps, and banana continue on without him. All of which led to him standing at the vending machine, squinting at the options as he decided upon a suitable replacement.

C9, Salt and Vinegar.

Toby reached into his pocket and pulled out some change, but as he held the coin to the slot, he noticed his hand was shaking. Toby noted a slight tremor in his hand recently, but he dismissed it as simply a case of low blood sugar, or stress, something that would fix itself on its own and certainly nothing to concern himself with.

However, as he grabbed his wrist with his other hand, trying to steady the tremor long enough to line the coin up with the slot, Toby doubted himself. Maybe it *was* something. His hand gave an involuntary jolt, and the coin slipped through his fingers, clinking as it rolled along the floor and underneath the vending machine.

Toby dropped to his knees to reach through the cave of dusty wiring in search of the coin. His body suddenly weakened, and as he clasped at empty air, the world shook beneath him. Toby's legs quivered and crumbled, and everything fell away, leaving Toby trembling and lying infantile on the cold tile floor. He saw the coin glinting beneath the vending machine, leaning against the back wall, now forever out of reach.

Then Toby felt a sharp knock on his spine. He shifted his unsteady body and saw that Dr Li had tripped over him. Dr Li quickly regained his footing and murmured something half apologetic as he continued on his way without a second glance. Toby opened his mouth to speak, to say something, but the strength in his voice drained from his body. Not that it would have mattered. This was already the longest interaction the pair shared in years.

PARKINSON'S. PARKINSON'S. PARK-IN-SON'S. PARKED sun. The word bounced around Toby's mind until it lost all meaning. He knew what Parkinson's was, of course, but never gave it much heed. Parkinson's fit into the same category as alzheimer's and arthritis, diseases reserved for other people, old people, not for him.

Toby peered past the doctor and quickly reviewed the results himself. There it was, clear as day in the scan of his brain, a labyrinth of grooves through his cerebral cortex, deep and thick, stretching along his basal ganglia and cascading down the substantia nigra falls. His brain was always his greatest asset, and now it was failing him.

"Are there any treatments available?" asked Toby.

"There's not much we can do for you, I'm afraid," said the doctor. "It's more a case of learning to live with the disease. For many people, it's just a part of getting old."

The word *old* stung Toby more than any diagnosis ever could. He wasn't old. Old people were old. He was still young. He had to be. Young people had things left to do, and Toby Cud had so much left to do.

TOBY LEFT THE DOCTOR'S OFFICE WITH A prescription for some tablets and a new perception of his own mortality. He spent the train ride home watching a young couple a few seats ahead of him. They had days to spare, yet Toby already burned most of his up, and the days remaining weren't looking promising, only the mounting loss of faculties to look forward to, and after that, the icy hand of the grave.

He continued staring at the couple, gossiping and laughing, as envy crept beneath his skin. They were wasting their gift; they weren't appreciating what they had. If he had their days, Toby would use them to improve mankind, help people and...

Toby's mind went blank as a fog descended around his thoughts, leaving them lost and unfinished.

AFTER SEVERAL ATTEMPTS, TOBY EVENTUALLY GOT his key in the lock to open his front door and found Paprika waiting for him inside, as she always did. His frustrations evaporated upon seeing his faithful cat, with her greying fur, slowly pad over to him, mewing as she sunk her face into him.

Toby knelt with considerable effort and ran his wrinkled hand through her soft coat. He felt a small area of Paprika's back and noticed a tuft of hair missing. The skin beneath was loose over her bony rib cage. So much changed without him even noticing.

Toby fetched a microwave dinner from the fridge and a can of cat food from the cupboard. He twisted the handle on the can opener as best he could, wrestling with it as it fumbled through his fingers. Everything was becoming a challenge, things he took for granted all his life.

Five minutes passed, and the can didn't open.

Ten minutes passed, and Paprika gave up her excitement and retreated to her bed. Finally, after half an hour, Toby made a decision. He decided it wasn't fair and caught the next train to Moonshot Labs.

HE WASN'T OLD. HE WAS A GENIUS. ONE WHO COULD fix anything, so of course he would fix himself. Toby began with his left hand, where he first noticed a problem.

A gyroscopic exoskeleton around it would undoubtedly counteract the shaking. Except the tremors weren't predictable. He needed to go deeper, to trace along the nerves directly and measure their signals. He couldn't allow the disease to have the slightest advantage over him.

Toby injected a syringe of local anesthetic into the arm, finally forcing it to sit still. Then, using only his right hand, he began the surgery, piercing the scalpel through the layers of skin and fatty tissue before intricately grafting wire along his nervous system. It was inelegant, but it worked, and the metal cage around his arm successfully dulled the shaking.

OVER THE FOLLOWING FEW MONTHS, TOBY REFINED the exoskeleton, making it smaller and stronger, continually unstitching his arm to access the inner workings of his body. However, the disease fought back and spread faster than Toby could keep up with.

It wasn't long before Toby was forced to extend the operation to his legs, his spinal cord and even his face until scarcely an inch of his body was free from mechanical protrusions, becoming a walking science experiment.

At first, people eyed him with wary curiosity, believing it to be some strange fashion statement. However, as his augmentations became more pronounced, they avoided him the way Dr Li did.

Toby often noticed people staring at him from a distance, but they would avert their gaze if he ever got too close. He would walk through the supermarket aisles and watch people's faces change as they caught a glimpse. Mothers would shield their children's eyes whilst failing to hide their own revulsion in time.

The teenagers at the bowling alley were far more vocal in their ridicule. Groups of them would turn up just to shout spiteful nicknames from across the lanes, '*The Iron Wanker*' being a particular favourite. Hoping to escape their torment, Toby began visiting the bowling alley at quieter times and would request the lane at the end, far away from anyone else, but try as he might, they would always find him.

He finally gave up the hobby after one of the more confident teens threw a discarded drink can at his head, telling Toby it was his son.

Even at his church, where Toby was always accepted, he soon felt like a pariah, outcast and ostracized by the other patrons. With each passing Sunday, Toby found people would sit further and further away from him, whispering about him from across the pews. Toby heard every scornful remark thanks to his newly augmented ear drums.

One day, the Vicar took Toby aside and voiced the concerns echoing through the church, recommending Toby find a different place to worship.

Even God abandoned Toby.

IT WAS FINE, TOBY TOLD HIMSELF. THE WORLD MAY have turned its back on him, but it didn't matter. He knew there was still someone who would always be happy to see him. Yet, as he opened his front door one night, she was nowhere to be seen.

"Paprika?"

She didn't come. Toby checked her bed, the litter tray, and the sunbeam by the window where she liked to sit. He eventually found her huddled in a ball under the sofa, shivering tightly.

"Paprika, what's wrong?" asked Toby, reaching his arm towards her.

She drew back, eyes wide and her body tense, as though he were a stranger. He slipped his hand around her and pulled the cat free, her claws scraping against the linoleum.

As he tried to kiss her head, the old feline hissed and tried to escape, wriggling through Toby's arms.

"It's ok," said Toby, attempting to soothe her, but his metallic voice box hissed back at her.

Paprika wriggled harder, padding her paws against Toby's face as he tried to hold her close. His arms tightened reflexively, the metal casing around his skin pressing into her.

"Shhh, everything's ok," repeated Toby, but her struggling only grew more desperate, now clawing at Toby's shirt. He gripped her tighter. All he needed was for her to calm down for a moment. He simply needed her to stop.

"Paprika, please..."

A sickening crack filled the air.

Paprika's body went limp, no longer struggling, as her head flopped back.

Toby froze, staring down at his arm, feeling a strange disconnect between himself and it. The metal limb clamped itself around Paprika with a force he didn't even know he was capable of. Perhaps he miscalculated the hydraulics. A simple miscalculation was all it was. It wasn't his fault. He didn't mean to do it.

Toby relinquished his grip, and Paprika fell lifeless to the floor with a shallow thud. Small pools of water collected in the silver divots around Toby's eyes, sizzling against his hardware. It wasn't fair. He didn't mean it!

She was gone, and nothing could bring her back. Except that wasn't true. There was something, something that could rebalance the scales in Toby's favour. *The time machine!*

The doors of Toby's mind flew open with possibility. How had he not thought of this before?

Dr Li must have finished it by now. Toby would simply borrow it, not that it would even be considered borrowing. After all, Toby dedicated years of his life to helping Dr Li, and he put his blood, sweat, and tears into it. That granted him some level of ownership.

He suffered for years, being used as a guinea pig. Every frequency of every wave bombarded his brain. Maybe that exacerbated his mental deterioration, perhaps it caused his Parkinson's altogether. It was only fair Toby use it to fix Paprika, and maybe even himself.

Toby laid Paprika's body gently onto her bed and hurried back to Moonshot Labs. He hadn't spoken to Dr Li in forever. Come to think of it, Toby hadn't even seen him for the past few months. It wouldn't matter anyway, he supposed. Toby didn't need to ask permission. The device belonged to him. He would use it once, maybe twice, and no one would even know it was gone.

Toby caught the last train and walked down the streets towards Moonshot Labs. The light of the lampposts reflected on the embedded ingots in his face, illuminating him in a lurid orange glow. Toby felt more comfortable at night. There were fewer people to stare and judge. All that was about to change.

Toby marched with newfound purpose through the corridors of Moonshot Labs, resisting the nervous urge to knock as he reached Dr Li's office. He pulled open the door handle, denting it under the force of his foreign strength.

Inside, newspapers, photographs, and half-scribed ideas littered the small office, but no time machine.

Toby checked every spot in the room, digging through filling cabinets and desks but found nothing, until he noticed something curious about the collage of scattered photographs. Discreetly, someone took each photograph from a distance, and each depicted the same child and his parents.

Then, his attention turned to the newspapers, boasting dates that had yet to happen and articles on events which wouldn't occur for years. This confirmed it. The time machine was functional. It was used.

Most importantly, it was kept from him. Why didn't Dr Li share this? They were supposed to be partners. They were supposed to be friends.

Li was gone without a trace. He abandoned Toby. This truth settled over Toby, and he realized they never truly were partners or friends.

They were enemies.

It wasn't just Dr Li.

Toby's fists clenched with a metallic groan, grinding his joints together as he relived every stare, and laugh, and whisper. They were all his enemies.

The entire world needed to pay for how it treated him.

68

Tim sucked down the final few sips of his Piña Colada. In the past, Tim wouldn't have strayed from beer and whiskey, the manliest of the drinks. Yet, here, on the precipice of death, all pretences were long gone. Plus, Piña Coladas were delicious, which is why Tim had seen off six of them.

Beside him, Sam grimaced as he took a sip from his own monstrosity of a drink, comprised tequila, rum, and a splash of absinthe, all swirling together into a radioactive potion which he proudly named '*The Sam Supreme.*'

Sam choked it down until all that remained was a frothy green moustache dripping down his top lip.

Miles sipped from a simple glass of water, the cleanest water he had in years, and to him, it tasted like the sweetest elixir to greet his lips. He held it up to the light, watching as the reflections scattered through it, uninterrupted by even a single rat's hair.

Tim tipped the last dregs of foam into his mouth and continued his story.

"So, then Sam pulls out the gun like an absolute madman.

What was it you were going to make them do? Sing or something, wasn't it?"

"Dance," said Sam, reaching for the bottle of absinthe to concoct another round.

"Yeah, dance, that was it. And then you were going to outrun the police in your mom's car." Tim shook his head, barely containing his laughter. "You couldn't even bloody drive!"

That was enough to set them all off, and the three of them burst into a fit of laughter.

"That doesn't surprise me one bit," said Miles. "Samuel has shown himself to be exceptionally capable in the face of danger."

"Not compared to Tim," said Sam. "He's done some properly cool stuff. Tell Miles about the time you beat up Pablo Escobar."

Tim hurriedly averted his gaze from Miles and took another sip of his empty glass.

"And, of course, Tim saved us from Greg," continued Sam. "He was trying to shoot us, and Tim blew him up with fireworks. Absolute legend."

Tim couldn't help but smile at that. He did save them.

"Greg was all like, '*You ain't got the balls.*' Then Tim looks him dead in the eyes and says, '*You do not bring a gun to a rocket fight,*' it was the coolest thing ever."

"It was alright," agreed Tim. "You'd have done the same."

Sam stewed on that for a moment. Would he have done the same?

He was sitting there drinking Sam Supremes whilst Jack was out there somewhere, lost in time as Dr Cud's prisoner and his family. Sam swept the thought away with another sip. Not now.

Instead, his mind turned to Tim, who may never see his

family again, never get the chance to save them, or even say goodbye.

"If anything happens to you," began Sam. "If we can't... y'know, stop it. Is there anyone you want us to find? Give them a message or something?"

"Nah," said Tim, taking another imaginary sip.

"Not even your family?" asked Miles.

Tim shrugged. "My dad died when I was little, and I haven't spoken to my mom in years."

The words fell bluntly from his mouth as though they held little weight, but his fingers tightened ever so slightly around his empty glass.

"No mates, no girlfriends?" asked Sam before venturing further. "No...Boyfriends?"

"Fuck off. I ain't gay!" snapped Tim, but his voice faltered.

What was the point of holding it in now, so close to the end? His voice softened.

"Well, actually, I am a bit." He gave a shy, almost embarrassed laugh, just in case he needed to backtrack.

Sam laughed with him, and Miles soon joined them. The three of them, sharing their laughter, a tiny moment of joy in the hurricane's eye.

Tim felt the weight lift from him and let out a warm sigh. He should've done it sooner, but at least he did it now.

69

It was 2015, and as the years passed, Toby grew more obsessed and paranoid. His sole goal now was to fix every problem that came with being human. He was above humanity now. Humans were flawed, and he long since surpassed them.

The lack of sun and constant augmentation caused Toby's skin to become a sickly shade of pale, stretched tightly over machinery. Not that anyone would ever see it, as he only dared to venture from his lab at night, slipping through the shadows to stock up on supplies and food.

Hunger, another flaw he would soon dispense with, every bite he took irritated him, a reminder that he still had a long way to go to escape the shackles of the flesh. There were too many problems to fix, and he was running out of time. He needed more manpower, but he would hardly find any around here.

Moonshot Labs shut down years ago, leaving Toby to haunt the building in isolation as it fell into disrepair, decaying as quickly as he was.

All that was about to change. Toby would repopulate this

place with a workforce of his own design, thanks to his newest creation: the small orange pill he now held in the palm of his silver hand.

A pill with the power to change the course of humanity for the better, precisely as he willed it.

All he needed was a test subject.

So Toby ventured out into the night.

———

IT DIDN'T TAKE LONG BEFORE TOBY SPOTTED THE perfect specimen. A dishevelled man staggering down an alleyway with a can of something or other in his hand, mumbling to himself.

Toby lurched from the shadows, his gait unnatural, like a spider devouring its prey. The man had barely enough time to register Toby before feeling the sharp prick of a syringe plunge into his neck.

The thick tranquillizer flowed through into his veins, and it was only a matter of seconds before he slipped away.

———

BY THE TIME THE MAN AWOKE, TOBY'S GRAND experiment had already began. The man tried to move, but found his wrists and ankles were bound to a large mahogany chair. He tried to see where he was but found only the blinding light of a torch, behind which stood the unholy silhouette of the devil himself.

"Pupil dilation normal," said the figure in a synthetic tone as it scribbled down notes onto a pad.

"Where am I?" asked the man.

The robotic beast said nothing, waiting, hoping.

The man swallowed, a strange certainty forming in his mind.

"I'm at Moonshot Labs," he said, recounting a newfound memory not there before.

"And who am I?"

"You're Doctor Tobias Cud."

"Wonderful," breathed Toby, the apertures in his eyes flicking with excitement. The basic knowledge imprinted itself successfully.

Next test. Obedience. Toby loosened the restraints around the man's wrists but found he did not attempt to escape, remaining completely still.

Good.

Toby presented a sewing needle and handed it to the man, who took it diligently, holding it between thumb and forefinger.

"Prick your finger," ordered Toby.

Without question, the man stabbed the tip of the needle into the end of his finger, and a tiny dot of blood grew around it.

Toby shuddered with ecstasy, but he needed to be sure. "Keep going."

The needle dug deeper, piercing the spongy flesh, slicing through nerves, and scratching against bone. The man recognized the pain sparking through his body, but felt no need to react. He only felt the compulsion to continue pushing the needle through, to do as he was instructed.

The man continued until the needle tip was visible through the underside of his fingernail. Still, Toby didn't tell him to stop. So the man kept pushing until the fingernail lifted from its bed, peeling away.

Toby stared, unblinking, salivating at his newfound power.

After countless more tests, Toby discovered how far the pill's influence would extend. The level of obedience was more than he could have hoped. They would literally die for him.

Unfortunately, learning this meant Toby would require some new test subjects. So, he began recruiting.

Soon, those he recruited began recruiting others, infiltrating drug dens and Narcotics Anonymous meetings, converting anyone and everyone who Toby believed the world wouldn't miss.

It spread like a virus until Toby amassed a small army, each equipped with a single objective: find Dr Li.

And after nearly a decade of searching, they found him.

Toby was enjoying a lobster dinner in the fanciest restaurant he knew when he found out, still yet to fully eliminate the need for food. The restaurant was empty apart from the twenty obedient staff waiting on his every command, moving as he moved. He savoured the power over them. That was far more delicious than any food could ever be.

A man approached his table, with his hands clasping a folder and his head bowed in respect to his master.

"What is it?" snapped Toby.

The man spoke in a tone which may have been mistaken for nervousness if Toby hadn't already eliminated that weakness.

"We've located him."

"Where?"

"He's started working as a physics lecturer at a university."

"Show me."

The man handed Toby a small bundle of photographs. Toby thumbed through them and felt the mechanized rhythm of his heart race faster.

There was Dr Li, captured within each blurry photo, walking through the university and living his life unburdened by what he did to Toby. Toby fixated on the man and his betrayal all these years, placing him on a pedestal of hate.

Everything bad that ever happened to Toby had something to do with Dr Li, and now revenge was within reach. As Toby turned to the final few photos, something curious caught his eye. He noticed many shots featured Dr Li standing beside a young man, a student perhaps?

No, he's seen this person before. Toby narrowed his gaze, recalling the pictures from Dr Li's office. That was it. It was him. He was the key to all this.

"What's your name?" asked Toby.

"Gregory Page."

"What's your job?"

"I'm a plumber, my lord."

"Congratulations, you've just earned yourself a promotion," said Toby, taking a slow sip of wine.

"You're going to become a lecturer, and you're going to find out where they're hiding my time machine."

70

Tim sat on his hand until it went numb, restraining it. Every few moments, it would twitch again, trying to move without his say-so, each digit fighting to act out Dr Cud's plans. However, Tim wouldn't let it. He would cut the hand off if he needed to.

"You're from the future, yeah?" asked Tim, his eyes fixed on Miles. "And you're not converted or dead or whatever, so that means we win, right?"

Miles hesitated. "Not exactly. I'm only alive because I was a coward."

The words stung his tongue, but he forced his way through them. "You see, my wife...she was one of the first. I used to work nights, and when I got home one morning, this very morning, in fact, I found her waiting for me."

Miles' voice wavered, and he took a steadying breath. "She'd already killed our two daughters in their sleep, Victoria and Emily. Twins, they were only six. They had my DNA running through them, and I was deemed imperfect." Miles gestured to his small stature.

"She was going to kill me, too. So I ran...When she needed

me most…I just ran. I've spent every day since digging through the bodies for any trace of my family. Not that it'd do any good." Miles wiped his eyes, *no tears*, he told himself.

As he glanced back up into Tim's darkening eyes, he asked the question he was dying to know all these years. "What's it like, him controlling you? Did she suffer?"

"Nah, you can't even feel it," lied Tim. "It's like falling asleep."

Miles faked a smile.

"There is just one thing," continued Tim. "Your wife. She was imperfect, too. She must have been if she couldn't even kill someone as worthless as you."

His mouth twisted into a snarled grin.

Miles rose to his feet, feeling for his gun. "Tim?"

"I won't make the same mistake she did." Tim jolted back, fighting it, convulsing as he pushed Dr Cud's thoughts back into their box.

Miles raised his weapon, loaded a pellet into the chamber, and watched as Tim collapsed to the floor, tearing himself free from the strings controlling him.

Then, Tim breathlessly coughed a tiny "Miles, mate, it's me. It's me."

Sam stumbled over, returning from what he just christened '*The Piss Corner.*' Although it wasn't particularly limited to a corner. Sam's blurry, half-drunken state limited his aim, not that it concerned him. The more of Dr Cud's possessions he could douse in urine, the better. Sam blinked at the sight of Miles, standing over Tim with his gun drawn, barrel directed at his chest.

"Miles, what are you doing?" said Sam, trying to stay calm and hoping this was some elaborate prank.

Miles didn't lower the gun. "It's started."

"We can find another way. Just put the gun down."

Miles didn't.

"Put the gun down," ordered Sam through gritted teeth, all drunken joviality falling from his voice.

"This has gone on long enough, Samuel."

"No, he's fighting it. He did it before. He'll do it again."

"It's unfair, I know. But Tim's already dead. Lord Cud saw to that. I'm simply stopping us from joining him."

"You're not killing him," said Sam as he tried to snatch the gun from Miles.

Miles ducked out of the way, narrowly avoiding Sam's grasp, but Sam wasn't about to relent, not this time.

He lost Jack. He lost Lucy. Tim was staying put. He needed more time. Tim would fight, and he would win. He needed to.

Sam kept fighting, kept trying to take the gun, but Miles avoided each advance. "Samuel, you need to understand. There's no cure, there's no way to save him, it's too late."

"No," declared Sam as he went for the gun again.

Miles stepped backwards through the lab, jumping out of Sam's reach, and as he did so, Miles' foot snagged on something. He stumbled back, falling over and landing face-to-face with what tripped him. Lucy, her vacant face staring up at him.

Miles found his gun was missing, escaping his grasp and skating along the floor before coming to rest beside Tim. Tim's hand reached out and wrapped around it like a python, raising it with eerie precision.

Miles sat up just in time to see Tim pull the trigger. It was the last thing he would ever see. The shot rang out, sharp and deafening. The pellet embedded itself between Miles' eyes, sending a shockwave through his body. Burnt streams of electricity seared across his face and down his arms, leaving him cooked and silent, resting motionless beside Lucy.

Tim came to. The bleached white canvas faded from his

eyes, and in its place, he saw Sam staring back at him in disbelieving silent stillness. He glanced down and saw Miles.

Dead. Unmistakably so. Finally, he saw the gun in his hand. It was him. He did this. He killed Miles.

"Tim?" pleaded Sam.

Tim stared down at the gun and rotated it, pointing it back at himself as he loaded a new pellet into the chamber. "I'm sorry."

Tim closed his eyes, and through the darkness, he saw Lucy; her face was soft and her smile gentle with understanding.

Tim pulled the trigger.

"No!" screamed Sam as the electricity swallowed Tim, killing him too.

PART 8

THE KING

71

Jack was struggling to keep his eyes open. His belly was full, and his father's bedtime story was making it impossible to stay awake.

His eyes surrendered and gently fluttered shut as his father watched him drift off to sleep. He thought it was probably for the best Jack didn't hear this part, anyway.

<h1 style="text-align:center">72</h1>

DR CUD AND JACK APPEARED IN THE SAME PLACE they left, but not the same time.

They were deep into the future, and the Moonshot Labs they knew was now long gone, reduced to nothing but the occasional stone tracing the outline of where it once stood. Beyond it lay only rubble, no plants, no moss. Even mold was too afraid to grow here. This was far from the haven of scientific endeavour Dr Cud expected. This wasn't right at all. The thriving metropolis he long envisioned was nowhere to be seen.

"This is a trick!" shouted Dr Cud, spittle spraying across Jack's face. "What did you do to the time machine? What did you do?!"

"Nothing," said Jack.

This future was as Jack remembered it: hell. A burning red sky hanging above the long-forgotten bones of society.

Dr Cud dragged Jack onward, each step crunching along the torn-up tarmac as the acrid chill of polluted ash rained down around them. His desperation grew as the backdrop of devastation failed to give way to a shining metropolis, no matter how far they walked. He would find it eventually. He was sure of it.

He would turn down a road, and suddenly, there it would be, gleaming brightly in the distance, everything he ever worked for, his utopia.

Eventually, Dr Cud found the first clue of his brave new world in a giant golden statue towering above them, a perfect recreation of himself. A crown perched on his head and a perfectly sculpted time machine in one hand, whilst the other hand was a great ruling fist pointed to the sky.

Beautifully detailed robes cascaded down, the individual fibres painstakingly carved, and one of many immortal monuments filling his brave new world. He excitedly pulled Jack over to it as he read the plinth.

"In honour of our bountiful provider, Lord Tobias Cud. Tomorrow is forever in our grasp."

Dr Cud stepped towards it, in awe of the likeness, hypnotized by his own image. It was perfect. He tossed Jack to the floor and stretched his arm out. He had to know it was true.

"Don't," warned Jack, having encountered another of these audacious monoliths the last time he was here. "Don't touch it."

Dr Cud ignored him, pressing his hand against the smooth gold, feeling every detail.

The eyes of the statue suddenly glowed red, bearing down on him. Dr Cud jumped back as the statue's arm swung forward, his electric reflexes narrowly avoiding its giant golden clutches.

"*Treason Detected,*" barked the statue.

Sirens hammered, and the surrounding rubble vibrated with the echo of footsteps charging their way.

They came. Some limped, some clanked, but within seconds, a cavalcade of half-decayed robotic corpses surrounded Jack and Dr Cud, husks of humanity in various states of ruin, each draped in an identical, frayed grey uniform.

Their leader stepped forward, who may have once been a young man, but was now little more than a roasted skeleton held together with cables.

"You have defiled the statue of Lord Cud. The punishment for your treason is death," said the leader as a series of artificial arms from the crowd grabbed hold of the pair.

"I *am* Dr Tobias Cud! Now get your hands off me!"

The leader tilted its skull curiously and stared through the deep black caverns where its eyes once were, a red light faintly flickering within.

"*Analysis complete.*" The leader turned to the crowd, raising its rusted arms in holy triumph. "*Lord Cud has returned!*"

The undead machines immediately loosened their grip, freeing Jack and Dr Cud. The horde of corpses stepped back in awed reverence of the man standing before them. They did their best to kneel in unison, creaking down in worship of their master. A few whose joints rusted could not kneel, so, instead, simply face-planted the ground.

"That's more like it," said Dr Cud, standing tall over his children. "Now, tell me, what happened here? I gave you simple instructions to follow."

His robotic flock exchanged blank stares, gears clicking in confusion.

"*We did as you asked, my lord. We are immortal,*" said the leader in a small synthetic voice.

Dr Cud scoffed, sickened by their twisted decay, a mockery of the perfection he asked of them. "You call this immortality?"

"What did you expect?" said Jack, the only one not kneeling. "You taught them only hatred. Of course, they wouldn't build something beautiful. All you do is destroy, and kill, and rip out anything human until all that's left is machinery. Why would they be any different?"

Dr Cud turned to Jack, his face contorting with rage.

"How dare you speak to me like that?!" he roared, smacking his hand against Jack and sending him sprawling to the floor.

Jack wiped the blood from his lip, checking his teeth were all still in place. He glared up at Dr Cud but said nothing.

Dr Cud turned to his army of the dead, thinking it over momentarily.

"I didn't give you all enough time. That's it. I need to go further."

For that, He would need power and a lot of it. Dr Cud turned to Jack with a cruel glint in his eye. He knew just the place to harvest this pathetic, insolent child's fear.

<h1 style="text-align:center">73</h1>

A strange silence surrounded Sam. He peered down at Tim, at the frozen sadness burnt into his charred face. Sam wanted to scream, swear, curse the world and vow revenge, but he didn't.

Instead, he gently reached down and closed Tim's eyes, partly out of respect, partly to avoid his silent judgement. Sam then turned to Miles.

Miles was right, and now he lay dead as well, because of Sam's selfishness. He knelt and closed Miles' eyes. Finally, Sam turned to Lucy. He should've let her arrest him.

Maybe they would all still be alive if she did. He closed her eyes, and Sam was alone. He sat back and stared off into the abyss, allowing the silence to take over.

The light of the afternoon sun reflected in Sam's eye, and he snapped from his trance. It was a while, hours maybe.

He glanced down at the three bodies by his feet.

Yep, still dead.

Sam noticed something affixed to Miles' temple, twinkling in the sunbeam. It was the small projector Miles used to alter his appearance. Sam plucked the singed gadget from his head and surveyed it, seeing no buttons, no controls, just a smooth chrome coin.

He pressed it against his own temple and found it stuck effortlessly in place. Sam tapped and jabbed at it, but to no avail. He tried to imagine what he wanted to look like, focusing with all his strength. After all, that worked with the time machine.

Right now, Sam wanted more than anything to be somebody else. As he stared at his reflection in the window, he only saw the same guilty face peering back. Peering deeper into the reflection, he noticed a tiny camera lens on the device, following his every movement, and it all became obvious. He needed to show it the face he wanted. So Sam quickly scanned the room. Tim, Lucy, Miles, none of those would work.

He pulled open drawers and threw open cupboards. There must be a picture here somewhere, something he could use. He found a stack of creepy pictures depicting Dr Li and Jack, but they were even less helpful. Eventually, Sam came across an ID card in the pocket of an old lab coat.

On it was a faded, worn-out photo of Dr Tobias Cud, his boyish face no older than Sam was now. That would have to do, he supposed. He held the card up to the camera, and the projector made a small triumphant ding. Sam then watched as his reflection changed, folding away and dissolving until he stared into the face of Dr Cud.

This was his way out.

How did Miles not think of doing this? He was smart, really smart…Then, it dawned on Sam as his eyes turned to the small corpse beneath him. There was only one mask, and Miles was anything but selfish.

Sam turned towards the door and sensed the army on the other side, still waiting for him. He pressed his ear against it and heard their shallow breathing.

Ten? A hundred? It didn't matter. The entire world outside the door was populated with Dr Cud zombies, and any of them would tear him to shreds, given the opportunity.

Yet, he needed to go out there. Sam needed to know his family was alive. He couldn't let them down, too.

His hand hovered over the door release panel as he composed himself.

He pressed it, and the door slid open. Before him stood an endless row of people extending down the halls, and at the front of the queue, in his inevitable bow tie, stood Amir, eager to get the first crack at Sam.

Sam stood a moment, waiting for them to attack, for them to shoot him dead, leaving him just another corpse, but they didn't, not even Amir. Instead, they only tilted their heads, eying him curiously like a pack of wild dogs.

He strode forward, playing the part of their master, mustering up all the arrogant condescension he could, and one by one, they stepped aside. Sam almost couldn't believe this was working, but it was likely a testament to his impeccable acting ability. Perhaps he should've studied drama rather than computing all along.

Their eyes followed Sam down the corridor, studying the face they were compelled to obey.

As Sam reached the end of the corridor, he stared back at the room housing the bodies of his friends, the inventions which brought the world to its knees, and enough alcohol to make a horse do the *Macarena*.

Sam's eyes met Amir's for the last time.

"Burn it down," commanded Sam.

Sam made his way out of Moonshot Labs, the only building left untouched by the destruction surrounding it.

The window Sam sat at, above the faded emblem of the moon, was now lit up with bright shades of orange and red. Sam watched for a moment as spirals of smoke leaked out from around the frame, drifting upward to join all the rest.

Not far away, Sam spotted a car with its door hung open, abandoned, mid-escape. The driver hastily tried to escape on foot but failed miserably, and now their body dangled halfway out of their seat and onto the road.

Sam dragged the body from the car, laying it down as gently as he could. He climbed into the car, grasped the bloodied steering wheel and fingered the key, luckily still in the ignition. Turning it, the vehicle churned to life.

He wouldn't need to hot-wire it after all. He fiddled with the stick, slotting it aimlessly into the gear that seemed most appropriate and began the long ride home.

<h1 style="text-align:center">74</h1>

DR CUD DRAGGED JACK BACK THROUGH THE VAST rivers of time until they found themselves in a child's bedroom. Familiar blue wallpaper surrounded Jack, lined with shelves of picture books, and beneath him lay a floor littered with toys.

The faint scent of laundry detergent and crayons tickled at a million dormant memories within Jack that he'd once thought lost.

"No," was all Jack could utter as he put the last pieces of Dr Cud's plan together.

It was him. It was always him, plaguing his nightmares, lurking in the shadows, the single dark constant shrouding Jack's life from the very start.

Dr Cud picked up a small wooden train by his feet and tutted.

"What an untidy child," laughed Dr Cud before crushing the train to dust in his hand.

"No," repeated Jack.

"Are you afraid?" asked Dr Cud.

Jack braced himself against the door to stop Dr Cud, but he batted Jack away with a swift, dismissive swipe. Before Jack caught his breath, Dr Cud drove the sharp heel of his smart, black dress shoe deep into Jack's chest, pinning him down. He followed with a brutal kick to Jack's ribs and another to his stomach.

Fury spilled from Dr Cud as feverish beads of angry sweat flicked from the few greasy strands of hair remaining atop his head.

"Are you afraid of me now, Jack?" hissed Dr Cud, barring his teeth tightly.

All Jack could do to respond was to suck in a tiny, painful rasp of breath and curl foetal-like into a ball.

There was nothing Jack could do to stop him, and with his point now made, Dr Cud recomposed himself, straightened his posture and opened the door a small way to listen.

A sweet serenade filled the room, the joyful sound of *"Happy Birthday To You"* being sung downstairs. Dr Cud fixed Jack with an icy stare and made his way out of the room, following the singing.

Jack crawled after him, trying to ignore the pain bursting through his abdomen. He reached the top of the stairs, and through the gaps in the bannisters, Jack could see the warm glow of his past downstairs.

His mother and father placed a cake before his younger self, who looked ready to burst with excitement as he sat surrounded by balloons, birthday cards and a pile of presents.

Jack didn't need to look at the large badge pinned to the boy's shirt to know that he was eight years old today, for this was the day that Jack had always vowed to return to.

Jack watched as Dr Cud reached the bottom step, gleefully joining the chorus of voices. He forced himself to his feet, through clenched fists and gritted teeth, and staggered after him.

On his way down the stairs, Jack heard the first scream. His mother noticed the mechanically mutilated monster who joined them and erupted into an outpouring of dreaded shrieks. There were stammerings of "Who are you?" and "What do you want?" as she held her son close, protecting him.

"Happy Birthday, Jack," whispered Dr Cud through the panic.

As Jack descended the stairs, he heard his father's voice, too.

"Please, you can have whatever you want. Just don't hurt my family."

"But what I want *is* to hurt your family," replied Dr Cud, the harsh rustling of his pistol filling the air.

"Mommy, what's happening?" asked the frightened birthday boy, burying his face in his mother's arms.

"Nothing, sweetheart, everything's fine."

Jack reached the bottom step, finally seeing the moment that would change the course of his life up close. It was all coming back to him now, the smells, the screams, and the fear, especially the fear. He remembered how afraid he was about to be, and it hurt far worse than anything physical Dr Cud could inflict on him.

"Do you know what's about to happen" asked Dr Cud, addressing both Jacks at once.

The older Jack knew all too well, and he wouldn't allow it, not while he still drew breath. He forced his body forward, throwing himself at Dr Cud, his fingers clawing desperately for the pistol in Dr Cud's hand. He needed to buy his family time, no matter what the cost.

"Get out of here! Go!" shouted Jack as he struggled against Dr Cud's iron grip.

Dr Cud effortlessly shoved Jack to the ground, leaving him sprawled at the feet of the terrified couple and their son. Each one of them were trapped in a frozen state of terror, eyes drawn to the pistol staring back at them.

"Are you scared, Jack?"

"No!"

"I wasn't talking to you."

Dr Cud turned to face the younger Jack, his shadow stretching over the table, swallowing up the cards, the presents, and the birthday cake. The candles still patiently burned away, wax dripping from them and forming small, translucent mountains atop the icing.

Dr Cud leant in close, looming over the flickering candlelight, lighting him up with a hellish glow and illuminating every grotesque detail of his face.

"Hello," said Dr Cud, grinning at the birthday boy.

"Leave him alone," shouted Jack.

"Why, you haven't blown out your candles yet," said Dr Cud in a sickly sweet tone. "Blow out your candles. Come here and blow your candles out."

The boy glanced at his mother for guidance.

"You stay away from my baby," she told Dr Cud and held her son tighter.

Without moving his eyes from the boy, Dr Cud pointed the gun at his mother, holding it inches from her head.

"Come here and blow out your candles, or I'll blow her brains out."

He would not ask a third time.

The birthday boy shook free from his mom, stood up, and took small determined steps towards Dr Cud. He snorted up his tears and wiped his cheeks and met Dr Cud's gaze. He was being brave.

Dr Cud knelt beside the child, placing a bony hand upon his trembling shoulder. The boy closed his eyes and leaned forward, trying desperately to blow the candles out, but couldn't calm his quivering breaths long enough to focus them.

"It's ok, I'll help you," said Dr Cud, extinguishing the candles with a single, steady breath. "I suppose that means I'm the one who gets to make a wish."

Dr Cud took the boy's hand and placed it delicately around the handle of the gun. He moved in close and whispered into the boy's ear.

"I wish for you to kill your parents."

Dr Cud glanced down and noticed the boy had wet himself, a dark patch spreading across his lap.

Oh, this was just too good. He hit the jackpot with this one. He pressed the boy's finger against the trigger and guided the aim.

Jack pulled himself up against the table, staring down the barrel of the gun, the only thing between it and his parents.

"No."

"I don't need you anymore," laughed Dr Cud. "I've found someone better."

He readied the small hand around the gun. He was three shots away from having all the fear the time machine could swallow.

Jack pressed his hand into his pocket and found the small metal disc Dr Li gave to him, the one that would free him from his fate.

"No," repeated Jack, straightening up. "This time's going to be different."

Jack hurled the disc at Dr Cud, and it detonated around him, exploding into a thick globe of swirling time energy. Everything within its radius slowed to a crawl as confusion trickled across Dr Cud's face like molasses.

Jack grabbed the cake and thrust it into the sphere, where it floated, rotating in near-suspended animation until it gracefully collided with Dr Cud in a leisured crash of sponge and icing.

Seizing the moment, Jack reached into the sphere, locked onto the hand of his younger self and yanked it free from the frozen football.

"Run!" shouted Jack as he pulled himself towards the front door.

Dr Cud scraped cake from his eyes with the speed of a sedated snail and reached for the middle of the orb, the epicentre of the explosion where the metal disc was situated.

Jack grabbed the car keys from the bowl and tore open the front door, not daring to look back. He and his younger self flew down the front path towards the family car. Frantically jabbing at the key fob, his relief was palpable when he heard the car's doors click open. They were actually about to make it.

"Where's mommy and daddy?" asked the boy, glancing anxiously back at the house.

"They were right behind us," agreed Jack, opening the backseat door and gently urging his younger self inside. "Get down. You can do that for me, can't you? Everything will be ok if you just hide."

Jack slammed the car door shut and spun back towards the house.

Where the hell were they?!

The sound of a gunshot rang out from inside the house, its echo bouncing through the walls of his childhood home and punching him squarely in the chest.

No.

Please no.

Jack's heart sank, the sound tearing through his soul.

Jack's father burst out of the front door, crying for help, his voice ragged with desperation. Jack pleaded with him to make it to the car, begging him to reach them, but when he saw Dr Cud appear in the doorway, Jack knew it was all in vain.

Dr Cud fired another round from his pistol, and Jack's father threw up his arms as the bullet tore into his back, collapsing face down onto the driveway. Jack rushed to him, falling to his side, but his father was already gone, his body still and lifeless. Blood continued to gurgle through his father's woollen jumper, flowing onto the pavement where it dripped between the stone slabs.

There were layers of blood on Jack's hands now. The blood Lucy spilt only just dried into a deep black glove, cracked like an oil painting, and now those cracks were being filled with a fresh coat of misery and pain.

Jack's parents died for the second time in his life. He spent all those years dreaming of returning to this place, protecting his parents from the forces that took them from him.

As he glanced down at his hands and the man lying beneath them, Jack realized it was he who caused this. Wherever Jack went, death followed him, and now he invited it to his parents' doorstep.

"Where's the boy?" asked Dr Cud.

Jack tore his eyes away, meeting Dr Cud's disinterested gaze.

"Gone," said Jack. "I told him to run far, far away."

"No matter," dismissed Dr Cud.

He glanced down at the time machine in his hand and couldn't help but smile. The device was fit to burst. Blue electricity filled the glass dome, bounding around like a hyperactive puppy.

"I got what I needed. Let's go."

Dr Cud held out his hand expectantly, beckoning Jack over. Jack obediently stepped around his father's corpse, giving one last glance to the car and its single, hidden passenger.

Without a word, Jack took Dr Cud's hand, sticky with cake debris, as they once more disappeared through time's doorway, leaving behind a little boy huddled in the car's footrest, waiting for his mommy and daddy to find him.

75

The time machine was pushed to its limits, rocketing Jack and Dr Cud further than Dr Li's pocket-sized creation could handle. Timelines buckled, dimensions bruised.

The years passed so quickly that light didn't just fold around them; it shattered, leaving only darkness in its wake. The cries of forgotten centuries wailed through the darkness in a frantic, discordant overture of history.

After somewhere between a second and a millennia, reality exploded back open, and the pair were thrown into the far future with a force that threatened to split their atoms apart.

Jack landed face-first in something soft. Disoriented, he squinted and was blinded by the harsh sunlight. Jack rubbed away the burning in his eyes and found it wasn't just his eyes that burned.

Everything did.

Every fibre of his being felt like it was on fire. It was as though he was sitting in a sauna, on the surface of the sun, whilst wearing a scarf. His shirt clung to his body, already soaked with sweat, as he tried to loosen the collar.

Everything ached, Jack's head felt full, and a profound nausea clawed its way up from his stomach. Even the pulse through his arms was painfully loud against the utter silence around him.

Jack tried to get to his feet but only slipped back down. The ground was silky and sank beneath him, shifting as his feet and hands pushed against it. Jack's eyes adjusted to the light, and he cupped a handful of ground, trying to inspect it before it slipped back through his fingers.

It was bleached white, shapeless, and continued all the way down, for as Jack looked out over the landscape of this future, he realized he was standing on a mountain of dust, boundless and bare, stretching far away.

Jack made out Dr Cud's silhouette shimmering ahead, cutting through the waves of heat like a mirage. With little alternative, Jack trudged after him, wading through the fine sand of an hourglass that had long run dry. Dr Cud remained out of reach, ploughing forward through the dust, unstoppable in his determination as he followed a singular blight on the white landscape, shining through the harsh sunlight and calling to him.

Dr Cud did not know how far away it was or any clue about what it might be. He just knew he needed to reach it. The goalpost was what he was rushing towards all his life, and it was nearly within reach.

Dr Cud continued on for minutes, maybe hours, maybe months; time had little meaning here, for nothing ever progressed, and nothing ever changed. As he drew closer, the tiny glint of hope glistened in a shower of light.

A perfect beacon, beckoning him home. Dr Cud ran, slipping on the frictionless dust and crawling on his hands and knees, pulling himself through until, finally, the treasure was all his.

There it was, a giant, half-sunk, golden chest comprising

five distinct sections, each marked by a ridge etched with meticulous precision. A sarcophagus, perhaps, imbued with the power to grant everlasting youth, free from pain and suffering and the judgement of others.

Dr Cud touched its smooth golden shell, and a muffled sound erupted up from below, cracked and distant through the dust. As Dr Cud listened closely, he made out two words, over and over.

"Treason detected."

With each repeat of its mantra, the words wavered and creaked and distorted until they finally gave up.

It wasn't a chest. Nor was it a sarcophagus.

It was a fist.

Jack caught up to Dr Cud, stumbling to a stop beside him. Jack didn't say a word. Neither of them did, for there was nothing left to say.

There they sat, their legs buried in the dust as they stared out over the endless horizon.

Jack glanced at his hands. The blood on them burnt away, leaving the skin beneath bright red and blistering under the relentless sun. He turned to Dr Cud, and for the first time, Jack saw a glimmer of humanity stretched over his robotic skull.

As soon as it appeared, it vanished, replaced by the viciousness Jack was well acquainted with.

"I don't need to be immortal," said Dr Cud. "I only need to outlive everybody else."

76

SAM STOOD ANXIOUSLY OUTSIDE HIS PARENTS' house, drenched in fear and exhaustion. Thankfully, the pungent smell of the future sewers masked the stench of his sweat. He abandoned the car a few miles back upon reaching an impasse of vehicles and corpses all piled together, like a *Scalextric* covered in jam. Sam couldn't manoeuvre the car any further, even with his skills, so he ran the rest of the way home.

Tapping the projector on the side of his head, he switched off his disguise, revealing the unfiltered worry beneath.

He surveyed the house. The curtains were drawn as they always were; the allotment stood as it always did, and the door remained the same shade of inviting rose red that had always offered nothing but safety. However, now, it all felt wrong, like the remnants of another life, one he could never have again.

Sam rang the doorbell, holding it down as it chimed away his fears. They needed to be ok, they just had to.

The front door opened, and time stood still as Sam finally saw the woman he hoped was still his mother. There she stood in the light of a million cozy lamps, yet the familiar warmth of her face outshone them all. A sob tore from her throat, and she threw her arms around Sam in an embrace so tight and loving that it made the entire world seem ok.

"Oh, Sammy," said his mother, showering him with kisses. "Where have you been? We were so worried about you. I was down at the police station shouting at whoever would listen that you were innocent, and then they tell me you've disappeared to God knows where, and no one can find you. Then there was all the stuff on the news..."

She pulled back briefly, studying Sam as if to ensure he was still there, then wrapped him up again, her hair flooding his senses with its familiar scent of hairspray and coconut shampoo.

"You're here now, and you're safe. That's all that matters."

Sam could barely squeeze in more than a "hello" as she held him in her arms, continuing to catch Sam up on every little detail he missed. But Sam didn't mind one bit. With every bit of gossip falling from his mother's lips, Sam's ragged breathing soothed a little more.

"Terry!" shouted his mother, far too close to Sam's ear. "You'll never guess who's here?"

"Who?" returned a muffled voice from the living room.

"Sam!" she yelled, louder this time.

"Who?"

"Sam!"

"Stan?"

"Sam!" She was screaming into Sam's ear at this point.

Sam wriggled free from his mom's embrace and walked through to the living room, where he found his dad sitting in his usual spot, burrowed into the sofa, eyes glued to the static image on TV.

"Hello, boy," said his father without turning from the screen. "Sam's here! Not Stan!"

"I'll pop the kettle on," said Sam's mom with a sigh.

"Where's Molly?" asked Sam.

"She's upstairs. She's fine. We're all fine now."

Sam sank into the sofa, allowing himself the very smallest of reprieves. Everything was terrible. His friends were missing or dead, and the world was ending, but his family was safe, and right at this moment, that was all he wanted to focus on.

"You seen this?" asked his father. "Every channel. They're saying we can't leave our homes. The same thing happened during the Cold War. At least back then, they told you what it was you had to fear. *H-bomb*, plain and simple. But now?" He shook his head, chuckling mirthlessly.

"Now it's all hush-hush. They're not telling us anything."

Sam glanced at the TV. The words *'EMERGENCY ANNOUNCEMENT'* was burned into the screen as the tinny accompaniment of a posh announcer droned on.

"Do not make any attempts to travel. All communication services in this area have been suspended. Avoid contact with others. Remain indoors unless it is vital to your survival that you do otherwise. We will offer more information as it becomes available. Do not make any attempts to travel. All communication services in this area have been suspended. Avoid..."

"I'm surprised he hasn't lost his voice," said Sam's dad. "He's been saying the same thing over and over all day long."

Sam's dad erupted with laughter at his own terrible joke.

"Lovely cup of tea for you, dear," said Sam's mom as she reentered the living room and handed Sam a mug. "Where's your friend?"

"Tim?" replied Sam, a lump in his throat forming. "He went home."

"Oh, that's lovely to hear."

"There he goes again," laughed Sam's dad, giving Sam a playful nudge. "You'd think he'd mix it up occasionally, do an accent or something."

"Terry, turn that bloody thing off, will you?" complained

Sam's mom. "All this fuss for a bit of flu going around. The man told us there was nothing to worry about."

"*The man*…What man?" asked Sam as he took a hollow sip from the mug.

He peered down into it and the facade of this haven cracked as he found the mug was empty.

"The government man, very official, had a suit and everything. He gave us some medicine to protect us from the flu."

"What did the medicine look like?" asked Sam as the lump in his throat grew.

"Tablets, only little ones. He left us some if you want one," said Sam's mother as she patted him on his shoulder. Sam couldn't help but recoil from her touch. "They're around here somewhere. Terry, where did you put them?"

"I don't know. You had them last."

Sam slowly rose from the sofa, trying his hardest to remain calm, or at least seem like he was.

"What colour were the pills?" he asked, his voice wavering ever so slightly.

"Red," said his dad.

"Yellow," said his mom.

"They were red," confirmed his dad.

"No, they weren't. They were yellow. I told you your eyes are going," argued his mom in the same way she always did. She turned to Sam.

"I keep telling him, he won't listen. I tell him, book up an appointment with the optician…"

Orange! They were orange! Sam wanted to scream but held it in and backed away from his bickering parents, edging towards the staircase.

"Where are you going?" asked his mom, her head twisting around to follow Sam with an uneasy urgency. "Those tablets are around here somewhere. I'll find them, don't you worry."

"I'm good. I don't need anything," said Sam, a gazelle in a lion's cage.

He just needed everyone to stay cool and calm and not try to kill him.

"They'll do you a world of good, Sammy. I'm feeling better than I have in years," said his mom, her smile a little too wide, her eyes a little too bright.

"It's fine, really."

"If you really don't want them..." she said, her smile dropping into a grave whisper. "I suppose we could always just kill you instead."

Shit.

Sam bolted up the stairs, scrabbling onto the landing as he heard his mother's footsteps following. He kicked open the door to his sister's bedroom, sending the sticky foam flowers adorning it flying.

"Molly! You need to come with me. We have to go right now."

Molly was sitting calmly at her desk. She turned to meet Sam, her face pale and her painted on smile unwavering.

"Why didn't you save us in time, Sam?" asked Molly, her vacant eyes locking onto him.

Sam's breath caught. "Please. Not you, too."

Molly rose, her body moving with an artificial, eerie grace.

"I was so scared, Sam, but you weren't there. You abandoned us. You left us to die. Is this what you wanted? Are you happy now, Sam?" she said, her voice cold as she marched toward her brother, the grin still glued to her face.

Sam stumbled back, colliding with the doorframe as he heard his parents following up the stairs. Their footsteps were slow, leisured even. They knew Sam had nowhere to go, so they could relish in his torment. They would toy with him until his spirit snapped in two.

Sam darted across the landing and into his bedroom,

slamming the door shut and pressing his full weight against it. Fists hammered against the door, vibrating through the wood and rattling Sam's bones with each strike.

"Sam! Come out here this instant!" demanded his mom.

"Listen to your mother, Sam," agreed his father.

The fists were joined by feet, kicking the door in and forcing Sam back. The last anchor to the life he once knew unmoored a little with every smack of the door.

"Please, please, please," Sam silently begged to what remained of his family, to himself, to God, to anyone who might make this ok.

Sam's hand brushed against the cold, rough outline of Miles' gun in his pocket. A final, terrible solution.

"Why are you trying to leave us again, Sam?" chimed his sister. "You were supposed to protect me."

The door nearly broke free from its hinges as Molly threw herself against it, enough to knock Sam to the ground as the door swung open.

Sam's fingers tightened around the gun's handle. He closed his eyes as tight as they would go, hiding in the darkness as he held the gun in front of him, and pulled the trigger again and again until the pellets ran dry.

The ringing in his ears, the electric screams, the thud of bodies, and soon, there was only that silence again. How Sam hated the silence. He slammed the door shut without looking back. He didn't need to check to know that he was now truly alone, not a single soul left on earth who was on his side. Sam desperately needed something to chase away the silence before it dug its sharp claws into him and never let him go.

His eyes landed on the old acoustic guitar by his bed. Sam picked it up and strummed a tentative chord. He let the untuned notes surround him, drowning out the world as he leaned against the bed frame and pretended he was fourteen again, spending his nights alone in his bedroom, learning chords and fumbling through songs.

He always believed learning the guitar would make him irresistible to women, envied by men and loved by all. Yet the only people who ever listened to him play were all gone now.

Sam put the guitar aside, serving as only a further reminder of those he lost, and instead searched for the cheap bottle of vodka he hid under his bed. His mother kept his room spotless in his absence, but the large glass bottle of half finished spirit had survived, concealed within a box of old school books. There the bottle sat, wedged between a pile of *Sherlock Holmes* novels and a well-worn copy of *Dracula*, patiently waiting for Sam all these years. Sam unscrewed the cap, and drank deeply, scarcely noticing the sting as it flowed into him.

Sam's gaze drifted to the photos along his window sill, mementos from a life lost. In one, Sam held his newborn sister in his arms, erupting with pride. In another, Sam stood with his family on holiday, their sunburnt faces all saying '*cheese*' as they squinted against the sunlight.

There, in the last frame, was Jack standing beside him, arms around each other's shoulders, with the blurry shape of a bouncy castle a little out of focus behind them, rendered in bold, carefree colours.

They weren't all gone, Sam realized as he held the last photo. Some were just lost.

Sam reached into his pocket and fished out the locator. On the screen, blinking dully, was Jack's location, right now, in the present and just outside of the city.

Sam slid open the window, the latch giving way with a reluctant squeak, and climbed over the photo frames. He grabbed hold of the thick branches of the tree, whose withered ends used to scrape against his window at night. When he was younger, Sam believed it was the hands of an alien or monster trying to snatch him away.

But Sam wasn't scared of monsters anymore. In fact, he was on his way to kill one.

Sam climbed along the branch, and from his new vantage point, he glanced out over the ghostly remains of the street beyond his garden. Rows of abandoned houses and hollow shells stood in silence. He spotted a lurid beacon in the distance.

Parked squarely in the middle of the road, fluorescent shades of pink and blue blazed through the empty, monochrome surroundings. He recognized the vehicle, and the taste of a million frozen memories soon hit his tongue. Hot summer days when it would pull up outside his house, and he and Jack would go running to its call.

Now, it called to Sam once more. The distorted cartoon faces painted across its sides grinned and gawked with exaggerated features, each begging him to take it for a spin.

Sam dropped from the tree, hopped the fence and approached the perfect monster-hunting machine: an ice cream truck.

77

So here we are, back where we started.

Jack stood on the edge of the cliff, a narrow stretch of unstable chalk jutting from the side of an unused road, as he watched over what was left of the city he once called home.

Buildings lay demolished, roads cluttered with abandoned cars and pillars of smoke stretched high into the sky like a forest. At least from up here, he couldn't make out the bodies.

"Front row seats," said the voice beside him. "I win."

The setting sun glowed through the veil of smoke, making it look like the sky was on fire. All across the world, everything was burning.

"So, new plan," continued Dr Cud. "Once my army is done converting, once they're all that's left, I'll tell them to kill themselves, too. Then it will just be me, and every resource on the planet, every human endeavour, every scrap of knowledge, will be mine alone." Dr Cud peered over at Jack, waiting.

"Nothing you'd like to say about that?"

Jack didn't answer.

Dr Cud twirled the time machine around in his hand as he thought.

"You know, seeing as I have no use for this anymore, I'm afraid that means I have no use for you either." He readied the pistol in his cold metal hand and aimed it at Jack. "Come on. I know you have something to say about that."

"Do it," said Jack. His voice didn't waver, nor did he turn to face his executioner.

"Do it," he said again and took a step closer to Dr Cud until the gun pressed into his chest.

"Do it," he demanded.

Jack's eyes locked onto Dr Cud's, daring him to shoot him, to end this. But he didn't. So Jack turned around and walked away from Dr Cud and the cliff side, heading towards the road.

"Where do you think you're going?" hissed Dr Cud.

Jack shrugged.

"Stop!" demanded Dr Cud.

Jack didn't stop.

"Kneel!"

Dr Cud fired the gun. The bullet shredded through the back of Jack's leg and embedded itself behind his kneecap. Jack fell to the knees, gripping tightly the small tufts of grass around the chalk to keep himself up.

The pain was fantastic, but with every shred of defiance left in him, he resisted the overwhelming urge to scream.

Dr Cud strolled over and held the gun to the back of Jack's head, boring it down into his scalp until he tasted metal.

"Are you scared?"

"Are you?" grunted Jack through the pain, and he closed his eyes.

He was done fighting.

Jack thought of all the people he loved, all the people he owed, all the people he could never apologize to. He thought of holidays in France, puzzles with his nan, early mornings with his mentor, and late nights with his best friend. He thought of all the days he spent building that stupid time machine, all the time he spent running and hiding, how it all led him here. Finally, he thought of that stupid essay that was technically still due tomorrow.

And he let it all go.

Jack heard heaven's chimes beckoning him to the afterlife. They were beautiful. They were filling his mind. They were... playing *Teddy Bear's Picnic*?

Jack opened his eyes. The music blared from an ice cream truck careening along the road towards them. Tyres screeched as it slammed on the brakes, skidding wildly before crashing into the roadside barrier beside the cliff's edge. The vehicle rocked and shuddered as something moved around inside.

Dr Cud yanked the pistol away from Jack's head, now aiming it towards the truck, his finger tense against the trigger. The back door kicked open, and standing there, with a gun in one hand and a half-eaten *cornetto* in the other, was Dr Cud. Again, only this one was younger.

"Yes, it is I. Dr Tobias...Cud." said the stranger, struggling to recall his own last name. He spoke in an overly grandiose tone as he hopped out from the truck.

"I command thee. Let Jack go."

Dr Cud's face hardened as he studied the young replica of himself standing before him.

"I am thee from the future," the newcomer continued. "I found immortality and have lived for millennia, but I decided it was wrong for me to have hurt all those people and for trying to rule the world. I should've just chilled out, y'know, dedicated my life to doing good. It's not too late for you. So put the gun down and just relax, yeah? What do you say?"

"What do I say?" repeated Dr Cud, narrowing his eyes. "Well, let's see, you're three inches shorter than I am, you don't sound anything like me, whatever disguise you're using to replicate my appearance doesn't extend beyond your face, and you're wearing the same garish outfit as that idiot Sam the last time we met."

The counterfeit Cud chucked the last of his cornetto cone into his mouth. "It was worth a shot," he shrugged, tapping the side of his head. His face folded and warped until it decided upon a new one, Sam's.

"Alright, Jack?" said Sam with a casual wink. "Like the new wheels? Can you believe I found it abandoned? Well, mostly abandoned."

Jack couldn't quite believe what he was seeing.

"Sam, you're alive," said Jack, disbelief shaking through his words. "But how did you find me?"

Sam whipped out the locator and waved it in the air.

"Nicked this off old Robo-dick, didn't I? Catch," said Sam as he tossed it vaguely in Jack's direction.

"So what now?" sneered Dr Cud. "Are you going to shoot me again?"

Sam raised Miles' gun to match Dr Cud's, answering his question without a word. The pair stood, locked in a standoff, each aiming at one another, fingers twitching just above the trigger.

The wind crackled between them, the only sound against their silence, as their eyes steadied in a fierce, unblinking challenge, each daring the other to make the first move.

Sam then burst out laughing. "Look how serious you are. No, I'm not here to shoot you. That'd be so boring. Anyway, this thing ran out of sci-fi bullets ages ago." He tossed the gun over his shoulder. "Nah, I've got something way better than a gun."

Sam reached into his pocket and drew out his secret weapon.

"A *Nobbly Bobbly*," announced Sam, unsheathing the ice lolly and thrusting it out like a fencer's blade.

"En garde," and laughed even harder. "You seriously need

to learn to chill out. *I'm Dr Cuddles. I'm so evil. I'm going to live forever. Then, I'm going to stand on the edge of a cliff and shoot people.* I mean, dial it back a little."

Dr Cud heard enough. He pulled the trigger without hesitation and fired a round into Sam's chest.

The gunshot shattered the silence, echoing across the chalky cliffs as Jack's heart jumped.

"Sam!" screamed Jack, before stopping, noticing that Sam hadn't fallen as so many others did. He was...still laughing, harder than before, and he didn't even drop his ice lolly.

Jack's confusion twisted into relief. Was Sam wearing a bulletproof vest, or had he used a magnet to divert the bullet, or was it something even more ingenious? Whatever Sam had done, it clearly worked.

"Don't worry," laughed Sam. "I'm so drunk I didn't even feel it."

The relief drained away from Jack's face, leaving only dread.

A bright red stain blossomed across Sam's chest, seeping through the hole in his shirt as he calmly took a lick of Nobbly Bobbly. He glanced down at the bullet hole, then back up at Dr Cud, relishing the surprise on his metal face.

"See what I mean, boring," continued Sam, staggering forward and taking another deliberate lick.

Each uneven step brought him closer to Dr Cud, his pace quickening with unyielding laughter.

Dr Cud growled with frustration and fired again, shot after shot, bursting into Sam, but Sam just kept coming, charging full pelt towards him. Brushing off the bullets as though they were little more than raindrops in a storm.

Dr Cud could only watch, his mechanical lips gawping open as Sam crashed into him. Sam jammed the Nobbly Bobbly deep into Dr Cud's open mouth, cramming it down his throat. Dr Cud gagged, the ice cream slowing his circuits and causing a very literal case of brain freeze, a little trick Sam had picked up from Amir.

Then, Sam charged again and, using all his drunken strength, clamped his arms around Dr Cud, forcing his entire weight into him, pressing them onward toward the cliff's edge.

"What the hell are you doing?" yelled Jack.

"I'm *Reichenbaching* this shit!" shouted Sam, his grin widening as he pulled Dr Cud with him off the edge, sending the pair tumbling into the abyss.

Sam clung onto Dr Cud as he struggled, blazing with rage that melted the ice cream into nothing. He wasn't about to let this idiot beat him, not when he still had a way out.

Jack crawled over to the edge just in time to see them disappear into a bright blue burst of light.

SAM AND DR CUD FIRED BACK INTO REALITY ABOVE A swimming pool, splashing into the water like a cannonball. Sam tried to snatch the time machine from Dr Cud as they fought beneath the water, their chlorine-filled eyes fixed on one another until the water between them turned a murky red.

Sam eventually brushed the time machine with the very tip of his finger, and the pool shone a luminous blue as electricity erupted through it, leaving only a half-singed lolly stick floating in their place.

"Everybody out of the pool!" shouted a very confused lifeguard, blowing his whistle.

BARRELING THROUGH TIME, SAM BROUGHT DR CUD to a place he knew all too well. The nightclub, close to the university, that Sam would so often drag Jack to, most recently for Jack's birthday.

The pair appeared on the dance floor beneath a chaotic swirl of techno music and disco lights. They were jostled by waves of people dancing around them, indifferent to the two soaking, bloodied men who appeared out of nowhere.

Sam went for the time machine again, grabbing it and yanking it firmly towards him, but Dr Cud's vice-like grip clamped down so tightly that the wood splintered. They both pulled back and forth on the device in a strange tango across the dance floor. Dr Cud shoved Sam back, sending him reeling into the path of a woman dancing with her friends, knocking her drink upwards, and causing a few drops to land on a certain purple blazer.

Sam and Dr Cud continued fighting over the device, both refusing to let go, as neither one of them had anything else left to fight for. All that mattered now was the time machine.

They fought their way from the dance floor and through the club until Sam's foot snagged on a barstool, sending him crashing down hard behind the bar and bringing Dr Cud down with him. People shouted, staff hid, and security came running over, but the pair were too preoccupied to notice. They wrestled along the bar's floor, rolling through puddles of spilt glasses.

Sam staggered to his feet on top of Dr Cud, who then reached up and smashed a glass into the side of Sam's face. The glass crunched into Sam, and blood sprayed from his cheek, dousing the bar like a human sprinkler. Sam barely registered the pain, retaliating with a sharp shove and driving Dr Cud's face down into something sticky. Sam reached for a bottle behind the bar to smack him with, but as he did so, he paused momentarily, seeing something impossible on the other side of the bar.

Sam saw himself.

A second Sam Higgs.

This other Sam was identical to him in every way, except he wasn't battered, bruised, and bleeding.

Then it all made sense. As Sam stared into the awe-struck face of his past, the paradox shined with destined prophecy. This was always going to happen. This was always going to be how it ended, so Sam had to make sure it ended right.

Sam swung the bottle down, heavy as his hand lost feeling, but before it could make contact, Dr Cud snatched Sam by his shirt collar and hauled him up, slamming him into the shelves of spirits behind the bar. Glass exploded into Sam's back, slicing through him as his head became light.

"Enough!" boomed Dr Cud.

"Never," choked Sam with a bloodied cough, and the pair disappeared, slingshot through the infinite time stream once more.

THEY LANDED ON SOMETHING SOFT AND SPRINGY, AN abrupt jolt that knocked Dr Cud off his footing and sent them both bouncing into the side of the colourful tomb Sam had brought them to. Dr Cud collided with the inflated red wall, and the jagged metal of his face pierced into it.

Air hissed out around Dr Cud's head in sharp bursts as children screamed and fled in every direction, retreating from the bouncy castle and back inside the nearby house.

All apart from one boy, who hesitantly approached the two broken men, wrapped entwined, each still clinging onto a cracked mess of wood and glass. The boy's wide eyes met Sam's, whose blood was now filling the crevices of the bouncy castle.

"Are you ok, mister?" asked the boy.

"Tip top," rasped Sam, forcing a bloodied smile.

"Are you magic?"

"Yeah."

"Sam, come on!" called another boy, poking his head out from the house.

"I've got to go, bye," he whispered and ran back to join his friend.

Sam watched the two boys as the walls of the bouncy castle collapsed around him. This was it. The adrenaline was wearing off or had spilt out somewhere across the bouncy castle. Either way, Sam could feel himself going. The lights were turning out, and he could now feel everything, the bullet embedded in his shoulder, the one buried in his chest and the hole in his thigh where a bullet had successfully made it all the way, not to mention the shards of glass piercing his eye and spine. With each weakening pulse of his heart, Sam's time grew shorter.

With all the energy he had left, Sam thought of Jack, alone on the cliff's edge, and how Sam just wanted to see him one last time. Sam clung to the memory of his face as time swallowed them up once more.

SAM AND DR CUD APPEARED IN THE SKY, HIGH ABOVE the cliff. Sam looked down, catching sight of Jack kneeling by the edge, only seconds from when they left. But they were still too far from him, just out of reach, precisely as Sam had intended. They plummeted down the cliff side once more, spiralling towards the ground below. Sam's grip on the time machine finally loosened, his fingers numb, and the device slipped from his hand as Dr Cud kicked him away.

Now, all Dr Cud had to do was think of somewhere, anywhere, and he'd win. So he thought hard, gritting his silver molars, willing himself away. But no matter how hard he tried, the world remained the same. The air rushed past, and the ground continued to grow closer. He looked over at Sam, still falling beside him, and watched him mouth the words "and sleep."

The last thing Dr Tobias Cud saw was the time machine, the one he'd fought all his life for, suffered and killed for. The last of its three LEDs blinked a dull green before falling dark completely. It was out of time, and so was he.

JACK WATCHED AS THEY HIT THE GROUND BELOW with a dull thud. He quickly hobbled over to the outgrowth of weeds where Sam had thrown the locator. On the screen, the map still flashed at Jack's location.

Jack crawled on to the blood-soaked gravel where Sam was shot. He ejected the locator's pin and pressed it into the darkest patch of blood before slotting it back inside the device.

The display flickered before cutting out completely. There was no signal, not to anything alive at least, not anymore.

Jack lay back against the side of the ice cream truck as the sun dipped beneath the horizon, and he felt the weight of the world crush him once more. Pain from his shattered kneecap pulsated through him, marking the seconds until the sky turned black. It was over, the world and everything in it that ever mattered.

Jack closed his eyes and gave up the fight.

78

Jack felt someone gently kicking him awake. He stirred, groggy, as it all started coming back to him, the rough gravel digging into his back, the icy chill of the night air, and the crippling pain in his leg. Now, to top it all off, someone was kicking him.

"Come on, up you get."

The words drifted through him, tugging Jack reluctantly back to life. Jack squinted through the pitch black as his eyes adjusted to the darkness.

Slowly, the dark shadow of a figure standing above him took shape as it cast the warm glow of torchlight over Jack and across the cliff's plateau.

Jack blinked, and the outline grew sharper, more familiar. Each detail slotted into place, the well-worn eyes surrounded by a patchwork of wrinkles and a bellowing white beard.

It was him, the proper him, as old as the day Jack had watched him die.

"Dr Li?" murmured Jack.

"That's right, now come on, we've got work to do," replied Dr Li, scanning the torch along the cliff with one hand, and in the other, he gripped a big brown leather bag, the type doctors always used in old movies.

"They all died," said Jack.

"I know," said Dr Li with a knowing sigh as he helped Jack to his feet.

Jack wrapped an arm around Dr Li's shoulder, and together, they trudged over to the ice cream truck, its gurning illustrations all the more unsettling under torchlight.

Dr Li found the keys were still inside, dangling from the ignition, and with a quick twist, the old vehicle clunked into life. Jack climbed into the passenger seat, wincing as he settled in, each jolt of the engine reminding him of the pain.

As they took the long, narrow road winding down around the cliff, Jack stared at the locator. The screen was still dark, the signal still lost, yet Jack watched it the entire way, waiting for it to flicker into life and show Sam was ok, that he escaped, like he always did.

<hr>

Eventually, Jack glanced up to find they'd reached the bottom of the cliff, the engine falling still as Dr Li parked. He helped Jack out of the truck, guiding him through the tangled weeds beyond the road.

Dr Li's torchlight swept through the darkness until its spotlight found a body sprawled out across the ground. Sam lay still in a peaceful, mangled heap. Surprisingly, after all that Jack went through, seeing the vacant body of someone he cared about never got any easier, especially not Sam's.

Jack felt the full magnitude of his grief hit him all over again, carving into his chest, hollowing him out, and leaving him almost as vacant as Sam.

Dr Li knelt beside Sam and, with clinical precision, gently removed the small projector fixed to his temple, hidden amongst the topography of broken glass buried into Sam's skin. He pocketed the projector and turned his torch to another body not far away.

The light scattered as it reflected off the mirrored corpse of Dr Cud, equally dead as Sam was. Dr Li didn't allow himself a moment to feel the swell of emotions that used to accompany his eternal foe. That would be for later. Right now, he had work to do.

Dr Li set his big brown bag down beside him, snapped open the clasps and fished out his buzz-saw from within. He switched it on and got to work. With the modifications he made to it and the lack of resistance from Dr Cud's synthetic cells, the saw went through with relative ease.

Grinding and sparking as it sliced through skin, metal and bone, carving through Dr Cud's neck until his head broke free with a final, crepitant crunch.

Dr Li reached down to extract the time machine from the dead man's hand. Even in death, Dr Cud put up a fight, and his wizened fingers locked around its wooden shell like a vice, still refusing to give up. Dr Li gripped the edge with both hands and, with all his might, he freed Excalibur from the stone. He shone his torch over what was left of its glass dome, crushed inwards, its jagged edges shone weakly against the light.

The hands of the clock face rattled free, unmoored from their temporal duty. Great cracks lined the wood, exposing the inner mechanisms and allowing cogs and gears to pour free like breakfast cereal. With a resigned sigh, he gathered up the broken pieces as best he could and tucked them carefully into his bag along with the buzz-saw. Dr Li returned to his feet, lifting his foe's severed head and cradling it under his arm like a football.

"Catch," he called as he tossed the head to Jack.

Dr Cud's head tumbled through the air, his cold features

frozen in perpetual rage, but Jack didn't even notice as it passed by. He was still staring at Sam, lost in the thought of a billion regrets. The head rolled along the ground like a ripening snowman, picking up gravel and dirt as it scraped along the path.

Dr Li retrieved the head, brushed some of the larger stones from Dr Cud's matted cotton wool hair, and stood beside Jack in the darkness.

Jack felt a hand on his shoulder, firm and reassuring, pulling him back from the storm inside his mind.

Dr Li walked Jack back to the ice cream truck, and together they continued driving off into the night to the tune of *Teddy Bear's Picnic*.

79

THEY REACHED MOONSHOT LABS, NOW A SMOKEY, twisted carcass, reduced to a burnt-out shell amongst an ocean of them. The doors had disintegrated into piles of crunchy debris, and everything beyond was stained black and burnt.

The leather chairs adorning the waiting area had shrivelled and cracked, cooked into jerky. Steel beams jutted down from the floors above, turning the entire reception into a macabre game of *kerplunk*.

Dr Li and Jack made their way inside, weaving through the razor-sharp climbing frame and along the corridors beyond. Dr Li shone the torch through the pitch-black halls, cutting thin beams of light through them. The once pristine walls bubbled with scorched paint, curling into twisted corals. It felt like they were walking through something organic, an endless intestine into the bowels of hell.

Jack sensed the familiar itch in his chest, growing as they descended further into the charred husk. Fallen plaster from the ceilings lay in large chunks on the floor, which crumbled like sand beneath their feet.

They climbed the stairs to the lab, each skeletal step

groaning and aching under their weight. Jack's foot slipped through one of the weaker slats, and a sickening vertigo filled his mind as his foot dangled above the concrete abyss below. Dr Li grabbed Jack by the arm, pulling him back up, and they pressed on, reaching the end of the intestines, the anus, also known as Dr Cud's lab.

Inside, the lab fared no better. A place Jack was once so scared of was now, too, reduced to charcoal. The dining table, the chairs, the piles of notebooks, all flaked into nothing.

A lifetime of Dr Cud's experiments and misdeeds were strewn around them, now only rubble adding to the pile. Jack turned to the rats in their cages and found their fried metal jaws locked around the bars as they tried to escape in their last moments.

Jack thought of Lucy, mummified and buried somewhere beneath his feet, along with Miles and Tim, whose pale skulls he pretended he hadn't noticed.

Amid the wreckage, one thing survived: a solitary metal dissection table, scarred and bruised and covered in empty bottles of spirits, but still intact.

Dr Li guided Jack over to the dissection table and helped him onto it, perching Jack on its edge. He gently rolled up the leg of Jack's trousers, revealing a mess of dark ooze and pus beneath. He touched it gently, fingers pressing around the swelling, and Jack fought hard to swallow the sharp shoot of pain back down. The pain only worsened as he saw Dr Li remove his miniature electromagnet from his bag. The item Jack handled the very first time he met Dr Li.

Jack gripped the end of the bench, bracing himself for what was about to come. He felt the bullet shift inside him, burrowing back through shattered bone and lighting up nerves along Jack's tender flesh. Gritting his teeth, he drove his fingernails into the bench as the pain turned to agony. Then, with a clank, it all subsided, and Jack let out a deep groan through his scrunched face.

Dr Li worked quickly, injecting the area with a syringe of something cold and numbing, before applying a layer of gel and finished up with a bandage.

"There, good as new."

With the starter complete, Dr Li returned to his magical Mary Poppins bag of horrors, rummaging through it for the main course. He hauled out several pieces of equipment of his own design: stacks of motherboards, buttons, and antennas, all knotted together in a tight tumbleweed of cable.

Dr Li hurriedly assembled them in a circle along the dissection table and placed Dr Cud's severed head in the centre. All the wrath of the universe remained embedded in that face, and his eyes were still open, still watching.

Bon appétit.

Dr Li dug through the deep mountains of ash until he found the helmet Dr Cud wore to transfer a copy of his brain into Tim's. The helmet was warped and blackened with soot. The insulation around the cables melted away, leaving only twisted wiring emerging through its pores. Dr Li revered the familiarity in its colander design for a moment before strapping the helmet around the severed head. He snapped a pair of crocodile clips to either side of the helmet and flicked a few switches on his makeshift machine, watching it spark to life.

Dr Cud's head twitched, a single eyelid spasming before growing into a full blink. Jack almost leapt from his skin at the sight of it, watching in horror as the head continued to move, its lips parting to release a small gurgled whisper, its tongue flickering within.

Nostrils flared, brows raised and eyes span in their sockets before landing on Jack, seeing him, recognizing him.

It was just electrical impulses flooding through his head,

Jack told himself, but the hatred in Dr Cud's convulsing expression said otherwise.

Dr Li's hands blurred across his controls, adjusting dials and switches with manic determination until the head slowed its movements, its muscles tightening just enough to imitate sleep.

"What are you doing?" asked Jack, edging along the dissection table and away from the reanimated head.

"The best I can." Dr Li didn't look up, distracting himself with his work. "I can't save everyone, but I can stop it."

Jack leant close, his voice almost a whisper as though afraid he might wake the head.

"You...you found a cure?"

"Something like that," said Dr Li, rubbing his eyes as he considered the best way to break this. "All the people Toby infected are linked to his brainwaves. Now that I have his brain. I can...switch them off."

"You mean kill them."

"If you want to put it like that. Then...Yes. It'll kill anyone exposed to Toby's pill."

Dr Li continued flicking switches and adjusting wires, avoiding Jack's gaze. He would not let Jack get to him. He was doing what needed to be done, and that was that.

"How many?" asked Jack.

"I don't know."

"How many?" pressed Jack, his voice firmer this time.

Dr Li rubbed his eyes again. He was so tired. "A million, maybe two, I don't know."

"You can't."

"Toby already killed them. I'm just stopping them."

"But..."

"But what, Jack? A million people die, or 8 billion people die. It's a simple decision. Anyone would do the same."

"I wouldn't."

Dr Li let out a small, exasperated sigh.

"Yes, you would," he said, turning to meet Jack's eyes.

It was time.

Dr Li tapped the side of his head, and suddenly, his features distorted as his face pixelated and folded away.

Jack watched in disbelief as the truth unfurled before his eyes, and everything suddenly made sense. As Dr Li's face reformed, a horrific realization sunk into Jack. He realized that this had always been his destiny. The linear path he struggled to escape was, in fact, inescapable.

Jack stared at the new man standing across from him, wearing the same projector affixed to his temple that both Miles and Sam had once worn. Where Dr Li stood was now someone different, yet more familiar. The man's irises were now the same kaleidoscope of greens and browns as his own. An identical mole lay above one eyebrow, although faded, and a nose and two ears completed the ensemble, matching Jack's too, albeit much larger.

Everything was the same, down to the most minute detail, like looking into a mirror. The one singular difference was time. Dr Li didn't lie about his age. He experienced an entire lifetime, and his face bore those marks well, but it was Jack's lifetime all along.

"Snap," said Dr Li finally.

"You're...You're me."

"I am. I was."

"You can't be," said Jack, staring his future in the eyes, hoping for this to be another trick.

"I'm afraid so. I told you this has all happened before. Over and over. Fifty-one attempts so far, and it always ends the same way. Everyone we care about dies. Every plan we ever try fails. This is the best I can do this time."

"Why didn't you tell me?"

Dr Li...

"Should I still call him Dr Li? Maybe Old Jack would be better? Jack 2? Or simply just Jack? No, that would make things more confusing than they already are. Let's just stick with Dr Li. So..."

Dr Li reached into his bag and removed one last item, an ancient leather-bound tome, the one Jack was once told housed instructions for the time machine but was forbidden from ever seeing inside. Dr Li handed the book to Jack.

"It's all in there," said Dr Li. "Attempts 2, 8, 19, 20 and 37 all involved you finding out the truth when you were young, and each time you ran away, or thought you were losing your mind, or both."

Jack opened the book, feeling the weight of it. The earliest pages were dark and stiff with the faded ink of his own handwriting, while the latter pages were still blank, yet to be filled.

As he flicked through, viewing each attempt and every failure, he read all the horrific ways his friends and loved ones died, each one unique.

Jack's mouth hung down, but only fragments of sentences fell out.

"When...? Why did...? What?" Jack struggled to fish out a question from the soupy mess of them sloshing in his head.

The questions ranged from specifics like: *In attempt 44, what circumstances led Sam to fall from a hot-air balloon?* To more general questions such as: *What the hell is going on?* Each question crowded together, clumping in his throat until Jack couldn't breathe.

"It's ok," said Dr Li, handing Jack his inhaler. "Calm down. I'll explain everything."

Jack took a few strained puffs and watched as Dr Li donned his lecturer's voice and began his lesson.

"One day, in about fifty years, you're going to become me, which gives you fifty years to study Toby, find his weaknesses and plan a way to stop him. And if it doesn't work, we'll try again. Just like that video game you always used to play, remember how you were stuck on that level with the boulder chasing you? You kept losing over and over again. But I told you to keep trying because each time, you'll get a little bit further, and eventually, you did it."

"That's not what happened at all," corrected Jack. "You boasted about how you could do it easily, then you got so frustrated when you couldn't that you smashed my *PlayStation* and used the parts for an electron destabilizer that you never finished."

"Well, maybe this time you can build a working electron destabilizer. You could try destabilizing Toby's electrons...I don't know, that's up to you."

Jack shook his head, desperately wanting to reject it, quit, and break this endless cycle. He knew he couldn't. If there was any possibility of bringing them all back, of saving Sam and Lucy and Tim and Miles and Mom and Dad and the millions of others about to die, his life would be a small price to pay for it. He couldn't say no, and fifty-one other versions of himself agreed.

Dr Li returned to the machinery, tinkering with a few more switches until a small red button at the heart of the controls glowed.

"It's ready," he said. "I need you to do it."

Jack shook his head harder. "Me? No, no, that's too much. Fifty years, fine, but I will not kill a million people. I can't."

"Please," said Dr Li. "You need to know what you're

fighting to stop, and it was hard enough the last time I had to press this button."

Every second Jack delayed it, countless more people would continue to suffer and fall. He needed this nightmare to end, to put one final full stop on this day. Jack stepped down from the table and limped over to the button. Accepting his fate, the same way he always did.

"I got it down to a million. I did better than most." Dr Li told himself.

Jack placed his hand over the button and took a deep breath. One final thought for the gravity of what he was about to do, and then he pushed the button.

***

Jack didn't truly see the weight of what he did, nor could he even imagine the heartbreak it would bring. A million people across the world collapsed, writhing in pain as their minds stung and exploded, leaving only more death.

People would eventually crawl out from their hiding spots, finally safe from Dr Cud's wrath, but there would be no celebration, no cheers, no joy. Instead, there would only be silence as the world mourned Jack's actions.

***

The circuit overloaded, sparking with one last gasp of energy and leaving Dr Cud's head as little more than a blackened crisp of corroded metal.

"Is it done?" asked Jack.

Dr Li nodded.

"Now what?"

"Well, we need to do something about this," said Dr Li,

presenting Jack with the mangled remains of the Time Machine, as dark and dead as everything else.

"You can fix it, can't you?" asked Jack.

Dr Li gave a kind, tired sigh. "It took over a decade to fix the last time you broke it, and I don't think I have another decade in me."

Jack remembered the last time it broke—not technically his fault, as Baby Toby was to blame. If he knew precisely the full extent of what that infant would do to him, maybe he could've gone through with it. Who was he kidding?

No, he couldn't. If the million people he just killed taught him anything, it's that he wasn't a killer.

"So it's up to you to fix it," finished Dr Li.

"Me? I can't do that. I know you think I can because you're me, and you did it, but I'm different. I can't fix it by myself."

Dr Li smiled. "I said the same thing at your age, but I never did it alone. I had you the second time I fixed it, right?"

"And the first?"

Dr Li waited a moment for Jack to figure out that terrible revelation for himself.

"No," said Jack, backing away from his responsibilities. "No, I refuse."

As Jack stepped back, he knocked into the dissection table, scattering the fragile remains of Dr Cud across it with a booming clatter, like the toll of some inevitable bell.

"It's the only way. He's the only person smart enough, and it's the best way to monitor him."

Jack was silent for a while, then he screamed, then he cried, and then he fell silent again.

"Ok," said Jack finally. "Let's go before I change my mind."

Jack took one last look at the world he was leaving behind. He'd reach it again one day, the long way round.

THEIR LAST TRIP THROUGH THE LANDSCAPE OF THE past brought Jack and Dr Li to the doorstep of a pristine Moonshot Labs fifty years earlier. Jack stared up at the building, a towering marvel crammed full of wide-eyed scientists working together to build a brighter tomorrow, as it was always meant to be.

The giant moon of the building's logo shone above like a beacon of youthful ambition, casting a gentle glow over Jack's face and promising him a future yet to be written.

Dr Li handed Jack the book, the broken time machine and an ID keycard. Three trinkets on which to build his new life. Jack inspected the ID card. On it was a picture of Dr Li, no older than Jack was now. *Moonshot Labs, Dr Lii, Room 14A*.

"Dr Li is spelt wrong," said Jack.

"It's not wrong. *Lii*, its Roman numerals. You're number 52,"

Dr Li mounted the projector onto Jack's temple, flicked it on, and Jack's bruised face and bloodied jaw folded and morphed into the man in the photo.

"What are you going to do now?" asked Jack.

"I'm sure you already know," said Dr Li with a sad smile.

Jack stared into the eyes of his future and remembered how he'd met his end. One last plea to Dr Cud to stop before having his neck snapped. Just how many of him died at Dr Cud's hands? Would *he* end the same way?

"It's your birthday tomorrow," continued Dr Li. "I need to get him something good."

Jack felt the locator weighing down his pocket, the one that only reminded him of Sam, the one Dr Li gave him for his birthday.

"Here," said Jack, handing it over.

"I'm sure he'll hate it," said Dr Li, tucking the device into his bag.

Dr Li reached into his boot, slipped out his own time machine, bustling with the knowing fear of his fate and gripped it tight.

The old Jack and the young Dr Li said their final farewell, gave each other one last knowing nod and then Jack was alone. The fading crackles of his old future slowly vanished, leaving only the front door to his new one.

Jack peered down at his keycard showing his new face, and then up at the face reflecting back at him through the glass doors. He wasn't convinced it suited him, but he'd grow into it. Jack took a step forward.

The pain in his leg had now reduced to a dull ache as the healing gel did its job. The sliding glass doors to Moonshot Labs opened automatically, and a receptionist greeted him with a friendly "Hi."

Jack didn't know what to say as he stood in stunned silence amidst the loud '70s decor. He briefly debated doing a voice, but didn't particularly like the idea of keeping that up for the next half-century. So he said nothing and handed over his ID.

"First day?" asked the receptionist. "You're in room 14A on the second floor. We actually have someone else starting today, too. They're next door to you."

"Thank you," mumbled Jack in an undecided accent as he took back the ID.

JACK WALKED THROUGH THE CORRIDORS HE KNEW well, his limp fading with each step down the familiar path. He felt a strange fusion of familiarity and detachment walking down the halls, both the same as he remembered, yet wholly different.

There were voices talking and laughing behind each door. This place teemed with life in every direction. Noticeboards lined the walls with schedules, photos, and adverts for badminton teams and science presentations.

Jack continued walking, like a bird returning to its nest, until he reached the lab he knew best. He stood outside the door momentarily, building up the courage to knock. He lightly tapped his fist against it, secretly hoping not to be heard, but as he felt movement on the other side, Jack knew he wasn't so lucky.

Jack wasn't sure what he would do. Perhaps he would hit him, and perhaps he wouldn't stop. Jack would get life in prison for sure. Preventing a future genocide was unlikely to hold up in a courtroom, but maybe that would be worth it. It would be over, and they would all be safe. Adrenaline fired around Jack's body, bubbling through him until his hands shook.

Then, the door opened, and a young man with floppy brown hair stood before Jack. "Hello," he said in a chipper tone. "You must be the other newbie, Lii something, right?"

"Er...yes," said Jack in his own voice.

"Nice to meet you. I'm Toby. It's my first day here, too. I was really nervous, but everyone's been so nice. Which room is yours?"

After a long moment, Jack realized he wasn't saying anything and was simply staring in bemusement at this kind young man. So Jack slowly raised a hand and pointed to the room next door.

"No way, we're lab neighbours."

"Lab neighbours," repeated Jack. "Yeah. I...I should go."

"Of course, I imagine you want to get straight to work,

changing the world and all. Well, it's a pleasure to meet you, Lii. I just know we're going to be great friends."

Toby held out his hand, ready to be shaken. Jack raised his with all the hesitation in the world to meet it. Toby shook it enthusiastically. His hand had an excited warmth to it, free of even the slightest trace of metal.

The door closed, and Jack exhaled deeply, fighting to hold on to the hate he harboured for the man. He wouldn't allow himself to forget the man he would become. Jack turned and stepped into the adjacent room, a mirror image of Dr Cud's, and took a seat at the empty table.

Jack reached into his bag and pulled out the ancient book. He set the well-worn tome down in front of him, peeled open its first ancient page and read.

80

Ten years ago, a biological weapon was released onto the population as a pill, the effects of which on the human body include hyper-aggression, alterations in personality and the formation of metallic structures within the brain.

Those infected appear to be connected via some form of hive mind, controlled by a man named Dr Tobias Cud, who I believe to be the perpetrator of this bio-weapon.

Implementing the bio-weapon has already claimed the lives of those closest to me. My parents, Gary and Geraldine Phoenix, my friends, Sam Higgs and Tim Watkins, a police officer who saved my life named Lucy Sparks and, most recently, the man helping me study this phenomenon, Miles Cross.

After studying these pills extensively, I have yet to find any discernible antidote to their effects. However, I have recently had an epiphany. If I cannot fix things in the present, perhaps I may find a way to do so in the past.

As such, I have studied the marvels of time travel to see if it may be more than simple whimsy. Escaping the constraints of the fourth dimension once seemed a ridiculous concept, but the world is different now, and the impossible has become commonplace.

JACK FLICKED AHEAD PAST SEVERAL PAGES OF indecipherable formulas and codes.

After half a lifetime of studying time travel, I have successfully overcome several dead ends. However, I appear to have reached an impasse and am unable to source the equipment to continue my work.

I require a particle collider and an instrument capable of stabilizing light photons into waves. Unfortunately, I doubt I will come across either while scavenging underground train stations and sewers.

As such, I have arrived at the difficult decision of seeking help from Lord Tobias Cud. The hive mind seems to have been given the singular goal of discovering the secrets to immortality, ensuring longevity for Lord Cud.

I believe I may be able to propose a truce in which he provides me with the resources, and in exchange, I will supply him with more time. That is so long as he doesn't kill me before I get the chance to ask him.

More formula, more code, a few schematics.

Tobias Cud has been of greater help than I could have anticipated. I may well detest the man and all he stands for, but I cannot fault his genius. He has been fully accommodating with resources and test subjects, as well as his own insights on quantum physics, which have been invaluable to my progress.

Unfortunately, I worry I may be running out of time to get the device working to a level at which I can stop him. I fear Tobias has been subjecting me to a micro-dose of his drug, small enough that I wouldn't initially detect it. However, I am now beginning to feel its effects taking hold.

Luckily, I have made more progress than Tobias is aware of. I believe that if I overload the circuits of the time machine, I may be able to pilot the device on a one-way trip into my past. Not nearly far enough to prevent his bio-weapon from being created in the first place, but perhaps far enough to supply my former self with my most recent progress so that he may continue my work.

I am not one to believe in any higher power, certainly not anymore, but I will pray that this endeavour of mine comes to fruition, and I pray my former self will prove better than I was.

There were fifty more accounts, or attempts, or failures just like it, and after that lay a series of blank pages, ready to be filled with attempt number 52.

81

Jack placed the broken time machine on the table and spent the next few decades trying to fix it. He would work all day and all night, barely sleeping.

Sleep was where the nightmares lived, and in them, Jack relived every terrible moment.

Some days, when it all got to him more than usual, and he could no longer keep the nightmares contained to sleep, Jack would sneak into Toby's lab late into the night and let it all out, destroying everything in his path.

It never stuck, however, as each time Toby would simply rebuild and continue his work.

Jack was forced to watch as the years passed and Toby became more obsessive and insane, bearing witness as the man mutilated his body in new and horrific ways in the pursuit of immortality.

One day, Jack fixed the last piece of the puzzle into place, and a faint blue glow flowed through the time machine's veins once more. He took his leave with no goodbyes and went to meet his new former self at his parents' wedding, and everything played out just as it had before.

He set up a new lab on an unassuming street in what was once a bakery. There, Jack worked on electromagnets, time dilation devices, and anything that may give himself a better chance this time.

Then he waited patiently for a couple more Jacks to show up at his door.

He took his younger self under his wing and taught him all he knew, preparing him as best he could for the trials he would one day face.

They soon outgrew the lab, and Jack used his savings to buy a cottage, going to great effort to install a sprinkler system in every room.

Events played out differently, but the result was the same. The sprinklers stopped the cottage from burning down, which only resulted in Tim and Lucy dying much sooner, killed by the horde of OAPs as they freed Dr Cud. After that, Sam used Miles' projector to pretend to be Jack long enough to trap himself and Dr Cud in the future with no way back.

Attempt 52 was a failure.

***

So he tried again. A new Jack became Dr Liii, and the cycle continued.

Over and over, Dr Liii became Dr Liv, who became Dr Ciixi, who became Dr Miicviixi. Some did better. Some did worse.

Attempt 679 resulted in only a single death. A venomous snake that Sam forgot to put back in its cage bit a passerby. But it wasn't good enough. Jack wouldn't stop until there wasn't a single death weighing down his conscience.

So he never stopped.

And that's where we get me.

Jack's father glanced down at his son. The medication took hold, and the young birthday boy was cooing softly in a contented sleep, curled up into a ball on the passenger seat of the ice cream truck.

His father smiled at him peacefully before tapping the side of his temple. Jack's father's face glitched and warped until it settled upon his true self.

"I'm attempting number 3564," he told his sleeping self. "I'll drop you off at Nan's house. Don't worry, you won't remember any of this. You won't remember me or what I told you, and you certainly won't remember what happened to mom and dad. The memory dampers in your ice cream will see to all that. Then, in a few years, we can do this whole thing again." He placed a gentle hand on his younger shoulder, feeling his sleepy, shallow breaths.

"I have a good feeling about this one."

***

JACK PARKED THE ICE CREAM TRUCK A SHORT distance from his grandmother's house. She would take good care of him. She always did.

As Jack lifted his younger self from the passenger seat, he felt the boy stir in his arms.

"Was it all real?" asked the young boy without opening his eyes.

"Shhhh," whispered Jack, carrying the boy down the moonlit road. But as they reached the doorstep of the house, the boy began murmuring again.

"I don't think Toby really is a baddie. I think he just needs a friend. You should be his friend."

Jack gave a small hum of "Wouldn't that be nice," before

dropping himself off on the doorstep and ringing the doorbell. Yet, as Jack walked back towards the ice cream truck, the idea lingered.

What if he just needs a friend?

Nowhere in the grand library of accounts did any book mention an attempt where a Jack became friends with a Toby. After all those years and all those repeats, not once did his former selves try something as crazy as that.

It was simply because it wouldn't work. It wouldn't change anything, would it?

Jack climbed into the ice cream truck, adjusted the wing mirror and stared intensely at his own reflection. Was it too late?

Time had only started to take hold of Jack, still yet to paint him into an ageing curmudgeon. What was he now? 30? 35?

It didn't take him too long to fix the time machine this time. A hundred thousand years of practice will do that.

He decided it wasn't too late and retrieved the small wooden device from inside his boot.

82

"Are you up too much tonight?" Jack asked Toby back at Moonshot Labs, trying to broach the subject over lunch.

Toby nearly choked on his sandwich. Jack, or Dr Miller as people knew him (a much more suitable name than Dr MMMDLXIV) had never once asked Toby about himself or what he was up to. If their conversations even slightly drifted away from work, he was always quick to correct it back to something more impersonal.

"Erm, no, not tonight, just a quiet one at home, I think," said Toby.

"Oh, right, because I was just wondering if you fancied getting a drink after work?"

"Really?" asked Toby, his cheeks flushing red, unable to conceal an excited smile.

"There's this good pub in town. It's got a stupid name, but if you fancy it-"

"Yes, definitely."

That evening, Jack and Toby sat and had drinks in The Bell's End, and it surprised Jack how much he enjoyed it. They had a surprising amount in common and the conversation flowed almost as well as the drinks.

They did it again the next week, and the next, and soon the pair spent most evenings playing pool in the pub, or bowling, or watching a film down at the cinema. They became almost inseparable.

Jack remained vigilant, worried that the day would still arrive when Toby would snap, reverting to his evil destiny and begin enacting his plan. Yet, as the years passed, the day never came.

One night, whilst the pair sat at their regular table in The Bell's End, Jack helped Toby muster up the courage to spark up a conversation with a woman named Angela and two years later, they were married. Jack was even named the best man at the wedding.

A few years after that, Jack became godfather to their daughter.

As time passed, Toby began spending less time in the lab and more time with his family, a family which Jack was now a part of.

The day of reckoning finally came, the day prophesied in each and every failed attempt, the day a young Jack, Sam, and Tim would confront Greg Page, and the first domino to the end of the world would fall. Except this time, it didn't.

Instead, Jack spent the evening at The Bell's End with

Toby for some birthday drinks. He was deep into his seventies now, though, with all the days spent in different timelines, it was impossible to truly calculate his age, and today likely wasn't his actual birthday, but if Toby wanted to buy him a drink, he would hardly complain.

JACK SPENT THE DAY ENSURING PLANS WERE IN place in case Toby still tried something, an instinct passed down from so many Jacks before him, which he simply couldn't shake.

Jack spied on Lucy excitedly over-preparing for her first day as a police officer that morning, memorizing every archaic law and daydreaming about all the good she would do. She had her mom and dad back, and she was happy.

Jack watched Miles dropping his two young daughters off at school, handing them their lunchboxes and giving both an extra long hug to last the day. Miles stood for a while as they ran off to meet their friends. He would never have to endure the pain of losing them, and he was happy.

Jack didn't need to go far to find Tim and Sam as they were currently sitting in The Bell's End at the very next table. They were drinking and arguing and celebrating a birthday of their own, that of Jack's younger self.

Tim was slurping down a Piña Colada, no longer worrying that opening up would allow in the world's harsh judgement, as he had two great friends who liked him for who he was, and he was happy.

A young Jack sat next to him, twenty years old today, as was clear from the big badge pinned to his shirt. He had everything: his parents, his friends, but best of all, he once more had a future that wasn't set.

Free from the endless game, he was no longer a snake

devouring its tail. He could choose to do whatever he wanted. The rest of his life was finally his own, and he was happy.

As for Sam, well, he was still very much Sam, but he was happy too.

"Well, it's official," said Sam, holding up his phone. "Just got the email. The university suspended me for two weeks."

"So, today's a double celebration then," said Jack sarcastically.

"What did you do?" asked Tim.

"He cheated on his coursework," answered Jack.

"I didn't cheat. It's the other way round. Amir copied off me."

"I saw your essay. It had Amir's name at the top," retorted Jack.

"That's not the point. I changed more than enough of that essay, so there was no way it should've been picked up for plagiarism in the first place," argued Sam.

"Everything apart from the name," said Jack with a smug sip of his drink.

"Oh, he's done you there," laughed Tim.

"I remember putting my name on it. I'm sure it got changed after I submitted it. I'm telling you, they've all got it out for me in that class. Amir probably hacked into the servers and changed the name." concluded Sam.

"This is pretty serious," said Jack, reading the email on Sam's phone. "They might actually kick you out."

"Well, I suppose you could always get a job here," said Tim. "You're here most of the time, anyway."

"I'm not working in a place called The Bell's End, and I certainly don't need career advice from you."

"Well, you still owe me for fireworks," said Tim.

"They were a gift. Look, it's all fine." dismissed Sam. "I'll hack into the university's mainframe tomorrow and delete myself from the suspension list. Simple."

"So you can't write an essay, but you're secretly a master hacker?" said Jack.

"You could always ask your mate Amir how he hacked into it and cheat off him again," laughed Tim.

"I didn't cheat!"

THE OLDER JACK WATCHED THE THREE BICKER, reminiscing on a life he never lived, until Toby returned from the bar, holding two pints of beer in his shaking hands.

The beers sloshed back and forth, reduced to half-pints by the time Toby placed what was left of them down onto the table with a smile and a wink.

Toby's Parkinson's joined forces with arthritis and, with no robotic enhancements, made most things either too painful or simply impossible. Still, he was determined to get these drinks for his best friend.

Jack helped Toby hold the glass up to his mouth as he took a long, deep sip.

"Thanks, that hit the spot," said Toby. "Happy Birthday. To many, many more."

Jack tapped his glass to Toby's and felt the pressures of all the Jacks who came before him fade away as they both said "cheers."

There was nothing to worry about, not anymore. The fight was over. Toby wasn't the same man. He was better. He may not live forever, but the man sitting across from Jack experienced a better life than any of Toby's past selves could have imagined, even with a million years at their disposal.

A brief life isn't something to waste your fear on, but a wasted life certainly is, a life without family, friendships, arguments down the pub, and kindness. Someone who hasn't tasted all that life offers will only become hungrier and hungrier until their starvation consumes them, leaving them a delirious husk.

But not Toby. He had enjoyed all of life's buffet. He was full, and Jack couldn't see how Toby could have lived any better.

Toby and Jack spoke long into the evening about science, television, books, the news, the weather, the good old days and everything else. They shared stories and reminisced about their time at Moonshot Labs and all the days since.

Toby proudly updated Jack all about how his family was doing, how his wife was becoming obsessed with crochet and how his granddaughter was starting a career as a doctor.

Eventually, it was time to go, so Jack picked up the duffle bag he brought with him and helped Toby out of his seat, steadying him as they made their way through the pub. Two happy old men.

As they passed the next table, Toby's leg seized, and he lost his balance, colliding into the table with a thud. Jack caught Toby before he hit the floor and helped him back up to his feet.

"You alright, mate?" asked Sam, jumping to attention.

Toby chuckled, brushing it off with a wave. "Grand, just not as steady on my feet as I used to be."

"You sure?" asked Tim, offering his chair. "Sit down for a bit if you need to."

Jack used this moment of distraction to slip a hand under their table, quietly swapping the duffle bag he knew would be there with the duplicate he was holding.

"Honestly, I've been through worse, but that's very kind of you boys," said Toby, offering a grateful nod as he recomposed himself.

"Have a good night," Jack called over his shoulder as he guided Toby towards the door.

The younger Jack watched the two men as they left. There

was something familiar about them he couldn't quite put his finger on. Before he could place them, Sam clapped him on the back.

"Come on, birthday boy, we should head off too," said Sam. "It's time we celebrated properly with some fireworks."

Jack grimaced. "I really don't think this is a good idea. Can't my birthday present be that we don't get our faces blown off?"

"It'll be fine," assured Sam. "Come on then, Tim. We've waited long enough. Let's see what we're working with."

Tim hauled the duffle bag onto the table, confusion growing as he lifted it; it felt much lighter than he remembered. Then, shielding it from any nosy onlookers, Tim leaned in and unzipped the bag. Instead of fireworks, he found only a collection of strange objects staring back at him.

Tim pulled out the first item, a sleek device which appeared to him like some futuristic phone, thick with technology and housing a screen that displayed a map.

Next, Tim retrieved a pocket-sized hard drive containing an entire library of lifetimes.

Beneath that, Tim found a curious wooden machine glowing with a faint blue hue, pulsing gently along the grains and knots in the wood. At one end was a glass ball encasing a clock face, an infinite number of possibilities concealed within its ancient mechanisms.

Lastly, tucked into the inside pocket, Tim felt something flat and rectangular. A green envelope bearing Jack's name.

The trio exchanged bewildered glances as they stared at the trinkets. Jack reached out and snatched the envelope addressed to him, surrendering to the impossible curiosity.

He eyed the lettering, each cursive stroke of his name written in his own handwriting, and tore it open.

The envelope contained a birthday card with a cheerful

otter holding a balloon, beneath a caption that read: '*Have an Otterly amazing day.*'

Jack opened the card.

Dear Jack,

Happy birthday.

I thought you might appreciate this more than fireworks.

Have a great life, fill it with adventure and don't be afraid.

Love,

Your Future.

ACKNOWLEDGEMENTS

My thanks go to Adam and Ray at Wicked Ink Publishing for taking a chance on me and my very first novel, and for their support and advice to get my story to reach its full potential.

To Deanna, for being the first person to read my story back when it was simply mad ramblings and non-sensical hieroglyphs.

To my family for their encouragement to pursue my dreams and whose many mannerisms and quirks inspired so many of the characters in this book.

To all my friends who've had to endure me droning on and on about this silly story for as long as they've known me.

To my school teacher Ms Claxton, who, at 8 years old, was the first of many people I promised to acknowledge in my book when I became a big shot author.

To the thousands of coffee shop baristas who looked the other way when I spent days typing away without being able to afford a single drink.

To Russell T Davies and Steven Moffat for inspiring a life-long obsession with time travel stories.

And most importantly, to you reading this right now for getting all the way to the last page, or at the very least skipping ahead to find out how it ends.

ABOUT THE AUTHOR

© Daniel Goy

Daniel Goy was raised amidst the picturesque landscapes of the English countryside and has always been a storyteller at heart. From crafting home movies with friends during his childhood to now releasing a series of science-fiction novels with Wicked Ink, his passion for narrative has been a lifelong journey.

Daniel graduated with a degree in biology, spent several years as a science teacher, and is currently training to become a doctor at St Bart's, London. As for the 'fiction' part, Daniel has dedicated his life to mastering the art of storytelling, immersing himself in films, TV, and novels, and even pursuing studies in film and drama at university.

His narratives often explore the funny side of the darkest aspects of humanity, placing relatable characters in impossible situations. Drawing inspiration from his own life and the characters he encountered growing up, Daniel aims to contribute to the collection of books that inspired him as a child, hoping to inspire future generations of storytellers.

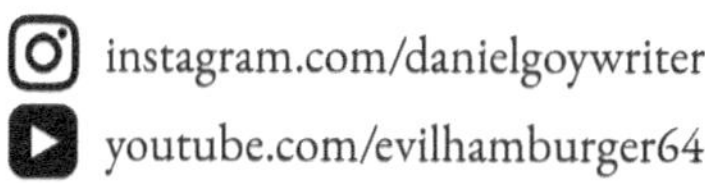

instagram.com/danielgoywriter

youtube.com/evilhamburger64